Born in the Kingdom of Fife in 1960, Ian Rankin graduated from the University of Edinburgh and has since been employed as grape-picker, swineherd, taxman, alcohol researcher, hi-fi journalist and punk musician. His first Rebus novel, *Knots & Crosses*, was published in 1987 and the Rebus books have now been translated into 26 languages. Ian Rankin has been elected a Hawthornden Fellow, and is a past winner of the prestigious Chandler-Fulbright Award, as well as two CWA short-story 'Daggers' and the 1997 CWA Macallan Gold Dagger for Fiction for *Black & Blue*, which was also shortlisted for the Mystery Writers of America 'Edgar' award for Best Novel. *Black & Blue*, *The Hanging Garden*, *Dead Souls* and *Mortal Causes* have been televised on ITV, starring John Hannah as Inspector Rebus. *Dead Souls*, the tenth novel in the series, was shortlisted for the CWA Gold Dagger Award in 1999. An Alumnus of the Year at Edinburgh University, he has also been awarded four honorary doctorates, from the University of Abertay Dundee in 1999, from the University of St Andrews in 2001, in 2003 from the University of Edinburgh and in 2005 from the Open University. In 2002 Ian Rankin was awarded an OBE for services to literature. In 2004 *Resurrection Men* won the Edgar Award for Best Novel. In 2005 *Fleshmarket Close* won the Crime Thriller of the Year award at the British Book Awards. Ian is the winner of the Crime Writers' Association Diamond Dagger 2005. In 2005 he was also awarded the Grand Prix du Littérature Policier (France), the Deutsche Krimi Prize (Germany) and the Icons of Scotland award. He lives in Edinburgh with his wife and two sons. Visit his website at www.ianrankin.net.

By Ian Rankin

The Inspector Rebus series
Knots & Crosses
Hide & Seek
Tooth & Nail
Strip Jack
The Black Book
Mortal Causes
Let It Bleed
Black & Blue
The Hanging Garden
Death Is Not The End (*novella*)
Dead Souls
Set in Darkness
The Falls
Resurrection Men
A Question of Blood
Fleshmarket Close

Other novels
The Flood
Watchman
Westwind

Writing as Jack Harvey
Witch Hunt
Bleeding Hearts
Blood Hunt

Short stories
A Good Hanging and Other Stories
Beggars Banquet

Omnibus editions
Rebus: The Early Years
(Knots & Crosses, Hide & Seek, Tooth & Nail)
Rebus: The St Leonard's Years
(Strip Jack, The Black Book, Mortal Causes)
Rebus: The Lost Years
(Let It Bleed, Black & Blue, The Hanging Garden)
Rebus: Capital Crimes (Dead Souls, Set in Darkness, The Falls)

All Ian Rankin's titles are available on audio. Also available:
Jackie Leven Said by Ian Rankin and Jackie Leven.

For Miranda

An Orion paperback
First published in Great Britain in 1998
by Orion
This paperback edition published in 1999
by Orion Books Ltd,
Orion House, 5 Upper St Martin's Lane,
London WC2H 9EA

A CIP catalogue record for this book
is available from the British Library.

ISBN-13 978-1-4072-0709-4

Printed and bound in the EU

The Orion Publishing Group's policy is to use papers
that are natural, renewable and recyclable products and made from
wood grown in sustainable forests. The logging and manufacturing
processes are expected to conform to the environmental
regulations of the country of origin.

www.orionbooks.co.uk

Ian Rankin

The Hanging Garden

ORION

'If all time is eternally present
All time is unredeemable.'

T.S. Eliot, 'Burnt Norton'

'I went to Scotland and found nothing
there that looks like Scotland'

Arthur Freed, Producer *Brigadoon*

INTRODUCTION

Having lived in France for six years, in the autumn of 1996 I moved back to Edinburgh with my family. I had left Scotland ten years previously, newly married and fresh from university. I was returning with two children and a full-time career as a novelist. Okay, so I wasn't earning enough for the mortgage on a three-bedroom flat, but some of the uncertainties of the past had gone. I felt like a proper, grown-up writer, able to take on big moral themes under the guise of writing whodunits. Academe and literary circles might not take the form seriously, but I knew that the crime novel could say as much about human nature and the state of the world as any other branch of writerly endeavour. My next project was already well under way as we unpacked and started coming to terms with driving on the left (in our French-registered Peugeot). The genesis of this project had been a day-trip I'd made to a place called Oradour – a town which had, quite literally, died.

All the six years I'd spent in France, I'd heard of this place, knew it was just over an hour's drive away from our home in north-east Dordogne. Friends' children went there on school trips, but I'd never made the effort. Then I remembered London. We'd lived there for four years before making the move to France. After we'd left, I'd thought with regret of all the things I hadn't done, places I hadn't bothered to visit. So, towards the end of our time in France, I took the drive north to Oradour.

And was stunned.

The town has been kept as a shrine to its victims. No one knows how many died there, the day the 3rd Company of the SS 'Der Führer' Regiment marched in and started rounding people up. Not far short of a thousand, the histories say. Corpses were set alight, or dropped down wells. Men, women, children: almost no one escaped the slaughter. During my time there, peering through windows into kitchens and living rooms, passing burned-out cars and the rusty carcass of the local tram, the overcast sky gave way to steady rain. I sought shelter in the church, but its roof was missing – torched by the Nazis. I got in close to one of its walls, and realised there were bullet-holes in the plaster all around me. This was where the women had been brought, a machine-gun pointed at them. So I headed for the small museum instead, with its displays of everyday objects: hairbrushes, pairs of spectacles . . . mementoes of the dead.

But what really affected me about Oradour was the fact that the man responsible – the general who'd given the order for the massacre – had been captured by the Allies, but was then sent back to Germany to live out the rest of his days in industry and comfort. What sort of justice was that? There would be reasons for it, of course: probably to do with politics, with diplomacy, with secret deals and information traded. There were usually reasons for these things. I started doing some research, and along the way learned of a network called the Rat-Line (which you'll read about in this book). I also became intrigued that the lessons of the past had not been learned. Atrocities were a daily occurrence in ex-Yugoslavia at this time. The West knew the identities of the men responsible, the men in charge – they were on our TV screens nightly, going about their butchers' business. Yet little or nothing was being done to stop them.

This sense of history repeating would form the basis for *The Hanging Garden*. Most of the book was written in France, but when I arrived in Edinburgh I knew I needed to do some final research on war criminals and how we have dealt with them in the past. So I went to the National Library on Edinburgh's George IV Bridge – a place I'd haunted as a student, back when I'd been writing my first two novels – and did a search.

And found something.

Having decided, months before, that I wanted to write about Oradour, I'd scratched my head for a while. The sticking point was: how could I do so from the point of view of Detective Inspector John Rebus? The answer came eventually: I would have Rebus investigate an alleged Nazi war criminal who has been living quietly in Edinburgh for forty years or more. In this way, I could question the validity of prosecuting old men for their crimes of half a century before.

Perfect, I thought.

But that day in the National Library, I found information on an alleged war criminal . . . a real one . . . living quietly in Edinburgh. A TV documentary had been made about him, and he'd taken legal action against the producers. And though he hadn't been successful, I knew I would have to be careful that he couldn't see himself in *my* portrait of a suspected monster . . .

The book went on to win the Cognac Prix du Roman Policier – not bad, considering I hadn't managed to find a French publisher during my long sojourn in that country! It also sneaked on to the margins of the bestseller lists in the UK, and was the third biggest-selling title in Scotland in 1999 (after two of the Harry Potter instalments). Having managed critical success with *Black & Blue*, I was now beginning to see some sales success, too. The mortgage on that three-bedroom flat couldn't be too far away . . .

Having borrowed from a song by The Cure for the title of *The Hanging Garden*, I decided I wanted to preface each section of my book with a couple of lines from the song. I had no idea how to go about seeking permission, so turned to the band's fan club for help. Eventually, I received a phone call from someone on the management side. They had, they told me, talked it over with Robert – meaning Robert Smith, the band's lyricist. Robert said it would be okay, but of course there would be a fee. I sucked in some air and asked how much.

'A few signed copies when the book comes out.'

I laughed – from relief, but also because it showed what a gentleman Mr Smith was – and was quick to accept. Only later did it dawn on me that I had no address to send the books to, and no record of the name of the person who'd phoned me. So if anyone out there knows Robert Smith, tell him to get in touch. There's a first edition waiting here with his name on. I'd like him to see the book some time, if only for the smile it might raise when he finds out what I've done with other songs of his – most notably 'Fascination Street' and 'Mr Pink Eyes' . . .

Now read on . . .

They were arguing in the living-room.

'Look, if your bloody job's so precious ...'

'What do you want from me?'

'You know bloody well!'

'I'm working my arse off for the three of us!'

'Don't give me that crap.'

And then they saw her. She was holding her teddy bear, Pa Broon, by one well-chewed ear. She was peering round the doorway, thumb in her mouth. They turned to her.

'What is it, sweetie?'

'I had a bad dream.'

'Come here.' The mother crouched down, opening her arms. But the girl ran to her father, wrapped herself around his legs.

'Come on, pet, I'll take you back to bed.'

He tucked her in, started to read her a story.

'Daddy,' she said, 'what if I fall asleep and don't wake up? Like Snow White or Sleeping Beauty?'

'Nobody sleeps forever, Sammy. All it takes to wake them up is a kiss. There's nothing the witches and evil queens can do about that.'

He kissed her forehead.

'Dead people don't wake up,' she said, hugging Pa Broon. 'Not even when you kiss them.'

1

John Rebus kissed his daughter.

'Sure you don't want a lift?'

Samantha shook her head. 'I need to walk off that pizza.'

Rebus put his hands in his pockets, felt folded banknotes beneath his handkerchief. He thought of offering her some money – wasn't that what fathers did? – but she'd only laugh. She was twenty-four and independent; didn't need the gesture and certainly wouldn't take the money. She'd even tried to pay for the pizza, arguing that she'd eaten half while he'd chewed on a single slice. The remains were in a box under her arm.

'Bye, Dad.' She pecked him on the cheek.

'Next week?'

'I'll phone you. Maybe the three of us …?' By which she meant Ned Farlowe, her boyfriend. She was walking backwards as she spoke. One final wave, and she turned away from him, head moving as she checked the evening traffic, crossing the road without looking back. But on the opposite pavement she half-turned, saw him watching her, waved her hand in acknowledgement. A young man almost collided with her. He was staring at the pavement, the thin black cord from a pair of earphones dribbling down his neck. Turn round and look at her, Rebus commanded. Isn't she incredible? But the youth kept shuffling along the pavement, oblivious to her world.

And then she'd turned a corner and was gone. Rebus could only imagine her now: making sure the pizza box was

3

secure beneath her left arm; walking with eyes fixed firmly ahead of her; rubbing a thumb behind her right ear, which she'd recently had pierced for the third time. He knew that her nose would twitch when she thought of something funny. He knew that if she wanted to concentrate, she might tuck the corner of one jacket-lapel into her mouth. He knew that she wore a bracelet of braided leather, three silver rings, a cheap watch with black plastic strap and indigo face. He knew that the brown of her hair was its natural colour. He knew she was headed for a Guy Fawkes party, but didn't intend staying long.

He didn't know nearly enough about her, which was why he'd wanted them to meet for dinner. It had been a tortuous process: dates rejigged, last-minute cancellations. Sometimes it was her fault, more often his. Even tonight he should have been elsewhere. He ran his hands down the front of his jacket, feeling the bulge in his inside breast pocket, his own little time-bomb. Checking his watch, he saw it was nearly nine o'clock. He could drive or he could walk – he wasn't going far.

He decided to drive.

Edinburgh on firework night, leaves blown into thick lines down the pavement. One morning soon he would find himself scraping frost from his car windscreen, feeling the cold like jabs to his kidneys. The south side of the city seemed to get the first frost earlier than the north. Rebus, of course, lived and worked on the south side. After a stint in Craigmillar, he was back at St Leonard's. He could make for there now – he was still on shift after all – but he had other plans. He passed three pubs on his way to his car. Chat at the bar, cigarettes and laughter, a fug of heat and alcohol: he knew these things better than he knew his own daughter. Two out of the three bars boasted 'doormen'. They didn't seem to be called bouncers these days. They were doormen or front-of-house managers, big guys with

4

short hair and shorter fuses. One of them wore a kilt. His face was all scar tissue and scowl, the scalp shaved to abrasion. Rebus thought his name was Wattie or Wallie. He belonged to Telford. Maybe they all did. Graffiti on the wall further along: Won't Anyone Help? Three words spreading across the city.

Rebus parked around the corner from Flint Street and started walking. The street was in darkness at ground level, except for a café and amusement arcade. There was one lamppost, its bulb dead. The council had been asked by police not to replace it in a hurry – the surveillance needed all the help it could get. A few lights were shining in the tenement flats. There were three cars parked kerbside, but only one of them with people in it. Rebus opened the back door and got in.

A man sat in the driver's seat, a woman next to him. They looked cold and bored. The woman was Detective Constable Siobhan Clarke, who had worked with Rebus at St Leonard's until a recent posting to the Scottish Crime Squad. The man, a Detective Sergeant called Claverhouse, was a Crime Squad regular. They were part of a team keeping twenty-four-hour tabs on Tommy Telford and all his deeds. Their slumped shoulders and pale faces bespoke not only tedium but the sure knowledge that surveillance was futile.

It was futile because Telford owned the street. Nobody parked here without him knowing who and why. The other two cars parked just now were Range Rovers belonging to Telford's gang. Anything but a Range Rover stuck out. The Crime Squad had a specially adapted van which they usually used for surveillance, but that wouldn't work in Flint Street. Any van parked here for longer than five minutes received close and personal attention from a couple of Telford's men. They were trained to be courteous and menacing at the same time.

'Undercover bloody surveillance,' Claverhouse growled. 'Only we're not undercover and there's nothing to survey.' He tore at a Snickers wrapper with his teeth and offered the first bite to Siobhan Clarke, who shook her head.

'Shame about those flats,' she said, peering up through the windscreen. 'They'd be perfect.'

'Except Telford owns them all,' Claverhouse said through a mouthful of chocolate.

'Are they all occupied?' Rebus asked. He'd been in the car a minute and already his toes were cold.

'Some of them are empty,' Clarke said. 'Telford uses them for storage.'

'But every bugger in and out of the main door gets spotted,' Claverhouse added. 'We've had meter readers and plumbers try to wangle their way in.'

'Who was acting the plumber?' Rebus asked.

'Ormiston. Why?'

Rebus shrugged. 'Just need someone to fix a tap in my bathroom.'

Claverhouse smiled. He was tall and skinny, with huge dark bags under his eyes and thinning fair hair. Slow-moving and slow-talking, people often underestimated him. Those who did sometimes discovered that his nickname of 'Bloody' Claverhouse was merited.

Clarke checked her watch. 'Ninety minutes till the changeover.'

'You could do with the heating on,' Rebus offered. Claverhouse turned in his seat.

'That's what I keep telling her, but she won't have it.'

'Why not?' He caught Clarke's eyes in the rearview. She was smiling.

'Because,' Claverhouse said, 'it means running the

6

engine, and running the engine when we're not going anywhere is wasteful. Global warming or something.'

'It's true,' Clarke said.

Rebus winked at her reflection. It looked like she'd been accepted by Claverhouse, which meant acceptance by the whole team at Fettes. Rebus, the perennial outsider, envied her the ability to conform.

'Bloody useless anyway,' Claverhouse continued. 'The bugger knows we're here. The van was blown after twenty minutes, the plumber routine didn't even get Ormiston over the threshhold, and now here we are, the only sods on the whole street. We couldn't blend in less if we were doing panto.'

'Visible presence as a deterrent,' Rebus said.

'Aye, right, a few more nights of this and I'm sure Tommy'll be back on the straight and narrow.' Claverhouse shifted in his seat, trying to get comfortable. 'Any word of Candice?'

Sammy had asked her father the same thing. Rebus shook his head.

'You still think Tarawicz snatched her? No chance she did a runner?'

Rebus snorted.

'Just because you want it to be them doesn't mean it was. My advice: leave it to us. Forget about her. You've got that Adolf thing to keep you busy.'

'Don't remind me.'

'Did you ever track down Colquhoun?'

'Sudden holiday. His office got a doctor's line.'

'I think we did for him.'

Rebus realised one of his hands was caressing his breast pocket. 'So is Telford in the café or what?'

'Went in about an hour ago,' Clarke said. 'There's a room at the back, he uses that. He seems to like the arcade, too. Those games where you sit on a motorbike and do the circuit.'

'We need someone on the inside,' Claverhouse said. 'Either that or wire the place.'

'We couldn't even get a plumber in there,' Rebus said. 'You think someone with a fistful of radio mikes is going to fare any better?'

'Couldn't do any worse.' Claverhouse switched on the radio, seeking music.

'Please,' Clarke pleaded, 'no country and western.'

Rebus stared out at the café. It was well-lit with a net curtain covering the bottom half of its window. On the top half was written 'Big Bites For Small Change'. There was a menu taped to the window, and a sandwich board on the pavement outside, which gave the café's hours as 6.30 a.m. – 8.30 p.m. The place should have been closed for an hour.

'How are his licences?'

'He has lawyers,' Clarke said.

'First thing we tried,' Claverhouse added. 'He's applied for a late-night extension. I can't see the neighbours complaining.'

'Well,' Rebus said, 'much as I'd love to sit around here chatting …'

'End of liaison?' Clarke asked. She was keeping her humour, but Rebus could see she was tired. Disrupted sleep pattern, body chill, plus the boredom of a surveillance you know is going nowhere. It was never easy partnering Claverhouse: no great fund of stories, just constant reminding that they had to do everything 'the right way', meaning by the book.

'Do us a favour,' Claverhouse said.

'What?'

'There's a chippy across from the Odeon.'

'What do you want?'

'Just a poke of chips.'

'Siobhan?'

'Irn-Bru.'

'Oh, and John?' Claverhouse added as Rebus stepped out of the car. 'Ask them for a hot-water bottle while you're at it.'

A car turned into the street, speeding up then screeching to a halt outside the café. The back door nearest the kerb opened, but nobody got out. The car accelerated away, door still hanging open, but there was something on the pavement now, something crawling, trying to push itself upright.

'Get after them!' Rebus shouted. Claverhouse had already turned the ignition, slammed the gear-shift into first. Clarke was on the radio as the car pulled away. As Rebus crossed the street, the man got to his feet. He stood with one hand against the café window, the other held to his head. As Rebus approached, the man seemed to sense his presence, staggered away from the café into the road.

'Christ!' he yelled. 'Help me!' He fell to his knees again, both hands scrabbling at his scalp. His face was a mask of blood. Rebus crouched in front of him.

'We'll get you an ambulance,' he said. A crowd had gathered at the window of the café. The door had been pulled open, and two young men were watching, like they were onlookers at a piece of street theatre. Rebus recognised them: Kenny Houston and Pretty-Boy. 'Don't just stand there!' he yelled. Houston looked to Pretty-Boy, but Pretty-Boy wasn't moving. Rebus took out his mobile, called in the emergency, his eyes fixing on Pretty-Boy: black wavy hair, eyeliner. Black leather jacket, black polo-neck, black jeans. Stones: 'Paint it Black'. But the face chalk-white, like it had been powdered. Rebus walked up to the door. Behind him, the man was beginning to wail, a roar of pain echoing into the night sky.

'We don't know him,' Pretty-Boy said.

'I didn't ask if you knew him, I asked for help.'

Pretty-Boy didn't blink. 'The magic word.'

Rebus got right up into his face. Pretty-Boy smiled and nodded towards Houston, who went to fetch towels.

Most of the customers had returned to their tables. One was studying the bloody palmprint on the window. Rebus saw another group of people, watching from the doorway of a room to the back of the café. At their centre stood Tommy Telford: tall, shoulders straight, legs apart. He looked almost soldierly.

'I thought you took care of your lads, Tommy!' Rebus called to him. Telford looked straight through him, then turned back into the room. The door closed. More screams from outside. Rebus grabbed the dishtowels from Houston and ran. The bleeder was on his feet again, weaving like a boxer in defeat.

'Take your hands down for a sec.' The man lifted both hands from his matted hair, and Rebus saw a section of scalp rise with them, like it was attached to the skull by a hinge. A thin jet of blood hit Rebus in the face. He turned away and felt it against his ear, his neck. Blindly he stuck the towel on to the man's head.

'Hold this.' Rebus grabbing the hands, forcing them on to the towel. Headlights: the unmarked police car. Claverhouse had his window down.

'Lost them in Causewayside. Stolen car, I'll bet. They'll be hoofing it.'

'We need to get this one to Emergency.' Rebus pulled open the back door. Clarke had found a box of paper hankies and was pulling out a wad.

'I think he's beyond Kleenex,' Rebus said as she handed them over.

'They're for you,' she said.

2

It was a three-minute drive to the Royal Infirmary. Accident & Emergency was gearing up for firework casualties. Rebus went to the toilets, stripped, and rinsed himself off as best he could. His shirt was damp and cold to the touch. A line of blood had dried down the front of his chest. He turned to look in the mirror, saw more blood on his back. He had wet a clump of blue paper towels. There was a change of clothes in his car, but his car was back near Flint Street. The door of the toilets opened and Claverhouse came in.

'Best I could do,' he said, holding out a black t-shirt. There was a garish print on the front, a zombie with demon's eyes, wielding a scythe. 'Belongs to one of the junior doctors, made me promise to get it back to him.'

Rebus dried himself off with another wad of towels. He asked Claverhouse how he looked.

'There's still some on your brow.' Claverhouse wiped the bits Rebus had missed.

'How is he?' Rebus asked.

'They reckon he'll be okay, if he doesn't get an infection on the brain.'

'What do you think?'

'Message to Tommy from Big Ger.'

'Is he one of Tommy's men?'

'He's not saying.'

'So what's his story?'

'Fell down a flight of steps, cracked his head at the bottom.'

'And the drop-off?'

'Says he can't remember.' Claverhouse paused. 'Eh, John ...?'

'What?'

'One of the nurses wanted me to ask you something.'

His tone told Rebus all he needed to know. 'AIDS test?'

'They just wondered.'

Rebus thought about it. Blood in his eyes, his ears, running down his neck. He looked himself over: no scratches or cuts. 'Let's wait and see,' he said.

'Maybe we should pull the surveillance,' Claverhouse said, 'leave them to get on with it.'

'And have a fleet of ambulances standing by to pick up the bodies?'

Claverhouse snorted. 'Is this sort of thing Big Ger's style?'

'Very much so,' Rebus said, reaching for his jacket.

'But not that nightclub stabbing?'

'No.'

Claverhouse started laughing, but there was no humour to the sound. He rubbed his eyes. 'Never got those chips, did we? Christ, I could use a drink.'

Rebus reached into his jacket for the quarter-bottle of Bell's.

Claverhouse didn't seem surprised as he broke the seal. He took a gulp, chased it down with another, and handed the bottle back. 'Just what the doctor ordered.'

Rebus started screwing the top back on.

'Not having one?'

'I'm on the wagon.' Rebus rubbed a thumb over the label.

'Since when?'

'The summer.'

'So why carry a bottle around?'

Rebus looked at it. 'Because that's not what it is.'

Claverhouse looked puzzled. 'Then what is it?'

'A bomb.' Rebus tucked the bottle back into his pocket. 'A little suicide bomb.'

They walked back to A&E. Siobhan Clarke was waiting for them outside a closed door.

'They've had to sedate him,' she said. 'He was up on his feet again, reeling all over the place.' She pointed to marks on the floor – airbrushed blood, smudged by footprints.

'Do we have a name?'

'He's not offered one. Nothing in his pockets to identify him. Over two hundred in cash, so we can rule out a mugging. What do you reckon for a weapon? Hammer?'

Rebus shrugged. 'A hammer would dent the skull. That flap looked too neat. I think they went for him with a cleaver.'

'Or a machete,' Claverhouse added. 'Something like that.'

Clarke stared at him. 'I smell whisky.'

Claverhouse put a finger to his lips.

'Anything else?' Rebus asked. It was Clarke's turn to shrug.

'Just one observation.'

'What's that?'

'I like the t-shirt.'

Claverhouse put money in the machine, got out three coffees. He'd called his office, told them the surveillance was suspended. Orders now were to stay at the hospital, see if the victim would say anything. The very least they wanted was an ID. Claverhouse handed a coffee to Rebus.

'White, no sugar.'

Rebus took the coffee with one hand. In the other he

held a polythene laundry-bag, inside which was his shirt. He'd have a go at cleaning it. It was a good shirt.

'You know, John,' Claverhouse said, 'there's no point you hanging around.'

Rebus knew. His flat was a short walk away across The Meadows. His large, empty flat. There were students through the wall. They played music a lot, stuff he didn't recognise.

'You know Telford's gang,' Rebus said. 'Didn't you recognise the face?'

Claverhouse shrugged. 'I thought he looked a bit like Danny Simpson.'

'But you're not sure?'

'If it's Danny, a name's about all we can hope to get out of him. Telford picks his boys with care.'

Clarke came towards them along the corridor. She took the coffee from Claverhouse.

'It's Danny Simpson,' she confirmed. 'I just got another look, now the blood's been cleaned off.' She took a swallow of coffee, frowned. 'Where's the sugar?'

'You're sweet enough already,' Claverhouse told her.

'Why did they pick on Simpson?' Rebus asked.

'Wrong place, wrong time?' Claverhouse suggested.

'Plus he's pretty low down the pecking order,' Clarke added, 'making it a gentle hint.'

Rebus looked at her. Short dark hair, shrewd face with a gleam to the eyes. He knew she worked well with suspects, kept them calm, listened carefully. Good on the street, too: fast on her feet as well as in her head.

'Like I say, John,' Claverhouse said, finishing his coffee, 'any time you want to head off ...'

Rebus looked up and down the empty corridor. 'Am I in the way or something?'

'It's not that. But your job's *liaison* – period. I know the way you work: you get attached to cases, maybe even over-attached. Look at Candice. I'm just saying ...'

'You're saying, don't butt in?' Colour rose to Rebus's cheeks: *Look at Candice.*

'I'm saying it's our case, not yours. That's all.'

Rebus's eyes narrowed. 'I don't get it.'

Clarke stepped in. 'John, I think all he means is –'

'Whoah! It's okay, Siobhan. Let the man speak for himself.'

Claverhouse sighed, screwed up his empty cup and looked around for a bin. 'John, investigating Telford means keeping half an eye on Big Ger Cafferty and his crew.'

'And?'

Claverhouse stared at him. 'Okay, you want it spelling out? You went to Barlinnie yesterday – news travels in our business. You met Cafferty. The two of you had a chinwag.'

'He asked me to go,' Rebus lied.

Claverhouse held up his hands. 'Fact is, as you've just said, he asked you and you went.' Claverhouse shrugged.

'Are you saying I'm in his pocket?' Rebus's voice had risen.

'Boys, boys,' Clarke said.

The doors at the end of the corridor had swung open. A young man in dark business suit, briefcase swinging, was coming towards the drinks machine. He was humming some tune. He stopped humming as he reached them, put down his case and searched his pockets for change. He smiled when he looked at them.

'Good evening.'

Early-thirties, black hair slicked back from his forehead. One kiss-curl looped down between his eyebrows.

'Anyone got change of a pound?'

They looked in their pockets, couldn't find enough coins.

'Never mind.' Though the machine was flashing EXACT

MONEY ONLY he stuck in the pound coin and selected tea, black, no sugar. He stooped down to retrieve the cup, but didn't seem in a hurry to leave.

'You're police officers,' he said. His voice was a drawl, slightly nasal: Scottish upper-class. He smiled. 'I don't think I know any of you professionally, but one can always tell.'

'And you're a lawyer,' Rebus guessed. The man bowed his head in acknowledgement. 'Here to represent the interests of a certain Mr Thomas Telford.'

'I'm Daniel Simpson's legal advisor.'

'Which adds up to the same thing.'

'I believe Daniel's just been admitted.' The man blew on his tea, sipped it.

'Who told you he was here?'

'Again, I don't believe that's any of your business, Detective ...?'

'DI Rebus.'

The man transferred his cup to his left hand so he could hold out his right. 'Charles Groal.' He glanced at Rebus's t-shirt. 'Is that what you call "plain clothes", Inspector?'

Claverhouse and Clarke introduced themselves in turn. Groal made great show of handing out business cards.

'I take it,' he said, 'you're loitering here in the hope of interviewing my client?'

'That's right,' Claverhouse said.

'Might I ask why, DS Claverhouse? Or should I address that question to your superior?'

'He's not my –' Claverhouse caught Rebus's look.

Groal raised an eyebrow. 'Not your superior? And yet he manifestly is, being an Inspector to your Sergeant.' He looked towards the ceiling, tapped a finger against his cup. 'You're not strictly colleagues,' he said at last, bringing his gaze back down to focus on Claverhouse.

'DS Claverhouse and myself are attached to the Scottish Crime Squad,' Clarke said.

'And Inspector Rebus isn't,' Groal observed. 'Fascinating.'

'I'm at St Leonard's.'

'Then this is quite rightly part of your division. But as for the Crime Squad ...'

'We just want to know what happened,' Rebus went on.

'A fall of some kind, wasn't it? How is he, by the way?'

'Nice of you to show concern,' Claverhouse muttered.

'He's unconscious,' Clarke said.

'And likely to be in an operating theatre fairly soon. Or will they want to X-ray him first? I'm not very up on the procedures.'

'You could always ask a nurse,' Claverhouse said.

'DS Claverhouse, I detect a certain hostility.'

'Just his normal tone,' Rebus said. 'Look, you're here to make sure Danny Simpson keeps his trap shut. We're here to listen to whatever bunch of shite the two of you eventually concoct for our delectation. I think that's a pretty fair summary, don't you?'

Groal cocked his head slightly to one side. 'I've heard about you, Inspector. Occasionally stories can become exaggerated but not, I'm pleased to say, in your case.'

'He's a living legend,' Clarke offered. Rebus snorted and headed back into A&E.

There was a woolly-suit in there, seated on a chair, his cap on his lap and a paperback book resting on the cap. Rebus had seen him half an hour before. The constable was sitting outside a room with its door closed tight. Quiet voices came from the other side. The woolly-suit was called Redpath and he worked out of St Leonard's. He'd been in the force a bit under a year. Graduate recruit. They called him 'The Professor'. He was tall and spotty and had a shy look about

17

him. He closed the book as Rebus approached, but kept a finger in his page.

'Science fiction,' he explained. 'Always thought I'd grow out of it.'

'There are a lot of things we don't grow out of, son. What's it about?'

'The usual: threats to the stability of the time continuum, parallel universes.' Redpath looked up. 'What do you think of parallel universes, sir?'

Rebus nodded towards the door. 'Who's in there?'

'Hit and run.'

'Bad?' The Professor shrugged. 'Where did it happen?'

'Top of Minto Street.'

'Did you get the car?'

Redpath shook his head. 'Waiting to see if she can tell us anything. What about you, sir?'

'Similar story, son. Parallel universe, you could call it.'

Siobhan Clarke appeared, nursing a fresh cup of coffee. She nodded a greeting towards Redpath, who stood up: a courtesy which gained him a sly smile.

'Telford doesn't want Danny talking,' she said to Rebus.

'Obviously.'

'And meantime he'll want to even the score.'

'Definitely.'

She caught Rebus's eyes. 'I thought he was a bit out of order back there.' Meaning Claverhouse, but not wanting to name names in front of a uniform.

Rebus nodded. 'Thanks.' Meaning: you did right not to say as much at the time. Claverhouse and Clarke were partners now. It wouldn't do for her to upset him.

A door slid open and a doctor appeared. She was young, and looked exhausted. Behind her in the room, Rebus could see a bed, a figure on the bed, staff milling around the various machines. Then the door slid closed.

'We're going to do a brain scan,' the doctor was telling Redpath. 'Have you contacted her family?'

'I don't have a name.'

'Her effects are inside.' The doctor slid open the door again and walked in. There was clothing folded on a chair, a bag beneath it. As the doctor pulled out the bag, Rebus saw something. A flat white cardboard box.

A white cardboard pizza box. Clothes: black denims, black bra, red satin shirt. A black duffel-coat.

'John?'

And black shoes with two-inch heels, square-toed, new-looking except for the scuff marks, like they'd been dragged along the road.

He was in the room now. They had a mask over her face, feeding her oxygen. Her forehead was cut and bruised, the hair pushed away from it. Her fingers were blistered, the palms scraped raw. The bed she lay on wasn't really a bed but a wide steel trolley.

'Excuse me, sir, you shouldn't be in here.'

'What's wrong?'

'It's this gentleman –'

'John? John, what is it?'

Her earrings had been removed. Three tiny pin-pricks, one of them redder than its neighbours. The face above the sheet: puffy blackened eyes, a broken nose, abrasions on both cheeks. Split lip, a graze on the chin, eyelids which didn't even flutter. He saw a hit and run victim. And beneath it all, he saw his daughter.

And he screamed.

Clarke and Redpath had to drag him out, helped by Claverhouse who'd heard the noise.

'Leave the door open! I'll kill you if you close that door!'

They tried to sit him down. Redpath rescued his book

from the chair. Rebus tore it from him and threw it down the hall.

'How could you read a fucking book?' he spat. 'That's Sammy in there! And you're out here reading a book!'

Clarke's cup of coffee had been kicked over, the floor slippy, Redpath going down as Rebus pushed at him.

'Can you jam that door open?' Claverhouse was asking the doctor. 'And what about a sedative?'

Rebus was clawing his hands through his hair, bawling dry-eyed, his voice hoarse and uncomprehending. Staring down at himself, he saw the ludicrous t-shirt and knew that's what he'd take away from this night: the image of an Iron Maiden t-shirt and its grinning bright-eyed demon. He hauled off his jacket and started tearing at the shirt.

She was behind that door, he thought, and I was out here chatting as casual as you like. She'd been in there all the time he'd been here. Two things clicked: a hit and run; the car speeding away from Flint Street.

He grabbed at Redpath. 'Top of Minto Street. You're sure?'

'What?'

'Sammy ... top of Minto Street?'

Redpath nodded. Clarke knew straight away what Rebus was thinking.

'I don't think so, John. They were headed the opposite way.'

'Could have doubled back.'

Claverhouse had caught some of the exchange. 'I just got off the phone. The guys who did Danny Simpson, we picked up the car. White Escort abandoned in Argyle Place.'

Rebus looked at Redpath. 'White Escort?'

Redpath was shaking his head. 'Witnesses say dark-coloured.'

Rebus turned to the wall, stood there with his palms

pressed to it, staring at the painting, it was like the child
had seen that year.

"I'm not sure I put a hand on his shoulder. Then, I'm sure
she's going to be fine. The doctor's sure in fact, you a
couple of tablets, but he can't... what about one of these?"

He spoke with Robert, and a folded in the crest of
his arm, the motion began in his hand.

"It's little, moving bomb."

He took the bomb and I lit it inside. A narrow lit top,
his eyes on the open doorway. I lifted the bottle to his lips.

"Drink."

pressed to it. Staring at the paintwork, it was like he could see *inside* the paint.

Claverhouse put a hand on his shoulder. 'John, I'm sure she's going to be fine. The doctor's gone to fetch you a couple of tablets, but meantime what about one of these?'

Claverhouse with Rebus's jacket folded in the crook of his arm, the quarter-bottle in his hand.

The little suicide bomb.

He took the bottle from Claverhouse. Unscrewed its top his eyes on the open doorway. Lifted the bottle to his li

Drank.

Book Two

'In the Hanging Garden/No one sleeps'

A seaside holiday: caravan park, long walks and sandcastles.
He sat in a deck-chair, trying to read. Cold wind blowing,
despite the sun. Rhona rubbed suntan lotion on Sammy, said
you couldn't be too careful. Told him to keep an eye open, she
was going back to the caravan for her book. Sammy was
burying her father's feet in the sand.

He was trying to read, but thinking about work. Every day
of the holiday, he sneaked off to a phone-box and called the
station. They kept telling him to go and enjoy himself, forget
about everything. He was halfway through a spy thriller. The
plot had already lost him.

Rhona was doing her best. She'd wanted somewhere foreign,
a bit of glamour and heat to go with the sunshine. Finances,
however, were on his side. So here they were on the Fife coast,
where he'd first met her. Was he hoping for something? Some
memory rekindled? He'd come here with his own parents,
played with Mickey, met other kids, then lost them again at the
end of the fortnight.

He tried the spy novel again, but case-work got in the way.
And then a shadow fell over him.

'Where is she?'

'What?' He looked down. His feet were buried in sand, but
Sammy wasn't there. How long had she been gone? He stood
up, scanned the seashore. A few tentative bathers, going in no
further than their knees.

'Christ, John, where is she?'

He turned round, looked at the sand dunes in the distance.

'The dunes …?'

They warned her. There were hollows in the dunes where the sand was eroding. Small dens had been created – a magnet for kids. Only they were prone to collapse. Earlier in the season, a ten-year-old boy had been dug out by frantic parents. He hadn't quite choked on the sand …

They were running now. The dunes, the grass, no sign of her.

'Sammy!'

'Maybe she went into the water.'

'You were supposed to be keeping an eye on her!'

'I'm sorry. I …'

'Sammy!'

A small shape in one of the dens. Hopping on its hands and knees. Rhona reached in, pulled her out, hugged her.

'Sweetie, we told you not to!'

'I was a rabbit.'

Rebus looked at the fragile roof: sand meshed with the roots of plants and grasses. Punched it with a fist. The roof collapsed. Rhona was looking at him.

End of holiday.

26

3

John Rebus kissed his daughter.

'See you later,' he said, watching her as she left the coffee shop. Espresso and a slice of caramel shortbread – that's all she'd had time for – but they'd fixed another date for dinner. Nothing fancy, just a pizza.

It was October 30th. By mid-November, if Nature were feeling bloody, it would be winter. Rebus had been taught at school that there were four distinct seasons, had painted pictures of them in bright and sombre colours, but his native country seemed not to know this. Winters were long, outstaying their welcome. The warm weather came suddenly, people stripping to t-shirts as the first buds appeared, so that spring and summer seemed entwined into a single season. And no sooner had the leaves started turning brown than the first frost came again.

Sammy waved at him through the cafe window then was gone. She seemed to have grown up all right. He'd always been on the lookout for evidence of instability, hints of childhood traumas or a genetic predisposition towards self-destruction. Maybe he should phone Rhona some day and thank her, thank her for bringing Samantha up on her own. It couldn't have been easy: that was what people always said. He knew it would be nice if he could feel some responsibility for the success, but he wasn't *that* hypocritical. The truth was, while she'd been growing up, he'd been elsewhere. It was the same with his marriage: even when in the same room as his wife, even out at the pictures or around the table at a dinner party ... the best part of him had been elsewhere, fixed on some case or other, some question that needed answering before he could rest.

Rebus lifted his coat from the back of his chair. Nothing left for it but to go back to the office. Sammy was headed back to her own office; she worked with ex-convicts. She had refused his offer of a lift. Now that it was out in the open, she'd wanted to talk about her man, Ned Farlowe. Rebus had tried to look interested, but found that his mind was half on Joseph Lintz – in other words, same problem as always. When he'd been given the Lintz case, he'd been told he was well-suited to it: his Army background for one thing; and his seeming affinity for historical cases – by which Farmer Watson, Rebus's chief superintendent, had meant Bible John – for another.

'With respect, sir,' Rebus had said, 'that sounds like a load of balls. Two reasons for me getting lumbered with this: one, no other bugger will touch it with a barge-pole; two, it'll keep me out of the way for a while.'

'Your remit,' the Farmer had said, unwilling to let Rebus rile him, 'is to sift through what there is, see if any of it amounts to evidence. You can interview Mr Lintz if it'll help. Do whatever you think necessary, and if you find enough to warrant a charge ...'

'I won't. You know I won't.' Rebus sighed. 'Sir, we've been through this before. It's the whole reason the War Crimes section was shut down. That case a few years back – lot of hoo-haa about bugger all.' He was shaking his head. 'Who wants it all dragged up, apart from the papers?'

'I'm taking you off the Mr Taystee case. Let Bill Pryde handle that.'

So it was settled: Lintz belonged to Rebus.

It had started with a news story, with documents handed over to a Sunday broadsheet. The documents had come from the Holocaust Investigation Bureau based in Tel Aviv.

They had passed on to the newspaper the name of Joseph Lintz, who had, they said, been living quietly in Scotland under an alias since the end of the war, and who was, in fact, Josef Linzstek, a native of Alsace. In June 1944, Lieutenant Linzstek had led the 3rd Company of an SS regiment, part of the 2nd Panzer Division, into the town of Villefranche d'Albarede in the Corrèze region of France. 3rd Company had rounded up everyone in the town – men, women, children. The sick were carried from their beds, the elderly pulled from their armchairs, babies hoisted from their cots.

A teenage girl – an evacuee from Lorraine – had seen what the Germans were capable of. She climbed into the attic of her house and hid there, watching from a small window in the roof-tiles. Everyone was marched into the village square. The teenager saw her schoolfriends find their families. She hadn't been in school that day: a throat infection. She wondered if anyone would tell the Germans …

There was a commotion as the mayor and other dignitaries remonstrated with the officer in charge. While machine guns were aimed at the crowd, these men – among them the priest, lawyer, and doctor – were set upon with rifle butts. Then ropes were produced, and strung over half a dozen of the trees which lined the square. The men were hauled to their feet, their heads pushed through the nooses. An order was given, a hand raised then dropped, and soldiers pulled on each rope, until six men were hanging from the trees, bodies writhing, legs kicking uselessly, the movements slowing by degrees.

As the teenager remembered it, it took an age for them to die. Stunned silence in the square, as if the whole village knew now, knew that this was no mere check of identity papers. More orders were barked. The men, separated from the women and children, were marched off to Prud-homme's barn, everyone else shepherded into the church. The square grew empty, except for a dozen or so soldiers, rifles slung over their shoulders. They chatted, kicked up dust and stones, shared jokes and cigarettes. One of them went into the bar and switched the radio on. Jazz music filled the air, competing with the rustle of leaves as a breeze twisted the corpses in the trees.

'It was strange,' the girl later said. 'I stopped seeing them as dead bodies. It was as if they'd become something else, parts of the trees themselves.'

Then the explosion, smoke and dust billowing from the church. A moment's silence, as though a vacuum had been created in the world, then screams, followed immediately by machine-gun fire. And when it finally stopped, she could still hear it. Because it wasn't just inside the church: it was in the distance, too.

Prudhomme's barn.

When she was finally found – by people from surround-ing villages – she was naked except for a shawl she had found in a trunk. The shawl had belonged to her grandmother, dead the previous year. But she was not alone in escaping the massacre. When the soldiers had opened fire in Prudhomme's barn, they'd aimed low. The first row of men to fall had been wounded in the lower body, and the bodies which fell on them shielded them from further fire. When straw was strewn over the mound and set alight, they'd waited as long as they could before starting to claw their way out from beneath, expecting at any moment to be shot. Four of them made it, two with their hair and clothes on fire, one dying later from his wounds.

Three men, one teenage girl: the only survivors.

The death toll was never finalised. No one knew how many visitors had been in Villefranche that day, how many refugees could be added to the count. A list was compiled of over seven hundred names, people who had most likely been killed.

Rebus sat at his desk and rubbed his eyes with his knuckles. The teenage girl was still alive, a pensioner now. The male survivors were all dead. But they'd been alive for the Bordeaux trial in 1953. He had summaries of their evidence. The summaries were in French. A lot of the material sitting on his desk was French, and Rebus didn't speak French. That was why he'd gone to the Modern Languages department at the university and found someone who could. Her name was Kirstin Mede, and she lectured in French, but also had a working knowledge of German, which was handy: the documents which weren't in French were in German. He had a one-page English summary of the trial proceedings, passed on from the Nazi hunters. The trial had opened in February 1953 and lasted just under a month. Of seventy-five men identified as having been part of the German force at Villefranche, only fifteen were present – six Germans and nine French Alsatians. Not one of them was an officer. One German received the death sentence, the others jail terms of between four and twelve years, but they were all released as soon as the trial finished. Alsace hadn't been enjoying the trial, and in a bid to unite the nation, the government had passed an amnesty. The Germans, meantime, were said to have already served their sentences.

The survivors of Villefranche had been horrified.

Even more extraordinary to Rebus's mind, the British had apprehended a couple of German officers involved in the massacre, but had refused to hand them over to the French authorities, returning them to Germany instead, where they lived long and prosperous lives. If Linzstek had been captured then, there would have been none of the present commotion.

Politics: it was all down to politics. Rebus looked up and

Kirstin Mede was standing there. She was tall, deftly constructed, and immaculately dressed. She wore make-up the way women usually did only in fashion adverts. Today she was wearing a check two-piece, the skirt just touching her knees, and long gold-coloured earrings. She had already opened her briefcase and was pulling out a sheaf of papers.

'Latest translations,' she said.

'Thanks.'

Rebus looked down at a note he'd made to himself: 'Corrèze trip necessary??' Well, the Farmer had said he could have whatever he wanted. He looked up at Kirstin Mede and wondered if the budget would stretch to a tour guide. She was sitting opposite him, putting on half-moon reading glasses.

'Can I get you a coffee?' he asked.

'I'm a bit pushed today. I just wanted you to see these.' She laid two sheets of paper on his desk so that they faced him. One sheet was the photocopy of a typed report, in German. The second sheet was her translation. Rebus looked at the German.

'– *Der Beginn der Vergeltungsmassnahmen hat ein merkbares Aufatmen hervorgerufen und die Stimmung sehr günstig beeinflusst.*'

'The beginning of reprisals,' he read, 'has brought about a marked improvement in morale, with the men now noticeably more relaxed.'

'It's supposed to be from Linzstek to his commander,' she explained.

'But no signature?'

'Just the typed name, underlined.'

'So it doesn't help us identify Linzstek.'

'No, but remember what we were talking about? It gives a reason for the assault.'

'A touch of R&R for the lads?'

Her look froze him. 'Sorry,' he said, raising his hands.

'Far too glib. And you're right, it's almost like the Lieutenant is trying to justify the whole thing in print.'

'For posterity?'

'Maybe. After all, they'd just started being the losing side.' He looked at the other papers. 'Anything else?'

'Some further reports, nothing too exciting. And some of the eyewitness testimony.' She looked at him with pale grey eyes. 'It gets to you after a while, doesn't it?'

Rebus looked at her and nodded.

The female survivor of the massacre lived in Juillac, and had been questioned recently by local police about the man in charge of the German troops. Her story hadn't changed from the one she'd told at the trial: she'd seen his face only for a few seconds, and looking down from the attic of a three-storey house. She'd been shown a recent photo of Joseph Lintz, and had shrugged.

'Maybe,' she'd said. 'Yes, maybe.'

Which would, Rebus knew, be turfed out by the Procurator-Fiscal, who knew damned well what any defence lawyer with half a brain would do with it.

'How's the case coming?' Kirstin Mede asked. Maybe she'd seen some look cross his face.

'Slowly. The problem is all this stuff.' He waved towards the strewn desk. 'On the one hand I've got all this, and on the other I've got a wee old man from the New Town. The two don't seem to go together.'

'Have you met him?'

'Once or twice.'

'What's he like?'

What was Joseph Lintz like? He was cultured, a linguist. He'd even been a Professor at the university, back in the early 70s. Only for a year or two. His own explanation: 'I was filling a vacuum until they could find someone of greater standing'. He'd been Professor of German. He'd lived in Scotland since 1945 or '46 – he was vague about

33

exact dates, blaming his memory. His early life was vague, too. He said papers had been destroyed. The Allies had had to create a duplicate set for him. There was only Lintz's word that these new papers were anything but an official record of lies he'd told and which had been believed. Lintz's story – birth in Alsace; parents and relatives all dead; forced enlistment in the SS. Rebus liked the touch about joining the SS. It was the sort of admission that would make officials decide: he's been honest about his involvement with that, so he's probably being honest about the other details. There was no actual record of a Joseph Lintz serving with any SS regiment, but then the SS had destroyed a lot of their own records once they'd seen the way the war was headed. Lintz's war record was vague, too. He mentioned shell-shock to explain the gaps in his memory. But he was vehement that he had never been called Linzstek and had never served in the Corrèze region of France.

'I was in the east,' he would say. 'That's where the Allies found me, in the east.'

The problem was that there was no convincing explanation as to how Lintz had found himself in the United Kingdom. He said he'd asked if he could go there and start a new life. He didn't want to return to Alsace, wanted to be as far away from the Germans as possible. He wanted water between him and them. Again, there was no documentation to back this up, and meantime the Holocaust investigators had come up with their own 'evidence', which pointed to Lintz's involvement in the 'Rat Line'.

'Have you ever heard of something called the Rat Line?' Rebus had asked at their first meeting.

'Of course,' Joseph Lintz had said. 'But I never had anything to do with it.'

Lintz: in the drawing-room of his Heriot Row home. An elegant four-storey Georgian edifice. A huge house for a man who'd never married. Rebus had said as much. Lintz had merely shrugged, as was his privilege. Where had the money come from?

'I've worked hard, Inspector.'

Maybe so, but Lintz had purchased the house in the late-1950s on a lecturer's salary. A colleague from the time had told Rebus everyone in the department suspected Lintz of having a private income. Lintz denied this.

'Houses were cheaper back then, Inspector. The fashion was for country properties and bungalows.'

Joseph Lintz: barely five foot tall, bespectacled. Parchment hands with liver spots. One wrist sported a pre-war Ingersoll watch. Glass-fronted bookcases lining his drawing-room. Charcoal-coloured suits. An elegant way about him, almost feminine: the way he lifted a cup to his lips; the way he flicked specks from his trousers.

'I don't blame the Jews,' he'd said. 'They'd implicate everyone if they could. They want the whole world feeling guilty. Maybe they're right.'

'In what way, sir?'

'Don't we all have little secrets, things we're ashamed of?' Lintz had smiled. 'You're playing their game, and you don't even know it.'

Rebus had pressed on. 'The two names are very similar, aren't they? Lintz, Linzstek.'

'Naturally, or they'd have absolutely no grounds for their accusations. Think, Inspector: wouldn't I have changed my name more radically? Do you credit me with a modicum of intelligence?'

'More than a modicum.' Framed diplomas on the walls, honorary degrees, photos taken with university chancellors, politicians. When the Farmer had learned a little more about Joseph Lintz, he'd cautioned Rebus to 'ca' canny'. Lintz was a patron of the arts – opera, museums, galleries – and a great giver to charities. He was a man with *friends*.

But also a solitary man, someone who was happiest when tending graves in Warriston Cemetery. Dark bags under his eyes, pushing down upon the angular cheeks. Did he sleep well?

'Like a lamb, Inspector.' Another smile. 'Of the sacrificial kind. You know, I don't blame you, you're only doing your job.'

'You seem to have no end of forgiveness, Mr Lintz.'

A careful shrug. 'Do you know Blake's words, Inspector? "And through all eternity/ I forgive you, you forgive me." I'm not so sure I can forgive the media.' This last word voiced with a distaste which manifested itself as a twist of facial muscles.

'Is that why you've set your lawyer on them?'

' "Set" makes me sound like a hunter, Inspector. This is a *newspaper*, with a team of expensive lawyers at its beck and call. Can an individual hope to win against such odds?'

'Then why bother trying?'

Lintz thumped both arms of his chair with clenched fists. 'For the principle, man!' Such outbursts were rare and short-lived, but Rebus had experienced enough of them to know that Lintz had a temper ...

'Hello?' Kirstin Mede said, angling her head to catch his gaze.

'What?'

She smiled. 'You were miles away.'

'Just across town,' he replied.

She pointed to the papers. 'I'll leave these here, okay? If you've any questions ...'

'Great, thanks.' Rebus got to his feet.

'It's okay, I know my way out.'

But Rebus was insistent. 'Sorry, I'm a bit ...' He waved his hands around his head.

'As I said, it gets to you after a while.'

As they walked back through the CID office, Rebus

could feel eyes following them. Bill Pryde came up, preening, wanting to be introduced. He had curly fair hair and thick blond eyelashes, his nose large and freckled, mouth small and topped with a ginger moustache – a fashion accessory he could well afford to lose.

'A pleasure,' he said, taking Kirstin Mede's hand. Then, to Rebus: 'Makes me wish we'd swopped.'

Pryde was working on the Mr Taystee case: an ice-cream man found dead in his van. Engine left running in a lock-up, looking initially like suicide.

Rebus steered Kirstin Mede past Pryde, kept them moving. He wanted to ask her out. He knew she wasn't married, but thought there might be a boyfriend in the frame. Rebus was thinking: what would she like to eat – French or Italian? She spoke both those languages. Maybe stick to something neutral: Indian or Chinese. Maybe she was vegetarian. Maybe she didn't like restaurants. A drink then? But Rebus didn't drink these days.

'... So what do you think?'

Rebus started. Kirstin Mede had asked him something. 'Sorry?'

She laughed, realising he hadn't been listening. He began to apologise, but she shook it off. 'I know,' she said, 'you're a bit ...' And she waved her hands around her head. He smiled. They'd stopped walking. They were facing one another. Her briefcase was tucked under one arm. It was the moment to ask her for a date, any kind of date – let *her* choose.

'What's that?' she said suddenly. It was a shriek, Rebus had heard it, too. It had come from behind the door nearest them, the door to the women's toilets. They heard it again. This time it was followed by some words they understood.

'Help me, somebody!'

Rebus pushed open the door and ran in. A WPC was pushing at a cubicle door, trying to force it with her shoulder. From behind the door, Rebus could hear choking noises.

'What is it?' he said.

'Picked her up twenty minutes ago, she said she needed the loo.' The policewoman's cheeks wore a flush of anger and embarrassment.

Rebus grabbed the top of the door and hauled himself up, peering over and down on to a figure seated on the pan. The woman there was young, heavily made-up. She sat with her back against the cistern, so that she was staring up at him, but glassily. And her hands were busy. They were busy pulling a streamer of toilet-paper from the roll, stuffing it into her mouth.

'She's gagging,' Rebus said, sliding back down. 'Stand back'. He shouldered the door, tried again. Stood back and hit the lock with the heel of his shoe. The door flew open, catching the seated woman on the knees. He pushed his way in. Her face was turning purple.

'Grab her hands,' he told the WPC. Then he started pulling the stream of white paper from her mouth, feeling like nothing so much as a cheap stage-show magician. There seemed to be half a roll in there, and as Rebus caught the WPC's eye, both of them let out a near-involuntary laugh. The woman had stopped struggling. Her hair was mousy-brown, lank and greasy. She wore a black skiing jacket and a tight black skirt. Her bare legs were mottled pink, bruising at one knee where the door had connected. Her bright red lipstick was coming off on Rebus's fingers. She had been crying, was crying still. Rebus, feeling guilty about the sudden laughter, crouched down so that he could look into her makeup-streaked eyes. She blinked, then held his gaze, coughing as the last of the paper was extracted.

'She's foreign,' the policewoman was explaining. 'Doesn't seem to speak English.'

'So how come she told you she needed the toilet?'

'There are ways, aren't there?'

'Where did you find her?'

'Down the Pleasance, brazen as you like.'

'That's a new patch on me.'

'Me, too.'

'Nobody with her?'

'Not that I saw.'

Rebus took the woman's hands. He was still crouching in front of her, aware of her knees brushing his chest.

'Are you all right?' She just blinked. He made his face show polite concern. 'Okay now?'

She nodded slightly. 'Okay,' she said, her voice husky. Rebus felt her fingers. They were cold. He was thinking: junkie? A lot of the working girls were. But he'd never come across one who couldn't speak English. Then he turned her hands, saw her wrists. Recent zigzag scar tissue. She didn't resist as he pushed up one sleeve of her jacket. The arm was a mass of similar inflictions.

'She's a cutter.'

The woman was talking now, babbling incoherently. Kirstin Mede, who had been standing back from proceedings, stepped forward. Rebus looked to her.

'It's not anything I understand ... not quite. Eastern European.'

'Try her with something.'

So Mede asked a question in French, repeating it in three or four other languages. The woman seemed to understand what they were trying to do.

'There's probably someone at the uni who could help,' Mede said.

Rebus started to stand up. The woman grabbed him by the knees, pulled him to her so that he nearly lost his balance. Her grip was tight, her face resting against his legs. She was still crying and babbling.

'I think she likes you, sir,' the policewoman said. They

wrested her hands free, and Rebus stepped back, but she was after him at once, throwing herself forwards, like she was begging, her voice rising. There was an audience now, half a dozen officers in the doorway. Every time Rebus moved, she came after him on all fours. Rebus looked to where his exit was blocked by bodies. The cheap magician had become straight man in a comedy routine. The WPC grabbed her, pulled her back on to her feet, one arm twisted behind her back.

'Come on,' she said through gritted teeth. 'Back to the cell. Show's over, folks.'

There was scattered applause as the prisoner was marched away. She looked back once, seeking Rebus, her eyes pleading. For what, he did not know. He turned towards Kirstin Mede instead.

'Fancy a curry some time?'

She looked at him like he was mad.

'Two things: one, she's a Bosnian Muslim. Two, she wants to see you again.'

Rebus stared at the man from the Slavic Studies department, who'd come here at Kirstin Mede's request. They were talking in the corridor at St Leonard's.

'Bosnian?'

Dr Colquhoun nodded. He was short and almost spherical, with long black hair which was swept back either side of a bald dome. His puffy face was pockmarked, his brown suit worn and stained. He wore suede Hush Puppies – same colour as the suit. *This*, Rebus couldn't help feeling, was how dons were supposed to look. Colquhoun was a mass of nervous twitches, and had yet to make eye contact with Rebus.

'I'm not an expert on Bosnia,' he went on, 'but she says she's from Sarajevo.'

'Does she say how she ended up in Edinburgh?'

'I didn't ask.'

'Would you mind asking her now?' Rebus gestured back along the corridor. The two men walked together, Colquhoun's eyes on the floor.

'Sarajevo was hit hard in the war,' he said. 'She's twenty-two, by the way, she told me that.'

She'd looked older. Maybe she was; maybe she was lying. But as the door to the Interview Room opened and Rebus saw her again, he was struck by how unformed her face was, and he revised her age downwards. She stood up abruptly as he came in, looked like she might rush forward to him, but he held up a hand in warning, and pointed to the chair. She sat down again, hands cradling the mug of sweetened black tea. She never took her eyes off him.

'She's a big fan,' the WPC said. The policewoman – same one as the toilet incident – was called Ellen Sharpe. She was sitting on the room's other chair. There wasn't much space in the Interview Room: a table and two chairs just about filled it. On the table were twin video recorders and a twin cassette-machine. The video camera pointed down from one wall. Rebus gestured for Sharpe to give her seat to Colquhoun.

'Did she give you a name?' he asked the academic.

'She told me Candice,' Colquhoun said.

'You don't believe her?'

'It's not exactly ethnic, Inspector.' Candice said something. 'She's calling you her protector.'

'And what am I protecting her from?'

The dialogue between Colquhoun and Candice was gruff, guttural.

'She says firstly you protected her from herself. And now she says you have to continue.'

'Continue protecting her?'

'She says you own her now.'

Rebus looked at the academic, whose eyes were on

41

Candice's arms. She had removed her skiing jacket. Underneath she wore a ribbed, short-sleeved shirt through which her small breasts were visible. She had folded her bare arms, but the scratches and slashes were all too apparent.

'Ask her if those are self-inflicted.'

Colquhoun struggled with the translation. 'I'm more used to literature and film than ... um ...'

'What does she say?'

'She says she did them herself.'

Rebus looked at her for confirmation, and she nodded slowly, looking slightly ashamed.

'Who put her on the street?'

'You mean ...?'

'Who's running her? Who's her manager?'

Another short dialogue.

'She says she doesn't understand.'

'Does she deny working as a prostitute?'

'She says she doesn't understand.'

Rebus turned to WPC Sharpe. 'Well?'

'A couple of cars stopped. She leaned in the window to talk with the drivers. They drove off again. Didn't like the look of the goods, I suppose.'

'If she can't speak English, how did she manage to "talk" to the drivers?'

'There are ways.'

Rebus looked at Candice. He began to speak to her, very softly. 'Straight fuck, fifteen, twenty for a blow job. Unprotected is an extra fiver.' He paused. 'How much is anal, Candice?'

Colour flooded her cheeks. Rebus smiled.

'Maybe not university tuition, Dr Colquhoun, but someone's taught her a few words of English. Just enough to get her working. Ask her again how she got here.'

Colquhoun mopped his face first. Candice spoke with her head lowered.

'She says she left Sarajevo as a refugee. Went to Amsterdam, then came to Britain. The first thing she remembers is a place with lots of bridges.'

'Bridges?'

'She stayed there for some time.' Colquhoun seemed shaken by the story. He handed her a handkerchief so she could wipe her eyes. She rewarded him with a smile. Then she looked at Rebus.

'Burger chips, yes?'

'Are you hungry?' Rebus rubbed his stomach. She nodded and smiled. He turned to Sharpe. 'See what the canteen can come up with, will you?'

The WPC gave him a hard stare, not wanting to leave. 'Would you like anything, Dr Colquhoun?'

He shook his head. Rebus asked for another coffee. As Sharpe left, Rebus crouched down by the table and looked at Candice. 'Ask her how she got to Edinburgh.'

Colquhoun asked, then listened to what sounded like a long tale. He scratched some notes on a folded sheet of paper.

'The city with the bridges, she says she didn't see much of it. She was kept inside. Sometimes she was driven to some rendezvous ... You'll have to forgive me, Inspector. I may be a linguist, but I'm no expert on colloquialisms.'

'You're doing fine, sir.'

'Well, she was used as a prostitute, that much I can infer. And one day they put her in the back of a car, and she thought she was going to another hotel or office.'

'Office?'

'From her descriptions, I'd say some of her ... work ... was done in offices. Also private apartments and houses. But mostly hotel rooms.'

'Where was she kept?'

'In a house. She had a bedroom, they kept it locked.'
Colquhoun pinched the bridge of his nose. 'They put her
in the car one day, and next thing she knew she was in
Edinburgh.'

'How long was the trip?'

'She's not sure. She slept part of the way.'

'Tell her everything's going to be all right.' Rebus
paused. 'And ask her who she works for now.'

The fear returned to Candice's face. She stammered,
shaking her head. Her voice sounded more guttural than
ever. Colquhoun looked like he was having trouble with the
translation.

'She can't tell you,' he said.

'Tell her she's safe.' Colquhoun did so. 'Tell her again,'
Rebus said. He made sure she was looking at him while
Colquhoun spoke. His face was set, a face she could trust.
She reached a hand out to him. He took it, squeezed.

'Ask her again who she works for.'

'She can't tell you, Inspector. They'd kill her. She's
heard stories.'

Rebus decided to try the name he'd been thinking of, the
man who ran half the city's working girls.

'Cafferty,' he said, watching for a reaction. There was
none. 'Big Ger. Big Ger Cafferty.' Her face remained
blank. Rebus squeezed her hand again. There was another
name ... one he'd been hearing recently.

'Telford,' he said. 'Tommy Telford.'

Candice pulled her hand away and broke into hysterics,
just as WPC Sharpe pushed open the door.

Rebus walked Dr Colquhoun out of the station, recalling
that just such a walk had got him into this in the first place.

'Thanks again, sir. If I need you, I hope you won't mind
if I call?'

'If you must, you must,' Colquhoun said grudgingly.

'Not too many Slavic specialists around,' Rebus said. He had Colquhoun's business card in his hand, a home phone number written on its back. 'Well,' Rebus put out his free hand, 'thanks again.' As they shook, Rebus thought of something.

'Were you at the university when Joseph Lintz was Professor of German?'

The question surprised Colquhoun. 'Yes,' he said at last. 'Did you know him?'

'Our departments weren't that close. I met him at a few social functions, the occasional lecture.'

'What did you think of him?'

Colquhoun blinked. He still wasn't looking at Rebus. 'They're saying he was a Nazi.'

'Yes, but back then ...?'

'As I say, we weren't close. Are you investigating him?'

'Just curious, sir. Thanks for your time.'

Back in the station, Rebus found Ellen Sharpe outside the Interview Room door.

'So what do we do with her?' she asked.

'Keep her here.'

'You mean charge her?'

Rebus shook his head. 'Let's call it protective custody.'

'Does *she* know that?'

'Who's she going to complain to? There's only one bugger in the whole city can make out what she's saying, and I've just packed him off home.'

'What if her man comes to get her?'

'Think he will?'

She thought about it. 'Probably not.'

'No, because as far as he's concerned, all he has to do is wait, and we'll release her eventually. Meantime, she doesn't speak English, so what can she give us? And she's here illegally no doubt, so if she talks, all *we'd* probably do is kick her out of the country. Telford's clever ... I hadn't

45

realised it, but he is. Using illegal aliens as prossies. It's sweet.'

'How long do we keep her?'

Rebus shrugged.

'And what do I tell my boss?'

'Direct all enquiries to DI Rebus,' he said, going to open the door.

'I thought it was exemplary, sir.'

He stopped. 'What?'

'Your knowledge of the charge-scale for prostitutes.'

'Just doing my job,' he said, smiling.

'One last question, sir … ?'

'Yes, Sharpe?'

'Why? What's the big deal?'

Rebus considered this, twitched his nose. 'Good question,' he said finally, opening the door and going in.

And he knew. He knew straight away. She looked like Sammy. Wipe away the make-up and the tears, get some sensible clothes on her, and she was the spitting image.

And she was scared.

And maybe he could help her.

'What can I call you, Candice? What's your real name?'

She took hold of his hand, put her face to it. He pointed to himself.

'John,' he said.

'Don.'

'John.'

'Shaun.'

'John.' He was smiling; so was she. 'John.'

'John.'

He nodded. 'That's it. And you?' He pointed at her now. 'Who are you?'

She paused. 'Candice,' she said, as a little light died behind her eyes.

4

Rebus didn't know Tommy Telford by sight, but he knew where to find him.

Flint Street was a passageway between Clerk Street and Buccleuch Street, near the university. The shops had mostly closed down, but the games arcade always did good business, and from Flint Street Telford leased gaming machines to pubs and clubs across the city. Flint Street was the centre of his eastern empire.

The franchise had until recently belonged to a man called Davie Donaldson, but he'd suddenly retired on 'health grounds'. Maybe he'd been right at that: if Tommy Telford wanted something from you and you weren't forthcoming, predictions of your future health could suddenly change. Donaldson was now in hiding somewhere: hiding not from Telford but from Big Ger Cafferty, for whom he had been holding the franchise 'in trust' while Cafferty bided his time in Barlinnie jail. There were some who said Cafferty ran Edinburgh as effectively from inside as he ever had done outside, but the reality was that gangsters, like Nature, abhorred a vacuum, and now Tommy Telford was in town.

Telford was a product of Ferguslie Park in Paisley. At eleven he'd joined the local gang; at twelve a couple of woolly-suits had visited him to ask about a spate of tyre slashings. They'd found him surrounded by other gang members, nearly all of them older than him, but he was at the centre, no doubt about it.

His gang had grown with him, taking over a sizeable chunk of Paisley, selling drugs and running prostitutes, doing a bit of extortion. These days he had shares in casinos and video shops, restaurants and a haulage firm, plus a property portfolio which made him landlord to several hundred people. He'd tried to make his mark in Glasgow, but had found it sealed down tight, so had gone exploring elsewhere. There were stories he'd become friendly with some big villain in Newcastle. Nobody could remember anything like it since the days when London's Krays had rented their muscle from 'Big Arthur' in Glasgow.

He'd arrived in Edinburgh a year ago, moving softly at first, buying a casino and hotel. Then suddenly he was inescapably *there*, like the shadow from a raincloud. With the chasing out of Davie Donaldson he'd given Cafferty a calculated punch to the gut. Cafferty could either fight or give up. Everyone was waiting for it to get messy ...

The games arcade called itself Fascination Street. The machines were all flashing insistence, in stark contrast to the dead facial stares of the players. Then there were shoot-'em-ups with huge video screens and digital imprecations.

'Think you're tough enough, punk?' one of them challenged as Rebus walked past. They had names like Harbinger and NecroCop, this latter reminding Rebus of how old he felt. He looked at the faces around him, saw a few he recognised, kids who'd been pulled into St Leonard's. They'd be on the fringes of Telford's gang, awaiting the call-up, hanging around like foster children, hoping The Family would take them. Most of them came from families who weren't families, latchkey kids grown old before their time.

One of the staff came in from the café.

'Who ordered the bacon sarnie?'

Rebus smiled as the faces turned to him. Bacon meant

pig meant him. A moment's examination was all he warranted. There were more pressing demands on their attention. At the far end of the arcade were the really big machines: half-size motorbikes you sat astride as you negotiated the circuit on the screen in front of you. A small appreciative coterie stood around one bike, on which sat a young man dressed in a leather jacket. Not a market-stall jacket, something altogether more special. Quality goods. Shiny sharp-toed boots. Tight black denims. White polo neck. Surrounded by fawning courtiers. Steely Dan: 'Kid Charlemagne'. Rebus found a space for himself in the midst of the glaring onlookers.

'No takers for that bacon sarnie?' he asked.

'Who are you?' the man on the machine demanded.

'DI Rebus.'

'Cafferty's man.' Said with conviction.

'What?'

'I hear you and him go back.'

'I put him inside.'

'Not every cop gets visiting rights though.' Rebus realised that though Telford's gaze was fixed on the screen, he was watching Rebus in its reflection. Watching him, talking to him, yet still managing to control the bike through hairpin bends.

'So is there some problem, Inspector?'

'Yes, there's a problem. We picked up one of your girls.'

'My what?'

'She calls herself Candice. That's about as much as we know. But foreign lassies are a new one on me. And you're fairly new around here, too.'

'I'm not getting your drift, Inspector. I supply goods and services to the entertainment sector. Are you accusing me of being a pimp?'

Rebus stuck out a foot and pushed the bike sideways. On

49

the screen, it spun and hit a crash barrier. A moment later, the screen changed. Back to the start of the race.

'See, Inspector,' Telford said, still not turning round. 'That's the beauty of games. You can always start again after an accident. Not so easy in real life.'

'What if I cut the power? Game over.'

Slowly, Telford swivelled from the hips. Now he was looking at Rebus. Close up, he looked so young. Most of the gangsters Rebus had known, they'd had a worn look, undernourished but overfed. Telford had the look of some new strain of bacteria, not yet tested or understood.

'So what is it, Rebus? Some message from Cafferty?'

'Candice,' Rebus said quietly, the slight tremor in his voice betraying his anger. With a couple of drinks in him, he'd have had Telford on the floor by now. 'From tonight, she's off the game, understood?'

'I don't know any Candice.'

'Understood?'

'Hang on, let's see if I've got this. You want me to agree with you that a woman I've never met should stop touting her hole?'

Smiles from the spectators. Telford turned back to his game. 'Where's this woman from anyway?' he asked, almost casually.

'We're not sure,' Rebus lied. He didn't want Telford knowing any more than was necessary.

'Must have been a great little chat the two of you had.'

'She's scared shitless.'

'Me, too, Rebus. I'm scared you're going to bore me to death. This Candice, did she give you a taste of the goods? I'm betting it's not every scrubber would get you this het up.'

Laughter, Rebus its brunt.

'She's off the game, Telford. Don't think about touching her.'

50

'Not with a bargepole, pal. Myself, I'm a clean-living sort of individual. I say my prayers last thing at night.'

'And kiss your cuddly bear?'

Telford looked at him again. 'Don't believe all the stories, Inspector. Here, grab a bacon sarnie on your way out, I think there's one going spare.' Rebus stood his ground a few moments longer, then turned away. 'And tell the mugs out front I said hello.'

Rebus walked back through the arcade and out into the night, heading for Nicolson Street. He was wondering what he was going to do with Candice. Simple answer: let her go, and hope she had the sense to keep moving. As he made to pass a parked car, its window slid down.

'Fucking well get in,' a voice ordered from the passenger seat. Rebus stopped, looked at the man who'd spoken, recognised the face.

'Ormiston,' he said, opening the back door of the Orion. 'Now I know what he meant.'

'Who?'

'Tommy Telford. I'm to tell you he said hello.'

The driver stared at Ormiston. 'Rumbled again.' He didn't sound surprised. Rebus recognised the voice.

'Hello, Claverhouse.'

DS Claverhouse, DC Ormiston: Scottish Crime Squad, Fettes's finest. On surveillance. Claverhouse: as thin as 'twa ply o' reek', as Rebus's father would have said. Ormiston: freckle-faced and with Mick McManus's hair – slick, pudding-bowl cut, unfeasibly black.

'You were blown before I walked in there, if that's any consolation.'

'What the fuck were you doing?'

'Paying my respects. What about you?'

'Wasting our time,' Ormiston muttered.

The Crime Squad were out for Telford: good news for Rebus.

'I've got someone,' he said. 'She works for Telford. She's frightened. You could help her.'

'The frightened ones don't talk.'

'This one might.'

Claverhouse stared at him. 'And all we'd have to do is ...?'

'Get her out of here, set her up somewhere.'

'Witness relocation?'

'If it comes to that.'

'What does she know?'

'I'm not sure. Her English isn't great.'

Claverhouse knew when he was being sold something. 'Tell us,' he said.

Rebus told them. They tried not to look interested.

'We'll talk to her,' Claverhouse said.

Rebus nodded. 'So how long has this been going on?'

'Ever since Telford and Cafferty squared off.'

'And whose side are we on?'

'We're the UN, same as always,' Claverhouse said. He spoke slowly, measuring each word and phrase. A careful man, DS Claverhouse. 'Meantime, you go charging in like some bloody mercenary.'

'I've never been a great one for tactics. Besides, I wanted to see the bastard close up.'

'And?'

'He looks like a kid.'

'And he's as clean as a whistle,' Claverhouse said. 'He's got a dozen lieutenants who'd take the fall for him.'

At the word 'lieutenants', Rebus's mind flashed to Joseph Lintz. Some men gave orders, some carried them out: which group was the more culpable?

'Tell me something,' he said, 'the teddy bear story ... is it true?'

Claverhouse nodded. 'In the passenger seat of his Range

Rover. A fucking huge yellow thing, sort they raffle in the pub Sunday lunchtime.'

'So what's the story?'

Ormiston turned in his seat. 'Ever hear of Teddy Willocks? Glasgow hardman. Carpentry nails and a claw-hammer.'

Rebus nodded. 'You welched on someone, Willocks came to see you with the carpentry bag.'

'But then,' Claverhouse took over, 'Teddy got on the wrong side of some Geordie bastard. Telford was young, making a name for himself, and he very badly wanted an in with this Geordie, so he took care of Teddy.'

'And that's why he carries a teddy around with him,' Ormiston said. 'A reminder to everyone.'

Rebus was thinking. Geordie meant someone from Newcastle. Newcastle, with its bridges over the Tyne ...

'Newcastle,' he said softly, leaning forward in his seat.

'What about it?'

'Maybe Candice was there. Her city of bridges. She might link Telford to this Geordie gangster.'

Ormiston and Claverhouse looked at one another.

'She'll need a safe place to stay,' Rebus told them. 'Money, somewhere to go afterwards.'

'A first-class flight home if she helps us nail Telford.'

'I'm not sure she'll want to go home.'

'That's for later,' Claverhouse said. 'First thing is to talk to her.'

'You'll need a translator.'

Claverhouse looked at him. 'And of course you know just the man ... ?'

She was asleep in her cell, curled under the blanket, only her hair visible. The Mothers of Invention: 'Lonely Little Girl'. The cell was in the women's block. Painted pink and blue, a slab to sleep on, graffiti scratched into the walls.

'Candice,' Rebus said quietly, squeezing her shoulder. She started awake, as if he'd administered an electric shock. 'It's okay, it's me, John.'

She looked round blindly, focused on him slowly. 'John,' she said. Then she smiled.

Claverhouse was off making phone calls, squaring things. Ormiston stood in the doorway, appraising Candice. Not that Ormiston was known to be choosy. Rebus had tried Colquhoun at home, but there'd been no answer. So now Rebus was gesturing, letting her know they wanted to take her somewhere.

'A hotel,' he said.

She didn't like that word. She looked from him to Ormiston and back again.

'It's okay,' Rebus said. 'It's just a place for you to sleep, that's all, somewhere safe. No Telford, nothing like that.'

She seemed to soften, came off the bed and stood in front of him. Her eyes seemed to say, I'll trust you, and if you let me down I won't be surprised.

Claverhouse came back. 'All fixed,' he said, his examination falling on Candice. 'She doesn't speak any English?'

'Not as practised in polite society.'

'In that case,' Ormiston said, 'she should be fine with us.'

Three men and a young woman in a dark blue Ford Orion, heading south out of the city. It was late now, past midnight, black taxis cruising. Students were spilling from pubs.

'They get younger every year.' Claverhouse was never short of a cliché.

'And more of them end up joining the force,' Rebus commented.

Claverhouse smiled. 'I meant prossies, not students. We pulled one in last week, said she was fifteen. Turned out she was twelve, on the run. All grown up about it.'

Rebus tried to remember Sammy at twelve. He saw her

54

scared, in the clutches of a madman with a grievance against Rebus. She'd had lots of nightmares afterwards, till her mother had taken her to London. Rhona had phoned Rebus a few years later. She just wanted to let him know he'd robbed Sammy of her childhood.

'I phoned ahead,' Claverhouse said. 'Don't worry, we've used this place before. It's perfect.'

'She'll need some clothes,' Rebus said.

'Siobhan can fetch her some in the morning.'

'How is Siobhan?'

'Seems fine. Hasn't half cut into the jokes and the language though.'

'Ach, she can take a joke,' Ormiston said. 'Likes a drink, too.'

This last was news to Rebus. He wondered how much Siobhan Clarke would change in order to blend with her new surroundings.

'It's just off the bypass,' Claverhouse said, meaning their destination. 'Not far now.'

The city ended suddenly. Green belt, plus the Pentland Hills. The bypass was quiet, Ormiston doing the ton between exits. They came off at Colinton and signalled into the hotel. It was a motorist's stop, one of a nationwide chain: same prices, same rooms. The cars which crowded the parking area were salesmen's specials, cigarette packets littering the passenger seats. The reps would be sleeping, or lying in a daze with the TV remote to hand.

Candice seemed reluctant to get out of the car, until she saw that Rebus was coming, too.

'You light up her life,' Ormiston offered.

At reception, they signed her in as one half of a couple – Mrs Angus Campbell. The two Crime Squad cops had the routine off pat. Rebus watched the hotel clerk, but a wink from Claverhouse told him the man was okay.

'Make it the first floor, Malcolm,' Ormiston said. 'Don't want anyone peeking in the windows.'

Room number 20. 'Will someone be with her?' Rebus asked as they climbed the stairs.

'Right there in the room,' Claverhouse said. 'The landing's too obvious, and we'd freeze our bums off in the car. Did you give me Colquhoun's number?'

'Ormiston has it.'

Ormiston was unlocking the door. 'Who's on first watch?'

Claverhouse shrugged. Candice was looking towards Rebus, seeming to sense what was being discussed. She snatched at his arm, jabbering in her native tongue, looking first to Claverhouse and then to Ormiston, all the time waving Rebus's arm.

'It's okay, Candice, really. They'll take care of you.'

She kept shaking her head, holding him with one hand and pointing at him with the other, prodding his chest to make her meaning clear.

'What do you say, John?' Claverhouse asked. 'A happy witness is a willing witness.'

'What time's Siobhan expected?'

'I'll hurry her up.'

Rebus looked at Candice again, sighed, nodded. 'Okay.' He pointed to himself, then to the room. 'Just for a little while, okay?'

Candice seemed satisfied with this, and went inside. Ormiston handed Rebus the key.

'I don't want you young things waking the neighbours now ...'

Rebus closed the door on his face.

The room was exactly as expected. Rebus filled the kettle and switched it on, dumped a tea-bag into a cup. Candice pointed to the bathroom, made turning motions with her hands.

56

'A bath?' He gestured with his arm. 'Go ahead.'

The curtain over the window was closed. He parted it and looked out. A grassy slope, occasional lights from the bypass. He made sure the curtains were closed tight, then tried adjusting the heating. The room was stifling. There didn't seem to be a thermostat, so he went back to the window and opened it a fraction. Cold night air, and the swish of nearby traffic. He opened the pack of custard creams, two small biscuits. Suddenly he felt ravenous. He'd seen a snack machine in the lobby. Plenty of change in his pockets. He made the tea, added milk, sat down on the sofa. For want of any other distractions, he turned the TV on. The tea was fine. The tea was absolutely fine, no complaints there. He picked up the phone and called Jack Morton.

'Did I wake you?'

'Not really. How's it going?'

'I wanted a drink today.'

'So what's new?'

Rebus could hear his friend making himself comfortable. Jack had helped Rebus get off the booze. Jack had said he could phone any time he liked.

'I had to talk to this scumbag, Tommy Telford.'

'I know the name.'

Rebus lit a cigarette. 'I think a drink would have helped.'

'Before or after?'

'Both.' Rebus smiled. 'Guess where I am now?'

Jack couldn't, so Rebus told him the story.

'What's your angle?' Jack asked.

'I don't know.' Rebus thought about it. 'She seems to need me. It's been a long time since anyone's felt like that.' As he said the words, he feared they didn't tell the whole story. He remembered another argument with Rhona, her screaming that he'd exploited every relationship he'd ever had.

'Do you still want that drink?' Jack was asking.

'I'm a long way from one.' Rebus stubbed out his cigarette. 'Sweet dreams, Jack.'

He was on his second cup of tea when she came back in, wearing the same clothes, her hair wet and hanging in rat's-tails.

'Better?' he asked, making the thumbs-up sign. She nodded, smiling. 'Do you want some tea?' He pointed to the kettle. She nodded again, so he made her a cup. Then he suggested a trip to the snack machine. Their haul included crisps, nuts, chocolate, and a couple of cans of Coke. Another cup of tea finished off the tiny cartons of milk. Rebus lay along the sofa, shoes off, watching soundless television. Candice lay on the bed, fully-clothed, sliding the occasional crisp from its packet, flicking channels. She seemed to have forgotten he was there. He took this as a compliment.

He must have fallen asleep. The touch of her fingers on his knee brought him awake. She was standing in front of him, wearing the t-shirt and nothing else. She stared at him, fingers still resting on his knee. He smiled, shook his head, led her back to bed. Made her lie down. She lay on her back, arms stretched. He shook his head again and pulled the duvet over her.

'That's not you any more,' he told her. 'Goodnight, Candice.'

Rebus retreated to the sofa, lay down again, and wished she would stop saying his name.

The Doors: 'Wishful Sinful' ...

A tapping at the door brought him awake. Still dark outside. He'd forgotten to close the window, and the room was cold. The TV was still playing, but Candice was asleep, duvet kicked off, chocolate wrappers strewn around her bare legs and thighs. Rebus covered her up, then tiptoed to the door, peered through the spyhole, and opened up.

'For this relief, much thanks,' he whispered to Siobhan Clarke.

She was carrying a bulging polythene bag. 'Thank God for the twenty-four-hour shop.' They went inside. Clarke looked at the sleeping woman, then went over to the sofa and started unpacking the bag.

'For you,' she whispered, 'a couple of sandwiches.'

'God bless the child.'

'For sleeping beauty, some of my clothes. They'll do till the shops open.'

Rebus was already biting into the first sandwich. Cheese salad on white bread had never tasted finer.

'How am I getting home?' he asked.

'I called you a cab.' She checked her watch. 'It'll be here in two minutes.'

'What would I do without you?'

'It's a toss-up: either freeze to death or starve.' She closed the window. 'Now go on, get out of here.'

He looked at Candice one last time, almost wanting to wake her to let her know he wasn't leaving for good. But she was sleeping so soundly, and Siobhan could take care of everything.

So he tucked the second sandwich into his pocket, tossed the room-key on to the sofa, and left.

Four-thirty. The taxi was idling outside. Rebus felt hungover. He went through a mental list of all the places he could get a drink at this time of night. He didn't know how many days it had been since he'd had a drink. He wasn't counting.

He gave his address to the cabbie, and settled back, thinking again of Candice, so soundly asleep, and protected for now. And of Sammy, too old now to need anything from her father. She'd be asleep too, snuggling into Ned Farlowe. Sleep was innocence. Even the city looked innocent in sleep. He looked at the city sometimes and saw a beauty his cynicism couldn't touch. Someone in a bar – recently? years back? – had challenged him to define romance. How could he do that? He'd seen too much of love's obverse: people killed for passion and from lack of it. So that now when he saw beauty, he could do little but respond to it with the realisation that it would fade or be brutalised. He saw lovers in Princes Street Gardens and imagined them further down the road, at the crossroads where betrayal and conflict met. He saw valentines in the shops and imagined puncture wounds, real hearts bleeding.

Not that he'd voiced any of this to his public bar inquisitor.

'Define romance,' had been the challenge. And Rebus's response? He'd picked up a fresh pint of beer and kissed the glass.

He slept till nine, showered and made some coffee. Then he phoned the hotel, and Siobhan assured him all was well.

'She was a bit startled when she woke up and saw me instead of you. Kept saying your name. I told her she'd see you again.'

'So what's the plan?'

'Shopping – one quick swoop on The Gyle. After that, Fettes. Dr Colquhoun's coming in at noon for an hour. We'll see what we get.'

Rebus was at his window, looking down on a damp Arden Street. 'Take care of her, Siobhan.'

'No problem.'

Rebus knew there'd be no problem, not with Siobhan. This was her first real action with the Crime Squad, she'd be doing her damnedest to make it a success. He was in the kitchen when the phone rang.

'Is that Inspector Rebus?'

'Who's speaking?' A voice he didn't recognise.

'Inspector, my name is David Levy. We've never met. I

apologise for calling you at home. I was given this number by Matthew Vanderhyde.'

Old man Vanderhyde: Rebus hadn't seen him in a while. 'Yes?'

'I must say, I was astonished when it transpired he knew you.' The voice was tinged with a dry humour. 'But by now nothing about Matthew should surprise me. I went to him because he knows Edinburgh.'

'Yes?'

Laughter on the line. 'I'm sorry, Inspector. I can't blame you for being suspicious when I've made such a mess of the introductions. I am a historian by profession. I've been contacted by Solomon Mayerlink to see if I might offer assistance.'

Mayerlink … Rebus knew the name. Placed it: Mayerlink ran the Holocaust Investigation Bureau.

'And exactly what "assistance" does Mr Mayerlink think I need?'

'Perhaps we could discuss it in person, Inspector. I'm staying in a hotel on Charlotte Square.'

'The Roxburghe?'

'Could we meet there? This morning, ideally.'

Rebus looked at his watch. 'An hour?' he suggested.

'Perfect. Goodbye, Inspector.'

Rebus called into the office, told them where he'd be.

5

They sat in the Roxburghe's lounge, Levy pouring coffee. An elderly couple in the far corner, beside the window, pored over sections of newspaper. David Levy was elderly, too. He wore black-rimmed glasses and had a small silver beard. His hair was a silver halo around a scalp the colour of tanned leather. His eyes seemed constantly moist, as if he'd just chewed on an onion. He sported a dun-coloured safari suit with blue shirt and tie beneath. His walking-stick rested against his chair. Now retired, he'd worked in Oxford, New York State, Tel Aviv itself, and several other locations around the globe.

'I never came into contact with Joseph Lintz, however. No reason why I should, our interests being different.'

'So why does Mr Mayerlink think you can help me?'

Levy put the coffee pot back on its tray. 'Milk? Sugar?' Rebus shook his head to both, then repeated his question.

'Well, Inspector,' Levy said, tipping two spoonfuls of sugar into his own cup, 'it's more a matter of moral support.'

'Moral support?'

'You see, many people before you have been in the same position in which you now find yourself. I'm talking about objective people, professionals with no axe to grind, and no real stake in the investigation.'

Rebus bristled. 'If you're suggesting I'm not doing my job ...'

A pained look crossed Levy's face. 'Please, Inspector,

I'm not making a very good job of this, am I? What I mean is that there will be times when you will doubt the validity of what you are doing. You'll doubt its worth.' His eyes gleamed. 'Perhaps you've already had doubts?'

Rebus said nothing. He had a drawerful of doubts, especially now that he had a real, living, breathing case – Candice. Candice, who might lead to Tommy Telford.

'You could say I'm here as your conscience, Inspector.' Levy winced again. 'No, I didn't put that right, either. You already have a conscience, that's not under debate.' He sighed. 'The question you've no doubt been pondering is the same one I've asked myself on occasions: can time wash away responsibility? For me, the answer would have to be no. The thing is this, Inspector.' Levy leaned forward. 'You are not investigating the crimes of an old man, but those of a young man who now happens to be old. Focus your mind on that. There have been investigations before, half-hearted affairs. Governments wait for these men to die rather than have to try them. But each investigation is an act of remembrance, and remembrance is never wasted. Remembrance is the only way we learn.'

'Like we've learned with Bosnia?'

'You're right, Inspector, as a species we've always been slow to take in lessons. Sometimes they have to be hammered home.'

'And you think I'm your carpenter? Were there Jews in Villefranche?' Rebus couldn't remember reading of any.

'Does it matter?'

'I'm just wondering, why the interest?'

'To be honest, Inspector, there is a slight ulterior motive.' Levy sipped coffee, considering his words. 'The Rat Line. We'd like to show that it existed, that it operated to save Nazis from possible tormentors.' He paused. 'That it worked with the tacit approval – the *more* than tacit approval – of several western governments and even the Vatican. It's a question of general complicity.'

'What you want is for everyone to feel guilty?'

'We want recognition, Inspector. We want the truth. Isn't that what you want? Matthew Vanderhyde would have me believe it is your guiding principle.'

'He doesn't know me very well.'

'I wouldn't be so sure of that. Meantime, there are people out there who want the truth to stay hidden.'

'The truth being …?'

'That known war criminals were brought back to Britain – and elsewhere – and offered new lives, new identities.'

'In exchange for what?'

'The Cold War was starting, Inspector. You know the old saying: My enemy's enemy is my friend. These murderers were protected by the secret services. Military Intelligence offered them jobs. There are people who would rather this did not become general knowledge.'

'So?'

'So a trial, an open trial, would expose them.'

'You're warning me about spooks?'

Levy put his hands together, almost in an attitude of prayer. 'Look, I'm not sure this has been a completely satisfactory meeting, and for that I apologise. I'll be staying here for a few days, maybe longer if necessary. Could we try this again?'

'I don't know.'

'Well, think about it, won't you?' Levy extended his right hand. Rebus took it. 'I'll be right here, Inspector. Thank you for seeing me.'

'Take care, Mr Levy.'

'*Shalom*, Inspector.'

At his desk, Rebus could still feel Levy's handshake. Surrounded by the Villefranche files, he felt like the curator of some museum visited only by specialists and cranks. Evil had been done in Villefranche, but had Joseph Lintz been responsible? And even if he had, had he perhaps atoned during the past half-century? Rebus phoned the Procurator-Fiscal's office to let them know how little progress he was making. They thanked him for calling. Then he went to see the Farmer.

'Come in, John, what can I do for you?'

'Sir, did you know the Crime Squad had set up a surveillance on our patch?'

'You mean Flint Street?'

'So you know about it?'

'They keep me informed.'

'Who's acting as liaison?'

The Farmer frowned. 'As I say, John, they keep me informed.'

'So there's no liaison at street level?' The Farmer stayed silent. 'By rights there should be, sir.'

'What are you getting at, John?'

'I want the job.'

The Farmer stared at his desk. 'You're busy on Villefranche.'

'I want the job, sir.'

'John, liaison means diplomacy. It's never been your strongest suit.'

So Rebus explained about Candice, and how he was already tied into the case. 'And since I'm already in, sir,' he concluded, 'I might as well act as liaison.'

'What about Villefranche?'

'That remains a priority, sir.'

The Farmer looked into his eyes. Rebus didn't blink. 'All right then,' he said at last.

'You'll let Fettes know?'

'I'll let them know.'

'Thank you, sir.' Rebus turned to leave.

'John …?' The Farmer was standing behind his desk. 'You know what I'm going to say.'

'You're going to tell me not to tread on too many toes, not to go off on my own little crusade, to keep in regular contact with you, and not betray your trust in me. Does that just about do it, sir?'

The Farmer shook his head, smiling. 'Bugger off,' he said.

Rebus buggered off.

When he walked into the room, Candice rose so quickly from her chair that it fell to the floor. She came forward and gave him a hug, while Rebus looked at the faces around them – Ormiston, Claverhouse, Dr Colquhoun, and a WPC.

They were in an Interview Room at Fettes, Lothian and Borders Police HQ. Colquhoun was wearing the same suit as the previous day and the same nervous look. Ormiston was picking up Candice's chair. He'd been standing against one wall. Claverhouse was seated at the table beside Colquhoun, a pad of paper in front of him, pen poised above it.

'She says she's happy to see you,' Colquhoun translated.

'I'd never have guessed.' Candice was wearing new clothes: denims too long for her and turned up four inches at the ankle; a black woollen v-neck jumper. Her skiing jacket was hanging over the back of her chair.

'Get her to sit down again, will you?' Claverhouse said. 'We're pushed for time.'

There was no chair for Rebus, so he stood next to Ormiston and the WPC. Candice went back to the story she'd been telling, but glanced regularly towards him. He noticed that beside Claverhouse's pad of paper sat a brown folder and an A4-sized envelope. On top of the envelope sat a black and white surveillance shot of Tommy Telford.

'This man,' Claverhouse asked, tapping the photo, 'she knows him?'

Colquhoun asked, then listened to her answer. 'She ...' He cleared his throat. 'She hasn't had any direct dealings with him.' Her two-minute commentary reduced to this. Claverhouse dipped into the envelope, spread more photos before her. Candice tapped one of them.

'Pretty-Boy,' Claverhouse said. He picked up the photo of Telford again. 'But she's had dealings with this man, too?'

'She's ...' Colquhoun mopped his face. 'She's saying something about Japanese people ... Oriental businessmen.'

Rebus shared a look with Ormiston, who shrugged.

'Where was this?' Claverhouse asked.

'In a car ... more than one car. You know, a sort of convoy.'

'She was in one of the cars?'

'Yes.'

'Where did they go?'

'They headed out of town, stopping once or twice.'

'Juniper Green,' Candice said, quite clearly.

'Juniper Green,' Colquhoun repeated.

'They stopped there?'

'No, they stopped before that.'

'To do what?'

Colquhoun spoke with Candice again. 'She doesn't know. She thinks one of the drivers went into a shop for some cigarettes. The others all seemed to be looking at a building, as if they were interested in it, but not saying anything.'

'What building?'

'She doesn't know.'

Claverhouse looked exasperated. She wasn't giving him much of anything, and Rebus knew that if there was nothing she could trade, Crime Squad would dump her straight back on the street. Colquhoun was all wrong for this job, completely out of his depth.

'Where did they go after Juniper Green?'

'Just drove around the countryside. For two or three hours, she thinks. They would stop sometimes and get out, but just to look at the scenery. Lots of hills and ...' Colquhoun checked something. 'Hills and flags.'

'Flags? Flying from buildings?'

'No, stuck into the ground.'

Claverhouse gave Ormiston a look of hopelessness.

'Golf courses,' Rebus said. 'Try describing a golf course to her, Dr Colquhoun.'

Colquhoun did so, and she nodded agreement, beaming at Rebus. Claverhouse was looking at him, too.

'Just a guess,' Rebus said with a shrug. 'Japanese businessmen, it's what they like about Scotland.'

Claverhouse turned back to Candice. 'Ask her if she ... accommodated any of these men.'

Colquhoun cleared his throat again, colour flooding his cheeks as he spoke. Candice looked down at the table, moved her head in the affirmative, started to speak.

'She says that's why she was there. She was fooled at first. She thought maybe they just wanted a pretty woman to look at. They had a nice lunch ... the beautiful drive ... But then they came back into town, dropped the Japanese off at a hotel, and she was taken up to one of the hotel rooms. Three of them ... she, as you put it yourself, DS Claverhouse, she "accommodated" three of them.'

'Does she remember the name of the hotel?'

She didn't.

'Where did they have lunch?'

'A restaurant next to flags and ...' Colquhoun corrected himself. 'Next to a golf course.'

'How long ago was this?'

'Two or three weeks.'

68

'And how many of them were there?'

Colquhoun checked. 'The three Japanese, and maybe four other men.'

'Ask her how long she's been in Edinburgh,' Rebus asked.

Colquhoun did so. 'She thinks maybe a month.'

'A month working the street ... funny we haven't picked her up.'

'She was put there as a punishment.'

'For what?' Claverhouse asked. Rebus had the answer.

'For making herself ugly.' He turned to Candice. 'Ask her why she cuts herself.'

Candice looked at him and shrugged.

'What's your point?' Ormiston asked.

'She thinks the scars will deter punters. Which means she doesn't like the life she's been leading.'

'And helping us is her only sure ticket out?'

'Something like that.'

So Colquhoun asked her again, then said: 'They don't like that she does it. That's why she does it.'

'Tell her if she helps us, she won't ever have to do anything like that again.'

Colquhoun translated, glancing at his watch.

'Does the name Newcastle mean anything to her?' Claverhouse asked.

Colquhoun tried the name. 'I've explained to her that it's a town in England, built on a river.'

'Don't forget the bridges,' Rebus said.

Colquhoun added a few words, but Candice only shrugged. She looked upset that she was failing them. Rebus gave her another smile.

'What about the man she worked for?' Claverhouse asked. 'The one before she came to Edinburgh.'

She seemed to have plenty to say about this, and kept touching her face with her fingers while she talked.

Colquhoun nodded, made her stop from time to time so he could translate.

'A big man ... fat. He was the boss. Something about his skin ... a birthmark maybe, certainly something distinctive. And glasses, like sunglasses but not quite.'

Rebus saw Claverhouse and Ormiston exchange another look. It was all too vague to be much use. Colquhoun checked his watch again. 'And cars, a lot of cars. This man crashed them.'

'Maybe he got a scar on his face,' Ormiston offered.

'Glasses and a scar aren't going to get us very far,' Claverhouse added.

'Gentlemen,' Colquhoun said, while Candice looked towards Rebus, 'I'm afraid I'm going to have to leave.'

'Any chance of coming back in later, sir?' Claverhouse asked.

'You mean today?'

'I thought maybe this evening ...?'

'Look, I do have other commitments.'

'We appreciate that, sir. Meantime, DC Ormiston will run you back into town.'

'My pleasure,' Ormiston said, all charm. They needed Colquhoun, after all. They had to keep him sweet.

'One thing,' Colquhoun said. 'There's a refugee family in Fife. From Sarajevo. They'd probably take her in. I could ask.'

'Thank you, sir,' Claverhouse said. 'Maybe later on, eh?'

Colquhoun seemed disappointed as Ormiston led him away.

Rebus walked over to Claverhouse, who was shuffling his photos together.

'Bit of an oddball,' Claverhouse commented.

'Not used to the real world.'

'Not much help either.'

Rebus looked towards Candice. 'Mind if I take her out?'

70

'What?'

'Just for an hour.' Claverhouse stared at him. 'She's been cooped up here, and only her hotel room to look forward to. I'll drop her back there in an hour, hour and a half.'

'Bring her back in one piece, preferably with a smile on her face.'

Rebus motioned for Candice to join him.

'Japanese and golf courses,' Claverhouse mused. 'What do you think?'

'Telford's a businessman, we know that. Businessmen do deals with other businessmen.'

'He runs bouncers and slot machines: what's the Japanese connection?'

Rebus shrugged. 'I leave the hard questions to the likes of you.' He opened the door.

'And, John?' Claverhouse warned, nodding towards Candice. 'She's Crime Squad property, okay? And remember, *you* came to *us*.'

'No bother, Claverhouse. And by the way, I'm your B Division liaison.'

'Since when?'

'With immediate effect. If you don't believe me, ask your boss. This might be your case, but Telford works out of *my* territory.'

He took Candice by the arm and marched her from the room.

He stopped the car on the corner of Flint Street.

'It's okay, Candice,' he said, seeing her agitation. 'We're staying in the car. Everything's all right.' Her eyes were darting around, looking for faces she didn't want to see. Rebus started the car again and drove off. 'Look,' he told her, 'we're leaving.' Knowing she couldn't understand. 'I'm guessing this is where you started from that day.' He looked at her. 'The day you went to Juniper Green. The

Japanese would be staying in a central hotel, somewhere pricey. You picked them up, then headed east. Along Dalry Road maybe?' He was speaking for his own benefit. 'Christ, I don't know. Look, Candice, anything you see, anything that looks familiar, just let me know, okay?'

'Okay.'

Had she understood? No, she was smiling. All she'd heard was that final word. All she knew was that they were heading away from Flint Street. He took her down on to Princes Street first.

'Was it a hotel here, Candice? The Japanese? Was it here?' She gazed from the window with a blank look.

He headed up Lothian Road. 'Usher Hall,' he said. 'Sheraton … Any of it ring a bell?' Nothing did. Out along the Western Approach Road, Slateford Road, and on to Lanark Road. Most of the lights were against them, giving her plenty of time to study the buildings. Each newsagent's they passed, Rebus pointed it out, just in case the convoy had paused there to buy cigarettes. Soon they were out of town and entering Juniper Green.

'Juniper Green!' she said, pointing at the signpost, delighted to have something to show him. Rebus attempted a smile. There were plenty of golf courses around the city. He couldn't hope to take her to every one of them, not in a week never mind an hour. He stopped for a few moments by the side of a field. Candice got out, so he followed, lit a cigarette. There were two stone gateposts next to the road, but no sign of a gate between them, or any sort of path behind them. Once there might have been a track, and a house at the end of it. Atop one of the pillars sat the badly worn representation of a bull. Candice pointed towards the ground behind the other pillar, where another lump of carved stone lay, half-covered by weeds and grass.

'Looks like a serpent,' Rebus said. 'Maybe a dragon.' He looked at her. 'It'll all mean something to somebody.' She looked back at him blankly. He saw Sammy's features, reminded himself that he wanted to help her. He was in danger of letting that slip, of focusing on how she might help them get to Telford.

Back in the car, he branched off towards Livingston, intending to head for Ratho and from there back into town. Then he noticed that Candice had turned to look out of the back window.

'What is it?'

She came out with a stream of words, her tone uncertain. Rebus turned the car anyway, and drove slowly back the way they'd just come. He stopped at the side of the road, opposite a low dry-stone wall, beyond which lay the undulations of a golf course.

'Recognise it?' She mumbled more words. Rebus pointed. 'Here? Yes?'

She turned to him, said something which sounded apologetic.

'It's okay,' he told her. 'Let's take a closer look anyway.' He drove to where a vast iron double-gate stood open. A sign to one side read POYNTINGHAME GOLF AND COUNTRY CLUB. Beneath it: 'Bar Lunches and A La Carte, Visitors Welcome'. As Rebus drove through the gates, Candice started nodding again, and when an oversized Georgian house came into view she almost bounced in her seat, slapping her hands against her thighs.

'I think I get the picture,' Rebus said.

He parked outside the main entrance, squeezing between a Volvo estate and a low-slung Toyota. Out on the course, three men were finishing their round. As the final putt went in, hands went to wallets and money changed hands.

Two things Rebus knew about golf: one, to some people it was a religion; two, a lot of players liked a bet. They'd bet on final tally, each hole, even every shot if they could.

And didn't the Japanese have a passion for gambling?

He took Candice's arm as he escorted her into the main building. Piano music from the bar. Panatella smoke and oak-panelling. Huge portraits of self-important unknowns. A few old wooden putters, framed behind glass. A poster advertised a Halloween dinner-dance for that evening. Rebus walked up to reception, explained who he was and what he wanted. The receptionist made a phone call, then led them to the Chief Executive's office.

Hugh Malahide, bald and thin, mid-forties, already had a slight stammer, which intensified when Rebus asked his first question. By throwing it back at the questioner, he seemed to be playing for time.

'Have we had any Japanese visitors recently? Well, we do get a few golfers.'

'These men came to lunch. Maybe a fortnight, three weeks back. There were three of them, plus three or four Scottish men. Probably driving Range Rovers. The table may have been reserved in the name of Telford.'

'Telford?'

'Thomas Telford.'

'Ah, yes ...' Malahide wasn't enjoying this at all.

'You know Mr Telford?'

'In a manner of speaking.'

Rebus leaned forward in his chair. 'Go on.'

'Well, he's ... look, the reason I seem so reticent is because we don't want this made common knowledge.'

'I understand, sir.'

'Mr Telford is acting as go-between.'

'Go-between?'

'In the negotiations.'

Rebus saw what Malahide was getting at. 'The Japanese want to buy Poyntinghame?'

'You understand, Inspector, I'm just the manager here. I mean, I run the day-to-day business.'

'But you're the Chief Executive.'

'With no personal share in the club. The actual owners were set against selling at first. But an offer has been made, and I believe it's a very good one. And the potential buyers ... well, they're persistent.'

'Have there been any threats, Mr Malahide?'

He looked horrified. 'What sort of threats?'

'Forget it.'

'The negotiations haven't been *hostile*, if that's what you mean.'

'So these Japanese, the ones who had lunch here ... ?'

'They were representing the consortium.'

'The consortium being ... ?'

'I don't know. The Japanese are always very secretive. Some big company or corporation, I'd guess.'

'Any idea why they want Poyntinghame?'

'I've wondered that myself.'

'And?'

'Everyone knows the Japanese love golf. It might be a prestige thing. Or it could be that they're opening a plant of some kind in Livingston.'

'And Poyntinghame would become the factory social club?'

Malahide shivered at the thought. Rebus got to his feet.

'You've been very helpful, sir. Anything else you can tell me?'

'Look, this has been off the record, Inspector.'

'I've no problem with that. I don't suppose you've got any names?'

'Names?'

'Of the diners that day.'

Malahide shook his head. 'I'm sorry, not even credit card details. Mr Telford paid cash as usual.'

'Did he leave a big tip?'

'Inspector,' smiling, 'some secrets are sacrosanct.'

'Let's keep this conversation that way, too, sir, all right?'

Malahide looked at Candice. 'She's a prostitute, isn't she? I thought as much the day they were here.' There was revulsion in his voice. 'Tarty little thing, aren't you?'

Candice stared at him, looked to Rebus for help, said a few words neither man understood.

'What's she saying?' Malahide asked.

'She says she once had a punter who looked just like you. He dressed in plus-fours and made her whack him with a mashie-niblick.'

Malahide showed them out.

6

Rebus telephoned Claverhouse from Candice's room.

'Could be something or nothing,' Claverhouse said, but Rebus could tell he was interested, which was good: the longer he stayed interested, the longer he'd want to hang on to Candice. Ormiston was on his way to the hotel to resume babysitting duties.

'What I want to know is, how the hell did Telford land something like this?'

'Good question,' Claverhouse said.

'It's way out of his previous sphere, isn't it?'

'As far as we know.'

'A chauffeur service for Jap companies ...'

'Maybe he's after the contract to supply their gaming machines.'

Rebus shook his head. 'I still don't get it.'

'Not your problem, John, remember that.'

'I suppose so.' There was a knock at the door. 'Sounds like Ormiston.'

'I doubt it. He's just left.'

Rebus stared at the door. 'Claverhouse, wait on the line.'

He left the receiver on the bedside table. The knock was repeated. Rebus motioned for Candice, who'd been flicking through a magazine on the sofa, to move into the bathroom. Then he crept up to the door and put his eye to the spy-hole. A woman: the day-shift receptionist. He unlocked the door.

'Yes?'

'Letter for your wife.'

He stared at the small white envelope which she was trying to hand him.

'Letter,' she repeated.

There was no name or address on the envelope, no stamp. Rebus took it and held it to the light. A single sheet of paper inside, and something flat and square, like a photograph.

'A man handed it in at reception.'

'How long ago?'

'Two, three minutes.'

'What did he look like?'

She shrugged. 'Tallish, short brown hair. He was wearing a suit, took the letter out of a briefcase.'

'How do you know who it's for?'

'He said it was for the foreign woman. He described her to a T.'

Rebus was staring at the envelope. 'Okay, thanks,' he mumbled. He closed the door, went back to the telephone.

'What is it?' Claverhouse asked.

'Someone's just dropped off a letter for Candice.' Rebus tore open the envelope, holding the receiver between shoulder and chin. There was a Polaroid photo and a single sheet, handwritten in small capitals. Foreign words.

'What does it say?' Claverhouse asked.

'I don't know.' Rebus tried a couple of words aloud. Candice had emerged from the bathroom. She snatched the paper from him and read it quickly, then fled back into the bathroom.

'It means something to Candice,' Rebus said. 'There's a photo, too.' He looked at it. 'She's on her knees gamming some fat bloke.'

'Description?'

'The camera's not exactly interested in his face. Claverhouse, we've got to get her away from here.'

'Hang on till Ormiston arrives. They might be trying to panic you. If they want to snatch her, one cop in a car isn't going to cause much of a problem. Two cops just might.'

'How did they know?'

'We'll think about that later.'

Rebus was staring at the bathroom door, remembering the locked cubicle at St Leonard's. 'I've got to go.'

'Be careful.'

Rebus put down the receiver.

'Candice?' He tried the door. It was locked. 'Candice?' He stood back and kicked. The door wasn't as strong as the one in St Leonard's; he nearly took it off its hinges. She was seated on the toilet, a plastic safety razor in her hand, slashing it across her arms. There was blood on her t-shirt, blood spraying the white tiled floor. She started screaming at him, the words collapsing into monosyllables. Rebus grabbed the razor, nicked his thumb in the process. He pulled her off the toilet, flushed the razor, and started wrapping towels around her arms. The note was lying in the bath. He waved it in her face.

'They're trying to scare you, that's all.' Not even half-believing it himself. If Telford could find her this quickly, if he had the means of writing to her in her own language, then he was much stronger, much cleverer than Rebus had suspected.

'It's going to be okay,' he went on. 'I promise. It's all okay. We'll look after you. We'll get you out of here, take you somewhere he can't get to you. I promise, Candice. Look, this is me talking.'

But she was bawling, tears dripping from her cheeks, head shaking from side to side. For a time, she'd actually believed in knights on white chargers. Now, she was realising how stupid she'd been ...

The coast seemed to be clear.

Rebus took her in his car, Ormiston tucked in behind. No other way to play it. It was a trade-off: a speedy exit versus hanging around for a cavalry escort. And the way Candice was bleeding, they couldn't afford to wait. The drive to the hospital was nerve-tingling, then there was the wait while her wounds were checked and some of them sewn up. Rebus and Ormiston waited in A&E, drinking coffee from beakers, asking one another questions they couldn't answer.

'How did he know?'

'Who did he get to write the note?'

'Why give us a warning? Why not just grab her?'

'What does the note say?'

It struck Rebus that they were near the university. He took Dr Colquhoun's card from his pocket and phoned his office. Colquhoun was in. Rebus read the message out to him, spelling some of the words.

'They sound like addresses,' Colquhoun said. 'Untranslatable.'

'Addresses? Are any towns named?'

'I don't think so.'

'Sir, we'll be taking her to Fettes if she's well enough … any chance you could meet us there? It's important.'

'Everything with you chaps is important.'

'Yes, sir, but this is *important*. Candice's life may be in danger.'

Colquhoun took time answering. 'I suppose in that case …'

'I'll send a car for you.'

After an hour, she was well enough to leave. 'The cuts weren't too deep,' the doctor said. 'Not life-threatening.'

'They weren't meant to be.' Rebus turned to Ormiston. 'She thinks she's going back to Telford, that's why she did it. She *knows* she's going back to him.'

Candice looked as though all the blood had been drained

from her. Her face seemed more skeletal than before, and her eyes darker. Rebus tried to recall what her smile looked like. He doubted he'd be seeing one for a while. She kept her arms folded protectively in front of her, and wouldn't meet his eyes. Rebus had seen suspects act that way in custody: people for whom the world had become a trap.

At Fettes, Claverhouse and Colquhoun were already waiting. Rebus handed over the note and photo.

'As I said, Inspector,' Colquhoun stated, 'addresses.'

'Ask her what they mean,' Claverhouse demanded. They were in the same room as before. Candice knew her place, and was already seated, her arms still folded, showing cream-coloured bandages and pink plasters. Colquhoun asked, but it was as though he'd ceased to exist. Candice stared at the wall in front of her, unblinking, her only motion a slight rocking to and fro.

'Ask her again,' Claverhouse said. But Rebus interrupted before Colquhoun could start.

'Ask her if people she knows live there, people who are important to her.'

As Colquhoun formed the question, the rocking grew slightly in intensity. There were fresh tears in her eyes.

'Her mother and father? Brothers and sisters?'

Colquhoun translated. Candice tried to stop her mouth trembling.

'Maybe she left a kid behind ...'

As Colquhoun asked, Candice flew from her chair, shouting and screaming. Ormiston tried to grab her, but she kicked out at him. When she'd calmed, she subsided in a corner of the room, arms over her head.

'She's not going to tell us anything,' Colquhoun translated. 'She was stupid to believe us. She just wants to go now. There's nothing she can help us with.'

Rebus and Claverhouse shared a look.

'We can't hold her, John, not if she wants to leave. It's

81

been dodgy enough keeping her away from a lawyer. Once she starts asking to go ...' He shrugged.

'Come on, man,' Rebus hissed, 'she's shit-scared, and with good reason. And now you've got all you're going to get out of her, you're just going to hand her back to Telford?'

'Look, it's not a question of –'

'He'll kill her, you know he will.'

'If he was going to kill her, she'd be dead.' Claverhouse paused. 'He's cleverer than that. He knows damned well all he had to do was give her a fright. He *knows* her. It sticks in my craw, too, but what can we do?'

'Just keep her a few days, see if we can't ...'

'Can't what? You want to hand her over to Immigration?'

'It's an idea. Get her the hell away from here.'

Claverhouse pondered this, then turned to Colquhoun. 'Ask her if she wants to go back to Sarajevo.'

Colquhoun asked. She slurred some answer, choking back tears.

'She says if she goes back, they'll kill everyone.'

Silence in the room. They were all looking at her. Four men, men with jobs, family ties, men with lives of their own. In the scheme of things, they seldom realised how well off they were. And now they realised something else: how helpless they were.

'Tell her,' Claverhouse said quietly, 'she's free to walk out of here at any time, if that's what she really wants. If she stays, we'll do our damnedest to help her ...'

So Colquhoun spoke to her, and she listened, and when he'd finished she pushed herself back on to her feet and looked at them. Then she wiped her nose on her bandages, pushed the hair out of her eyes, and walked to the door.

'Don't go, Candice,' Rebus said.

She half-turned towards him. 'Okay,' she said.

Then she opened the door and was gone.

82

Rebus grabbed Claverhouse's arm. 'We've got to pull Telford in, warn him not to touch her.'

'You think he needs telling?'

'You think he'd listen?' Ormiston added.

'I can't believe this. He scared her half to death, and as a result we let her walk? I really can't get my head round this.'

'She could always have gone to Fife,' Colquhoun said. With Candice out of the room, he seemed to have perked up a bit.

'Bit late now,' Ormiston said.

'He beat us this time, that's all,' Claverhouse said, his eyes on Rebus. 'But we'll take him down, don't worry.' He managed a thin, humourless smile. 'Don't think we're giving up, John. It's not our style. Early days yet, pal. Early days ...'

She was waiting for him out in the car park, standing by the passenger-door of his battered Saab 900.

'Okay?' she said.

'Okay,' he agreed, smiling with relief as he unlocked the car. He could think of only one place to take her. As he drove through The Meadows, she nodded, recognising the tree-lined playing fields.

'You've been here before?'

She said a few words, nodded again as Rebus turned into Arden Street. He parked the car and turned to her.

'You've been *here*?'

She pointed upwards, fingers curled into the shape of binoculars.

'With Telford?'

'Telford,' she said. She made a show of writing something down, and Rebus took out his notebook and pen, handed them over. She drew a teddy bear.

'You came in Telford's car?' Rebus interpreted. 'And he

watched one of the flats up there?' He pointed to his own flat.

'Yes, yes.'

'When was this?' She didn't understand the question. 'I need a phrasebook,' he muttered. Then he opened his door, got out and looked around. The cars around him were all empty. No Range Rovers. He signalled for Candice to get out and follow him.

She seemed to like his living-room, went straight to the record collection but couldn't find anything she recognised. Rebus went into the kitchen to make coffee and to think. He couldn't keep her here, not if Telford knew about the place. Telford ... why had he been watching Rebus's flat? The answer was obvious: he knew the detective was linked to Cafferty, and therefore a potential threat. He thought Rebus was in Cafferty's pocket. Know your enemy: it was another rule Telford had learned.

Rebus phoned a contact from the *Scotland on Sunday* business section.

'Japanese companies,' Rebus said. 'Rumours pertaining to.'

'Can you narrow that down?'

'New sites around Edinburgh, maybe Livingston.'

Rebus could hear the reporter shuffling papers on his desk. 'There's a whisper going round about a microprocessor plant.'

'In Livingston?'

'That's one possibility.'

'Anything else?'

'Nope. Why the interest?'

'Cheers, Tony.' Rebus put down the receiver, looked across at Candice. He couldn't think where else to take her. Hotels weren't safe. One place came to mind, but it would be risky ... Well, not so very risky. He made the call.

'Sammy?' he said. 'Any chance you could do me a favour … ?'

Sammy lived in a 'colonies' flat in Shandon. Parking was almost impossible on the narrow street outside. Rebus got as close as he could.

Sammy was waiting for them in the narrow hallway, and led them into the cramped living-room. There was a guitar on a wicker chair and Candice lifted it, setting herself on the chair and strumming a chord.

'Sammy,' Rebus said, 'this is Candice.'

'Hello there,' Sammy said. 'Happy Halloween.' Candice was putting chords together now. 'Hey, that's Oasis.'

Candice looked up, smiled. 'Oasis,' she echoed.

'I've got the CD somewhere …' Sammy examined a tower of CDs next to the hi-fi. 'Here it is. Shall I put it on?'

'Yes, yes.'

Sammy switched the hi-fi on, told Candice she was going to make some coffee, and beckoned for Rebus to follow her into the kitchen.

'So who is she?' The kitchen was tiny. Rebus stayed in the doorway.

'She's a prostitute. Against her will. I don't want her pimp getting her.'

'Where's she from again?'

'Sarajevo.'

'And she doesn't have much English?'

'How's your Serbo-Croat?'

'Rusty.'

Rebus looked around. 'Where's your boyfriend?'

'Out working.'

'On the book?' Rebus didn't like Ned Farlowe. Partly it was that name: 'Neds' were what the *Sunday Post* called hooligans. They robbed old ladies of their pension books

85

and walking-frames. Those were the Neds of this world. And Farlowe meant Chris Farlowe: 'Out of Time', a number one that should have belonged to the Stones. Farlowe was researching a history of organised crime in Scotland.

'Sod's law,' Sammy said. 'He needs money to buy the time to write the thing.'

'So what's he doing?'

'Just some freelance stuff. How long am I babysitting?'

'A couple of days at most. Just till I find somewhere else.'

'What will he do if he finds her?'

'I'm not that keen to find out.'

Sammy finished rinsing the mugs. 'She looks like me, doesn't she?'

'Yes, she does.'

'I've got some time off coming. Maybe I'll phone in, see if I can stay here with her. What's her real name?'

'She hasn't told me.'

'Has she any clothes?'

'At a hotel. I'll get a patrol car to bring them.'

'She's really in danger?'

'She might be.'

Sammy looked at him. 'But I'm not?'

'No,' her father said. 'Because it'll be our secret.'

'And what do I tell Ned?'

'Keep it short, just say you're doing your dad a favour.'

'You think a journalist's going to be content with that?'

'If he loves you.'

The kettle boiled, clicked off. Sammy poured water into three mugs. Through in the living-room, Candice's interest had shifted to a pile of American comic books.

Rebus drank his coffee, then left them to their music and their comics. Instead of going home, he made for Young Street and the Ox, ordering a mug of instant. Fifty pee.

Pretty good deal, when you thought about it. Fifty pence for … what, half a pint? A pound a pint? Cheap at twice the price. Well, one-point-seven times the price, which would take it to the price of a beer … give or take.

Not that Rebus was counting.

The back room was quiet, just somebody scribbling away at the table nearest the fire. He was a regular, a journalist of some kind. Rebus thought of Ned Farlowe, who would want to know about Candice, but if anyone could keep him at bay, Sammy could. Rebus took out his mobile, phoned Colquhoun's office.

'Sorry to bother you again,' he said.

'What is it now?' The lecturer sounded thoroughly exasperated.

'Those refugees you mentioned. Any chance you could have a word with them?'

'Well, I …' Colquhoun cleared his throat. 'Yes, I suppose I could talk to them. Does that mean …?'

'Candice is safe.'

'I don't have their number here.' Colquhoun sounded fuddled again. 'Can it wait till I go home?'

'Phone me when you've talked to them. And thanks.'

Rebus rang off, finished his coffee, and called Siobhan Clarke at home.

'I need a favour,' he said, feeling like a broken record.

'How much trouble will it get me in?'

'Almost none.'

'Can I have that in writing?'

'Think I'm stupid?' Rebus smiled. 'I want to see the files on Telford.'

'Why not just ask Claverhouse?'

'I'd rather ask you.'

'It's a lot of stuff. Do you want photocopies?'

'Whatever.'

'I'll see what I can do.' Voices were raised in the front bar. 'You're not in the Ox, are you?'

'As it happens, yes.'

'Drinking?'

'A mug of coffee.'

She laughed in disbelief and told him to take care. Rebus ended the call and stared at his mug. People like Siobhan Clarke, they could drive a man to drink.

7

It was 7 a.m. when the buzzer sounded, telling him there was someone at his tenement's main door. He staggered along the hall to the intercom, and asked who the bloody hell it was.

'The croissant man,' a rough English voice replied.

'The what?'

'Come on, dick-brain, wakey-wakey. Memory's not so hot these days, eh?'

A name tilted into Rebus's head. 'Abernethy?'

'Now open up, it's perishing down here.'

Rebus pushed the buzzer to let Abernethy in, then jogged back to the bedroom to put on some clothes. His mind felt numb. Abernethy was a DI in Special Branch, London. The last time he'd been in Edinburgh had been to chase terrorists. Rebus wondered what the hell he was doing here now.

When the doorbell sounded, Rebus tucked in his shirt and walked back down the hall. True to his word, Abernethy was carrying a bag of croissants. He hadn't changed much: same faded denims and black leather bomber, same cropped brown hair spiked with gel. His face was heavy, pockmarked, and his eyes an unnerving, psychopath's blue.

'How've you been, mate?' Abernethy slapped Rebus's shoulder and marched past him into the kitchen. 'Get the kettle on then.' Like they did this every day of the week. Like they didn't live four hundred miles apart.

'Abernethy, what the hell are you doing here?'

'Feeding you, of course, same thing the English have always done for the Jocks. Got any butter?'

'Try the butter-dish.'

'Plates?'

Rebus pointed to a cupboard.

'Bet you drink instant: am I right?'

'Abernethy ...'

'Let's get this ready first, then talk, okay?'

'The kettle boils quicker if you switch it on at the plug.'

'Right.'

'And I think there's some jam.'

'Any honey?'

'Do I look like a bee?'

Abernethy smirked. 'Old Georgie Flight sends his love, by the way. Word is, he'll be retiring soon.'

George Flight: another ghost from Rebus's past. Abernethy had unscrewed the top from the coffee jar and was sniffing the granules.

'How fresh is this?' He wrinkled his nose. 'No class, John.'

'Unlike you, you mean? When did you get here?'

'Hit town half an hour ago.'

'From London?'

'Stopped a couple of hours in a lay-by, got my head down. That A1 is murder though. North of Newcastle, it's like coming into a third-world country.'

'Did you drive four hundred miles just to insult me?'

They took everything through to the table in the living-room, Rebus shoving aside books and notepads, stuff about the Second World War.

'So,' he said, as they sat down, 'I'm assuming this isn't a social call?'

'Actually it is, in a way. I could have just telephoned, but I suddenly thought: wonder how the old devil's getting on?

Next thing I knew, I was in the car and heading for the North Circular.'

'I'm touched.'

'I've always tried to keep track of what you're up to.'

'Why?'

'Because last time we met ... well, you're different, aren't you?'

'Am I?'

'I mean, you're not a team player. You're a loner, bit like me. Loners can be useful.'

'Useful?'

'For undercover, jobs that are a bit out of the ordinary.'

'You think I'm Special Branch material?'

'Ever fancied moving to London? It's where the action is.'

'I get action enough up here.'

Abernethy looked out of the window. 'You couldn't wake this place with a fifty-megaton warhead.'

'Look, Abernethy, not that I'm not enjoying your company or anything, but why *are* you here?'

Abernethy brushed crumbs from his hands. 'So much for the social niceties.' He took a gulp of coffee, squirmed at its awfulness. 'War Crimes,' he said. Rebus stopped chewing. 'There's a new list of names. You know that, because you've got one of them living on your doorstep.'

'So?'

'So I'm heading up the London HQ. We've established a temporary War Crimes Unit. My job's to collate gen on the various investigations, create a central register.'

'You want to know what I know?'

'That's about it.'

'And you drove through the night to find out? There's got to be more to it.'

Abernethy laughed. 'Why's that?'

'There just has. A collator's job is for someone good at office work. That's not you, you're only happy in the field.'

'What about you? I'd never have taken you for a historian.' Abernethy tapped one of the books on the table.

'It's a penance.'

'What makes you think it's any different with me? So, what's the score with Herr Lintz?'

'There's no score. So far all the darts have missed the board. How many cases are there?'

'Twenty-seven originally, but eight of those are deceased.'

'Any progress?'

Abernethy shook his head. 'We got one to court, trial collapsed first day. Can't prosecute if they're ga-ga.'

'Well, for your information, here's where the Lintz case stands. I can't prove he was and is Josef Linzstek. I can't disprove his story of his participation in the war, or how he came to Britain.' Rebus shrugged.

'Same tale I've been hearing up and down the country.'

'What did you expect?' Rebus was picking at a croissant.

'Shame about this coffee,' Abernethy said. 'Any decent caffs in the neighbourhood?'

So they went to a café, where Abernethy ordered a double espresso, Rebus a decaf. There was a story on the front of the *Record* about a fatal stabbing outside a nightclub. The man reading the paper folded it up when he'd finished his breakfast and took it away with him.

'Any chance you'll be talking to Lintz today?' Abernethy asked suddenly.

'Why?'

'Thought I might tag along. It's not often you get to meet someone who might have killed seven hundred Frenchies.'

'Morbid attraction?'

'We're all a bit that way inclined, aren't we?'

'I've nothing new to ask him,' Rebus said, 'and he's already been muttering to his lawyer about harassment.'

'He's well–connected?'

Rebus stared across the table. 'You've done your reading.'

'Abernethy the Conscientious Cop.'

'Well, you're right. He has friends in high places, only a lot of them have been hiding behind the curtains since this all started.'

'Sounds like you think he's innocent.'

'Until proven guilty.'

Abernethy smiled, lifted his cup. 'There's a Jewish historian been going around. Has he contacted you?'

'What's his name?'

Another smile. 'How many Jewish historians have you been in touch with? His name's David Levy.'

'You say he's been going around?'

'A week here, a week there, asking how the cases are going.'

'He's in Edinburgh just now.'

Abernethy blew on his coffee. 'So you've spoken with him?'

'Yes, as it happens.'

'And?'

'And what?'

'Did he try his "Rat Line" story?'

'Again, why the interest?'

'He's tried it with everyone else.'

'What if he has?'

'Jesus, do you always answer a question with a question? Look, as collator, this guy Levy's name has popped up on my computer screen more than once. That's why I'm interested.'

'Abernethy the Conscientious Cop.'

'That's right. So shall we go see Lintz?'

'Well, seeing you've come all this way ...'

On the way back to the flat, Rebus stopped at a newsagent's and bought the *Record*. The stabbing had taken place outside Megan's Nightclub, a new establishment in Portobello. The fatality had been a 'doorman', William Tennant, aged 25. The story had made the front page because a Premier League footballer had been on the periphery of the incident. A friend who'd been with him had received minor cuts. The attacker had fled on a motorbike. The footballer had offered no comment to reporters. Rebus knew him. He lived in Linlithgow and a year or so back had been caught speeding in Edinburgh, with – in his own words – a 'wee bitty Charlie', meaning cocaine, on his person.

'Anything interesting?' Abernethy asked.

'Someone killed a bouncer. Quiet little backwater, eh?'

'A story like that, in London it wouldn't rate a column inch.'

'How long are you staying here?'

'I'll be off today, want to drop in on Carlisle. They're supposed to have another old Nazi. After that, it's Blackpool and Wolverhampton before home.'

'A sucker for punishment.'

Rebus drove them the tourist route: down The Mound and across Princes Street. He double parked in Heriot Row, but Joseph Lintz wasn't home.

'Never mind,' he said. 'I know where he'll probably be.' He took them down Inverleith Row and turned right into Warriston Gardens, stopping at the cemetery gates.

'What is he, a gravedigger?' Abernethy got out of the car and zipped his jacket.

'He plants flowers.'

'Flowers? What for?'

'I'm not sure.'

A cemetery should have been about death, but Warriston

didn't feel that way to Rebus. Much of it resembled a rambling park into which some statuary had been dropped. The newer section, with stone driveway, soon gave way to an earthen path between fading inscriptions. There were obelisks and Celtic crosses, lots of trees and birds, and the electric movements of squirrels. A tunnel beneath a walkway took you to the oldest part of the cemetery, but between tunnel and driveway sat the heart of the place, with its roll-call of Edinburgh's past. Names like Ovenstone, Cleugh, and Flockhart, and professions such as actuary, silk merchant, ironmonger. There were people who'd died in India, and some who'd died in infancy. A sign at the gate informed visitors that the place had been the subject of a compulsory purchase by the City of Edinburgh, because previous private owners had let it fall into neglect. But that same neglect was at least part of its charm. People walked their dogs here, or came to practise photography, or just mused among the tombstones. Gays came looking for company, others for solitude.

After dark, of course, the place had another reputation entirely. A Leith prostitute – a woman Rebus had known and liked – had been found murdered here earlier in the year. Rebus wondered if Joseph Lintz knew about that ...

'Mr Lintz?'

He was trimming the grass around a headstone, doing so with a half-sized pair of garden shears. There was a sheen of sweat on his face as he forced himself upright.

'Ah, Inspector Rebus. You have brought a colleague?'

'This is DI Abernethy.'

Abernethy was examining the headstone, which belonged to a teacher called Cosmo Merriman.

'They let you do this?' he asked, his eyes finally finding Lintz's.

'No one has tried to stop me.'

'Inspector Rebus tells me you plant flowers, too.'

'People assume I am a relative.'

'But you're not, are you?'

'Only in so far as we are the family of man, Inspector Abernethy.'

'You're a Christian then?'

'Yes, I am.'

'Born and bred?'

Lintz took out a handkerchief and wiped his nose. 'You're wondering if a Christian could commit an atrocity like Villefranche. It's perhaps not in my interest to say this, but I think it entirely possible. I've been explaining this to Inspector Rebus.'

Rebus nodded. 'We've had a couple of talks.'

'Religious belief is no defence, you see. Look at Bosnia, plenty of Catholics involved in the fighting, plenty of good Muslims, too. "Good" in that they are believers. And what they believe is that their faith gives them the right to kill.'

Bosnia: Rebus saw a sharp image of Candice escaping the terror, only to end up more terrified still, and more trapped than ever.

Lintz was stuffing the large white handkerchief into the pocket of his baggy brown cord trousers. In the outfit – green rubber overshoes, green woollen jersey, tweed jacket – he did look like a gardener. Little wonder he attracted so little attention in the cemetery. He blended in. Rebus wondered how artful it was, how deeply he'd learned the skill of invisibility.

'You look impatient, Inspector Abernethy. You're not a man for theories, am I right?'

'I wouldn't know about that, sir.'

'In that case, you must not know very much. Now Inspector Rebus, he listens to what I have to say. More than that, he looks *interested*. Whether he is or not, I can't judge, but his performance – if performance it be – is exemplary.' Lintz always spoke like this, like he'd been rehearsing each line. 'Last time he visited my home, we discussed human duality. Would you have any opinion on *that*, Inspector Abernethy?'

The look on Abernethy's face was cold. 'No, sir.'

Lintz shrugged: case against the Londoner proven. 'Atrocities, Inspector, occur by an effort of the collective will.' Spelling it out; sounding like the lecturer he had once been. 'Because sometimes all it takes to turn us into devils is the fear of being an outsider.'

Abernethy sniffed, hands in pockets. 'Sounds like you're justifying war crimes, sir. Sounds to me like you might even have been there yourself.'

'Do I need to be a spaceman to imagine Mars?' He turned to Rebus, gave him the fraction of a smile.

'Well, maybe I'm just a bit too simple, sir,' Abernethy said. 'I'm also a bit parky. Let's walk back to the car and carry on our discussion there, all right?'

While Lintz packed his few small tools into a canvas bag, Rebus looked around, saw movement in the distance, between headstones. The crouched figure of a man. Split-second glimpse of a face he recognised.

'What is it?' Abernethy asked.

Rebus shook his head. 'Nothing.'

The three men walked in silence back to the Saab. Rebus opened the back door for Lintz. To his surprise, Abernethy got into the back, too. Rebus took the driver's seat, felt warmth returning slowly to his toes. Abernethy had his arm along the back of the seat, his body twisted towards Lintz.

'Now, Herr Lintz, my role in all this is quite straightforward. I'm collating all the information on this latest outbreak of alleged old Nazis. You understand that with allegations such as these, very serious allegations, we have a duty to investigate?'

'Spurious allegations rather than "serious" ones.'

'In which case you've nothing to worry about.'

'Except my reputation.'

'When you're exonerated, we'll take care of that.'

Rebus was listening closely. None of this sounded like Abernethy. The hostile graveside tone had been replaced by something much more ambiguous.

'And meantime?' Lintz seemed to be picking up whatever the Londoner was saying between the lines. Rebus felt deliberately excluded from the conversation, which was why Abernethy had got into the back seat in the first place. He'd placed a physical barrier between himself and the officer investigating Joseph Lintz. There was something going on.

'Meantime,' Abernethy said, 'co-operate as fully as you can with my colleague. The sooner he's able to reach his conclusions, the sooner this will all be over.'

'The problem with conclusions is that they should be conclusive, and I have so little proof. This was wartime, Inspector Abernethy, a lot of records destroyed ...'

'Without proof either way, there's no case to answer.'

Lintz was nodding. 'I see,' he said.

Abernethy hadn't voiced anything Rebus himself didn't feel; the problem was, he'd voiced it to the suspect.

'It would help if your memory improved,' Rebus felt obliged to add.

'Well, Mr Lintz,' Abernethy was saying, 'thanks for your time.' His hand was on the elderly man's shoulder: protective, comforting. 'Can we drop you somewhere?'

'I'll stay here a little longer,' Lintz said, opening the door and easing himself out. Abernethy handed the bag of tools to him.

'Take care now,' he said.

Lintz nodded, gave a small bow to Rebus, and shuffled back towards the gate. Abernethy climbed into the passenger seat.

'Rum little bugger, isn't he?'

'You as good as told him he was off the hook.'

'Bollocks,' Abernethy said. 'I told him where he stands, let him know the score. That's all.' He saw the look on Rebus's face. 'Come on, do you really want to see him in court? An old professor who keeps cemeteries tidy?'

'It doesn't make it any easier if you sound like you're on his side.'

'Even supposing he *did* order that massacre – you think a trial and a couple of years in clink till he snuffs it is the answer? Better to just give them all a bloody good scare, stuff the trial, and save the taxpayer millions.'

'That's not our job,' Rebus said, starting the engine.

He took Abernethy back to Arden Street. They shook hands, Abernethy trying to sound like he wanted to stay a little longer.

'One of these days,' he said. And then he was gone. As his Sierra drew away, another car pulled into the space he'd just vacated. Siobhan Clarke got out, bringing with her a supermarket carrier-bag.

'For you,' she said. 'And I think I'm owed a coffee.'

She wasn't as fussy as Abernethy, accepted the mug of instant with thanks and ate a spare croissant. There was a message on the answering machine, Dr Colquhoun telling him the refugee family could take Candice tomorrow. Rebus jotted down the details, then turned his attention to the contents of Siobhan's carrier-bag. Maybe two hundred sheets of paper, photocopies.

'Don't get them out of order,' she warned. 'I didn't have time to staple them.'

'Fast work.'

'I went back into the office last night. Thought I'd get it done while no one was about. I can summarise, if you like.'

'Just tell me who the main players are.'

She came to the table and pulled a chair over beside him,

found a sequence of surveillance shots. Put names to the faces.

'Brian Summers,' she said, 'better known as "Pretty-Boy". He runs most of the working girls.' Pale, angular face, thick black lashes, a pouting mouth. Candice's pimp.

'He's not very pretty.'

Clarke found another picture. 'Kenny Houston.'

'From Pretty-Boy to Plug-Ugly.'

'I'm sure his mother loves him.' Prominent teeth, jaundiced skin.

'What does he do?'

'He runs the doormen. Kenny, Pretty-Boy and Tommy Telford grew up on the same street. They're at the heart of The Family.' She sifted through more photos. 'Malky Jordan ... he keeps the drugs flowing. Sean Haddow ... bit of a brainbox, runs the finances. Ally Cornwell ... he's muscle. Deek McGrain ... There's no religious divide in The Family, Prods and Papes working together.'

'A model society.'

'No women though. Telford's philosophy: relationships get in the way.'

Rebus picked up a sheaf of paper. 'So what have we got?'

'Everything but the evidence.'

'And surveillance is supposed to provide that?'

She smiled over the top of her mug. 'You don't agree?'

'It's not my problem.'

'And yet you're interested.' She paused. 'Candice?'

'I don't like what happened to her.'

'Well, just remember: you didn't get this stuff from me.'

'Thanks, Siobhan.' He paused. 'Everything going all right?'

'Fine. I like Crime Squad.'

'Bit livelier than St Leonard's.'

'I miss Brian.' Meaning her one-time partner, now out of the force.

'You ever see him?'

'No, do you?'

Rebus shook his head, got up to show her out.

He spent about an hour sifting through the paperwork, learning more about The Family and its convoluted workings. Nothing about Newcastle. Nothing about Japan. The core of The Family – eight or nine of them – had been at school together. Three of them were still based in Paisley, taking care of the established business. The rest were now in Edinburgh, and busy prying the city away from Big Ger Cafferty.

He went through lists of nightclubs and bars in which Telford had an interest. There were incident reports attached: arrests in the vicinity. Drunken brawls, swings taken at bouncers, cars and property damaged. Something caught Rebus's eye: mention of a hot-dog van, parked outside a couple of the clubs. The owner questioned: possible witness. But he'd never seen anything worth the recall. Name: Gavin Tay.

Mr Taystee.

Recent dodgy suicide. Rebus gave Bill Pryde a bell, asked how that investigation was going.

'Dead end street, pal,' Pryde said, not sounding too concerned. Pryde: too long the same rank, and not going anywhere. Beginning the long descent into retirement.

'Did you know he ran a hot-dog stall on the side?'

'Might explain where he got the cash from.'

Gavin Tay was an ex-con. He'd been in the ice-cream business a little over a year. Successful, too: new Merc parked outside his house. His financial records hadn't hinted at money to spare. His widow couldn't account for the Merc. And now: evidence of a job on the side, selling food and drink to punters stumbling out of nightclubs.

Tommy Telford's nightclubs.

Gavin Tay: previous convictions for assault and reset. A

persistent offender who'd finally gone straight ... The room began to feel stuffy, Rebus's head clotted and aching. He decided to get out.

Walked through The Meadows and down George IV Bridge, took the Playfair Steps down to Princes Street. A group was sitting on the stone steps of the Scottish Academy: unshaven, dyed hair, torn clothes. The city's dispossessed, trying their best not to be ignored. Rebus knew he had things in common with them. In the course of his life, he'd failed to fit several niches: husband, father, lover. He hadn't fit in with the Army's ideas of what he should be, and wasn't exactly 'one of the lads' in the police. When one of the group held out a hand, Rebus offered a fiver, before crossing Princes Street and heading for the Oxford Bar.

He settled into a corner with a mug of coffee, got out his mobile, and called Sammy's flat. She was home, all was well with Candice. Rebus told her he had a place for Candice, she could move out tomorrow.

'That's fine,' Sammy said. 'Hold on a second.' There was a rustling sound as the receiver was passed along.

'Hello, John, how are you?'

Rebus smiled. 'Hello, Candice. That's very good.'

'Thank you. Sammy is ... uh ... I am teaching how to ...' She broke into laughter, handed the receiver back.

'I'm teaching her English,' Sammy said.

'I can tell.'

'We started with some Oasis lyrics, just went from there.'

'I'll try to come round later. What did Ned say?'

'He was so shattered when he came home, I think he barely noticed.'

'Is he there? I'd like to talk to him.'

'He's out working.'

'What did you say he was doing again?'

'I didn't.'

'Right. Thanks again, Sammy. See you later.'

He took a swig of coffee, washed it around his mouth. Abernethy: he couldn't just let it go. He swallowed the coffee and called the Roxburghe, asked for David Levy's room.

'Levy speaking.'

'It's John Rebus.'

'Inspector, how good to hear from you. Is there something I can do?'

'I'd like to talk to you.'

'Are you in your office?'

Rebus looked around. 'In a manner of speaking. It's a two-minute walk from your hotel. Turn right out of the door, cross George Street, and walk down to Young Street. Far end, the Oxford Bar. I'm in the back room.'

When Levy arrived, Rebus bought him a half of eighty-bob. Levy eased himself into a chair, hanging his walking-stick on the back of it. 'So what can I do for you?'

'I'm not the only policeman you've spoken to.'

'No, you're not.'

'Someone from Special Branch in London came to see me today.'

'And he told you I'd been travelling around?'

'Yes.'

'Did he warn you against speaking to me?'

'Not in so many words.'

Levy took off his glasses, began polishing them. 'I told you, there are people who'd rather this was all relegated to history. This man, he came all the way from London just to tell you about me?'

'He wanted to see Joseph Lintz.'

'Ah.' Levy was thoughtful. 'Your interpretation, Inspector?'

'I was hoping for yours.'

'My utterly subjective interpretation?' Rebus nodded. 'He wants to be sure of Lintz. This man works for Special Branch, and as everyone knows Special Branch is the public arm of the secret services.'

'He wanted to be confident I wasn't going to get anything out of Lintz?'

Levy nodded, staring at the smoke from Rebus's cigarette. This case was like that: one minute you could see it, the next you couldn't. Like smoke.

'I have a little book with me,' Levy said, reaching into his pocket. 'I'd like you to read it. It's in English, translated from the Hebrew. It's about the Rat Line.'

Rebus took the book. 'Does it prove anything?'

'That depends on your terms.'

'Concrete proof.'

'Concrete proof exists, Inspector.'

'In this book?'

Levy shook his head. 'Under lock and key in Whitehall, kept from scrutiny by the Hundred Year Rule.'

'So there's no way to prove anything.'

'There's one way ...'

'What?'

'If someone talks. If we can get just *one* of them to talk ...'

'That's what this is all about: wearing down their resistance? Looking for the weakest link?'

Levy smiled again. 'We have learned patience, Inspector.' He finished his drink. 'I'm so grateful you called. This has been a much more satisfactory meeting.'

'Will you send your bosses a progress report?'

Levy chose to ignore this. 'We'll talk again, when you've read the book.' He stood up. 'The Special Branch officer ... I've forgotten his name?'

'I didn't give it.'

Levy waited a moment, then said, 'Ah, that explains it

then. Is he still in Edinburgh?' He watched Rebus shake his head. 'Then he's probably on his way to Carlisle, yes?'

Rebus sipped coffee, offered no comment.

'My thanks again, Inspector,' Levy said, undeterred.

'Thanks for dropping by.'

Levy took a final look around. 'Your office,' he said, shaking his head.

8

The Rat Line was an 'underground railway', delivering Nazis – sometimes with the help of the Vatican – from their Soviet persecutors. The end of the Second World War meant the start of the Cold War. Intelligence was necessary, as were intelligent, ruthless individuals who could provide a certain level of expertise. It was said that Klaus Barbie, the 'Butcher of Lyons', had been offered a job with British Intelligence. It was rumoured that high-profile Nazis had been spirited away to America. It wasn't until 1987 that the United Nations released its full list of fugitive Nazi and Japanese war criminals, forty thousand of them.

Why so late in releasing the list? Rebus thought he could understand. Modern politics had decreed that Germany and Japan were part of the global brotherhood of capital-ism. In whose interests would it be to reopen old wounds? And besides, how many atrocities had the Allies themselves hidden? Who fought a war with clean hands? Rebus, who'd grown to adulthood in the Army, could comprehend this. He'd done things … He'd served time in Northern Ireland, seen trust disfigured, hatred replace fear.

Part of him could well believe in the existence of a Rat Line.

The book Levy had given him went into the mechanics of how such an operation might have worked. Rebus wondered: was it really possible to disappear completely, to change identity? And again, the recurring question: did any of it matter? There did exist sources of identification, and there *had* been court cases – Eichmann, Barbie, Demjanjuk – with others ongoing. He read about war criminals who, rather than being tried or extradited, were allowed to return home, running businesses, growing rich, dying of old age. But he also read of criminals who served their sentences and became 'good people', people who *had* changed. These men said war itself was the real culprit. Rebus recalled one of his first conversations with Joseph Lintz, in the drawing-room of Lintz's home. The old man's voice was hoarse, a scarf around his throat.

'At my age, Inspector, a simple throat infection can feel like death.'

There didn't seem to be many photographs around. Lintz had explained that a lot had gone missing during the war.

'Along with other mementoes. I do have these photos though.'

He'd shown Rebus half a dozen framed shots, dating back to the 1930s. As he'd explained who the subjects were, Rebus had suddenly thought: what if he's making it up? What if these are just a bunch of old photos he picked up somewhere and had framed? And the names, the identities he now gave to the faces – had he invented them? He'd seen in that instant, for the first time, how easy it might be to construct another life.

And then, later in their conversation that day, Lintz, sipping honeyed tea, had started discussing Villefranche.

'I've been thinking a lot about it, Inspector, as you might imagine. This Lieutenant Linzstek, he was in charge on the day?'

'Yes.'

'But presumably under orders from above. A lieutenant is not so very far up the pecking order.'

'Perhaps.'

'You see, if a soldier is under orders ... then they must carry out those orders, no?'

'Even if the order is insane?'

'Nevertheless, I'd say the person was at the very least *coerced* into committing the crime, and a crime that very many of us would have carried out under similar circumstances. Can't you see the hypocrisy of trying someone, when you'd probably have done the same thing yourself? One soldier standing out from the crowd ... saying no to the massacre: would you have made that stand yourself?'

'I hope so.' Rebus thinking back to Ulster and the 'Mean Machine' ...

Levy's book didn't prove anything. All Rebus knew was that Josef Linzstek's name was on a list as having used the Rat Line, posing as a Pole. But where had the list originated? In Israel. Again, it was highly speculative. It wasn't *proof*.

And if Rebus's instincts told him Lintz and Linzstek were one and the same, they were still failing to tell him whether it mattered.

He dropped the book back to the Roxburghe, asked the receptionist to see that Mr Levy got it.

'I think he's in his room, if you'd like to ...'

Rebus shook his head. He hadn't left any message with the book, knowing Levy might interpret this as a message in itself. He went home for his car, drove down to Haymarket and along to Shandon. As usual, parking near Sammy's flat was a problem. Everyone was home from work and tucked in front of their televisions. He climbed the stone steps, wondering how treacherous they'd get when the frosts came, and rang the bell. Sammy herself led him into the living room, where Candice was watching a game show.

'Hello, John,' she said. 'Are you my wonderwall?'

'I'm nobody's wonderwall, Candice.' He turned to Sammy. 'Everything all right?'

'Just fine.'

At that moment, Ned Farlowe walked in from the kitchen. He was eating soup from a bowl, dunking a folded slice of brown bread into it.

'Mind if I have a word?' Rebus said.

Farlowe shook his head, then jerked it in the direction of the kitchen.

'Can I eat while we talk? I'm starving.' He sat down at the foldaway table, got another slice of bread from the packet and spread margarine on it. Sammy put her head round the doorway, saw the look on her father's face, and made a tactical retreat. The kitchen was about seven foot square and too full of pots and appliances. Swinging a cat, you could have done a lot of damage.

'I saw you today,' Rebus said, 'skulking in Warriston Cemetery. Coincidence?'

'What do you think?'

'I'm asking you.' Rebus leaned his back against the sink unit, folded his arms.

'I'm watching Lintz.'

'Why?'

'Because I'm being paid to.'

'By a newspaper?'

'Lintz's lawyer has interim interdicts flying around. Nobody can afford to be seen near him.'

'But they still want him watched?'

'If there's a court case coming, they want to know as much as possible, stands to reason.'

By court case, Farlowe didn't mean any trial of Lintz, but rather of the newspapers themselves, for libel.

'If he catches you ...'

'He doesn't know me from Adam. Besides, there'd

always be somebody to take my place. Now do I get to ask a question?'

'Let me say something first. You know I'm investigating Lintz?' Farlowe nodded. 'That means we're too close. If you find out anything, people might think it came from me.'

'I haven't told Sammy what I'm doing, *specifically* so there's no conflict of interests.'

'I'm just saying others might not believe it.'

'A few more days, I'll have enough money to fund the book for another month.' Farlowe had finished his soup. He carried the empty bowl over to the sink, stood next to Rebus.

'I don't want this to be a problem, but the bottom line is: what can you do about it?'

Rebus stared at him. His instinct was to stuff Farlowe's head into the sink, but how would that look with Sammy?

'Now,' Farlowe said, 'do I get to ask my question?'

'What is it?'

'Who's Candice?'

'A friend of mine.'

'So what's wrong with *your* flat?'

Rebus realised he was no longer dealing with his daughter's boyfriend. He was confronted with a journalist, someone with a nose for a story.

'Tell you what,' said Rebus, 'say I didn't see you in the cemetery. Say we didn't just have this little chat.'

'And I don't ask about Candice?' Rebus stayed quiet. Farlowe considered the deal. 'Say I get to ask you a few questions for my book.'

'What sort of questions?'

'About Cafferty.'

Rebus shook his head. 'I could talk about Tommy Telford though.'

'When?'

'When we've got him behind bars.'

Farlowe smiled. 'I could be on the pension by then.' He waited, saw Rebus was going to give him nothing.

'She's only here till tomorrow anyway,' Rebus said.

'Where's she off to?'

Rebus just winked. Left the kitchen, returned to the living-room. Talked to Sammy while Candice's game show reached its climax. Whenever she heard audience laughter, she joined in. Rebus made arrangements for the following day, then left. There was no sign of Farlowe. He'd either hidden himself in the bedroom or else gone back out. It took Rebus a few moments to remember where he'd parked his car. He drove home carefully; stopped for all the lights.

The parking spaces were all taken in Arden Street. He left the Saab on a yellow line. As he approached his tenement door, he heard a car door open and spun towards the sound.

It was Claverhouse. He was on his own. 'Mind if I come in?'

Rebus thought of a dozen reasons for saying yes. But he shrugged and made for the door. 'Any news of the stabbing at Megan's?' he asked.

'How did you know we'd be interested?'

'A bouncer gets stabbed, the attacker flees on a waiting motorbike. It was premeditated. And the majority of the bouncers work for Tommy Telford.'

They were climbing the stairs. Rebus's flat was on the second floor.

'Well, you're right,' Claverhouse said. 'Billy Tennant worked for Telford. He controlled the traffic in and out of Megan's.'

'Traffic as in dope?'

'The footballer's friend, the one who got wounded, he's a known dealer. Works out of Paisley.'

'Therefore connected to Telford, too.'

'We're speculating he was the target, Tennant just got in the way.'

'Leaving only one question: who was behind it?'

'Come on, John. It was Cafferty, obviously.'

'Not Cafferty's style,' Rebus said, unlocking his door.

'Maybe he's learned a thing or two from the Young Pretender.'

'Make yourself at home,' Rebus said, walking down the hall. The breakfast things were still on the dining table. Siobhan's bag of goodies was down the side of a chair.

'A guest.' Claverhouse had noticed the two mugs, two plates. He looked around. 'She's not here now though?'

'She wasn't here for breakfast either.'

'Because she's at your daughter's.'

Rebus froze.

'I went to settle up with the hotel. They said a police car had come and taken all her things away. So then I asked around, and the driver gave me Samantha's address as the drop-off.' Claverhouse sat down on the sofa, crossed one leg over the other. 'So what's the game, John, and how come you've seen fit to leave me on the bench?' He sounded calm now, but Rebus could tell there'd been a storm.

'Do you want a drink?'

'I want an answer.'

'When she walked out ... she waited beside my car. I couldn't think where to take her, so I brought her here. But she recognised the street. Telford had been watching my flat.'

Claverhouse looked interested. 'Why?'

'Maybe because I know Cafferty. I couldn't let Candice stay here, so I took her to Sammy's.'

'Is she still there?' Rebus nodded. 'So what happens now?'

'There's a place she can go, the refugee family.'

'For how long?'

'What do you mean?'

Claverhouse sighed. 'John, she's … the only life she's known here is prostitution.'

Rebus went over to the hi-fi for something to do, looked through his tapes. He needed to do *some*thing.

'What's she going to do for money? Are you going to provide? What does that make you?'

Rebus dropped a CD, turned on his heels. 'Nothing like that,' he spat.

Claverhouse had his hands up, palms showing. 'Come on, John, you know yourself there's –'

'I don't know anything.'

'John …'

'Look, get out, will you?' It wasn't just that it had been a long day, more that it felt like the day would never end. He could feel the evening stretch to infinity, no rest available to him. In his head, bodies were swaying gently from trees while smoke engulfed a church. Telford was on his arcade motorbike, cannoning off spectators. Abernethy was touching an old man's shoulder. Soldiers were rifle-butting civilians. And John Rebus … John Rebus was in every frame, trying hard to remain an onlooker.

He put Van Morrison on the hi-fi: *Hardnose the Highway*. He'd played this music on East Neuk beaches and tenement stakeouts. It always seemed to heal him, or at least patch the wounds. When he turned back into the room, Claverhouse was gone. He looked out of his window. Two kids lived in the second-floor flat across from his. He'd watched them often from this window, and they never once saw him, for the simple reason that they never so much as glanced outside. Their world was complete and all-absorbing, anything outside their window an irrelevance. They were in bed now, their mother closing the shutters. Quiet city. Abernethy was right about that. There were large chunks of Edinburgh where you could live your whole life and never encounter a spot of bother. Yet the murder rate in Scotland was double that of its southern neighbour, and half those murders took place in the two main cities.

Not that the statistics mattered. A death was a death. Something unique had disappeared from the world. One murder or several hundred ... they all meant something to the survivors. Rebus thought of Villefranche's sole existing survivor. He hadn't met her, probably never would. Another reason it was hard to get passionate about a historical case. In a contemporary one, you had many of the facts to hand, and could talk to witnesses. You could gather forensic evidence, question people's stories. You could measure guilt and grief. You became part of the whole story. This was what interested Rebus. The people interested him; their stories fascinated him. When part of their lives, he could forget his own.

He noticed the answering-machine was flashing: one message.

'Oh, hello there. I'm ... um, I don't know how to put this ...' Placed the voice: Kirstin Mede. She sighed. 'Look, I can't do this any more. So please don't ... I'm sorry, I just can't. There are other people who can help you. I'm sure one of them ...'

End of message. Rebus stared down at the machine. He didn't blame her. *I can't do this any more.* That makes two of us, Rebus thought. The only thing was, *he* had to keep going. He sat down at his table and pulled the Villefranche paperwork towards him: lists of names and occupations, ages and dates of birth. Picat, Mesplede, Rousseau, Deschamps. Wine merchant, china painter, cartwright, housemaid. What did any of it mean to a middle-aged Scot? He pushed it aside and lifted Siobhan's paperwork on to the table.

Off with Van the Man; on with side one of *Wish You*

Were Here. Scratched to hell. He remembered it had come in a black polythene wrapper. When opened, there'd been this smell, which afterwards he'd learned was supposed to be burning flesh …

'I need a drink,' he said to himself, sitting forward in his chair. 'I want a drink. A few beers, maybe with whiskies attached.' Something to smooth the edges …

He looked at his watch; not even near to closing time. Not that it mattered much in Edinburgh, the land that closing time forgot. Could he make it to the Ox before they shut up shop? Yes, too easily. It was nicer to have a challenge. Wait an hour or so and then repeat the debate.

Or call Jack Morton.

Or go out, right now.

The telephone rang. He picked it up.

'Hello?'

'John?' Making it sound like 'Sean'.

'Hello, Candice. What's up?'

'Up?'

'Is there a problem?'

'Problem, no. I just wanting … I say to you, see you tomorrow.'

He smiled. 'Yes, see you tomorrow. You speak very good English.'

'I was chained to a razor blade.'

'What?'

'Line from song.'

'Oh, right. But you're not chained to it now?'

She didn't seem to understand. 'I'm … uh …'

'It's okay, Candice. See you tomorrow.'

'Yes, see you.'

Rebus put down the receiver. Chained to a razor blade … Suddenly he didn't want a drink any more.

9

He picked Candice up the next afternoon. She had two carrier bags, her worldly belongings. She gave Sammy as much of a hug as her bandaged arms would allow.

'See you again, Candice,' Sammy said.

'Yes, see you. Thanks ...' Lost for an ending to the sentence, Candice opened her arms wide, bags swinging.

They stopped off at McDonald's (her choice) for something to eat. Zappa and the Mothers: 'Cruising for Burgers'. The day was bright and crisp, just right for crossing the Forth Bridge. Rebus took it slowly, so Candice could take in the view. He was heading towards Fife's East Neuk, a cluster of fishing villages popular with artists and holidaymakers. Out of season, Anstruther seemed practically deserted. Though Rebus had an address, he stopped to ask directions. Finally, he parked in front of a small terraced house. Candice stared at the red door until he gestured for her to follow him. He hadn't been able to make her understand what they were doing here. Hoped Mr and Mrs Drinic would make a better job of it.

The door was opened by a woman in her early forties. She had long black hair, and peered at him over half-moon glasses. Then her attention shifted to Candice, and she said something in a language both women understood. Candice replied, looking a little shy, not sure what was going on.

'Come in, please,' Mrs Drinic said. 'My husband is in the kitchen.'

They sat around the kitchen table. Mr Drinic was heavily

built, with a thick brown moustache and wavy brown and silver hair. A pot of tea was produced, and Mrs Drinic drew her chair beside Candice's and began talking again.

'She's explaining to the girl,' Mr Drinic said.

Rebus nodded, sipped the strong tea, listened to a conversation he could not understand. Candice, cautious at first, grew more animated as she told her story, and Mrs Drinic was a skilled listener, sympathising, showing shared horror and exasperation.

'She was taken to Amsterdam, told there would be a job there for her,' Mr Drinic explained. 'I know this has happened to other young women.'

'I think she left a child behind.'

'A son, yes. She's telling my wife about him.'

'What about you?' Rebus asked. 'How did you end up here?'

'I was an architect in Sarajevo. No easy decision, leaving your whole life behind.' He paused. 'We went to Belgrade first. A refugee bus brought us to Scotland.' He shrugged. 'That was nearly five years ago. Now I am a carpenter.' A smile. 'Distance no object.'

Rebus looked at Candice, who had started crying, Mrs Drinic comforting her.

'We will look after her,' Mrs Drinic said, staring at her husband.

Later, at the door, Rebus tried to give them some money, but they wouldn't take it.

'Is it all right if I come and see her sometime?'

'But of course.'

He stood in front of Candice.

'Her real name is Karina,' Mrs Drinic said quietly.

'Karina.' Rebus tried out the word. She smiled, her eyes softer than Rebus remembered them, as if some transformation were beginning. She bent forward.

'Kiss the girl,' she said.

A peck on both cheeks. Her eyes filling with tears again. Rebus nodded, to let her know he understood everything.

At his car, he waved once, and she blew him another kiss. Then he drove around the corner and stopped, gripping the steering-wheel hard. He wondered if she'd cope. If she'd learn to forget. He thought again of his ex-wife's words. What would she think of him now? Had he exploited Karina? No, but he wondered if that was only because she hadn't been able to give him anything on Telford. He felt he had somehow failed to do the right thing. So far, the only choice she'd had to make was when she'd waited for him by his car rather than going back to Telford. Before then and after, all the decisions had been taken for her. In a sense, she was still as trapped as ever, because the locks and chains were in her mind; they were what she expected from life. It would take time for her to change, to begin trusting the world again. The Drinics would help her.

Heading south down the coast, thinking about families, he decided to visit his brother.

Mickey lived on an estate in Kirkcaldy, his red BMW parked in the driveway. He was just home from work and suitably surprised to see Rebus.

'Chrissie and the kids are at her mum's,' he said. 'I was going to grab a curry for dinner. How about a beer?'

'Maybe just a coffee,' Rebus said. He sat in the lounge until Mickey returned, toting a couple of old shoe-boxes.

'Look what I dug out of the attic last weekend. Thought you might like a look. Milk and sugar?'

'A spot of milk.'

While Mickey went to the kitchen to fetch the coffee, Rebus examined the boxes. They were filled with packets of photographs. The packets had dates on them, some with questionmarks. Rebus opened one at random. Holiday snaps. A fancy dress parade. A picnic. Rebus didn't have any pictures of his parents, and the photos startled him. His mother had thicker legs than he remembered, but a tidy body, too. His father used the same grin in every shot, a grin Rebus shared with Mickey. Digging further into the box, he found one of himself with Rhona and Sammy. They were on a beach somewhere, the wind playing havoc. Peter Gabriel: 'Family Snapshot'. Rebus couldn't place it at all. Mickey came back through with a mug of coffee and a bottle of beer.

'There are some,' he said, 'I don't know who the people are. Relatives maybe? Grandma and Grandad?'

'I'm not sure I'd be much help.'

Mickey handed over a menu. 'Here,' he said, 'best Indian in town. Pick what you want.'

So Rebus chose, and Mickey phoned the order in. Twenty minutes till delivery. Rebus was on to another packet. These photos were older still, the 1940s. His father in uniform. The soldiers wore hats like McDonald's counter staff. They also wore long khaki shorts. 'Malaya' written on the backs of some, 'India' on the others.

'Remember, the old man got himself wounded in Malaya?' Mickey said.

'No, he didn't.'

'He showed us the wound. It was in his knee.'

Rebus was shaking his head. 'Uncle Jimmy told me it was a cut Dad got playing football. He kept picking the scab off, ended with a scar.'

'He told us it was a war wound.'

'He was fibbing.'

Mickey had started on the other box. 'Here, look at these ...' Handing over an inch-thick collection of post-cards and photographs, secured with an elastic band. Rebus pulled the band off, turned the cards over, saw his own writing. The photos were of him, too: posed snaps, badly taken.

'Where did you get these?'

'You always used to send me a card or a photo, don't you remember?'

They were all from Rebus's own Army days. 'I'd forgotten,' he said.

'Once a fortnight, usually. A letter to Dad, a card for me.'

Rebus sat back in his chair and started to go through them. Judging by the postmarks, they were in chronological sequence. Training, then service in Germany and Ulster, more exercises in Cyprus, Malta, Finland, and the desert of Saudi Arabia. The tone of each postcard was breezy, so that Rebus failed to recognise his own voice. The cards from Belfast consisted of almost nothing but jokes, yet Rebus remembered that as one of the most nightmarish periods of his life.

'I used to love getting them,' Mickey said, smiling. 'I'll tell you, you almost had me joining up.'

Rebus was still thinking of Belfast: the closed barracks, the whole compound a fortress. After a shift out on the streets, there was no way to let off steam. Booze, gambling and fights – all taking place within the same four walls. All culminating in the Mean Machine ... And here were these postcards, here was the image of Rebus's past life that Mickey had lived with these past twenty-odd years.

And it was all a lie.

Or was it? Where did the reality lie, other than in Rebus's own head? The postcards were fake documents, but they were also the only ones in existence. There was nothing to contradict them, nothing except Rebus's word. It was the same with the Rat Line, the same with Joseph Lintz's story. Rebus looked at his brother and knew he could break the spell right now. All he had to do was tell him the truth.

'What's the matter?' Mickey asked.

'Nothing.'

'Ready for that beer yet? The food'll be here any second.'

Rebus stared at the cooling mug of coffee. 'More than ready,' he said, putting the rubber band back around his past. 'But I'll stick to this.' He lifted the mug, toasted his brother.

10

Next morning, Rebus went to St Leonard's, telephoned the NCIS centre at Prestwick and asked if they had anything connecting British criminals to European prostitution. His reasoning: *someone* had brought Candice – she was still Candice to him – from Amsterdam to Britain, and he didn't think it was Telford. Whoever it was, Rebus would get to them somehow. He wanted to show Candice her chains could be broken.

He got NCIS to fax him what information they had. Most of it concerned the 'Tippelzone', a licensed car park where drivers went for sex. It was worked by foreign prostitutes mainly, most of them lacking work permits, many smuggled in from Eastern Europe. The main gangs seemed to be from former Yugoslavia. NCIS had no names for any of these kidnappers-cum-pimps. There was nothing about prostitutes making the trip from Amsterdam to Britain.

Rebus went into the car park to smoke his second cigarette of the day. There were a couple of other smokers out there, a small brotherhood of social pariahs. Back in the office, the Farmer wanted to know if there was any progress on Lintz.

'Maybe if I brought him in and slapped him around a bit,' Rebus suggested.

'Be serious, will you?' the Farmer growled, stalking back to his office.

Rebus sat down at his desk and pulled forward a file.

'Your problem, Inspector,' Lintz had said to him once, 'is that you're afraid of being taken seriously. You want to give people what you think they expect. I mention the Ishtar gate, and you talk of some Hollywood movie. At first I thought this was meant to rouse me to some indiscretion, but now it seems more a game you are playing against *yourself*.'

Rebus: seated in his usual chair in Lintz's drawing-room. The view from the window was of Queen Street Gardens. They were kept locked: you had to pay for a key.

'Do educated people frighten you?'

Rebus looked at the old man. 'No.'

'Are you sure? Don't you perhaps wish you were more like them?' Lintz grinned, showing small, discoloured teeth. 'Intellectuals like to see themselves as history's victims, prejudiced against, arrested for their beliefs, even tortured and murdered. But Karadzic thinks himself an intellectual. The Nazi hierarchy had its thinkers and philosophers. And even in Babylon ...' Lintz got up, poured himself more tea. Rebus declined a refill.

'Even in Babylon, Inspector,' Lintz continued, getting comfortable again, 'with its opulence and its artistry, with its enlightened king ... do you know what they did? Nebuchadnezzar held the Jews captive for seventy years. This splendid, awe-inspiring civilisation ... Do you begin to see the madness, Inspector, the flaws that run so deep in us?'

'Maybe I need glasses.'

Lintz threw his cup across the room. 'You need to listen and to learn! You need to understand!'

The cup and saucer lay on the carpet, still intact. Tea was soaking into the elaborate design, where it would become all but invisible ...

He parked on Buccleuch Place. The Slavic Studies

department was housed in one of the tenements. He tried the secretary's office first, asked if Dr Colquhoun was around.

'I haven't seen him today.'

When Rebus explained what he wanted, the secretary tried a couple of numbers but didn't find anyone. Then she suggested he take a look in their library, which was one floor up and kept locked. She handed him a key.

The room was about sixteen feet by twelve, and smelled stuffy. The shutters across the windows were closed, giving the place no natural light. A No Smoking sign sat on one of four desks. On another sat an ashtray with three butts in it. One entire wall was shelved, filled with books, pamphlets, magazines. There were boxes of press cuttings, and maps on the walls showing Yugoslavia's changing demarcation lines. Rebus lifted down the most recent box of cuttings.

Like a lot of people he knew, Rebus didn't know much about the war in ex-Yugoslavia. He'd seen some of the news reports, been shocked by the pictures, then had got on with his life. But if the cuttings were to be believed, the whole region was being run by war criminals. The Implementation Force seemed to have done its damnedest to avoid confrontation. There had been a few arrests recently, but nothing substantial: out of a meagre seventy-four suspects charged, only *seven* had been apprehended.

He found nothing about slave traders, so thanked the secretary and gave her back her key, then crawled through the city traffic. When the call came on his mobile, he nearly went off the road.

Candice had disappeared.

Mrs Drinic was distraught. They'd had dinner last night, breakfast this morning, and Karina had seemed fine.

'There was a lot she said she couldn't tell us,' Mr Drinic

said, standing behind his seated wife, hands stroking her shoulders. 'She said she wanted to forget.'

And then she'd gone out for a walk down to the harbour, and hadn't returned. Lost maybe, though the village was small. Mr Drinic had been working; his wife had gone out, asking people if they'd seen her.

'And Mrs Muir's son,' she said, 'he told me she'd been taken away in a car.'

'Where was this?' Rebus asked.

'Just a couple of streets away,' Mr Drinic said.

'Show me.'

Outside his home on Seaford Road, Eddie Muir, aged eleven, told Rebus what he'd seen. A car stopping beside a woman. A bit of chat, though he couldn't hear it. The door opening, the woman getting in.

'Which door, Eddie?'

'One of the back ones. Had to be, there were two of them in the car already.'

'Men?'

Eddie nodded.

'And the woman got in by herself? I mean, they didn't grab her or anything?'

Eddie shook his head. He was straddling his bike, keen to be going. One foot kept testing a pedal.

'Can you describe the car?'

'Big, a bit flash. Not from round here.'

'And the men?'

'Didn't really get a good look. Driver was wearing a Pars shirt.'

Meaning a football shirt, Dunfermline Athletic. Which would mean he was from Fife. Rebus frowned. A pick-up? Could that be it? Candice back to her old ways so soon? Not likely, not in a place like this, on a street like this. It was no chance encounter. Mrs Drinic was right: she'd been snatched. Which meant someone had known where to find her. Had Rebus been followed yesterday? If he had, they'd been invisible. Some device on his car? It seemed unlikely, but he checked wheel-arches and the underbody: nothing. Mrs Drinic had calmed a little, her husband having administered medicinal vodka. Rebus could use a shot himself, but turned down the offer.

'Did she make any phone calls?' he asked. Drinic shook his head. 'What about strangers hanging around the street?'

'I would have noticed. After Sarajevo, it's hard to feel safe, Inspector.' He opened his arms. 'And here's the proof – nowhere's safe.'

'Did you tell anyone about Karina?'

'Who would we tell?'

Who knew? That was the question. Rebus did. And Claverhouse and Ormiston knew about the place, because Colquhoun had mentioned it.

Colquhoun knew. The nervy old Slavic Studies specialist knew ... On the way back to Edinburgh, Rebus tried phoning him at office and home: no reply. He'd told the Drinics to let him know if Candice came back, but he didn't think she'd be coming back. He remembered the look she'd given him early on when he'd asked her to trust him. *I won't be surprised if you let me down.* Like she'd known back then that he'd fail. And she'd given him a second chance, waiting for him beside his car. And he'd let her down. He got back on his mobile and called Jack Morton.

'Jack,' he said, 'for Christ's sake, talk me out of having a drink.'

He tried Colquhoun's home address and the Slavic Studies office: both locked up tight. Then he drove to Flint Street and looked for Tommy Telford in the arcade. But Telford wasn't there. He was in the café's back office, surrounded as usual by his men.

'I want to talk to you,' Rebus said.

'So talk.'

'Without the audience.' Rebus pointed to Pretty-Boy. 'That one can stay.'

Telford took his time, but finally nodded, and the room began to empty. Pretty-Boy stood against a wall, hands behind his back. Telford had his feet up on his desk, leaning back in his chair. They were relaxed, confident. Rebus knew what *he* looked like: a caged bear.

'I want to know where she is.'

'Who?'

'Candice.'

Telford smiled. 'Still on about her, Inspector? How should I know where she is?'

'Because a couple of your boys grabbed her.' But as he spoke, Rebus realised he was making a mistake. Telford's gang was a *family*: they'd grown up together in Paisley. Not many Dunfermline supporters that distant from Fife. He stared at Pretty-Boy, who ran Telford's prostitutes. Candice had arrived in Edinburgh from a city of bridges, maybe Newcastle. Telford had Newcastle connections. And the Newcastle United strip – vertical black and white lines – was damned close to Dunfermline's. Probably only a kid in Fife could make the mistake.

A Newcastle strip. A Newcastle car.

Telford was talking, but Rebus wasn't listening. He walked straight out of the office and back to the Saab. Drove to Fettes – the Crime Squad offices – and started looking. He found a contact number for a DS Miriam Kenworthy. Tried the number but she wasn't there.

'Fuck it,' he told himself, getting back into his car.

The A1 was hardly the country's fastest road – Abernethy was right about that. Still, without the daytime traffic Rebus made decent time on his way south. It was late evening when he arrived in Newcastle, pubs emptying, queues forming outside clubs, a few United shirts on display, looking like prison bars. He didn't know the city. Drove around it in circles, passing the same signs and landmarks, heading further out, just cruising.

Looking for Candice. Or for girls who might know her.

After a couple of hours, he gave up, headed back into the centre. He'd had the idea of sleeping in his car, but when he found a hotel with an empty room, the thought of en-suite facilities suddenly seemed too good to miss.

He made sure there was no mini-bar.

A long soak with his eyes closed, mind and body still racing from the drive. He sat in a chair by his window and listened to the night: taxis and yells, delivery lorries. He couldn't sleep. He lay on the bed, watching soundless TV, remembering Candice in the hotel room, asleep under sweet wrappers. Deacon Blue: 'Chocolate Girl.'

He woke up to breakfast TV. Checked out of the hotel and had breakfast in a café, then called Miriam Kenworthy's office, relieved to find she was an early starter.

'Come right round,' she said, sounding bemused. 'You're only a couple of minutes away.'

She was younger than her telephone voice, face softer than her attitude. It was a milkmaid's face, rounded, the cheeks pink and plump. She studied him, swivelling slightly in her chair as he told her the story.

'Tarawicz,' she said when he'd finished. 'Jake Tarawicz. Real name Joachim, probably.' Kenworthy smiled. 'Some of us around here call him Mr Pink Eyes. He's had dealings – meetings anyway – with this guy Telford.' She opened the brown folder in front of her. 'Mr Pink Eyes has a lot of European connections. You know Chechnia?'

'In Russia?'

'It's Russia's Sicily, if you know what I mean.'

'Is that where Tarawicz comes from?'

'It's one theory. The other is that he's Serbian. Might explain why he set up the convoy.'

'What convoy?'

'Running aid lorries to former Yugoslavia. A real humanitarian, our Mr Pink.'

'But also a way of smuggling people out?'

Kenworthy looked at him. 'You've been doing your homework.'

'Call it an educated guess.'

'Well, it gets him noticed. He got a papal blessing six months ago. Married to an Englishwoman – not for love. She was one of his girls.'

'But it gives him residency here.'

She nodded. 'He hasn't been around that long, five or six years ...'

Like Telford, Rebus thought.

'But he's built himself a rep, muscled in where there used to be Asians, Turks ... Story is, he started with a nice line in stolen icons. A ton of stuff has been lifted out of the Soviet bloc. And when that operation started drying, he moved into prossies. Cheap girls, and he could keep them docile with a bit of crack. The crack comes up from London – the Yardies control that particular scene. Mr Pink spreads their goods around the north-east. He also deals heroin for the Turks and sells some girls to Triad brothels.' She looked at Rebus, saw she had his attention. 'No racial barriers when it comes to business.'

'So I see.'

'Probably also sells drugs to your friend Telford, who distributes them through his nightclubs.'

' "Probably"?'

'We've no hard proof. There was even a story going around that Pink wasn't selling to Telford, he was *buying*.'

Rebus blinked. 'Telford's not that big.'

She shrugged.

'Where would he get the stuff?'

'It was a story, that's all.'

But it had Rebus thinking, because it might help explain the relationship between Tarawicz and Telford ...

'What does Tarawicz get out of it?' he asked, making his thoughts flesh.

'You mean apart from money? Well, Telford trains a good bouncer. Jock bouncers get respect down here. Then, of course, Telford has shares in a couple of casinos.'

'A way for Tarawicz to launder his cash?' Rebus thought about this. 'Is there anything Tarawicz *doesn't* have a finger in?'

'Plenty. He likes businesses which are fluid. And he's still a relative newcomer.'

Eagles: 'New Kid in Town'.

'We think he's been dealing arms: a lot of stuff crossing into Western Europe. The Chechens seem to have weaponry to spare.' She sniffed, gathered her thoughts.

'Sounds like he's one step ahead of Tommy Telford.' Which would explain why Telford was so keen to do business with him. He was on a learning curve, learning how to fit into the bigger picture. Yardies and Asians, Turks and Chechens, and all the others. Rebus saw them as spokes on a huge wheel which was trundling mercilessly across the world, breaking bones as it went.

'Why "Mr Pink Eyes"?' he asked.

She'd been awaiting the question, slid a colour photo towards him.

It was the close-up of a face, the skin pink and blistered, white lesions running through it. The face was puffy, bloated, and in its midst sat eyes hidden by blue-tinted glasses. There were no eyebrows. The hair above the jutting forehead was thin and yellow. The man looked like some monstrous shaved pig.

'What happened to him?' he asked.

'We don't know. That's the way he looked when he arrived.'

Rebus remembered the description Candice had given: sunglasses, looks like a car-crash victim. Dead ringer.

'I want to talk to him,' Rebus said.

But first, Kenworthy gave him a guided tour. They took her car, and she showed him where the street girls worked. It was mid-morning, no action to speak of. He gave her a description of Candice, and she promised she'd put the word out. They spoke with the few women they met. They all seemed to know Kenworthy, weren't hostile towards her.

'They're the same as you or me,' she told him, driving away. 'Working to feed their kids.'

'Or their habit.'

'That too, of course.'

'In Amsterdam, they've got a union.'

'Doesn't help the poor sods who're shipped there.' Kenworthy signalled at a junction. 'You're sure he has her?'

'I don't think Telford does. Someone knew addresses back in Sarajevo, addresses that were important to her. Someone shipped her out of there.'

'Sounds like Mr Pink all right.'

'And he's the only one who can send her back.'

She looked at him. 'Why would he do a thing like that?'

Just as Rebus was thinking their surroundings couldn't get any grimmer – all industrial decay, gutted buildings and pot-holes – Kenworthy signalled to turn in at the gates of a scrapyard.

'You're kidding?' he said.

Three Alsatians, tethered by thirty-foot chains, barked and bounded towards the car. Kenworthy ignored them, kept driving. It was like being in a ravine. Either side of them stood precarious canyon walls of car wrecks.

'Hear that?'

Rebus heard it: the sound of a collision. The car entered a wide clearing, and he saw a yellow crane, dangling a huge grab from its arm, pluck up the car it had dropped and lift it high, before dropping it again on to the carcass of another. A few men were standing at a safe distance, smoking cigarettes and looking bored. The grab dropped on to the roof of the top car, denting it badly. Glass shimmered on the oily ground, diamonds against black velvet.

Jake Tarawicz – Mr Pink Eyes – was in the crane, laughing and roaring as he picked up the car again, worrying it the way a cat might play with a mouse without noticing it was dead. If he'd seen the new additions to his audience, it didn't show. Kenworthy hadn't got out of her car immediately. First, she'd fixed on a face from her repertoire. When finally she was ready, she nodded to Rebus and they opened their doors simultaneously.

As Rebus stood upright, he saw that the grab had dropped the car and was swinging towards them. Kenworthy folded her arms and stood her ground. Rebus was reminded of those arcade games where you had to pick up a prize. He could see Tarawicz in the cab, manipulating the controls like a kid with a toy. He remembered Tommy Telford on his arcade bike, and saw at once something the two men had in common: neither had ever really grown up.

The motorised hum stopped suddenly, and Tarawicz dropped from the cab. He was wearing a cream suit and emerald shirt, open at the neck. He'd borrowed a pair of green wellies from somewhere, so as to keep his trousers clean. As he walked towards the two detectives, his men stepped into line behind him.

'Miriam,' he said, 'always a pleasure.' He paused. 'Or so

the rumour goes.' A couple of his men grinned. Rebus recognised one face: 'The Crab', that's what he'd been called in central Scotland. His grip could crush bones. Rebus hadn't seen him in a long time, and had never seen him so smartly groomed and dressed.

'All right, Crab?' Rebus said.

This seemed to disconcert Tarawicz, who half-turned towards his minion. The Crab stayed quiet, but colour had risen to his neck.

Up close, it was hard not to stare at Mr Pink Eyes's face. His eyes demanded that you meet them, but you really wanted to study the flesh in which they sat.

He was looking at Rebus now.

'Have we met?'

'No.'

'This is Detective Inspector Rebus,' Kenworthy explained. 'He's come all the way from Scotland to see you.'

'I'm flattered.' Tarawicz's grin showed small sharp teeth with gaps between them.

'I think you know why I'm here,' Rebus said.

Tarawicz made a show of astonishment. 'Do I?'

'Telford needed your help. He needed a home address for Candice, a note to her in Serbo–Croat ...'

'Is this some sort of riddle?'

'And now you've taken her back.'

'Have I?'

Rebus took a half-step forward. Tarawicz's men fanned out either side of their boss. There was a sheen on Tarawicz's face which could have been sweat or some medical cream.

'She wanted out,' Rebus told him. 'I promised I'd help her. I never break a promise.'

'She wanted out? She told you that?' Tarawicz's voice was teasing.

One of the men behind cleared his throat. Rebus had been wondering about this man, so much smaller and more reticent than the others, better dressed and with sad drooping eyes and sallow skin. Now he knew: lawyer. And the cough was his way of warning Tarawicz that he was saying too much.

'I'm going to take Tommy Telford down,' Rebus said quietly. 'That's my promise to you. Once he's in custody, who knows what he'll say?'

'I'm sure Mr Telford can look after himself, Inspector. Which is more than can be said for Candice.' The lawyer coughed again.

'I want her kept off the streets,' Rebus said.

Tarawicz stared at him, tiny black pupils like spots of absolute darkness.

'Can Thomas Telford go about his daily business unfettered?' he said at last. Behind him, the lawyer almost choked.

'You know I can't promise that,' Rebus said. 'It's not me he has to worry about.'

'Take a message to your friend,' Tarawicz said. 'And afterwards, stop being his friend.'

Rebus realised then: Tarawicz was talking about *Cafferty*. Telford had told him that Rebus was Cafferty's man.

'I think I can do that,' Rebus said quietly.

'Then do it.' Tarawicz turned away.

'And Candice?'

'I'll see what I can do.' He stopped, slid his hands into his jacket pockets. 'Hey, Miriam,' he said, his back still to them, 'I like you better in that red two-piece.'

Laughing, he walked away.

'Get in the car,' Kenworthy said through gritted teeth. Rebus got into the car. She looked nervous, dropped her keys, bent to retrieve them.

'What's wrong?'

'Nothing's wrong,' she snapped.

'The red two-piece?'

She glared at him. 'I don't have a red two-piece.' She did a three point-turn, hitting brakes and accelerator with a little more force than necessary.

'I don't get it.'

'Last week,' she said, 'I bought some red underwear ... bra and pants.' She revved the engine. 'Part of his little game.'

'So how does he know?'

'That's what I'm wondering.' She shot past the dogs and out of the gate. Rebus thought of Tommy Telford, and how he'd been watching Rebus's flat.

'Surveillance isn't always one-way,' he said, knowing now who'd taught Telford the skill. A little later he asked about the scrapyard.

'He owns it. He's got a compacter, but before the cars get squashed he likes to play with them. And if you cross him, he welds your seatbelt shut.' She looked at him. 'You become part of his game.'

Never get personally involved: it was *the* golden rule. And practically every case he worked, Rebus broke it. He sometimes felt that the reason he became so involved in his cases was that he had no life of his own. He could only live *through* other people.

Why had he become so involved with Candice? Was it down to her physical resemblance to Sammy? Or was it that she had seemed to need *him*? The way she'd clung to his leg that first day ... Had he wanted – just for a little while – to be someone's knight in shining armour, the real thing, not some mockery?

John Rebus: complete bloody sham.

He phoned Claverhouse from his car, filled him in. Claverhouse told him not to worry.

'Thanks for that,' Rebus said. 'I feel a whole lot better now. Listen, who's Telford's supplier?'

'For what? Dope?'

'Yes.'

'That's the real joker in the pack. I mean, he does business with Newcastle, but we can't be certain who's dealing and who's buying.'

'What if Telford's selling?'

'Then he's got a line from the continent.'

'What do Drugs Squad say?'

'They say not. If he's landing the stuff from a boat, it means transporting it from the coast. Much more likely he's buying from Newcastle. Tarawicz has the contacts in Europe.'

'Makes you wonder why he needs Tommy Telford at all ...'

'John, do yourself a favour, switch off for five minutes.'

'Colquhoun seems to be keeping his head down ...'

'Did you hear me?'

'I'll talk to you soon.'

'Are you heading back?'

'In a manner of speaking.' Rebus cut the call and drove.

11

'Strawman,' said Morris Gerald Cafferty, as he was escorted into the room by two prison guards.

Earlier in the year, Rebus had promised Cafferty he would put a Glasgow gangster, Uncle Joe Toal, behind bars. It hadn't worked, despite Rebus's best efforts. Toal, pleading old age and illness, was still a free man, like a war criminal excused for senility. Ever since then, Cafferty had felt Rebus owed him.

Cafferty sat down, rolled his neck a few times, loosening it.

'So?' he asked.

Rebus nodded for the guards to leave, waited in silence until they'd gone. Then he slipped a quarter-bottle of Bell's from his pocket.

'Keep it,' Cafferty told him. 'From the look of you, I'd say your need was greater than mine.'

Rebus put the bottle back in his pocket. 'I've brought a message from Newcastle.'

Cafferty folded his arms. 'Jake Tarawicz?'

Rebus nodded. 'He wants you to lay off Tommy Telford.'

'What does he mean?'

'Come on, Cafferty. That bouncer who got stabbed, the dealer wounded ... There's war breaking out.'

Cafferty stared at the detective. 'Not my doing.'

Rebus snorted, but looking into Cafferty's eyes, he found himself almost believing.

'So who was it?' he asked quietly.

'How do I know?'

'Nevertheless, war is breaking out.'

'That's as may be. What's in it for Tarawicz?'

'He does business with Tommy.'

'And to protect that, he needs to have *me* warned off by a cop?' Cafferty was shaking his head. 'You really buy that?'

'I don't know,' Rebus said.

'One way to finish this.' Cafferty paused. 'Take Telford out of the game.' He saw the look on Rebus's face. 'I don't mean top him, I mean put him away. That should be *your* job, Strawman.'

'I only came to deliver a message.'

'And what's in it for you? Something in Newcastle?'

'Maybe.'

'Are you Tarawicz's man now?'

'You know me better than that.'

'Do I?' Cafferty sat back in his chair, stretched out his legs. 'I wonder about that sometimes. I mean, it doesn't keep me awake at night, but I wonder all the same.'

Rebus leaned on the table. 'You must have a bit salted away. Why can't you just be content with that?'

Cafferty laughed. The air felt charged; there might have been only the two of them left in the world. 'You want me to retire?'

'A good boxer knows when to stop.'

'Then neither of us would be much cop in the ring, would we? Got any plans to retire, Strawman?'

Despite himself, Rebus smiled.

'Thought not. Do I have to say something for you to take back to Tarawicz?'

Rebus shook his head. 'That wasn't the deal.'

'Well, if he does come asking, tell him to get some life insurance, the kind with death benefits.'

Rebus looked at Cafferty. Prison might have softened him, but only physically.

'I'd be a happy man if someone took Telford out of the game,' Cafferty went on. 'Know what I mean, Strawman? It'd be worth a lot to me.'

Rebus stood up. 'No deal,' he said. 'Personally, I'd be happy if you wiped one another out. I'd be jumping for joy at ring-side.'

'Know what happens at ring-side?' Cafferty rubbed at his temples. 'You tend to get spattered with blood.'

'As long as it's someone else's.'

The laughter came from deep within Cafferty's chest. 'You're not a spectator, Strawman. It's not in your nature.'

'And you're some kind of psychologist?'

'Maybe not,' said Cafferty. 'But I know what gets people excited.'

Book Three

'Cover my face as the animals cry.'

Book Two

Running through the hospital, stopping nurses to ask directions. Sweat dripping off him, tie hanging loose around his neck. Taking right turns, left turns, looking for signs. Whose fault? He kept asking himself that. A message which failed to reach him. Because he was on a surveillance. Because he wasn't in radio contact. Because the station didn't know how important the message was.

Now running, a stitch in his side. He'd run all the way from the car. Up two flights of stairs, down corridors. The place was quiet. Middle of the night.

'Maternity!' he called to a man pushing a trolley. The man pointed to a set of doors. He pushed through them. Three nurses in a glass cubicle. One of them came out.

'Can I help?'

'I'm John Rebus. My wife …'

She gave him a hard look. 'Third bed along.' Pointing … Third bed along, curtains closed around it. He pulled the curtains open. Rhona lay on her side, face still flushed, hair sticking to her brow. And beside her, nuzzling into her, a tiny perfection with wisps of brown hair and black, unfocused eyes.

He touched the nose, ran a finger round the curves of an ear. The face twitched. He bent past it to kiss his wife.

'Rhona … I'm really sorry. They didn't get the message to me until ten minutes ago. How did it … ? I mean … he's beautiful.'

'He's a she,' his wife said, turning away from him.

12

Rebus was sitting in his boss's office. It was nine-fifteen and he had slept for probably forty-five minutes the previous night. There'd been the hospital vigil and Sammy's operation: something about a blood clot. She was still unconscious, still 'critical'. He'd called Rhona in London. She'd told him she'd catch the first train she could. He'd given her his mobile number, so she could let him know when she arrived. She'd started to ask ... her voice had cracked. She'd put down the receiver. He'd tried to find some feeling for her. Richard and Linda Thompson: 'Withered and Died'.

He'd called Mickey, who said he'd drop by the hospital some time today. And that was it for the family. There were other people he could call, people like Patience, who had been his lover for a time, and Sammy's landlady until far more recently. But he didn't. He knew in the morning he'd call the office where Sammy worked. He wrote it in his notebook so he wouldn't forget. And then he'd called Sammy's flat and given Ned Farlowe the news.

Farlowe had asked a question nobody else had: 'How about you? Are you all right?'

Rebus had looked around the hospital corridor. 'Not exactly.'

'I'll be right there.'

So they'd spent a couple of hours in one another's company, not really saying very much at first. Farlowe smoked, and Rebus helped him empty the pack. He couldn't reciprocate with whisky – there was nothing in the bottle – but he'd bought the young man several cups of coffee, since Farlowe had spent nearly all his money on the taxi from Shandon ...

'Wakey-wakey, John.'

Rebus's boss was shaking him gently. Rebus blinked, straightened in his chair.

'Sorry, sir.'

Chief Superintendent Watson went around the desk and sat down. 'Hellish sorry to hear about Sammy. I don't really know what to say, except that she's in my prayers.'

'Thank you, sir.'

'Do you want some coffee?' The Farmer's coffee had a reputation throughout the station, but Rebus accepted a mug gladly. 'How is she anyway?'

'Still unconscious.'

'No sign of the car?'

'Not the last I heard.'

'Who's handling it?'

'Bill Pryde started the ball rolling last night. I don't know who's taken it from him.'

'I'll find out.' The Farmer made an internal call, Rebus watching him over the rim of his mug. The Farmer was a big man, imposing behind a desk. His cheeks were a mass of tiny red veins and his thin hair lay across the dome of his head like the lines of a well-furrowed field. There were photos on his desk: grandchildren. The photos had been taken in a garden. There was a swing in the background. One of the children was holding a teddy bear. Rebus felt his throat start to ache, tried to choke it back.

The Farmer put down the receiver. 'Bill's still on it,' he said. 'Felt if he worked straight through we might get a quicker result.'

'That's good of him.'

'Look, we'll let you know the minute we get something, but meantime you'll probably want to go home ...'

'No, sir.'

'Or to the hospital.'

Rebus nodded slowly. Yes, the hospital. But not right this minute. He had to talk to Bill Pryde first.

'And meantime, I'll reassign your cases.' The Farmer started writing. 'There's this War Crimes thing, and your liaison on Telford. Are you working on anything else?'

'Sir, I'd prefer it if you ... I mean, I want to keep working.'

The Farmer looked at him, then leaned back in his chair, pen balanced between his fingers.

'Why?'

Rebus shrugged. 'I want to keep busy.' Yes, there was that. And he didn't want anyone else taking his work. It was *his*. He owned it; it owned him.

'Look, John, you're going to want some time off, right?'

'I can handle things, sir.' His gaze met the Farmer's. 'Please.'

Across the hall in the CID room he nodded as everyone came up to say how sorry they were. One person stayed at their desk – Bill Pryde knew Rebus was coming to see him.

'Morning, Bill.'

Pryde nodded. They'd met in the wee small hours at the Infirmary. Ned Farlowe had been napping in a chair, so they'd stepped into the corridor to talk. Pryde looked tireder now. He had loosened the top button of his dark green shirt. His brown suit looked lived-in.

'Thanks for sticking with it,' Rebus said, drawing over a chair. Thinking: *I'd rather have had someone else, someone sharper ...*

'No problem.'

'Any news?'

'A couple of good eyewitnesses. They were waiting to cross at the lights.'

'What's their story?'

Pryde considered his reply. He knew he was dealing with a father as well as a cop. 'She was crossing the road. Looked like she was heading down Minto Street, maybe making for the bus stop.'

Rebus shook his head. 'She was walking, Bill. Going to a friend's in Gilmour Road.'

She'd said as much over the pizza, apologising that she couldn't stay longer. Just one more coffee at the end of the meal … one more coffee and she wouldn't have been there at that moment. Or if she'd accepted his offer of a lift … When you thought about life, you thought of it as chunks of time, but really all it was was a series of connected moments, any one of which could change you completely.

'The car was heading south out of town,' Pryde went on. 'Looks like he ran a red light. Motorist sitting behind him seemed to think so.'

'Reckon he was drunk?'

Pryde nodded. 'Way he was driving. I mean, could be he just lost control, but in that case why didn't he stop?'

'Description?'

Pryde shook his head. 'We've got a dark car, a bit sporty. Nobody caught the licence plate.'

'It's a busy enough street, must've been other cars around.'

'A couple of people have called in.' Pryde flicked through his notes. 'Nothing helpful, but I'm going to interview them, see if I can jog a memory or two.'

'Could the car have been nicked? Maybe that's why he was in a hurry.'

'I can check.'

'I'll help you.'

Pryde considered this. 'You sure?'

'Try and stop me, Bill.'

'No skid marks,' Pryde said, 'no sign that he tried braking, either before or after.'

They were standing at the junction of Minto Street and Newington Road. The cross-streets were Salisbury Place and Salisbury Road. Cars, vans and buses queued at the traffic lights as pedestrians crossed the road.

It could have been any one of you, Rebus thought. Any one of them could have taken Sammy's place ...

'She was about here,' Pryde went on, pointing to a spot where, just past the lights, a bus lane started. The carriageway was wide, a four-lane road. She hadn't crossed at the lights. She'd been lazy, carrying on down Minto Street a few strides, then crossing in a diagonal. When she'd been a child, they'd taught her about crossing the road. Green Cross Code, all of that. Drummed it into her. Rebus looked around. At the top of Minto Street were some private houses and Bed & Breakfasts. On one corner stood a bank, on another a branch of Remnant Kings, with a takeaway next door.

'The takeaway would have been open,' Rebus said, pointing. On the third corner stood a Spar. 'That place, too. Where did you say she was?'

'The bus lane.' She'd crossed three lanes, been only a yard or two from safety. 'Witnesses say she was nearly at the kerb when he hit her. I think he was drunk, lost it for a second.' Pryde nodded towards the bank. There were two phone boxes in front of it. 'Witness called from there.' The wall behind the phone boxes had a poster glued to it. Grinning maniac behind a steering-wheel, and some writing: 'So many pedestrians, so little time'. A computer game ...

'It would have been so easy to avoid her,' Rebus said quietly.

'Sure you're okay? There's a café up the road.'

'I'm fine, Bill.' He looked around, took a deep breath. 'Looks like offices behind the Spar, doubtful anyone would have been there. But there are flats above Remnant Kings and the bank.'

'Want to talk to them?'

'And the Spar and the kebab shop. You take the B&Bs and the houses, meet back here in half an hour.'

Rebus talked to everyone he could find. In the Spar, there was a new shift on, but he got home phone numbers from the manager and called up the workers from the previous night. They hadn't seen or heard anything. First they'd known had been the flashing lights of the ambulance. The kebab shop was closed, but when Rebus banged on the door a woman came through from the back, wiping her hands on a tea-towel. He pressed his warrant card to the glass door, and she let him in. The shop had been busy last night. She didn't see the accident – she called it that, 'the accident'. And that's what it was: the word really hadn't sunk in until she said it. Elvis Costello: 'Accidents Will Happen'. Was the next line really 'It's only hit and run'?

'No,' the woman said, 'the first thing that caught my attention was the crowd. I mean, only three or four people, but I could see they were standing around something. And then the ambulance came. Will she be all right?'

The look in her eyes was one Rebus had encountered before. It almost wanted the victim dead, because then there was a story to be told.

'She's in hospital,' he said, unable to look at the woman any longer.

'Yes, but the paper said she's in a coma.'

'What paper?'

She brought him the first edition of the day's *Evening News*. There was a paragraph on one of the inside pages – 'Hit and Run Coma Victim'.

It wasn't a coma. She was unconscious, that was all. But Rebus was thankful for the story. Maybe someone would read it and come forward. Maybe guilt would begin to press down on the driver. Maybe there'd been a passenger ... It was hard to keep secrets, usually you told *some*one.

He tried Remnant Kings, but of course they had been closed last night, so he climbed to the flats above. There was no one home at the first flat. He wrote a brief message on the back of a business card and pushed it through the letterbox, then jotted down the surname on the door. If they didn't call him, he'd call them. A young man answered the second door. He was just out of his teens and pushed a thick lock of black hair away from his eyes. He wore Buddy Holly glasses and had acne scars around his mouth. Rebus introduced himself. The hand went to the hair again, a backward glance into the flat.

'Do you live here?' Rebus asked.

'Mm, yeah. Like, I'm not the owner. We rent it.'

There were no names on the door. 'Anyone else in at the moment?'

'Nope.'

'Are you all students?'

The young man nodded. Rebus asked his name.

'Rob. Robert Renton. What's this about?'

'There was an accident last night, Rob. A hit and run.' So many times he'd been in this situation, passing on the bland news of another changed life. It was a whole hour since he'd telephoned the hospital. In the end, they'd taken his mobile number, said it might be easier if they phoned him whenever there was news. They meant easier for them, not him.

'Oh, yes,' Renton was saying, 'I saw it.'

Rebus blinked. 'You saw it?'

Renton was nodding, hair bobbing in front of his eyes. 'From the window. I was up changing a CD, and –'

'Is it okay if I come in for a minute? I want to see what kind of view you had.'

Renton puffed out his cheeks, exhaled. 'Well, I suppose ...'

And Rebus was in.

The living-room was fairly tidy. Renton went ahead of him, crossed to where a hi-fi rack sat between two windows. 'I was putting on a new CD, and I looked out of the window. You can see the bus stop, and I wondered if I might catch Jane coming off a bus.' He paused. 'Jane's Eric's girlfriend.'

The words washed over Rebus. He was looking down on the street, where Sammy had been walking. 'Tell me what you saw.'

'This girl was crossing the road. She was nice-looking ... I thought so anyway. Then this car came through the lights, swerved and sent her flying.'

Rebus closed his eyes for a second.

'She must have gone ten feet in the air, hit that hedge, bounced back on to the pavement. She didn't move after that.'

Rebus opened his eyes. He was at the window, Renton standing just behind his left shoulder. Down on the street, people were crossing the road, walking over the spot where Sammy had been hit, the spot where she'd landed. Flicking ash on to the pavement where she'd lain.

'I don't suppose you saw the driver?'

'Not from this angle.'

'Any passengers?'

'Couldn't tell.'

He wears glasses, Rebus thought. How reliable is he?

'When you saw it happen, you didn't go down?'

'I'm not a medical student or anything.' He nodded towards an easel in the corner, and Rebus noticed a shelf of paints and brushes. 'Someone ran to the phone box, so I knew help was coming.'

Rebus nodded. 'Anyone else see it?'

'They were in the kitchen.' Renton paused. 'I know what you're thinking.' Rebus doubted it. 'You're thinking I wear specs, so maybe I didn't see it right. But he definitely swerved. You know ... deliberately. I mean, like he was aiming for her.' He nodded to himself.

'*Aiming* for her?'

Renton made a movement with his hand, imitating a car gliding off one course and on to another. 'He steered straight for her.'

'The car didn't lose control?'

'That would have been jerkier, wouldn't it?'

'What colour was the car?'

'Dark green.'

'And the make?'

Renton shrugged. 'I'm hopeless with cars. Tell you what though ...'

'What?'

Renton took off his glasses, started polishing them. 'Why don't I try sketching it for you?'

He moved the easel over to the window and got to work. Rebus went into the hall and called the hospital. The person he got through to didn't sound too surprised.

'No change, I'm afraid. She's got a couple of visitors with her.'

Mickey and Rhona. Rebus terminated the call, made another to Pryde's mobile.

'I'm in one of the flats over Remnant Kings. I've got an eyewitness.'

'Yes?'

'He saw the whole thing. And he's an art student.'

'Yes?'

'Come on, Bill. Do you want me to draw it for you?'
There was silence for a moment, then Pryde said 'Ah'.

13

Rebus held the mobile to his ear as he walked through the hospital.

'Joe Herdman's put together a list,' Bill Pryde was saying. 'Rover 600 series, the newer Ford Mondeos, Toyota Celica, plus a couple of Nissans. Rank outsider is the BMW 5-series.'

'It narrows things down a bit, I suppose.'

'Joe says the Rover, Mondeo and Celica are favourites. He's given me a few more details – chrome around the number-plates, stuff like that. I'm going to call our artist friend, see if anything clicks.'

A nurse was glaring at Rebus as he walked towards her.

'Let me know what he says. Talk to you later, Bill.' Rebus slipped the phone back into his pocket.

'You're not supposed to use those things in here,' the nurse snapped.

'Look, I'm in a bit of a hurry …'

'They can interfere with the machines.'

Rebus pulled up, colour leaving his face. 'I forgot,' he said. He put a shaking hand to his forehead.

'Are you all right?'

'Fine, fine. Look, I won't do it again, okay?' He started to move off. 'You can rely on that.'

Rebus took a photocopy of Renton's drawing from his pocket. Joe Herdman was a desk sergeant who knew everything about cars. He'd been useful before, turning a vague description into something more concrete. Rebus looked at the drawing as he walked. All the details were there: buildings in the background, the hedge, the onlookers. And Sammy, caught at the point of impact. She'd half-turned, was stretching out her hands as if she could push the car to a stop. But Renton had drawn fine lines issuing from the back of the car, representing the air being pushed, representing speed. Where there should have been a face, he had left a blank oval. The back half of the car was very clearly defined, the front a blur of disappearing perspective. Renton said he'd left out anything he couldn't be sure of. He promised he hadn't let his imagination fill in the blanks.

It was the face, or the lack of it … it disturbed Rebus more than anything else in the picture. He drew himself into the scene, wondered what he'd have done. Would he have concentrated on the car, caught its licence plate? Or would his attention have been focused on Sammy? Which would have prevailed: cop instincts or fatherhood? Someone at the station had said, 'Don't worry, we'll get him.' Not, 'Don't worry, she'll be all right.' Which brought it all down to two things: him – meaning the driver – and retribution, rather than her – the victim – and recovery.

'I'd just have been another witness,' Rebus said quietly. Then he folded the drawing and put it away.

Sammy had a room to herself, all tubes and machinery, the way he'd seen it in films and on TV. Only here the room was dingier, paint flaking from the walls and around the window-frames. The chairs had metal legs and rubber feet and moulded plastic seats. A woman rose as he came in. They embraced. He kissed the side of her forehead.

Aiming for her. Didn't anyone say that?

'Hello, Rhona.'

'Hello, John.'

She looked tired, of course, but her hair was stylishly cut and dyed the colour of a dull golden harvest. Her clothes were smart and she wore jewellery. He studied her eyes. Their colour was wrong. Coloured contacts. Not even her eyes were going to betray her past.

'Christ, Rhona, I'm sorry.'

He was whispering, not wanting to disturb Sammy. Which was ludicrous, because right now all he wanted in the world was for her to wake up.

'How is she?' he asked.

'Much the same.'

Mickey stood up. There were three chairs arranged in a sort of semi-circle. Mickey and Rhona had been sitting with an empty chair between them. As Rhona broke from Rebus's embrace, his brother took her place.

'This is so fucking awful,' Mickey said, his voice low. He looked the same as ever: a party animal who'd stopped getting the invites.

Niceties dispensed with, Rebus went to Sammy's bed-side. Her face was still bruised, and now he could place the probable cause of each abrasion: hedge, wall, pavement. One leg was broken, both arms heavily bandaged. A teddy bear, missing one ear, lay by her head. Rebus smiled.

'You brought Pa Broon.'

'Yes.'

'Do they know yet if there's any … ?' His eyes were on Sammy as he spoke.

'What?' Rhona wanted him to spell it out. No hiding place.

'Brain damage,' he said.

'Nobody's told us anything,' she said, sounding snubbed.

Aiming for her. Didn't anyone say that? No, none of the other onlookers had even hinted as much, but then they hadn't had Renton's grandstand view.

'Has nobody been in?'

'Not since I got here.'

'And I was here before Rhona,' Mickey added. 'Haven't seen a soul.'

It was enough. Rebus strode from the room. A doctor and two nurses were standing chatting at the end of the corridor. One of the nurses was leaning against a wall.

'What's going on?' Rebus exploded. 'Nobody's been near my daughter all morning!'

The doctor was young, male. Blond hair cut short with a parting.

'We're doing everything we can.'

'What does that mean?'

'I can appreciate that you're –'

'Fuck you, pal. Why hasn't the big man been to look at her? Why's she just lying there like a –' Rebus choked back the words.

'Your daughter was seen by two specialists this morning,' the doctor said quietly. 'We're waiting for some test results to determine whether to operate again. There's some brain swelling. The tests take a little time to process, there's nothing we can do about it.'

Rebus felt cheated: still angry, but nothing to feel angry *about*, not here. He nodded, turned away.

Back in the room, he explained the situation to Rhona. A suitcase and large holdall were sitting behind one of the machines.

'Listen,' he told her, 'it'd make sense if you stayed at the flat. It's only ten minutes away, and I could let you have the car.'

She was shaking her head. 'We're booked into the Sheraton.'

'The flat's nearer, and I tend not to charge ...' *We?* Rebus looked at Mickey, whose eyes were on the bed. Then the door opened and a man came in. Short, thickly built, breathing hard. He was rubbing his hands to let everyone know he'd been to the toilet. Loose folds of flesh furrowed his brow and bulged from his shirt collar. His hair was thick and black, like an oil-slick. He stopped when he saw Rebus.

'John,' Rhona said, 'this is a friend of mine, Jackie.'

'Jackie Platt,' the man said, reaching out a plump hand. 'When Jackie heard, he insisted on driving me up.'

Platt shrugged, his head almost disappearing into his shoulders. 'Couldn't have her training it up on her ownio.'

'Hell of a drive,' Mickey said, his tone hinting at repetition.

'Could have done without the roadworks,' Jackie Platt agreed. Rebus's eyes caught Rhona's; she looked away quickly, dodging reproach.

To Rebus, this bulk didn't belong. It was as if a character had wandered on to the wrong set. Platt hadn't been in the script.

'She looks so peaceful, don't she?' the Londoner was saying, making for the bed. He touched her arm, Sammy's bandaged arm, grazing it with the back of his hand. Rebus's fingernails dug into his palms.

Then Platt yawned. 'You know, Rhona, it might not be good manners, but I think I'm about to crash. See you back at the hotel?' She nodded, relieved. Platt picked up the suitcase. As he passed her, his hand went into his trouser pocket, came out with a fold of banknotes.

'Get a cab back, all right?'

'All right, Jackie. See you later.'

'Cheers, pet.' And he squeezed her hand. 'Take care, Mickey. All the best, John.' A huge, face-creasing wink, then he was gone. They waited in silence for a few seconds. Rhona held up her free hand, the one without the wad of notes.

'Not a word, okay?'

'Furthest thing from my mind,' Rebus said, sitting down. ' "Think I'm about to crash". Tactful or what?'

'Come on, Johnny,' Mickey said. Johnny: only Mickey could do that, using the name so that the years fell from both of them. Rebus looked at his brother and smiled. Mickey was a therapist by profession; he knew the things to say.

'Why the cases?' Rebus asked Rhona.

'What?'

'You're going to a hotel, why not leave them in his car?'

'I thought about staying here. They said I could if I wanted to. Only then I saw her ... and I changed my mind.' Tears started down her face, smudging already-smudged mascara. Mickey had a handkerchief ready.

'John, what if she ... ? Oh, Jesus Christ, why did this have to happen?' She was wailing now. Rebus went over to her chair, crouched in front of it, his hands resting on hers. 'She's all we've got, John. She's all we ever had.'

'She's still here, Rhona. She's right here.'

'But why her? Why Samantha?'

'I'll ask him when I find him, Rhona.' He kissed her hair, his eyes on Mickey. 'And believe me, I'm going to find him.'

Later, when Ned Farlowe visited, Rebus took him outside. There was drizzle falling, but the air felt good.

'One of the eye-witnesses,' Rebus said, 'thinks it was deliberate.'

'I don't understand.'

'He thinks the driver meant to hit Sammy.'

'I still don't get it.'

'Look, there are two scenarios. One, he was intent on hitting a pedestrian, and anyone would have done. Two, Sammy was his target. He'd been following her, saw his chance when she crossed the road, only the lights were against him so he had to jump them. Then she was so close to the kerb he had to switch lanes.'

'But why?'

Rebus stared at him. 'This is Sammy's dad and her lover, right? For the purposes of what follows, I want you to stop being a reporter.'

Farlowe stared back, nodded slowly.

'I've had a few run-ins with Tommy Telford,' Rebus said. He was seeing teddy bears: Pa Broon, and the one Telford kept in his car. 'This might have been a message for me.' Telford or Tarawicz: flip a coin. 'Or for you, if you've been asking questions about Telford.'

'You think my book ...'

'I'm keeping an open mind. I've been working the Lintz case ... and so have you.'

'Someone warning us off Lintz?'

Rebus thought of Abernethy, shrugged. 'Then there's Sammy's job, working with ex-cons. Maybe one of them had a grudge.'

'Jesus.'

'She hadn't mentioned anyone following her? Nobody odd in the area?' Same question he'd put to the Drinics, only different victim ...

Farlowe shook his head. 'Look,' he said, 'until five minutes ago I thought this was an accident. Now you're saying it was attempted murder. Are you *sure*?'

'I'm trusting a witness.' But he knew what Bill Pryde thought: a drunk driver, a crazy man. And a grandstand spectator who wore glasses and had read it wrong. He took out the drawing again.

'What's that?'

Rebus handed it over. 'This is what someone saw last night.'

'What kind of car is it?'

'Rover 600, Ford Mondeo, something like that. Dark green. Ring any bells?'

Ned Farlowe shook his head, then looked at Rebus. 'Let me help. I can ask around.'

'One kid in a coma's enough.'

The rest of the office had packed up and gone home. Now there were only Rebus and Sammy's boss, a woman called Mae Crumley. The light from half a dozen desk-lamps illuminated the haphazard office, which was on the top floor of an old four-storey building off Palmerston Place. Rebus knew Palmerston Place: there was a church there where the AA held meetings. He'd been to a couple. He could still taste whisky at the back of his throat. Not that he'd had any so far today, not in daylight hours. But then he hadn't phoned Jack Morton either.

The address might have been posher than Rebus was expecting, but the accommodation was cramped. The office was in the eaves of the building, so that you couldn't stand up in half the available space, which hadn't stopped desks being sited in the most awkward corners.

'Which is hers?' Rebus asked. Mae Crumley pointed to the desk next to her own. There was a computer there somewhere, but only its screen was showing. Loose sheets of paper, books and pamphlets and reports, the whole lot spilled on to the chair and from there down on to the floor.

'She works too hard,' Crumley said. 'We all do.'

Rebus sipped the coffee she'd made him. Cafe Hag.

'When Sammy came here,' she went on, 'the first thing she said was that her father was CID. She never tried to hide it.'

'And you'd no qualms about taking her on?'

'None at all.' Crumley folded her arms. They were big arms; she was a big woman. Her hair was a fiery red, long and frizzy and tied back with a black ribbon. She wore an oatmeal linen shirt with a denim jacket over the top of it. Her eyebrows had been plucked into thin arches over pale grey eyes. Her desk was relatively tidy, but only, as she'd explained to Rebus, because she tended to stay later than anyone else.

'What about her clients?' Rebus asked. 'Could any of them have held a grudge?'

'Against her or against you?'

'Against me *through* her.'

Crumley considered this. 'To the extent that they'd run her over just to make a point? I very much doubt it.'

'I'd be interested to see her client list.'

She shook her head. 'Look ... you shouldn't be doing this. It's too personal, you know that. I mean, who am I talking to here: Sammy's father, or a copper?'

'You think I've a score to settle?'

'Well haven't you?'

Rebus put down the coffee mug. 'Maybe.'

'And that's why you shouldn't be doing this.' She sighed. 'Number one on my wish list: Sammy back on her feet and back here. But what about if meantime I do a bit of poking around? I stand a better chance of getting them to talk than you do.'

Rebus nodded. 'I'd appreciate that.' He got to his feet. 'Thanks for the coffee.'

Outside, he checked the list the Juice Church had given him. He kept it in his pocket, didn't refer to it often. There was a meeting at Palmerston Place in about an hour and a half. No good. He knew he'd spend the time beforehand in a pub. Jack Morton had introduced him to Al-Anon, but Rebus hadn't really taken to it, though the stories had affected him.

'See,' one man had told the group, 'I had problems at work, problems with my wife, my kids. I had money problems and health problems and everything else. Practically the only problem I didn't have was with the drink. And that's because I was a drunk.'

Rebus lit himself a cigarette and drove home.

He sat in his chair and thought about Rhona. They'd shared so much over so many years ... and then it had all stopped. He'd chosen his job over his marriage, and that could not be forgiven. Last time he'd seen her had been in London, wearing her new life like armour. Nobody had warned him about Jackie Platt. His phone rang, and he snatched it from the floor.

'Rebus.'

'It's Bill.' Pryde sounded halfway to excited, which was as far as he ever ventured.

'What have you got?'

'Dark green Rover 600 – I think the owner called it "Sherwood Green" – stolen yesterday evening about an hour before the collision.'

'Where from?'

'Metered parking on George Street.'

'What do you reckon?'

'My advice is, keep an open mind. Having said that, at least now we've got a licence plate. Owner reported it at six-forty last night. It hasn't turned up anywhere, so I've upped the alert status.'

'Give me the reg.' Pryde read out the letters and numbers. Rebus thanked him and put down the phone. He was thinking of Danny Simpson, dumped outside Fascination Street around the time Sammy was being hit. Coincidence? Or a double message, Telford and Rebus. Which put Big Ger Cafferty in the frame. He called the hospital, was told there was no change. Farlowe was in visiting. The nurse said he had his laptop with him.

Rebus recalled Sammy growing up – a series of isolated images. He hadn't been there for her. He saw her in a series of fast jerky impressions, as if the film had been spliced. He tried not to think about the hell she had gone through at the hands of Gordon Reeve ...

He saw good people doing bad things and bad people doing good, and he tried dividing the two into groups. He saw Candice and Tommy Telford and Mr Pink Eyes. And encompassing it all, he saw Edinburgh. He saw the mass of the people just getting on with their lives, and he saluted them. They *knew* things and felt things, things he'd never feel. He used to think he knew things. As a kid, he'd known *everything*. Now he knew differently. The only thing you could be sure of was the inside of your head, and even that could deceive you. I don't even know myself, he thought. So how could he ever hope to know Sammy? And with each year, he understood less.

He thought of the Oxford Bar. Even on the wagon, he'd stayed a regular, drinking cola and mugs of coffee. A pub like the Ox was about so much more than just the hooch. It was therapy and refuge, entertainment and art. He checked his watch, thinking he could head down there now. Just a couple of whiskies and a beer, something to make him feel good about himself until the morning.

The phone rang again. He picked it up.

'Evening, John.'

Rebus smiled, leaned back in his chair. 'Jack, you must be a bloody mind reader ...'

14

Mid-morning, Rebus walked through the cemetery. He'd been to the hospital to check on Sammy – no change. Now, he felt he had time to kill ...

'A bit cooler today, Inspector.' Joseph Lintz rose from his knees and pushed his glasses back up to the bridge of his nose. There were damp patches on his trousers from where he'd been kneeling. He dropped his trowel on to a white polythene bag. Beside the bag stood pots of small green plants.

'Won't the frost get them?' Rebus asked. Lintz shrugged.

'It gets all of us, but we're allowed to bloom for a while.'

Rebus turned away. Today, he wasn't in the mood for games. Warriston Cemetery was vast. In the past, it had been a history lesson to Rebus – headstones telling the story of nineteenth-century Edinburgh – but now he found it a jarring reminder of mortality. They were the only living souls in the place. Lintz had pulled out a handkerchief.

'More questions?' he asked.

'Not exactly.'

'What then?'

'Truth is, Mr Lintz, I've got other things on my mind.'

The old man looked at him. 'Maybe all this archaeology is beginning to bore you, Inspector?'

'I still don't get it, planting things before the first frost?'

'Well, I can't plant very much afterwards, can I? And at my age ... any day now I could be lying in the ground. I like to think there might be a few flowers surviving above me.' He'd lived in Scotand the best part of half a century, but there was still something lurking beneath the local accent, peculiarities of phrasing and tone that would be with Joseph Lintz until he died, reminders of his far less recent history.

'So,' he said now, 'no questions today?' Rebus shook his head. 'You're right, Inspector, you do seem preoccupied. Is it something I can help with?'

'In what way?'

'I don't really know. But you've come here, questions or no. I take it there's a reason?'

A dog was bounding through the long grass, crunching on the fallen leaves, nose brushing the ground. It was a yellow labrador, short-haired and overweight. Lintz turned towards it and almost growled. Dogs were the enemy.

'I was just wondering,' Rebus was saying, 'what you're capable of.' Lintz looked puzzled. The dog began to paw at the ground. Lintz reached down, picked up a stone, and hurled it. It didn't reach the dog. The labrador's owner was rounding the corner. He was young, crop-haired and skinny.

'That thing should be kept on its lead!' Lintz roared.

'*Jawohl!*' the owner snapped back, clicking his heels. He was laughing as he passed them.

'I am a famous man now,' Lintz reflected, back to his old self after the outburst. 'Thanks to the newspapers.' He looked up at the sky, blinked. 'People send me hate by the Royal Mail. A car was parked outside my home the other night ... they put a brick through the windscreen. It wasn't my car, but they didn't know that. Now my neighbours keep clear of that spot, just in case.'

He spoke like the old man he was, a little tired, a little defeated.

'This is the worst year of my life.' He stared down at the border he'd been tending. The earth, newly turned, looked dark and rich, like crumbs of chocolate cake. A few worms and wood lice had been disturbed and were still looking for their old homes. 'And it's going to get worse, isn't it?'

Rebus shrugged. His feet were cold, the damp seeping in through his shoes. He was standing on the rough roadway, Lintz six inches above him on the grass. And still Lintz didn't reach his height. A little old man: that's what he was. And Rebus could study him, talk with him, go to his home and see what few photographs remained – according to Lintz – from the old days.

'What did you mean back there?' he said. 'What was it you said? Something about what I was capable of?'

Rebus stared at him. 'It's okay, the dog just showed me.'

'Showed you what?'

'What you're like with the enemy.'

Lintz smiled. 'I don't like dogs, it's true. Don't read too much into it, Inspector. That's the journalists' job.'

'Your life would be easier without dogs, wouldn't it?'

Lintz shrugged. 'Of course.'

'And easier without me, too?'

Lintz frowned. 'If it weren't you, it would be someone else, a boor like your Inspector Abernethy.'

'What do you think he was telling you?'

Lintz blinked. 'I'm not sure. Someone else came to see me. A man called Levy. I refused to talk to him – one privilege still open to me.'

Rebus shuffled his feet, trying to get some warmth into them. 'I have a daughter, did I ever tell you that?'

Lintz looked baffled. 'You might have mentioned it.'

'You know I have a daughter?'

'Yes ... I mean, I think I knew before today.'

'Well, Mr Lintz, the night before last, someone tried to kill her, or at least do her some serious damage. She's in hospital, still unconscious. And *that* bothers me.'

'I'm so sorry. How did it ... ? I mean, how do you ... ?'

'I think maybe someone was trying to send me a message.'

Lintz's eyes widened. 'And you believe *me* capable of such a thing? My God, I thought we had come to understand one another, at least a little.'

Rebus was wondering. He was wondering how easy it would be to put on an act, when you'd spent half a century practising. He was wondering how easy it would be to steel yourself to killing an innocent ... or at least ordering their death. All it took was an order. A few words to someone else who would carry out your bidding. Maybe Lintz had it in him. Maybe it wouldn't be any more difficult than it had been for Josef Linzstek.

'Something you should know,' Rebus said. 'Threats don't scare me off. Quite the opposite.'

'It's good that you are so strong.' Rebus looked for meaning behind the words. 'I'm on my way home. Can I offer you some tea?'

Rebus drove, and then sat in the drawing-room while Lintz busied himself in the kitchen. Started flicking through a pile of books on a desk.

'Ancient History, Inspector,' Lintz said, bringing in the tray – he always refused offers of help. 'Another hobby of mine. I'm fascinated by that intersection at which history and fiction meet.' The books were all about Babylonia. 'Babylon is an historical fact, you see, but what about the Tower of Babel?'

'A song by Elton John?' Rebus offered.

'Always making jokes.' Lintz looked up. 'What is it you're afraid of?'

Rebus took one of the cups. 'I've heard of the Gardens of Babylon,' he admitted, putting the book down. 'What other hobbies do you have?'

'Astrology, hauntings, the unknown.'

'Have you ever been haunted?'

Lintz seemed amused. 'No.'

'Would you like to be?'

'By seven hundred French villagers? No, Inspector, I wouldn't like that at all. It was astrology that first brought me to the Chaldeans. They came from Babylonia. Have you ever heard of Babylonian numbers ...?'

Lintz had a way of turning conversations in directions *he* wanted them to take. Rebus wasn't going to be deflected this time. He waited till Lintz had the cup to his lips.

'Did you try to kill my daughter?'

Lintz paused, then sipped, swallowed.

'No, Inspector,' he said quietly.

Which left Telford, Tarawicz and Cafferty. Rebus thought of Telford, surrounded by his Family but wanting to play with the big boys. How different was a gang war from any other kind? You had soldiers, and orders given to them. They had to prove themselves, or lose face, show themselves cowards. Shoot a civilian, run down a pedestrian. Rebus realised that he didn't want the driver as such – he wanted the person who'd *driven* them to do it. Lintz's defence of Linzstek was that the young lieutenant had been under orders, that war itself was the real culprit, as though humans had no say in the matter ...

'Inspector,' the old man was saying, 'do *you* think I'm Linzstek?'

Rebus nodded. 'I know you are.'

A wry smile. 'Then arrest me.'

'Here comes the blue-nose,' Father Conor Leary said. 'Out to steal Ireland's God-given Guinness.' He paused, eyes narrowing. 'Or are you still on that abstention kick?'

'I'm trying,' Rebus said.

'Well, I won't tempt you then.' Leary smiled. 'But you know me, John. I'm not one to judge, but a wee drop never harmed a soul.'

'Problem is, you put lots of wee drops together and you get a bloody big fall.'

Father Leary laughed. 'But aren't we all the fallen? Come away in.'

Father Leary was priest of Our Lady of Perpetual Help. Years back, someone had defaced the board outside to turn 'Help' into 'Hell'. The board had been corrected many times, but Rebus always thought of the place as 'Perpetual Hell': it was what the followers of Knox and Calvin would have believed. Father Leary took him through to the kitchen.

'Here, man, sit yourself down. I haven't seen you in so long, I thought you'd renounced me.' He went to the fridge and lifted out a can of Guinness.

'Are you operating a pharmacy on the side?' Rebus asked. Father Leary looked at him. Rebus nodded towards the fridge. 'The shelves of medicine.'

Father Leary rolled his eyes. 'At my age, you go to the doctor with angina and they dose you for every conceivable ailment. They think it makes old folk feel better.' He brought a glass to the table, placed it next to his can. Rebus felt a hand fall on his shoulder.

'I'm hellish sorry about Sammy.'

'How did you hear?'

'Her name was in one of the rags this morning.' Father Leary sat down. 'Hit and run, they said.'

'Hit and run,' Rebus echoed.

Father Leary shook his head wearily, one hand rubbing slowly over his chest. He was probably in his late-sixties, though he'd never said. Well-built, with a thatch of silver hair. Tufts of grey sprouted from his ears, nose and dog-collar. His hand seemed to smother the can of Guinness. But when he poured, he poured gently, almost with reverence.

'It's a terrible thing,' he said quietly. 'Coma, is it?'

'Not until the doctors say so.' Rebus cleared his throat. 'It's only been a day and a half.'

'You know what we believers say,' Father Leary went on. 'When something like this happens, it's a test for all of us. It's a way of making us stronger.' The head on his Guinness was perfect. He took a swallow, licked his lips thoughtfully. 'That's what we *say*; it may not be what we think.' He looked into his drink.

'It didn't make me strong. I went back to the whisky.'

'I can understand that.'

'Until a friend reminded me it was the lazy way out, the cowardly way.'

'And who's to say he's not right?'

' "Faint-Heart and the Sermon",' Rebus said with a smile.

'What's that?'

'A song. But maybe it's us, too.'

'Get away, we're just two old boys having a natter. So how are you holding up, John?'

'I don't know.' He paused. 'I don't think it was an accident. And the man I think is behind it ... Sammy isn't the first woman he's tried to destroy.' Rebus looked into the priest's eyes. 'I want to kill him.'

'But so far you haven't?'

'I haven't even talked to him.'

'Because you're worried what you might do?'

'Or not do.' Rebus's mobile sounded. He gave a look of apology and switched it on.

'John, it's Bill.'

'Yes, Bill?'

'Green Rover 600.'

'Yes?'

'We've got it.'

The car had been parked illegally on the street outside

Piershill Cemetery. There was a parking ticket on its windscreen, dated the previous afternoon. If anyone had checked, they'd have found the driver's-side door unlocked. Maybe someone had: the car was empty, no coins, no map-books or cassettes. The fascia had been removed from the radio/cassette. There were no keys in the ignition. A car transporter had arrived, and the Rover was being winched aboard.

'I called in a favour at Howdenhall,' Bill Pryde was saying, 'they've promised to fingerprint it today.'

Rebus was studying the front passenger side. No dents, nothing to suggest this car had been used as a battering-ram against his daughter.

'I think maybe we need your permission, John.'

'What for?'

'Someone should go to the Infirmary and print Sammy.'

Rebus stared at the front of the car, then got out the drawing. Yes, she'd put out a hand. Her prints might be there, invisible to him.

'Sure,' he said. 'No problem. You think this is it?'

'I'll tell you once we print it.'

'You steal a car,' Rebus said, 'then you hit someone with it, and leave it a couple of miles away.' He looked around. 'Ever been on this street before?' Pryde shook his head. 'Me neither.'

'Someone local?'

'I'm wondering why they stole it in the first place.'

'Stick false plates on and sell it,' Pryde suggested. 'Spot of joy-riding maybe.'

'Joy-riders don't leave cars looking like this.'

'No, but they'd had a fright. They'd just knocked someone down.'

'And they drove all the way over here before deciding to dump it?'

'Maybe it was stolen for a job, turn over a petrol station.

Then they hit Sammy and decide to jump ship. Maybe the job was this side of town.'

'Or Sammy *was* the job.'

Pryde put a hand on his shoulder. 'Let's see what the boffins turn up, eh?'

Rebus looked at him. 'You don't go for it?'

'Look, it's a feeling you've got, and that's fair enough, but right now all you've got is that student's word for it. There were other witnesses, John, and I asked them all again, and they told me the same thing: it looked like the driver lost control, that's all.'

There was an edge of irritation to Pryde's voice. Rebus knew why: long hours.

'Will Howdenhall let you know tonight?'

'They promised. And I'll phone you straight away, okay?'

'On my mobile,' Rebus said. 'I'm going to be on the move.' He looked around. 'There was something about Piershill Cemetery recently, wasn't there?'

'Kids,' Pryde said, nodding. 'They pushed over a load of gravestones.'

Rebus remembered now. 'Just the Jewish headstones, wasn't it?'

'I think so.'

And there, sprayed on the wall near the gates, the same piece of graffiti: Won't Anyone Help?

It was late evening, and Rebus was driving. Not the M90 into Fife: tonight, he was on the M8, heading west, heading for Glasgow. He'd spent half an hour at the hospital, followed by an hour and a half with Rhona and Jackie Platt, their guest for dinner at the Sheraton. He'd worn a fresh suit and shirt. He hadn't smoked. He'd drunk a bottle of Highland Spring.

They were planning yet more tests on Sammy. The

neurologist had taken them into his office and talked them through the procedures. There would probably be another operation at the end of it. Rebus could barely remember what the man had said. Rhona had asked for the occasional explanation, but these seemed no more lucid than what had gone before.

Dinner had been a subdued affair. Jackie Platt, it turned out, sold second-hand cars.

'See, John, where I really score is the obituaries. Check the local paper, hare round there and see if they've left a car behind. Quick cash offer.'

'Sammy doesn't drive, sorry,' Rebus had said, causing Rhona to drop her cutlery on to her plate.

At the end of the meal, she'd seen him out to his car, gripped one of his arms hard.

'Get the bastard, John. I want to look him in the face. Just get the bastard who did this to us.' Her eyes were blazing.

He nodded. Stones: 'Just Wanna See His Face'. Rebus wanted it, too.

The M8, which could be a nightmare at rush-hour, was a quiet drive in the evenings. Rebus knew he was making good time, and that he would soon see the outline of the Easterhouse estate against the sky. When his phone sounded, he didn't hear it at first: blame Wishbone Ash. As *Argus* finished, he picked up.

'Rebus.'

'John, it's Bill.'

'What've you got?'

'Forensics were good as gold. There are prints all over the car, interior and exterior. Several sets.' He paused, and Rebus thought the connection had gone. 'One good palm and finger set on the front of the bonnet ...'

'Sammy's?'

'For definite.'

'So we've got our car.'

'The owner's given us a set so we can eliminate him. When we've done that ...'

'We're still not home and dry, Bill. The car sat unlocked outside that cemetery, we don't know someone didn't clean it out.'

'Owner says the radio/cassette fascia was there when he left it. Also half a dozen tapes, a packet of Paracetamol, receipts for petrol and a road map. So someone cleaned it out, whether it's the bastard we want or just some scavenger.'

'At least we know it's the car.'

'I'll check again with Howdenhall tomorrow, collect any other prints and start trying to match them. Plus I'll ask around Piershill, see if anyone saw someone dumping it.'

'Meantime get some sleep, eh?'

'Try and stop me. What about you?'

'Me?' Two cups of espresso after dinner. And with the knowledge of what lay ahead. 'I'll get my head down soon enough, Bill. Talk to you tomorrow.'

On the outskirts of Glasgow, headed for Barlinnie Prison.

He'd phoned ahead, made sure they were expecting him. It was way outside any visiting hours, but Rebus had made up a story about a murder inquiry. 'Follow-up questions,' was what he'd said.

'At this time of night?'

'Lothian and Borders Police, pal. Motto: Justice Never Sleeps.'

Morris Gerald Cafferty probably didn't sleep much either. Rebus imagined him lying awake at night, hands under his head, staring into the darkness.

Scheming.

Running things through his mind: how to keep his

empire from falling, how best to combat threats like Tommy Telford. Rebus knew that Cafferty employed a lawyer – a middle-aged pinstripe from the New Town – to carry messages back to his gang in Edinburgh. He thought of Charles Groal, Telford's lawyer. Groal was young and sharp, like his paymaster.

'Strawman.'

He was waiting in the Interview Room, arms folded, chair set well away from the table. And of course his opening gambit was his nickname for Rebus.

'A lovely surprise, two visits in a week. Don't tell me you've another message from the Pole?'

Rebus sat down opposite Cafferty. 'Tarawicz isn't Polish.' He glanced towards the guard who stood by the door, lowered his voice. 'Another of Telford's boys got a doing.'

'How clumsy.'

'He was all but scalped. Are you looking for war?'

Cafferty drew his chair in to the table, leaned across towards Rebus. 'I've never backed down from a fight.'

'My daughter got hurt. Funny that, so soon after we'd had our little chat.'

'Hurt how?'

'Hit and run.'

Cafferty was thoughtful. 'I don't pick on civilians.'

Yes, Rebus thought, but she wasn't a civilian, because *he* had lured her on to the battlefield.

'Convince me,' Rebus said.

'Why should I bother?'

'The conversation we had ... What you asked me to do.'

'Telford?' A whisper. Cafferty sat back for a moment to consider. When he leaned forward again, his eyes bored into Rebus's. 'There's something you've forgotten. I lost a son, remember. Think I could do that to another father? I'd do a lot of things, Rebus, but not that, never that.'

Rebus held the stare. 'All right,' he said.

'You want me to find who did it?'

Rebus nodded slowly.

'That's your price?'

Rhona's words: *I want to look him in the face*. Rebus shook his head. 'I want them *delivered* to me. I want you to do that, whatever it takes.'

Cafferty placed his hands on his knees, seemed to take his time positioning them just so. 'You know it's probably Telford?'

'Yes. If it's not you.'

'You'll be going after him then?'

'Any way I can.'

Cafferty smiled. 'But your ways aren't my ways.'

'You might get to him first. I want him *alive*.'

'And meantime, you're my man?'

Rebus stared at him. 'I'm your man,' he said.

15

Rebus got a phone call early the next morning from Leith CID, telling him Joseph Lintz was dead. The bad news was, it looked like murder: the body found hanging from a tree in Warriston Cemetery.

By the time Rebus appeared at the scene, they were cordoning it off, the doctor having concluded that most suicides wouldn't have bothered administering a violent blow to their own head before commencing with operations.

The corpse of Joseph Lintz was being zipped into a body bag. Rebus got a look at the face. He'd seen elderly corpses before, and mostly they'd looked wonderfully at peace, their faces shiny and child-like. But Joseph Lintz looked like he'd suffered. He didn't look to be at rest at all.

'You'll have come to thank us, no doubt,' a man said, walking towards Rebus. His shoulders were hunched inside a navy raincoat and he walked with head bowed, hands in pockets. His hair was thick and silver and wiry, his skin an almost jaundiced yellow – the remains of an autumn holiday tan.

'Hiya, Bobby,' Rebus said.

Bobby Hogan was Leith CID.

'To get back to my initial observation, John ...'

'What am I supposed to be thanking you for?'

Hogan nodded towards the body bag. 'Taking Mr Lintz off your hands. 'Don't tell me you were *enjoying* digging into all that?'

'Not exactly.'

'Any idea who might have wanted him dead?'

Rebus puffed out his cheeks. 'Where do you want me to start?'

'I mean, I'm right to rule out the usual, aren't I?' Hogan held up three fingers. 'It wasn't suicide, muggers aren't quite this creative, and it surely wasn't an accident.'

'Someone was making a point, no doubt about it.'

'But what sort of point?'

Scene of Crime officers were busying themselves, filling the *locus* with noise and movement. Rebus gestured for Hogan to walk with him. They were deep in the cemetery, the part Lintz had loved so much. As they walked, the place grew wilder, more overgrown.

'I was here with him yesterday morning,' Rebus said. 'I don't know if he had a routine exactly, but he came here most days.'

'We found a bag of gardening tools.'

'He planted flowers.'

'So if someone knew he'd be coming, they could have been waiting?'

Rebus nodded. 'An assassination.'

Hogan was thoughtful. 'Why hang him?'

'It's what happened at Villefranche. The town elders were strung up in the square.'

'Jesus.' Hogan stopped walking. 'I know you've got other stuff on the go, but can you help out on this, John?'

'Any way I can.'

'A list of possibles would do for a start.'

'How about an old woman living in France, and a Jewish historian who walks with a stick?'

'Is that all you've got?'

'Well, there's always me. Yesterday I as good as accused him of trying to kill my daughter.' Hogan stared at him. 'I don't think he did it.' Rebus paused, thinking of Sammy:

he'd called the hospital first thing. She was still unconscious; they still weren't using the word 'coma'. 'One more
thing,' he said. 'Special Branch, a guy called Abernethy. He
was here talking to Lintz.'

'What's the connection?'

'Abernethy's co-ordinating the various war crimes investigations. He's street-tough, not your typical desk-jockey.'

'A strange choice for the job?' Rebus nodded. 'Which
hardly makes him a suspect.'

'I'm doing my best, Bobby. We could check Lintz's
house, see if we can turn up any of the hate mail he claimed
he'd been getting.'

' "Claimed"?'

Rebus shrugged. 'You were never sure where you were
with Lintz. Do you have any idea what happened?'

'From what you've told me, I'd guess he came down here
as usual to do his gardening stint – he's certainly dressed
for it. Someone was waiting. They smacked him over the
head, stuck his neck in a noose, and hauled him up into the
tree. The rope was tied around a headstone.'

'Did the hanging kill him?'

'Doctor says yes. Haemorrhages in the eyes. What do
you call them?'

'Tardieu spots.'

'That's it. The blow to the head was just to knock him
out. Something else – bruising and cuts on the face. Looks
like someone kicked him when he was down.'

'Knock him cold, thump him in the face, then string him
up.'

'Big-time grudge.'

Rebus looked around. 'Someone with a flair for theatre.'

'And not afraid to take risks. This place might never get
exactly crowded, but it's a public space and that tree's in
open view. Anyone could have walked past.'

'What time are we talking about?'

'Eight, eight-thirty. I'm guessing Mr Lintz would have wanted to do his digging in daylight.'

'Could have been earlier,' Rebus suggested. 'A pre-arranged meeting.'

'Then why the tools?'

'Because by the time it got light, the meeting would be over.'

Hogan looked doubtful.

'And if it *was* a meeting,' Rebus said, 'there might be some record of it at Lintz's home.'

Hogan looked at him, nodded. 'My car or yours?'

'Better get his keys first.'

They started back up the slope.

'Searching through a dead man's pockets,' Hogan said to himself. 'Why is that never mentioned during recruitment?'

'I was here yesterday,' Rebus said. 'He invited me back for tea.'

'No family?'

'None.'

Hogan looked around the hallway. 'Big place. What happens to the money when it's sold?'

Rebus looked at him. 'We could split it two ways.'

'Or we could just move ourselves in. Basement and ground for me, you can have first and second.'

Hogan smiled, tried one of the doors off the hall. It opened on to an office. 'This could be my bedroom,' he said, going in.

'When I came here before, he always took me upstairs.'

'On you go. We'll take a floor each, then swop.'

Rebus headed up the staircase, running his hand over the varnished banister: not a speck of dust. Cleaning ladies could be invaluable informants.

'If you find a chequebook,' he called down to Hogan, 'look for regular payments to a Mrs Mop.'

Four doors led off the first-floor landing. Two were bedrooms, one a bathroom. The last door led into the huge drawing-room, where Rebus had asked his questions and listened to the stories and philosophy that Lintz had used in place of answers.

'Do you think guilt has a genetic component, Inspector?' he'd asked one time. 'Or are we taught it?'

'Does it matter, so long as it's there?' Rebus had said, and Lintz had nodded and smiled, as if the pupil had given some satisfactory answer.

The room was big, not too much furniture. Huge sash windows – recently cleaned – looked down on to the street. There were framed prints and paintings on the walls. They could have been priceless originals or junk-store stuff – Rebus was no expert. He liked one painting. It showed a ragged white-haired man seated on a rock, surrounded by a barren plain. He had a book open on his lap, but was staring skywards in horror or awe as a shining light appeared there, picking him out. It had a Biblical look, but Rebus couldn't quite place it. He knew the look on the man's face though. He'd seen it before when some suspect's carefully crafted alibi had suddenly come tumbling down.

Over the marble fireplace was a large gilt-framed mirror. Rebus studied himself in it. Behind him he could see the room. He knew he didn't fit here.

One bedroom was for guests, the other was Lintz's. A faint smell of embrocation, half a dozen medicine bottles on the bedside table. Books, too, a pile of them. The bed had been made, a dressing-gown draped across it. Lintz was a creature of habit; he'd been in no special hurry this morning.

The next floor up, Rebus found two further bedrooms and a toilet. There was a slight smell of damp in one room, and the ceiling was discoloured. Rebus didn't suppose Lintz got many visitors; no impetus to redecorate. Out on the landing again, he saw that one of the stair-rails was missing. It had been propped against the wall, awaiting repair. A house this size, things would always be going wrong.

He went back downstairs. Hogan was in the basement. The kitchen had a door on to a back garden – stone patio, lawn covered in rotting leaves, an ivy-covered wall giving privacy.

'Look what I found,' Hogan said, coming back from the utility room. He was holding a length of rope, frayed at one end where it had been cut.

'You think it'll match with the noose? That would mean the killer got it from here.'

'Meaning Lintz knew them.'

'Anything in the office?'

'It's going to take a bit of time. There's an address book, lots of entries, but most of them seem to go back a while.'

'How can you tell?'

'Old STD codes.'

'Computer?'

'Not even a typewriter. He used carbons. Lots of letters to his solicitor.'

'Trying to shut the media up?'

'You get a couple of mentions, too. Anything upstairs?'

'Go take a look. I'll check the office.'

Rebus climbed upstairs and stood in the office doorway, looking around. Then he sat down at the desk and imagined the room was his. What did he do here? He conducted his daily business. There were two filing-cabinets, but to get to them he'd have to stand up from the desk. And he was an old man. Say the cabinets were for dead correspondence. More recent stuff would be closer to hand.

He tried the drawers. Found the address book Hogan had mentioned. A few letters. A small snuff-box, its contents turned solid. Lintz hadn't even allowed himself that small vice. In a bottom drawer were some files. Rebus lifted out the one marked 'General/Household'. It comprised bills and guarantees. A large brown envelope was marked BT. Rebus opened it and took out the phone bills. They went back to the beginning of the year. The most recent bill was at the front. Rebus was disappointed to find that it wasn't itemised. Then he noticed that all the other statements *were*. Lintz had been meticulous, placing names beside calls made, double-checking British Telecom's totals at the foot of each page. The whole year was like that ... right up until recently. Frowning, Rebus realised that the penultimate statement was missing. Had Lintz mislaid it? Rebus couldn't see him mislaying anything. A missing bill would have hinted at chaos in his ordered world. No, it had to be somewhere.

But Rebus was damned if he could find it.

Lintz's correspondence was all business, either to lawyers or else to do with local charities and committees. He'd been resigning from his committees. Rebus wondered if pressure had been applied. Edinburgh could be cruel and cold that way.

'Well?' Hogan said, sticking his head round the door.

'I'm just wondering ...'

'What?'

'Whether to add on a conservatory and knock through from the kitchen.'

'We'd lose some garden space,' Hogan said. He came in, rested against the desk. 'Anything?'

'A missing phone bill, and a sudden change from being itemised.'

'Worth a call,' Hogan admitted. 'I found a chequebook in his bedroom. Stubs show payments of £60 a month to E. Forgan.'

'Where in the bedroom?'

'Marking his place in a book.' Hogan reached into the desk's top drawer, lifted out the address book.

Rebus got up. 'Pretty rich street this. Wonder how many of them do their own dusting.'

Hogan shut the book. 'No listing for an E. Forgan. Think the neighbours will know?'

'Edinburgh neighbours know *everything*. It's just that they most often keep it to themselves.'

16

Joseph Lintz's neighbours: an artist and her husband on one side; a retired advocate and his wife on the other. The artist used a cleaning lady called Ella Forgan. Mrs Forgan lived in East Claremont Street. The artist gave them a telephone number.

Conclusions drawn from the two interviews: shock and horror that Lintz was dead; praise for the quiet, considerate neighbour. A Christmas card every year, and an invitation to drinks one Sunday afternoon each July. Hard to tell when he'd been at home and when he'd been out. He went off on holiday without telling anyone except Mrs Forgan. Visitors to his home had been few – or few had been noticed, which wasn't quite the same thing.

'Men? Women?' Rebus had asked. 'Or a mixture?'

'A mixture, I'd say,' the artist had replied, measuring her words. 'Really, we knew very little about him, to say we've been neighbours these past twenty-odd years ...'

Ah, and that was Edinburgh for you, too, at least in this price bracket. Wealth was a very private thing in the city. It wasn't brash and colourful. It stayed behind its thick stone walls and was at peace.

Rebus and Hogan held a doorstep conference.

'I'll call the cleaning lady, see if I can meet her, preferably here.' Hogan looked back at Lintz's front door.

'I'd love to know where he got the money to buy this place,' Rebus said.

'That could take some excavating.'

Rebus nodded. 'Solicitor would be the place to start. What about the address book? Worth tracking down some of these elusive friends?'

'I suppose so.' Hogan looked dispirited at the prospect.

'I'll follow up on the phone bills,' Rebus said. 'If that'll help.'

Hogan was nodding. 'And remember to get me copies of your files. Are you busy otherwise?'

'Bobby, if time was money, I'd be in hock to every lender in town.'

Mae Crumley reached Rebus on his mobile.

'I thought you'd forgotten me,' he told Sammy's boss.

'Just being methodical, Inspector. I'm sure you'd want no less.' Rebus stopped at traffic lights. 'I've been in to see Sammy. Is there any news?'

'Nothing much. So you've talked to her clients?'

'Yes, and they all seemed genuinely upset and surprised. Sorry to disappoint you.'

'What makes you think I'm disappointed?'

'Sammy has a good rapport with all her clients. None of them would have wanted her hurt.'

'What about the ones who didn't want to be her clients?'

Crumley hesitated. 'There was one man ... When he was told Sammy had a police inspector for a father, he'd have nothing to do with her.'

'What's his name?'

'It couldn't have been him though.'

'Why not?'

'Because he killed himself. His name was Gavin Tay. He used to drive an ice-cream van ...'

Rebus thanked her for her call, and put down the phone. If someone had tried to kill Sammy on purpose, the question was: why? Rebus had been investigating Lintz; Ned Farlowe had been following him. Rebus had twice confronted Telford; Ned was writing a book about organised crime. Then there was Candice ... Could she have *told* Sammy something, something which might have threatened Telford, or even Mr Pink Eyes? Rebus just didn't know. He knew the most likely culprit – the most vicious – was Tommy Telford. He remembered their first meeting, and the young gangster's words to him: *That's the beauty of games. You can always start again after an accident. Not so easy in real life.* At the time it had sounded like bravado, a performance for the troops. But now it sounded like a plain threat.

And now there was Mr Taystee, connecting Sammy to Telford. Mr Taystee had worked Telford's clubs; Mr Taystee had rejected Sammy. Rebus knew he'd have to talk to the widow.

There was just the one problem. Mr Pink Eyes had intimated that if Telford wasn't left alone, Candice would suffer. He kept seeing images of Candice: torn from home and homeland; used and abused; abusing herself in the hope of respite; clinging to a stranger's legs ... He recalled Levy's words: *Can time wash away responsibility?* Justice was a fine and noble thing, but revenge ... revenge was an *emotion*, and so much stronger than an abstract like justice. He wondered if Sammy would want revenge. Probably not. She'd want him to help Candice, which meant yielding to Telford. Rebus didn't think he could do that.

And now there was Lintz's murder, unconnected but resonant.

'I've never felt comfortable with the past, Inspector,' Lintz had said once. Funny, Rebus felt the same way about the present.

Joanne Tay lived in Colinton: a newish three-bedroomed semi with the Merc still parked in the drive.

'It's too big for me,' she explained to Rebus. 'I'll have to sell it.'

He wasn't sure if she meant the house or the car. Having declined her offer of tea, he sat in the busy living-room, ornaments on every flat surface. Joanne Tay was still in mourning: black skirt and blouse, dark grooves beneath her eyes. He'd interviewed her back at the start of the inquiry.

'I still don't know why he did it,' she said now, reluctant to see her husband's death as anything other than suicide.

But the pathology and forensic tests had cast this into doubt.

'Have you ever heard,' Rebus asked, 'of a man called Tommy Telford?'

'He runs a nightclub, doesn't he? Gavin took me there once.'

'So Gavin knew him?'

'Seemed to.'

Yes: because no way was Mr Taystee setting up his hot-dog pitch outside Telford's premises without Telford's okay. And Telford's okay almost certainly meant payment of some kind. A percentage maybe ... or a favour.

'The week before Gavin died,' Rebus went on, 'you said he'd been busy?'

'Working all hours.'

'Days as well as nights?' She nodded. 'The weather was lousy that week.'

'I know. I told him: you'll never get them buying ice-cream, a day like this. Pelting down outside. But still he went out.'

Rebus shifted in his chair. 'Did he ever mention SWEEP, Mrs Tay?'

'He had some woman would visit him ... red hair.'

'Mae Crumley?'

She nodded, eyes staring at the coal-effect fire. She asked him again if he wanted some tea. Rebus shook his head and made to leave. Did pretty well: knocked over just the two ornaments on his way to the door.

*

The hospital was quiet. When he pushed open the door to Sammy's room, he saw that another bed had been added, a middle-aged woman sleeping in it. Her hands lay on the bedcovers, a white identity tag around one wrist. She was hooked up to a machine, and her head was bandaged.

Two women were sitting by Sammy's bed. Rhona, and Patience Aitken. Rebus hadn't seen Patience in a while. The women were sitting close together. Their whispered conversation stopped as he came in. He lifted a chair and placed it beside Patience's. She leaned over and squeezed his hand.

'Hello, John.'

He smiled at her, spoke to Rhona. 'How is she?'

'The specialist says those last tests were very positive.'

'What does that mean?'

'It means there's brain activity. She's not in deep coma.'

'Is that his version?'

'He thinks she'll come out of it, John.' Her eyes were bloodshot. He noticed a handkerchief gripped in one hand.

'That's good,' he said. 'Which doctor was it?'

'Dr Stafford. He's just back from holiday.'

'I can't keep track of them all.' Rebus rubbed his forehead.

'Look,' Patience said, checking her watch, 'I really should be going. I'm sure the two of you ...'

'Stay as long as you like,' Rebus told her.

'I'm already late for an appointment, actually.' She got to her feet. 'Nice to meet you, Rhona.'

'Thanks, Patience.' The two women shook hands a little awkwardly, then Rhona got up and they hugged, and the awkwardness vanished. 'Thanks for coming.'

Patience turned to Rebus. She looked radiant, he decided. Light really seemed to emanate from her skin. She was wearing her usual perfume, and had had her hair restyled.

'Thanks for looking in,' he said.

'She's going to be fine, John.' She took his hands in hers, leaned towards him. A peck on the cheek, a kiss between friends. Rebus saw Rhona watching them.

'John,' she said, 'see Patience out, will you?'

'No, that's all –'

'Of course, yes,' Rebus said.

They left the room together. Walked the first few steps in silence. Patience spoke first.

'She's great, isn't she?'

'Rhona?'

'Yes.'

Rebus was thoughtful. 'She's terrific. Have you met her paramour?'

'He's gone back to London. I've … I asked Rhona if she wanted to come stay with me. Hotels can be …'

Rebus smiled tiredly. 'Good idea. Then all you'd have to do is invite my brother over and you'd have the whole set.'

Her face cracked into an embarrassed grin. 'I suppose it must look a bit like I'm collecting you all.'

'The perfect hand of Unhappy Families.'

She turned to him. They were at the main doors of the hospital. She touched his shoulder. 'John, I'm really sorry about Sammy. Anything I can do, you've only got to ask.'

'Thanks, Patience.'

'But asking for things has never been your strong point, has it? You just sit in silence and hope they come to you.' She sighed. 'I can't believe I'm saying this, but I miss you. I think that's why I took in Sammy. If I couldn't be close to you, at least I could be close to someone who was. Does that make any sense? Is this where you say something about not deserving me?'

'You've seen the script.' He pulled back a little from her, just so he could look at her face. 'I miss you, too.'

All the nights slumped at the bar, or in his chair at home,

the long midnight drives so he could keep his restlessness alive. He'd have the TV and the hi-fi on at the same time, and the flat would still feel empty. Books he tried reading, finding he was ten pages in and couldn't remember anything. Gazing from his window at the darkened flats across the street, imagining lives at rest.

All because he didn't have *her*.

They embraced in silence for a while. 'You're going to be late,' he said.

'God, John, what are we going to do?'

'See one another?'

'That sounds like a start.'

'Tonight? Mario's at eight?' She nodded and they kissed again. He squeezed her hand. Her head was turned to look at him as she pushed open the doors.

Emerson, Lake and Palmer: 'Still ... You Turn Me On.'

Rebus felt a little giddy as he walked back to Sammy's room. Only it wasn't any more, wasn't 'Sammy's room'. Now there was another patient there. They'd said there was always that possibility – shortage of space, cutbacks. The woman was still asleep or unconscious, breathing noisily. Rebus ignored her and sat where Patience had been sitting.

'I've got a message for you,' Rhona said. 'From Dr Morrison.'

'Who's he when he's at home?'

'I've no idea. All he said was, could he have his t-shirt back?'

The ghoul with the scythe ... Rebus picked up Pa Broon, turned the bear in his hands. They sat in silence for a while, until Rhona shifted in her chair. 'Patience is really nice.'

'Did the two of you have a good chat?' She nodded. 'And you told her what a perfect husband I'd been?'

'You must be crazy, walking out on her.'

'Sanity's never exactly been my strong point.'

'But you used to know a good thing when you saw it.'

'Trouble is, that's never what I see when I look in the mirror.'

'What do you see?'

He looked at her. 'Sometimes I don't see anything at all.'

Later, they took a coffee-break, went to the machine.

'I lost her, you know,' Rhona said.

'What?'

'Sammy, I lost her. She came back here. She came back to you.'

'We hardly see one another, Rhona.'

'But she's *here*. Don't you get it? It's you she wants, not me.' She turned away from him, fumbled for her handkerchief. He stood close behind her, then couldn't think of anything to say. He was all out of words; every line of sympathy rang hollow to him, just another cliché. He touched the back of her neck, rubbed it. She lowered her head a little, didn't resist. Massage: there'd been a lot of massage early on in their relationship. By the end, he hadn't even given her time for a handshake.

'I don't know why she came back, Rhona,' he said at last. 'But I don't think she was running away, and I don't think it had much to do with seeing me.'

A couple of nurses ran past, urgency in their movements.

'I'd better get back,' Rhona said, rubbing a hand over her face, pulling it into something resembling composure.

Rebus went with her to the room, then said he had to be going. He bent down to kiss Sammy, feeling the breath from her nostrils against his cheek.

'Wake up, Sammy,' he cajoled. 'You can't stay in bed all your life. Time to get up.'

When there was no movement, no response, he turned and left the room.

17

David Levy was no longer in Edinburgh. At least, he wasn't at the Roxburghe Hotel. Rebus could think of only one way of contacting him. Seated at his desk, he called the Holocaust Investigation Bureau in Tel Aviv and asked to speak with Solomon Mayerlink. Mayerlink wasn't available, but Rebus identified himself and said he needed to contact him as a matter of urgency. He got a home telephone number.

'Is there news on Linzstek, Inspector?' Mayerlink's voice was a harsh rasp.

'Of a kind, yes. He's dead.'

Silence on the line, then a slow release of breath. 'That's a pity.'

'It is?'

'People die, a little bit of history dies with them. We would have preferred to see him in court, Inspector. Dead, he's worthless.' Mayerlink paused. 'I take it this ends your inquiry?'

'It changes the nature of the investigation. He was murdered.'

Static on the line; an eight-beat pause. 'How did it happen?'

'He was hung from a tree.'

There was a longer silence on the line. 'I see,' Mayerlink said at last. There was a slight echo on his voice. 'You think the allegations led to his murder?'

'What would you say?'

'I'm not a detective.'

But Rebus knew Mayerlink was lying: detection was *exactly* the role he'd chosen in life. A detective of history.

'I need to talk to David Levy,' Rebus said. 'Do you have his address and phone number?'

'He came to see you?'

'You know he did.'

'It's not that simple with David. He doesn't work for the Bureau. He's self-motivated. I ask him for help occasionally. Sometimes he helps, sometimes he doesn't.'

'But you do have some way of contacting him?'

It took Mayerlink a full minute to come up with the details. An address in Sussex, plus telephone number.

'Is David your number one suspect, Inspector?'

'Why do you ask?'

'I could tell you you're barking up the wrong tree.'

'The same tree Joseph Lintz swung from?'

'Can you really see David Levy as a murderer, Inspector?'

Safari suit, walking stick. 'It takes all sorts,' Rebus said, putting down the phone.

He tried Levy's number. It rang and rang. He gave it a couple of minutes, drank a coffee, tried again. Still no answer. He called British Telecom instead, explained what he needed, was finally put through to the right person.

'My name's Justine Graham, Inspector. How can I help?'

Rebus gave her Lintz's details. 'He used to get itemised bills, then he switched.'

He heard her fingers hammer a keyboard. 'That's right,' she told him. 'The customer asked for itemised billing to be discontinued.'

'Did he say why?'

'No record of that. You don't need to give an excuse, you know.'

'When was this?'

195

'A couple of months back. The customer had requested monthly billing several years previously.'

Monthly billing: because he was meticulous, kept his accounts by the month. A couple of months back – September – the Lintz/Linzstek story had blown up in the media. And, suddenly, he hadn't wanted his phone calls to be a matter of record.

'Do you have records of his calls, even the *un*itemised ones?'

'Yes, we should have that information.'

'I'd like to see a list. Everything from the first unitemised call through to this morning.'

'Is that when he died – this morning?'

'Yes.'

She was thoughtful. 'Well, I'll need to check.'

'Please do. But remember, Ms Graham, this is a murder inquiry.'

'Yes, of course.'

'And your information could be absolutely crucial.'

'I'm quite aware of –'

'So if I could have that by the end of today ...?'

She hesitated. 'I'm not sure I can promise that.'

'And one last thing. The bill for September is missing. I'd like a copy of it. Let me give you the fax number here, speed things up.'

Rebus congratulated himself with another cup of coffee and a cigarette in the car park. She might or might not deliver later in the day, but he was confident she'd be trying her best. Wasn't that all you could ask of anybody?

Another call: Special Branch in London. He asked for Abernethy.

'I'll just put you through.'

Someone picked up: a grunt in place of an acknowledgement.

'Abernethy?' Rebus asked. He heard liquid being swallowed. The voice became clearer.

'He's not here. Can I help?'

'I really need to speak to him.'

'I could have him paged, if it's urgent.'

'My name's DI Rebus, Lothian and Borders Police.'

'Oh, right. Have you lost him or something?'

Rebus's expression turned quizzical. His voice carried a false note of humour. 'You know what Abernethy's like.'

A snort. 'Don't I just.'

'So any help appreciated.'

'Yeah, right. Look, give me your number. I'll get him to call you.'

Have you lost him or something? 'You've no idea where he is then?'

'It's your city, chum. Take your best shot.'

He's up here, Rebus thought. *He's right here.*

'I bet the office is quiet without him.'

Laughter on the line, then the sounds of a cigarette being lit. A long exhalation. 'It's like being on holiday. Keep him as long as you like.'

'So how long have you been without him?'

A pause. As the silence lengthened, Rebus could feel the change of atmosphere.

'What did you say your name was?'

'DI Rebus. I was only asking when he left London.'

'This morning, soon as he heard. So what have I won: the hatchback or the hostess trolley?'

Rebus's turn to laugh. 'Sorry, I'm just nosy.'

'I'll be sure to tell him that.' A single click, then the sound of an open line.

Later that afternoon, Rebus chased up British Telecom, then tried Levy's house again. This time he got through to a woman.

'Hello, Mrs Levy? My name's John Rebus. I was wondering if I could have a word with your husband?'

'You mean my father.'

'I'm sorry. Is your father there?'

'No, he's not.'

'Any idea when ... ?'

'Absolutely none.' She sounded peeved. 'I'm just his cook and cleaner. Like I don't have a life of my own.' She caught herself. 'Sorry, Mr ... ?'

'Rebus.'

'It's just that he never says how long he's going to be away.'

'He's away just now?'

'Has been for the best part of a fortnight. He rings two or three times a week, asks if there've been any calls or letters. If I'm lucky, he *might* remember to ask how *I'm* doing.'

'And how are you doing?'

A smile in her voice. 'I know, I know. I sound like I'm his mother or something.'

'Well, you know, fathers ...' Rebus stared into the middle distance ... 'if you don't tell them anything's wrong, they're happy to assume the best and hold their peace.'

'You speak from experience?'

'Too much experience.'

She was thoughtful. 'Is it something important?'

'Very.'

'Well, give me your name and number, and next time he calls I'll have him phone you.'

'Thanks.' Rebus reeled off two numbers: home and mobile.

'Got that,' she said. 'Any other message?'

'No, just have him call me.' Rebus thought for a moment. 'Has he had any other calls?'

'You mean, people trying to reach him? Why do you ask?'

'I just ... no real reason.' He didn't want to say he was a policeman; didn't want her spooked. 'No reason,' he repeated.

As he came off the phone, someone handed him another coffee. 'That receiver must be red hot.'

He touched it with the tips of his fingers. It was pretty warm. Then it rang and he picked it up again.

'DI Rebus,' he said.

'John, it's Siobhan.'

'Hiya, how's tricks?'

'John, you remember that guy?' Her tone was warning him of something.

'What guy?' The humour was gone from his voice.

'Danny Simpson.' He of the flappy skull; Telford's lackey.

'What about him?'

'I've just found out he's HIV positive. His GP let the hospital know.'

Blood in Rebus's eyes, his ears, dribbling down his neck ...

'Poor guy,' he said quietly.

'He should have said something at the time.'

'When?'

'When we got him to the hospital.'

'Well, he had other things on his mind, and some of them were in danger of falling off.'

'Christ, John, be serious for a minute!' Her voice was loud enough to have people glance up from their desks. 'You need to get a blood test.'

'Fine, no problem. How is he, by the way?'

'Back home but poorly. And sticking to his story.'

'Do I detect the influence of Telford's lawyer?'

'Charles Groal? That one's so slimy, he's practically primordial.'

'Saves you the cost of a valentine.'

'Look, just phone the hospital. Talk to a Dr Jones. She'll fix an appointment. They can do a test right away. Not that it'll be the last word – there's a three-month incubation.'

'Thanks, Siobhan.'

Rebus put down the receiver, drummed his fingers against it. Wouldn't *that* be a nice irony? Rebus out to get Telford, does the Good Samaritan bit for one of his men, gets AIDS and dies. Rebus stared at the ceiling.

Nice one, Big Man.

The phone rang again. Rebus snatched it up.

'Switchboard,' he said.

'Is that you, John?' Patience Aitken.

'The one and only.'

'Just wanted to check we're still on for tonight.'

'To be honest, Patience, I'm not sure I'll be at my most sparkling.'

'You want to cancel?'

'Absolutely not. But I have something to take care of. At the hospital.'

'Yes, of course.'

'No, I don't think you understand. It's not Sammy this time, it's me.'

'What's wrong?'

So he told her.

She went with him. Same hospital Sammy was in, different department. Last thing he wanted was to bump into Rhona, have to explain everything to her. Possibly HIV-infected: chances were, she'd red-card him from the bedside.

The waiting room was white, clean. Lots of information on the walls. Leaflets on every table, as if paperwork was the real virus.

'I must say, it's very pleasant for a leper colony.'

Patience didn't say anything. They were alone in the room. Someone on reception had dealt with him first, then a nurse had come out and taken some details. Now another door opened.

'Mr Rebus?'

A tall thin woman in a white coat, standing in the doorway: Dr Jones, he presumed. Patience took his arm as they walked towards her. Halfway across the floor, Rebus turned on his heels and bolted.

Patience caught up with him outside, asked what was wrong.

'I don't want to know,' he told her.

'But, John …'

'Come on, Patience. All I got was a bit of blood splashed on me.'

She didn't look convinced. 'You need to take the test.'

He looked back towards the building. 'Fine.' Started walking away. 'But some other time, eh?'

It was one in the morning when he drove back into Arden Street. No dinner date with Patience: instead, they'd visited the hospital, sat with Rhona. He'd made a silent pact with the Big Man: bring her back and I'll keep off the booze. He'd driven Patience home. Her last words to him: 'Take that test. Get it over and done with.'

As he locked his car, a figure appeared from nowhere.

'Mr Rebus, long time no see.'

Rebus recognised the face. Pointy chin, misshapen teeth, the breathing a series of small gasps. The Weasel: one of Cafferty's men. He was dressed like a down-and-out, perfect camouflage for his role in life. He was Cafferty's eyes and ears on the street.

'We need to talk, Mr Rebus.' His hands were deep in the

pockets of a tweed coat meant for someone eight inches taller. He glanced towards the tenement door.

'Not in my flat,' Rebus stated. Some things were sacrosanct.

'Cold out here.'

Rebus just shook his head, and the Weasel sniffed hard.

'You think it was a hit?' he said.

'Yes,' Rebus answered.

'She was meant to die?'

'I don't know.'

'A pro wouldn't fuck up.'

'Then it was a warning.'

'We could do with seeing your notes.'

'Can't do that.'

The Weasel shrugged. 'Thought you wanted Mr Cafferty's help?'

'I can't give you the notes. What about if I summarise?'

'It'd be a start.'

'Rover 600, stolen from George Street that afternoon. Abandoned on a street by Piershill Cemetery. Radio and some tapes lifted – not necessarily by the same person.'

'Scavengers.'

'Could be.'

The Weasel was thoughtful. 'A warning ... That would mean a professional driver.'

'Yes,' Rebus said.

'And not one of ours ... Doesn't leave too many candidates. Rover 600 ... what colour?'

'Sherwood Green.'

'Parked on George Street?'

Rebus nodded.

'Thanks for that.' The Weasel made to turn away, then paused. 'Nice doing business with you again, Mr Rebus.'

Rebus was about to say something, then remembered he needed the Weasel more than the Weasel needed him. He wondered how much crap he'd take from Cafferty ... how long he'd have to take it. All his life? Had he made a contract with the devil?

For Sammy, he'd have done much, much worse ...

In his flat, he stuck on the CD of *Rock 'n' Roll Circus*, skipping to the actual Stones tracks. His answering machine was flashing. Three messages. The first: Hogan.

'Hello, John. Just thought I'd check, see if there's been any word from BT.'

Not by the time Rebus had left the office. Message two: Abernethy.

'Me again, bad penny and all that. Heard you've been trying to catch me. I'll call you tomorrow. Cheers.'

Rebus stared at the machine, willing Abernethy to say more, to give some hint of a location. But the machine was on to the final message. Bill Pryde.

'John, tried you at the office, left a message. But I thought you'd want to know, we've had final word on those prints. If you want to try me at home, I'm on ...'

Rebus took down the number. Two in the morning, but Bill would understand.

After a minute or so, a woman picked up. She sounded groggy.

'Sorry,' Rebus said. 'Is Bill there?'

'I'll get him.'

He heard background dialogue, then the receiver being hoisted.

'So what's this about prints?' he asked.

'Christ, John, when I said you could call, I didn't mean the middle of the night!'

'It's important.'

'Yes, I know. How's she doing anyway?'

'Still out cold.'

Pryde yawned. 'Well, most of the prints inside the car

belong to the owner and his wife. But we found one other set. Problem is, looks like they belong to a kid.'

'What makes you so sure?'

'The size.'

'Plenty of adults around with small hands.'

'I suppose so ...'

'You sound sceptical.'

'More likely to be one of two scenarios. One, Sammy was hit by a joyrider. I know what you think, but it does happen. Two, the prints belong to whoever rifled the car after it was left at the cemetery.'

'The kid who took the cassette player and tapes?'

'Exactly.'

'No other prints? Not even partials?'

'The car was clean, John.'

'Exterior?'

'Same three sets on the doors, plus Sammy's on the bonnet.' Pryde yawned again. 'So what about your grudge theory?'

'Still holds. A pro would be wearing gloves.'

'That's what I was thinking. Not too many pros out there though.'

'No.' Rebus was thinking of the Weasel: *I'm dealing with slime to catch a slug*. Nothing he hadn't done before, only this time there were personal reasons.

And he didn't think there'd be a trial.

18

Breakfast was on Hogan: bacon rolls in a brown paper bag. They ate them in the CID room at St Leonard's. A Murder Room had been established in Leith, and that's where Hogan should have been.

Only he wanted Rebus's files, and he knew better than to trust Rebus to deliver them.

'Thought I'd save you the hassle,' was what he said.

'You're a gentleman,' Rebus answered, examining the interior of his roll. 'Tell me, are pigs an endangered species?'

'I lifted half a slice from you.' Hogan pulled a string of fat from his mouth, tossed it into a bin. 'Thought I was doing you a favour: cholesterol and all that.'

Rebus put the roll to one side, took a swig from the can of Irn-Bru – Hogan's idea of a morning beverage – and swallowed. What was sugar consumption compared to HIV? 'What did you get from the cleaning lady?'

'Grief. Soon as she heard her employer was dead, the taps were on.' Hogan brushed flour from his fingers: mealtime over. 'She never met any of his friends, never had occasion to answer his telephone, hadn't noticed any change in him recently, and doesn't think he was a mass murderer. Quote: "If he'd killed that many people, I'd have known".'

'What is she, psychic or something?'

Hogan shrugged. 'About all I got from her was a glowing character reference and the fact that as she was paid in advance, she owes his estate a partial refund.'

'There's your motive.'

Hogan smiled. 'Speaking of motives ...'

'You've got something?'

'Lintz's lawyer has come up with a letter from the deceased's bank.' He handed Rebus a photocopy. 'Seems our man made a cash withdrawal of five grand ten days ago.'

'*Cash?*'

'We found ten quid on his person, and about another thirty bar in the house. No five grand. I'm beginning to think blackmail.'

Rebus nodded. 'What about his address book?'

'Slow work. A lot of old numbers, people who've moved on or died. Plus a few charities, museums ... an art gallery or two.' Hogan paused. 'What about you?'

Rebus opened his drawer, pulled out the fax sheets. 'Waiting for me this morning. The calls Lintz wanted kept secret.'

Hogan looked down the list. 'Calls plural, or one in particular?'

'I've just started going through them. Best guess: there'll be callers he spoke to regularly. Those numbers will show up on the other statements. We're looking for anomalies, one-offs.'

'Makes sense.' Hogan looked at his watch. 'Anything else I should know?'

'Two things. Remember I told you about the Special Branch interest?'

'Abernethy?'

Rebus nodded. 'I tried calling him yesterday.'

'And?'

'According to his office, he was on his way up here. He'd already heard the news.'

'So I've got Abernethy sniffing around, and you don't trust him? Terrific. What's the other thing?'

'David Levy. I spoke with his daughter. She doesn't know where he is. He could be anywhere.'

'With a grudge against Lintz?'

'It's possible.'

'What's his phone number?'

Rebus patted the topmost file on his desk. 'Ready for you to take away.'

Hogan studied the foot-high pile, looking glum.

'I whittled it down to what's absolutely necessary,' Rebus told him.

'There's a month's reading there.'

Rebus shrugged. 'My case is your case, Bobby.'

With Hogan gone, Rebus went back to the British Telecom list. It was as detailed as he could have wished for. Lots of calls to Lintz's solicitor, a few to one of the city's taxi firms. Rebus tried a couple of numbers, found himself connected to charity offices: Lintz would have been phoning to tender his resignation. There were a few calls that stood out from the crowd: the Roxburghe Hotel – duration four minutes; Edinburgh University – twenty-six minutes. The Roxburghe had to mean Levy. Rebus knew Levy had talked to Lintz – Lintz himself had admitted it. Talking to him – being confronted by him – was one thing; calling him at his hotel quite another.

The number for Edinburgh University connected Rebus to the main switchboard. He asked to be put through to Lintz's old department. The secretary was very helpful. She'd been in the job over twenty years, was due to retire. Yes, she remembered Professor Lintz, but he hadn't contacted the department recently.

'Every call that comes through here, I know about it.'

'He might have got straight through to a tutor though?' Rebus suggested.

'No one's mentioned speaking to him. There's nobody here from the Professor's day.'

'He doesn't keep in touch with the department?'

'I haven't spoken to him in years, Inspector. Too many years for me to remember ...'

So who had he been talking to for over twenty minutes? Rebus thanked the secretary and put down the phone. He went through the other numbers: a couple of restaurants, a wine shop, and the local radio station. Rebus told the receptionist what he was after, and she said she'd do her best. Then he went back to the restaurants, asked them to check if Lintz had been making a reservation.

Within half an hour, the calls started coming in. First restaurant: a booking for dinner, just the one cover. The radio station: they'd asked Lintz to appear on a programme. He'd said he'd consider it, then had called back to decline. Second restaurant: a lunch reservation, two covers.

'Two?'

'Mr Lintz and one other.'

'Any idea who the "other" might have been?'

'Another gentleman, quite elderly, I think ... I'm sorry, I don't really remember.'

'Did he walk with a stick?'

'I wish I could help, but it's a madhouse here at lunchtime.'

'You remember Lintz though?'

'Mr Lintz is a regular ... was a regular.'

'Did he usually eat alone, or with company?'

'Mostly alone. He didn't seem to mind. He'd bring a book with him.'

'Do you happen to recall any of his other guests?'

'I remember a young woman ... his daughter maybe? Or granddaughter?'

'So when you say "young" ...?'

'Younger than him.' A pause. 'Maybe much younger.'

'When was this?'

'I really don't remember.' The voice impatient now.

'I appreciate your help, sir. Just one more minute of your time ... This woman, did he bring her more than once?'

'I'm sorry, Inspector. The kitchen needs me.'

'Well, if you think of anything else ...'

'Of course. Goodbye.'

Rebus put the phone down, made some notes. Just one number left. He waited for an answer.

'Yeah?' The voice grudging.

'Who's this?'

'This is Malky. Who the fuck are you?'

A voice in the background: 'Tommy says that new machine's fucked.' Rebus put the phone down. His hand was shaking. *That new machine* ... Tommy Telford on his arcade motorbike. He remembered The Family mugshots: Malky Jordan. Tiny nose and eyes in a balloon of a face. *Joseph Lintz talking to one of Telford's men? Phoning Telford's office??* Rebus found the number of Hogan's mobile.

'Bobby,' he said. 'If you're driving, better slow down right now ...'

Hogan's notion: five in cash was just Telford's style. Blackmail? But where was the connection? Something else ...?

Hogan's play: he'd talk to Telford.

Rebus's notion: five was a bit steep for a hit-man. All the same, he wondered about Lintz ... paying five thou' to Telford to set up the 'accident'. Motive: give Rebus a fright, scare him off? It put Lintz back in the frame, potentially.

Rebus had fixed up another meeting, one he didn't want

anyone knowing about. Haymarket Station was nice and anonymous. The bench on platform one. Ned Farlowe was already waiting. He looked tired: worry over Sammy. They talked about her for a couple of minutes. Then Rebus got down to business.

'You know Lintz has been murdered?'

'I didn't think this was a social call.'

'We're looking at a blackmail angle.'

Farlowe looked interested. 'And he didn't pay up?'

Oh, he paid up all right, Rebus thought. He paid up, and someone still took him out of the game.

'Look, Ned, this is *all* off the record. By rights I should take you in for questioning.'

'Because I followed him for a few days?'

'Yes.'

'And that makes me a suspect?'

'It makes you a possible witness.'

Farlowe thought about it. 'One evening. Lintz left his house, walked down the road, made a call from a phone-box, then went straight back home.'

Not wanting to use his home phone ... afraid it was bugged? Afraid of the number being traced? Telephone bugging: a favourite ploy of Special Branch.

'And something else,' Farlowe was saying. 'He met this woman on his doorstep. Like she was waiting for him. They had a few words. I think she was crying when she left.'

'What did she look like?'

'Tall, short dark hair, well-dressed. She had a briefcase with her.'

'Wearing?'

Farlowe shrugged. 'Skirt and jacket ... matching. Black and white check. You know ... elegant.'

He was describing Kirstin Mede. Her phone message to Rebus: *I can't do this any more ...*

'There's something I want to ask you,' Farlowe was saying. 'That girl Candice.'

'What about her?'

'You asked me if anything unusual had happened just before Sammy got hit.'

'Yes?'

'Well, *she* happened, didn't she?' Farlowe's eyes narrowed. 'Does she have anything to do with it?'

Rebus looked at Farlowe, who started nodding.

'Thanks for the confirmation. Who was she?'

'One of Telford's girls.'

Farlowe leaped to his feet, paced the platform. Rebus waited for him to sit down again. When he did, there could be no doubting the fury in his eyes.

'You hid one of Telford's girls with your own *daughter*?'

'I didn't have much choice. Telford knows where I live. I ...'

'You were using us!' He paused. 'Telford did this, didn't he?'

'I don't know,' Rebus said. Farlowe leaped to his feet again. 'Look, Ned, I don't want you –'

'Quite frankly, *Inspector*, I don't think you're in any position to give advice.' He started walking, and though Rebus called after him, he never once looked back.

As Rebus walked into the Crime Squad office, a paper plane glided past and crashed into the wall. Ormiston had his feet up on the desk. Country and western music was playing softly in the background, its source a tape player on the window ledge behind Claverhouse's desk. Siobhan Clarke had pulled a chair over beside him. They were poring over some report.

'Not exactly the "A-Team" in here, is it?' Rebus retrieved the plane, straightened its crumpled nose, and sent it back to Ormiston, who asked what he was doing there.

'Liaising,' Rebus told him. 'My boss wants a progress report.'

Ormiston glanced towards Claverhouse, who was tipping himself back in his chair, hands behind his head.

'Want to take a guess at the headway we've made?'

Rebus sat down opposite Claverhouse, nodded a greeting to Siobhan.

'How's Sammy?' she asked.

'Just the same,' Rebus answered. Claverhouse looked abashed, and Rebus suddenly realised that he could use Sammy as a lever, play on people's sympathy. Why not? Hadn't he used her in the past? Wasn't Ned Farlowe on the nail there?

'We've pulled the surveillance,' Claverhouse said.

'Why?'

Ormiston snorted, but it was Claverhouse who answered.

'High maintenance, low returns.'

'Orders from above?'

'It isn't as if we were close to getting a result.'

'So we just let him get on with getting on?'

Claverhouse shrugged. Rebus wondered if news would get back to Newcastle. Jake Tarawicz would be happy. He'd think Rebus was fulfilling his part of the bargain. Candice would be safe. Maybe.

'Any news on that nightclub killing?'

'Nothing to link it to your chum Cafferty.'

'He's *not* my chum.'

'Whatever you say. Stick the kettle on, Ormie.' Ormiston glanced towards Clarke, then rose grudgingly from his chair. Rebus had thought the tension in the office was all to do with Telford. Not a bit of it. Claverhouse and Clarke close together, *involved*. Ormiston off on his own, a kid making paper planes, seeking attention. An old Status Quo song: 'Paper Plane'. But the status quo here had been disturbed: Clarke had usurped Ormiston. The office junior was absolved from making the tea.

Rebus could see why Ormiston was pissed off.

'I hear Herr Lintz was a bit of a swinger,' Claverhouse said.

'Now there's a joke I haven't heard before.' Rebus's pager sounded. The display gave him a number to call.

He used Claverhouse's phone. It sounded like he was connected to a pay-phone. Street sounds, heavy traffic close by.

'Mr Rebus?' Placed the voice at once: the Weasel.

'What is it?'

'A couple of questions. The tape player from the car, any idea of the make?'

'Sony.'

'The front bit detachable?'

'That's right.'

'So all they got was the front bit?'

'Yes.' Claverhouse and Clarke, back at their report, pretending they weren't listening.

'What about the tapes? You said some tapes got stolen?'

'Opera – *The Marriage of Figaro* and Verdi's *Macbeth*.' Rebus squeezed his eyes shut, thinking. 'And another tape with film music on it, famous themes. Plus Roy Orbison's *Greatest Hits*.' This last the wife's. Rebus knew what the Weasel was thinking: whoever took the stuff, they'd try flogging it round the pubs or at a car boot sale. Car boot sales were clearing houses for knock-off. But getting whoever had lifted the stuff from the unlocked car wasn't going to nail the driver ... Unless the kid – the one who'd lifted the stuff, whose prints were on the car – had *seen* something: been hanging around on the street, watched the car screeching to a stop, a man getting out and hoofing it ...

An eye witness, someone who could describe the driver.

'The only prints we got were small, maybe a kid's.'

'That's interesting.'

'Anything else I can do,' Rebus said, 'just let me know.'

The Weasel hung up.

'Sony's a good make,' Claverhouse said, fishing.

'Some stuff lifted from a car,' Rebus told him. 'It might have turned up.'

Ormiston had made the tea. Rebus went to fetch himself a chair, saw someone walk past the open doorway. He dropped the chair and ran into the corridor, grabbed at an arm.

Abernethy spun quickly, saw who it was and relaxed.

'Nice one, son,' he said. 'You almost had knuckles for teeth.' He was working on a piece of chewing gum.

'What are you doing here?'

'Visiting.' Abernethy looked back at the open door, walked towards it. 'What about you?'

'Working.'

Abernethy read the sign on the door. 'Crime Squad,' he said, sounding amused, taking in the office and the people in it. Hands in pockets, he sauntered in, Rebus following.

'Abernethy, Special Branch,' the Londoner said by way of introduction. 'That music's a good idea: play it at interrogations, sap the suspect's will to live.' He was smiling, surveying the premises like he was thinking of moving in. The mug meant for Rebus was on the corner of the desk. Abernethy picked it up and slurped, made a face, started chewing again. The three Crime Squad officers were like a frozen tableau. Suddenly they looked like a unit: it had taken Abernethy to do that.

Had taken him all of ten seconds.

'What you working on?' No one answered. 'Must've got the sign on the door wrong,' Abernethy said. 'Should be Mime Squad.'

'Is there something we can do for you?' Claverhouse asked, his voice level, hostility in his eyes.

'I don't know. It was John pulled me in here.'

'And I'm pulling you out again,' Rebus said, taking his arm. Abernethy shrugged free, bunched his fists. 'A word in the corridor ... please.'

Abernethy smiled. 'Manners maketh the man, John.'

'What does that maketh you?'

Abernethy turned his head slowly, looked at Siobhan Clarke who'd just spoken.

'I'm just a regular guy with a heart of gold and twelve big inches of ability.' He grinned at her.

'To go with your twelve big points of IQ,' she said, going back to the report. Ormiston and Claverhouse weren't trying too hard to conceal their laughter as Abernethy stormed out of the room. Rebus hung back long enough to watch Ormiston pat Clarke on the back, then headed off after the Special Branch man.

'What a bitch,' Abernethy said. He was making for the exit.

'She's a friend of mine.'

'And they say you can choose your friends ...' Abernethy shook his head.

'What brings you back?'

'You have to ask?'

'Lintz is dead. Case closed as far as you're concerned.'

They emerged from the building.

'So?'

'So,' Rebus persisted, 'why come all the way back here? What is there that couldn't be done with a phone or fax?'

Abernethy stopped, turned to face him. 'Loose ends.'

'What loose ends?'

'There aren't any.' Abernethy gave a cheerless smile and took a key from his pocket. As they approached his car, he used the remote to unlock it and disable the alarm.

'What's going on, Abernethy?'

'Nothing to worry your pretty little head about.' He opened the driver's-side door.

'Are you glad he's dead?'

'What?'

'Lintz. How do you feel about him being murdered?'

'I've no feelings either way. He's dead, which means I can cross him off my list.'

'That last time you came up here, you were warning him.'

'Not true.'

'Was his phone bugged?' Abernethy just snorted. 'Did you know he might be killed?'

Abernethy turned on Rebus. 'What's it to you? I'll tell you: nothing. Leith CID are on the murder, and you're out of it. End of story.'

'Is it the Rat Line? Too embarrassing if it all came to light?'

'Christ, what *is* it with you? Just give it a rest.' Abernethy got into the car, closed the door. Rebus didn't move. The engine turned and caught, Abernethy's window slid down. Rebus was ready.

'They sent you four hundred miles just to check there were no loose ends.'

'So?'

'So there's rather a large loose end, isn't there?' Rebus paused. 'Unless you know who Lintz's killer was.'

'I leave that sort of thing to you guys.'

'Heading down to Leith?'

'I have to talk to Hogan.' Abernethy stared at Rebus. 'You're a hard bastard, aren't you? Maybe even a bit selfish.'

'How's that?'

'If I'd a daughter in hospital, police work would be the last thing on my mind.'

As Rebus lunged towards the open window, Abernethy gunned the car. Footsteps behind: Siobhan Clarke.

'Good riddance,' she said, watching the car speed off. A finger appeared from Abernethy's window. She gave a two-fingered reply. 'I didn't want to say anything in the office ...' she began.

'I took the test yesterday,' Rebus lied.

'It'll be negative.'

'Are you positive?'

She smiled a little longer than the joke merited. 'Ormiston chucked your tea away, said he was going to disinfect the mug.'

'Abernethy has that effect on people.' He looked at her. 'Remember, Ormiston and Claverhouse go back years.'

'I know. I think Claverhouse has a crush on me. It'll pass, but until it does ...'

'Tread carefully.' They started walking back towards the main entrance. 'And don't let him tempt you into the broom cupboard.'

19

Rebus went back to St Leonard's, saw that the office was coping quite well without him, and headed over to the hospital with Dr Morrison's Iron Maiden t-shirt in a plastic bag. A third bed had been moved into Sammy's room. An elderly woman lay in it. Though awake, she stared fixedly at the ceiling. Rhona was at Sammy's bedside, reading a book.

Rebus stroked his daughter's hair. 'How is she?'

'No change.'

'Any more tests planned?'

'Not that I know of.'

'That's it then? She just stays like this?'

He lifted a chair over, sat down. It had turned into a sort of ritual now, this bedside vigil. It felt almost ... the word he wanted to use was 'comfortable'. He squeezed Rhona's hand, sat there for twenty minutes, saying almost nothing, then went to find Kirstin Mede.

She was in her office at the French Department, marking scripts. She sat at a big desk in front of the window, but moved from this to a coffee-table with half a dozen chairs arranged around it.

'Sit down,' she said. Rebus sat down.

'I got your message,' he told her.

'Hardly matters now, does it? The man's dead.'

'I know you spoke with him, Kirstin.'

She glanced towards him. 'I'm sorry?'

'You waited for him outside his house. Did the two of you have a nice chat?'

Colour had risen to her cheeks. She crossed her legs, tugged the hem of her skirt towards her knee. 'Yes,' she said at last, 'I went to his house.'

'Why?'

'Because I wanted to see him close up.' Her eyes were on his now, challenging him. 'I thought maybe I could tell from his face ... the look in his eyes. Maybe something in his tone of voice.'

'And could you?'

She shook her head. 'Not a damned thing. No window to the soul.'

'What did you say to him?'

'I told him who I was.'

'Any reaction?'

'Yes.' She folded her arms. 'His words: "My dear lady, will you kindly piss off".'

'And did you?'

'Yes. Because I knew then. Not whether he was Linzstek or not, but something else.'

'What?'

'That he was at the end of his tether.' She was nodding. 'Absolutely at breaking point.' She looked at Rebus again. 'And capable of anything.'

The problem with the Flint Street surveillance was that it had been so open. A hidden operation – deep cover – that's what was needed. Rebus had decided to scout out the territory.

The tenement flats across the road from Telford's café and arcade were served by a single main door. It was locked, so Rebus chose a buzzer at random – marked HETHERINGTON. Waited, pushed again. An elderly voice came on the intercom.

'Who is it, please?'

'Mrs Hetherington? Detective Inspector Rebus, I'm your Community CID officer. Can I talk to you about home security? There've been a few break-ins around here, especially with elderly victims.'

'Gracious, you'd better come up.'

'Which floor?'

'The first.' The door buzzed, and Rebus pushed it open.

Mrs Hetherington was waiting for him in her doorway. She was tiny and frail-looking, but her eyes were lively and her movements assured. The flat was small, well-maintained. The sitting-room was heated by a two-bar electric fire. Rebus wandered over to the window, found himself looking down on to the arcade. Perfect location for a surveillance. He pretended to check her windows.

'These seem fine,' he said. 'Are they always locked?'

'I open them a bit in the summer,' Mrs Hetherington said, 'and when they need washing. But I always lock them again afterwards.'

'One thing I should warn you about, and that's bogus officials. People coming to your door, telling you they're so-and-so. Always ask to see some ID, and don't open up until you're satisfied.'

'How can I see it without opening the door?'

'Ask them to push it through the letterbox.'

'I didn't see *your* identification, did I?'

Rebus smiled. 'No, you didn't.' He took it out and showed her. 'Sometimes the fake stuff can look pretty convincing. If you're unsure, keep the door locked and call the police.' He looked around. 'You have a phone?'

'In the bedroom.'

'Any windows in there?'

'Yes.'

'Can I take a look?'

The bedroom window also looked out on to Flint Street.

Rebus noticed travel brochures on the dressing-table, a small suitcase standing near the door.

'Off on holiday, eh?' With the flat empty, maybe he could move the surveillance in.

'Just a long weekend,' she said.

'Somewhere nice?'

'Holland. Wrong time of year for the bulb-fields, but I've always wanted to go. It's a nuisance flying from Inverness, but so much cheaper. Since my husband died ... well, I've done a bit of travelling.'

'Any chance of taking me with you?' Rebus smiled. 'This window's fine, too. I'll just check your door, see if it could do with more locks.' They went into the narrow hall.

'You know,' she said, 'we've always been very lucky here, no break-ins or anything like that.'

Hardly surprising with Tommy Telford as proprietor.

'And with the panic button, of course ...'

Rebus looked at the wall next to the front door. A large red button. He'd assumed it was for the stairhead lights or something.

'Anyone who calls, anyone at all, I'm supposed to press it.'

Rebus opened the door. 'And do you?'

Two very large men were standing right outside.

'Oh, yes,' Mrs Hetherington said. 'I always do.'

For thugs, they were very polite. Rebus showed them his warrant card and explained the nature of his visit. He asked them who they were, and they told him they were 'representatives of the building's owner'. He knew the faces though: Kenny Houston, Ally Cornwell. Houston – the ugly one – ran Telford's doormen; Cornwell, with his wrestler's bulk, was general muscle. The little charade was carried out with humour and good nature on both sides. They accompanied him downstairs. Across the street,

Tommy Telford was standing in the café doorway, wagging his finger. A pedestrian crossed Rebus's line of vision. Too late, Rebus saw who it was. Had his mouth open to shout something, then saw Telford hang his head, hands going to his face. Screeching.

Rebus ran across the road, pulled the pedestrian round: Ned Farlowe. A bottle dropped from Farlowe's hand. Telford's men were closing in. Rebus held tight to Farlowe.

'I'm placing this man under arrest,' he said. 'He's *mine*, understood?'

A dozen faces glaring at him. And Tommy Telford down on his knees.

'Get your boss to the hospital,' Rebus said. 'I'm taking this one to St Leonard's ...'

Ned Farlowe sat on the ledge in one of the cells. The walls were blue, smeared brown near the toilet-pan. Farlowe was looking pleased with himself.

'Acid?' Rebus said, pacing the cell. '*Acid*? All this research must have gone to your head.'

'It's what he deserved.'

Rebus glared at him. 'You don't know what you've done.'

'I know *exactly* what I've done.'

'He'll kill you.'

Farlowe shrugged. 'Am I under arrest?'

'You'd better believe it, son. I want you kept out of harm's way. If I hadn't been there ...' But he didn't want to think about that. He looked at Farlowe. Looked at Sammy's lover, who'd just staged a full-frontal assault on Telford, the kind of assault Rebus knew wouldn't work.

Now Rebus would have to redouble his efforts. Because otherwise, Ned Farlowe was a dead man ... and when Sammy came round, he didn't want news like that to be waiting for her.

*

He drove back towards Flint Street, parked at a distance from it, and headed there on foot. Telford had the place sewn up, no doubt about it. Letting his flats to old folk might have been a charitable act but he'd made damned sure it served its purpose. Rebus wondered if, given the same circumstances, Cafferty would have been clever enough to think of panic-buttons. He suspected not. Cafferty wasn't thick, but most of what he did he did by instinct. Rebus wondered if Tommy Telford had ever made a rash move in his life.

He was staking out Flint Street because he needed an *in*, needed to find the weak link in the chain around Telford. After ten minutes of windchill, he thought of a better idea. On his mobile, he called one of the city's taxi firms. Identified himself and asked if Henry Wilson was on shift. He was. Rebus told the switchboard to put a call out to Henry. It was as simple as that.

Ten minutes later, Wilson turned up. He drank in the Ox occasionally, which was his problem really. Drunk in charge of a taxi-cab. Luckily Rebus had been around to smooth things over, as a result of which Wilson owed him a lifetime of favours. He was tall, heavily built, with short black hair and a long black beard. Ruddy-faced, and he always wore check shirts. Rebus thought of him as 'The Lumberjack'.

'Need a lift?' Wilson said, as Rebus got into the front passenger-seat.

'First thing I need is a blast of the heater.' Wilson obliged. 'Second thing I need is to use your taxi as cover.'

'You mean, sit here?'

'That's what I mean.'

'With the meter running?'

'You've got an engine problem, Henry. Your cab's out of the game for the rest of the afternoon.'

'I'm saving up for Christmas,' Wilson complained.

Rebus stared him out. The big man sighed and lifted a newspaper from the side of his seat. 'Help me pick a few winners then,' he said, turning to the racing pages.

They sat for over an hour at the end of Flint Street, and Rebus stayed in the front of the cab. His reasoning: a cab parked with a passenger in the back looked suspicious. A cab parked with two guys in the front, and you'd just think they were on their break, or at shift's end – two cabbies sharing stories and a flask of tea.

Rebus took one sip from the plastic cup and winced. Half a bag of sugar in the flask.

'I've always had a sweet tooth,' Wilson explained. He had a packet of crisps open on his lap: pickled onion flavour.

Finally, Rebus saw two Range Rovers being driven into Flint Street. Sean Haddow – Telford's money man – was driving the lead car. He got out and went into the arcade. On the passenger seat, Rebus could see a huge yellow teddy bear. Haddow was coming out again, bringing Telford with him. Telford: back from the hospital already, hands bandaged, gauze patches on his face like he'd had a particularly ropey shave. But not about to let a little thing like an acid attack get in the way of business. Haddow held the back door open, and Telford got in.

'This is us, Henry,' Rebus said. 'You're going to be following those two Range Rovers. Stay back as far as you like. Those things are so high off the ground, we'll be able to see them over anything smaller than a double-decker.'

Both Range Rovers headed out of Flint Street. The second car carried three of Telford's 'soldiers'. Rebus recognised Pretty-Boy. The other two were younger recruits, well-dressed with groomed hair. One hundred percent business.

The convoy headed for the city centre, stopped outside a

hotel. Telford had a word with his men, but entered the building alone. The cars stayed where they were.

'Are you going in?' Wilson asked.

'I think I'd be noticed,' Rebus said. The drivers of both Range Rovers had got out and were enjoying a smoke, but keeping a keen eye on people entering and leaving the hotel. A couple of prospects looked into the cab, but Wilson shook his head.

'I could be making a mint here,' he muttered. Rebus offered him a Polo. Wilson accepted with a snort.

'Brilliant,' Rebus said. Wilson looked back towards the hotel. A parking warden was talking to Haddow and Pretty-Boy. She had her notebook out. They were tapping their watches, attempting charm. Double yellow lines kerbside: no parking any time.

Haddow and Pretty-Boy held up their hands in surrender, had a quick confab, then it was back into the Range Rovers. Pretty-Boy made circling motions with one hand, letting his passengers know they were going to circle the block. The warden stood her ground till they'd moved off. Haddow was on his mobile: doubtless letting his boss know the score.

Interesting: they hadn't tried to strongarm the warden, or bribe her, nothing like that. Law-abiding citizens. Telford's rules, no doubt. Again, Rebus couldn't see any of Cafferty's men giving in so quickly.

'You going in then?' Wilson asked.

'Not much point, Henry. Telford will already be in a bedroom or somebody's suite. If he's doing business, it'll be behind closed doors.'

'So that was Tommy Telford?'

'You've heard of him?'

'I'm a taxi driver, we hear things. He's after Big Ger's cab business.' Wilson paused. 'Not that Big Ger *has* a cab business, you understand.'

'Any idea how Telford plans to wrest it away from Cafferty?'

'Scare off the drivers, or get them to switch sides.'

'What about your company, Henry?'

'Honest, legal and decent, Mr Rebus.'

'No approach by Telford?'

'Not yet.'

'Here they come again.' They watched as the two Range Rovers turned back into the street. There was no sign of the warden. A couple of minutes later, Telford emerged from the hotel, bringing with him a Japanese man with spiky hair and a shiny aquamarine suit. He carried a briefcase but didn't look like a businessman. Maybe it was the sunglasses, worn in late-afternoon twilight; maybe it was the cigarette slouching from the corner of the downturned mouth. Both men got into the back of the lead car. The Japanese leaned forward and ruffled the teddy bear's ears, making some joke. Telford didn't look amused.

'Do we follow them?' Wilson asked. He saw the look on Rebus's face, turned the key in the ignition.

They were heading west out of town. Rebus already had an inkling of their ultimate destination, but he wanted to know what route they'd take. Turned out it was much the same route he'd taken with Candice. She hadn't recognised anything until Juniper Green, but it wasn't as if there were many landmarks. On Slateford Road the back car signalled that it was pulling over.

'What do I do?' Wilson asked.

'Keep going. Make the first left you can, and turn the cab round. We'll wait for them to go past us.'

Haddow had gone into a newspaper shop. Same story as with Candice. Strange, during what was a business trip, that Telford would allow a stop. And what about the building which, according to Candice, he'd seemed so interested in? There it was: an anonymous brick edifice. A warehouse maybe? Rebus could think of reasons why a warehouse might be of interest to Tommy Telford. Haddow stayed in the shop three minutes – Rebus timed him. No one else came out, so it wasn't as if he'd had to queue. Back into the car, and the little convoy set off again. They were heading for Juniper Green, and after that Poyntinghame Country Club. Little point in tagging along: the further they got out of town, the more conspicuous the cab would be. Rebus told Henry to turn around.

He got the cabbie to drop him off at the Oxford Bar. Wilson slid down his window as he was about to move off.

'Are we square now?' he called.

'Till next time, Henry.' Rebus pushed open the door and walked into the pub.

Perched on a stool, daytime TV and Margaret the barmaid for company, Rebus ordered a mug of coffee and a corned beef and beetroot roll. For his main course Margaret suggested a bridie.

'Excellent choice,' Rebus agreed. He was thinking about the Japanese businessman. Who hadn't really looked like a businessman at all. He'd been all sharp edges, chiselled face. Fortified, Rebus walked from the Ox back to the hotel, and kept watch on it from an overpriced bar across the street. He passed the time making calls on his mobile. By the time the battery died, he'd spoken with Hogan, Bill Pryde, Siobhan Clarke, Rhona and Patience, and had been about to call Torphichen cop-shop, see if anyone there could identify the building on Slateford Road. Two hours crawled by. He broke his 'personal best' for slow drinking: two Cokes. The bar wasn't exactly crowded; no one seemed to mind. The music was on a tape-loop. 'Psycho Killer' was coming round for the third time when the Range Rovers stopped outside the hotel. Telford and the Jap shook hands, made slight bows. Telford and his men drove off.

Rebus left the bar, crossed the road, and entered the

hotel. The lift doors were closing on Mr Aquamarine. Rebus walked up to reception, showed his ID.

'The guest who just came in, I need his name.'

The receptionist had to check. 'Mr Matsumoto.'

'First name?'

'Takeshi.'

'When did he arrive?'

She checked the register again. 'Yesterday.'

'How long's he staying?'

'Three more days. Look, I should call my supervisor ...'

Rebus shook his head. 'That's all I needed to know, thanks. Mind if I sit in the lounge for a while?'

She shook her head, so Rebus wandered into the residents' lounge. He settled on a sofa – perfect view of the reception area through the glass double-doors – and picked up a newspaper. Matsumoto was in town on Poyntinghame business, but Rebus had a whiff of something altogether less savoury. Hugh Malahide's story had been that a corporation wanted to buy the club, but Matsumoto didn't look like he worked in any above-board business. When he finally emerged into reception, he'd changed into a white suit, black open-necked shirt, and Burberry trenchcoat, topped off with a woollen tartan scarf. He had a cigarette in his mouth, but didn't light it until he was outside the hotel. With the collar of his coat turned up, he started walking. Rebus followed him for the best part of a mile, and kept checking that no one was following *him*. It was possible, after all, that Telford would want to keep tabs on Matsumoto. But if there was surveillance, it was exceptional. Matsumoto wasn't playing the tourist, wasn't dawdling. He kept his head down, protecting his face from the wind, and seemed to have some destination in mind.

When he disappeared into a building, Rebus paused, studying the glass door behind which stood a flight of red-carpeted stairs. He knew where he was, didn't need the sign above the door to tell him. He was outside the Morvena Casino. The place used to be owned by a local villain called Topper Hamilton and managed by a man called Mandelson. But Hamilton was in retirement, and Mandelson had scarpered. The new owner was still an unknown quantity – or had been till now. Rebus guessed he wouldn't be far wrong if he placed Tommy Telford and his Japanese friends in the frame. He looked around, checking the parked cars: no Range Rovers.

'What the hell,' he said to himself, pushing open the door and starting to climb the stairs.

In the upstairs foyer he was eyeballed by security: two of them looking uncomfortable in their black suits and bowties, white shirts. One skinny – he'd be all about speed and manoeuvres; one a real heavyweight – slow muscle to back up the fast moves. Rebus seemed to pass whatever test they'd just given him. He bought a twenty's worth of chips and walked into the gaming room.

At one time, it would have been the drawing-room of a Georgian house. There were two huge bay windows, and ornate cornicing connected the twenty-foot-high cream walls to the pastel-pink ceiling. Now it was home to gaming tables: blackjack, dice, roulette. Hostesses moved between the tables, taking orders for drinks. There was very little noise: the gamblers took their work seriously. Rebus wouldn't have called the place busy, but what clientele there was comprised a veritable United Nations. Matsumoto's coat had disappeared into the cloakroom, and he was seated at the roulette table. Rebus sat down beside two men at the blackjack table, nodded a greeting. The dealer – young, but obviously sure of himself – smiled. Rebus won with his first hand. Lost with his second and third. Won again with his fourth. There was a voice just behind his right ear.

'Something to drink, sir?'

The hostess had bent forward to speak to him, showing plenty of cleavage.

'Coke,' he told her. 'Ice and lemon.' He pretended to watch her move away. Really, he was scoping the room. He'd sat in on the game quickly: walking around the room would have attracted everyone's interest, and he couldn't be sure if there'd be anyone here who'd know him.

He needn't have worried. The only person he recognised was Matsumoto, rubbing his hands as the croupier pushed chips towards him. Rebus stuck on eighteen. The dealer got twenty. Rebus had never been a great gambler. He'd tried the football pools, sometimes the horses, and now occasionally the lottery. But fruit machines didn't interest him; the poker sessions organised in the office didn't interest him. He had other ways of losing money.

Matsumoto lost and gave what sounded like a curse, a little bit louder than the room liked. The skinny security ape put his head around the door, but Matsumoto ignored him, and when Mr Skinny saw who was making the noise, he retreated fast. Matsumoto laughed: he might not have much English, but he knew he had power in this place. He told everyone something in a stream of Japanese, nodding, trying for eye contact. Then a hostess brought him a big tumbler of whisky and ice. He handed her a couple of chips as a tip. The croupier was telling everyone to place their bets. Matsumoto quietened down and went back to work.

Rebus's drink was a while coming, Coke the unlikely beverage of the high roller. He'd won a couple of hands, felt a bit better. Stood up to accept the drink. The table knew to leave him out of the next deal.

'Where are you from?' he asked the hostess. 'I can't place your accent.'

'I am from Ukraine.'

'You speak good English.'

'Thank you.' She turned away. Conversation was not house policy, it kept the punters away from their games. Ukraine: Rebus wondered if she was another of Tarawicz's imports. Like Candice ... A few things seemed clear to him. Matsumoto was comfortable here, therefore known. And the staff were wary of him, therefore he had clout, had Telford behind him. Telford wanted him kept sweet. It wasn't much return for all Rebus's work, but it was something.

Then someone walked in. Someone Rebus knew. Dr Colquhoun. He saw Rebus immediately and fear jumped into his face. Colquhoun: with his sick line to the university; his enforced holiday; no forwarding address. Colquhoun: who'd known Rebus was taking Candice to the Drinics.

Rebus watched him back towards the doors. Watched him turn and run.

Options: go after him, or stay with Matsumoto? Which was the more important to him now, Candice or Telford? Rebus stayed. But now Colquhoun was back in town, he'd track him down.

For definite.

After an hour and a quarter's play, he was considering cashing a cheque for more chips. Twenty quid down in a little over an hour, and Candice fighting for some space in his crowded head. He took a break, moved to a row of fruit machines, but the lights and buttons defeated him. He wasted three nudges and ran out of time on some accumulator. Another two quid gone – this time in a couple of minutes. Little wonder clubs and pubs wanted slot machines. Tommy Telford was in the right business. His hostess came to see him again, asked if he wanted another drink.

'I'm fine,' he said. 'Not much action tonight.'

'It's early,' she told him. 'Wait till after midnight ...'

No way was he sticking around that long. But Matsumoto surprised him, threw up his hands and came out with another rush of Japanese, nodding and grinning, gathering up his chips. He cashed them and left the casino. Rebus waited all of thirty seconds, then followed. He said a breezy goodnight to the security men, felt their eyes on him all the way back down the stairs.

Matsumoto was buttoning his coat, wrapping the scarf tight around his neck. He was headed back in the direction of the hotel. Rebus, suddenly bone-tired, stopped in his tracks. He was thinking of Sammy and Lintz and the Weasel, thinking of all the time he seemed to be wasting.

'Fuck this for a game of soldiers.'

Turned on his heels and went to collect his car. Ten Years After: 'Goin' Home'.

It was a twenty-minute walk to Flint Street, a lot of it uphill and with the wind doing nobody any favours. The city was quiet: people huddled at bus stops; students munching on baked potatoes, chips with curry sauce. A few souls marching home with the concentrated tread of the sozzled. Rebus stopped, frowned, looked around. This was where he'd left the Saab. He was positive ... no, not 'positive' – the word had taken on malign overtones. He was *sure*, yes, sure he'd left the Saab right here. Where now a black Ford Sierra was parked, and behind that a Mini. But no sign of Rebus's car.

'Aw, Christ,' he exploded. There were no signs of glass by the roadside, which meant they hadn't taken a brick to one of his windows. Oh, there'd be jokes in the office about this though, whether he got the car back or not. A taxi came along and he flagged it down, then remembered he'd no cash, so waved it off again.

His flat in Arden Street wasn't that far off, but had he been a camel, he'd have been keeping well clear of any straw.

20

He was asleep in his chair by the living-room window, duvet pulled up to his neck, when the buzzer sounded. He couldn't remember setting the alarm. Consciousness brought the dawning realisation that it was his door. He staggered to his feet, found his trousers and put them on.

'All right, all right,' he called, heading for the hall. 'Keep your hair on.'

He opened the door and saw Bill Pryde.

'Jesus, Bill, is this some sort of twisted revenge?' Rebus looked at his watch: two-fifteen.

'Afraid not, John,' Pryde said. His face and voice told Rebus something bad had happened.

Something very bad indeed.

'I've been off the booze for weeks.'

'Sure about that?'

'Definite.' Rebus's eyes burned into those of DCI Gill Templer. They were in her office at St Leonard's. Pryde was there, too. His jacket was off and his sleeves rolled up. Gill Templer looked bleary from interrupted sleep. Rebus was pacing what floor there was, unable to stay seated.

'I've had nothing to drink all day but coffee and Coke.'

'Really?'

Rebus ran his hands through his hair. He felt groggy, and his head was throbbing. But he couldn't ask for Paracetamol and water: they'd assume hangover.

'Come on, Gill,' he said, 'I'm being shafted here.'

'Who authorised your surveillance?'

'Nobody. I did it in my own time.'

'How do you work that out?'

'The Chief Super said I could take a bit of time off.'

'He meant so you could visit your daughter.' She paused. 'Is that what this was all about?'

'Maybe.'

'This Mr ...' she checked her notes '... Matsumoto, he was connected to Thomas Telford. And your theory is that Telford was behind the attack on your daughter?'

Rebus thumped the wall with his fists. 'It's a set-up, oldest trick in the book. I've yet to see one perfected. There's got to be something at the scene ... something out of kilter.' He turned to his colleagues. 'You've got to let me go there, take a look around.'

Templer looked to Bill Pryde. Pryde folded his arms, shrugged assent. But it was Templer's play, she was the senior officer here. She tapped her pen against her teeth, then dropped it on to the desk.

'Will you submit to a blood test?'

Rebus swallowed. 'Why not?' he said at last.

'Come on then,' she said, getting to her feet.

The story was: Matsumoto had been on his way back to his hotel. Crossing the road, he'd been hit by a car travelling at speed. The driver hadn't stopped, not right away. But the car had travelled only another couple of hundred yards before mounting the pavement with its front wheels. It had been abandoned there, driver's door open.

A Saab 900, its identity known to half the Lothian and Borders force.

The interior reeked of whisky, the screw-top from a bottle lying on the passenger seat. No sign of the bottle, no sign of the driver. Just the car, and two hundred yards further back, the body of the Japanese businessman, growing cold by the roadside.

Nobody had seen anything. Nobody had heard anything. Rebus could believe it: never one of the city centre's busier routes, at this hour the place was dead.

'When I followed him from his hotel, he didn't come this way,' Rebus told Templer. She stood with shoulders hunched, hands deep in her coat pockets, keeping out the cold.

'So?' she asked.

'Long way round for a short-cut.'

'Maybe he wanted to see the sights,' Pryde suggested.

'What time's this supposed to have happened?' Rebus asked.

Templer hesitated. 'There's a margin of error.'

'Look, Gill, I know this is awkward. You shouldn't have brought me here, you shouldn't answer my questions. I'm the number one suspect, after all.' Rebus knew how much she had to lose. Over two hundred male Chief Inspectors in Scotland; only *five* women. Bad odds, and a lot of people waiting for her to fail. He held up his hands. 'Look, if I was blind drunk and I hit somebody, think I'd leave the car at the scene?'

'You might not know you'd hit anyone. You hear a thunk, lose control and mount the kerb, and some survival instinct tells you it's time to get out and walk.'

'Only I hadn't been drinking. I left the car near Flint Street, and that's where they took it from. Any signs it was broken into?'

She didn't say anything.

'I'll guess not,' Rebus went on. 'Because professionals don't leave marks. But to get it started, they must have wired it or got into the steering column. That's what you should be looking for.'

The car had been towed. First thing in the morning, forensics would be all over it.

Rebus laughed, shaking his head. 'It's nice though, isn't it? First they make Sammy look like a hit and run, and now they try to pin me for the same thing.'

'Who's "they"?'

'Telford and his men.'

'I thought you said they were doing business with Matsumoto?'

'They're all gangsters, Gill. Gangsters fall out.'

'What about Cafferty?'

Rebus frowned. 'What about him?'

'He's got an old grudge against you. This way, he stitches you up *and* annoys Telford.'

'So you do think I'm being stitched up?'

'I'm giving you the benefit of the doubt.' She paused. 'Not everyone will. What was Matsumoto's business with Telford?'

'Something to do with a country club – on the surface at least. Some Japanese were buying it, and Telford was clearing the way.' He shivered: should have worn a coat over his jacket. He rubbed his arm where the blood sample had been taken to test his alcohol level. 'Of course, a check of the deceased's hotel room might throw up something.'

'We've already been there,' Pryde said. 'Nothing out of the ordinary.'

'Which deadbeat did you send?'

'I went myself,' Gill Templer said, voice as icy as the wind. Rebus bowed his head in apology. She had a point though: Matsumoto and Telford had been doing business. There had been nothing about their farewell to one another to suggest a break-up, and Matsumoto had seemed happy and confident at the casino. What had Telford to gain by bumping him off?

Apart from maybe getting Rebus off his back.

Templer had mentioned Cafferty: was Big Ger capable of such a move? What did *he* stand to gain? Apart from settling a long-held grudge against Rebus, giving Telford a headache, and maybe gaining Poyntinghame and the Japanese deal for himself.

Balance the two – Telford against Cafferty. Cafferty's side tipped, went clunk as it hit the ground.

'Let's get back to the station,' Templer said. 'I'm reaching the early stages of frostbite.'

'Can I go home then?'

'We're not done with you yet, John,' she said, getting into the car. 'Not by a long chalk.'

But eventually they had to let him go. He wasn't being charged, not yet. There was work still to be done. He knew they could make a case against him if they wanted to, knew it only too well. *He'd* followed Matsumoto out of the club. *He* was the one with the grudge against Telford. *He* was the one who'd see poetic justice in sending Telford a message by driving over one of his associates.

He, John Rebus, was firmly in the frame. It was tightly constructed and quite elegant in its way. The scales suddenly tipped back towards Telford again, so much subtler than Cafferty.

Telford.

Rebus visited Farlowe in his cell. The reporter wasn't asleep.

'How long do I have to stay here?' he asked.

'As long as possible.'

'How's Telford?'

'Minor burns. Don't expect him to press charges. He'll want you on the outside.'

'Then you'll have to let me go.'

'Don't bet on it, Ned. *We* can press charges. We don't need Telford.'

Farlowe looked at him. 'You're going to prosecute me?'

'I saw the whole thing. Unwarranted attack on an innocent man.'

Farlowe snorted, then smiled. 'Ironic, isn't it? Charging me for my own good.' He paused. 'I won't be able to see Sammy, will I?'

Rebus shook his head.

'I didn't think of that. Fact is, I didn't *think*.' He looked up from his ledge. 'I just did. And right up until the moment I did it, it felt ... brilliant.'

'And afterwards?'

Farlowe shrugged. 'What does afterwards matter? It's only the rest of my life.'

Rebus didn't go home, knew he wouldn't sleep. And he'd no car, so he couldn't go driving. Instead, he visited the hospital, sat down by Sammy's bedside. He took her hand, rested it against his face.

When a nurse came in and asked if he wanted anything, he asked if she'd any Paracetamol.

'In a hospital?' she said, smiling. 'I'll see what I can do.'

21

Rebus was due for further questioning at St Leonard's at ten o'clock, so when his pager sounded at eight-fifteen, he assumed it was a reminder. But the phone number it wanted him to call was the mortuary down in the Cowgate. He called from the hospital payphone, and was put through to Dr Curt.

'Looks like I've drawn the short straw,' Curt told him. 'You're about to start work on Matsumoto?'

'For my sins. Look, I've heard the stories ... don't suppose there's any truth in them?'

'I didn't kill him.'

'Glad to hear it, John.' Curt seemed to be struggling to say something. 'There are questions of ethics, of course, so I can't suggest that you come down here ...'

'There's something you think I should see?'

'That I can't say.' Curt cleared his throat. 'But if you happened to be here ... and the place is always very quiet this time of the morning ...'

'I'm on my way.'

The Infirmary to the mortuary: a ten-minute walk. Curt himself was waiting to lead Rebus to the body.

The room was all white tile, bright light and stainless steel. Two of the dissecting-tables lay empty. Matsumoto's naked body lay on the third. Rebus walked around it, stunned by what he saw.

Tattoos.

And not just the kilted piper on a sailor's arm. These

were works of art, and they were massive. A scaly green dragon, breathing pink and red fire, covered one shoulder and crept down the arm towards the wrist. Its back legs reached around the body's neck, while its front ones rested on the chest. There were other smaller dragons, and a landscape – Mount Fuji reflected in water. There were Japanese symbols and the visored face of a kendo champion. Curt put on rubber gloves, and had Rebus do the same. Then the two men rolled the body over, displaying a further gallery across Matsumoto's back. A masked actor, something out of a Noh play, and a warrior in full armour. Some delicate flowers. The effect was mesmerising.

'Stunning, aren't they?' Curt said.

'Phenomenal.'

'I've visited Japan a few times, given papers at conferences.'

'So you recognise some of these?'

'A few of the references, yes. Thing is, tattoos – especially on this scale – usually mean you're a gang member.'

'Like the Triads?'

'The Japanese are called Yakuza. Look here.' Curt held up the left hand. The pinkie had been severed at the first joint, the skin healed in a rough crust.

'That's what happens when they screw up, isn't it?' Rebus said, the word 'Yakuza' bouncing around in his head. 'Someone cuts off a finger every time.'

'I think so, yes,' Curt said. 'Just thought you might like to know.'

Rebus nodded, eyes glued to the corpse. 'Anything else?'

'Well, I haven't started on him yet, really. All looks fairly standard: evidence of impact with a moving vehicle. Crushed ribcage, fractures to the arms and legs.' Rebus noticed that a bone was protruding from one calf, obscenely white against the skin. 'There'll be a lot of internal damage.

Shock probably killed him.' Curt was thoughtful. 'I must let Professor Gates know. Doubt he'll have seen anything like it.'

'Can I use your phone?' Rebus asked.

He knew one person who might know about the Yakuza – she'd seemed knowledgeable about every other country's criminal gangs. So he spoke to Miriam Kenworthy in Newcastle.

'Tattoos and missing fingers?' she said.

'Bingo.'

'That's Yakuza.'

'Actually, it's only the top bit missing from one little finger. That's done to them when they step out of line, isn't it?'

'Not quite. They do it to *themselves* as a way of saying they're sorry. I'm not sure I know much more than that.' There was the sound of papers being shifted. 'I'm just looking for my notes.'

'What notes?'

'When I was connecting all these gangs, different cultures, I did some research. Might be something on the Yakuza … Look, can I call you back?'

'How long?'

'Five minutes.'

Rebus gave her Curt's number, then sat and waited. Curt's room wasn't so much an office as a walk-in cupboard. Files were stacked high on his desk, and a dictaphone lay on top of them, along with a fresh pack of tapes. The room reeked of cigarettes and bad ventilation. On the walls: schedules of meetings, postcards, a couple of framed prints. The place was a bolt-hole, a necessity; Curt spent most of his time elsewhere.

Rebus took out Colquhoun's business card, tried home

and office. As far as his secretary was concerned, Dr Colquhoun was still off sick.

Maybe, but he was well enough to visit a casino. One of Telford's casinos. No coincidence surely ...

Kenworthy was good as gold.

'Yakuza,' she said, sounding like she was lifting from her script. 'Ninety thousand members split into something like two and a half thousand groupings. Utterly ruthless, but also highly intelligent and sophisticated. Very hierarchical structure, almost impenetrable to outsiders. Like a secret society. They even have a sort of middle management level, called the Sokaiya.'

Rebus was writing it all down. 'How do you spell that?'

She told him. 'Back in Japan they run *pachinko* parlours – that's a sort of gaming thing – and have fingers in most other illegal pies.'

'Unless they've lopped them off. What about outside Japan?'

'Only thing I've got down here is that they ship expensive designer stuff back home to sell on the black market, also stolen art, ship it back to wealthy buyers ...'

'Wait a minute, you told me Jake Tarawicz started out smuggling icons out of Russia.'

'You're saying Pink Eyes might connect to the Yakuza?'

'Tommy Telford's been chauffeuring them around. There's a warehouse everyone seems interested in, plus a country club.'

'What's in the warehouse?'

'I don't know yet.'

'Maybe you should find out.'

'It's on my list. Something else, these *pachinko* parlours ... would those be like amusement arcades?'

'Pretty much.'

'Another connection with Telford: he puts gaming machines into half the pubs and clubs on the east coast.'

'You think the Yakuza saw someone they could do a deal with?'

'I don't know.' He tried stifling a yawn.

'Too early in the morning for big questions?'

He smiled. 'Something like that. Thanks for your help, Miriam.'

'No problem. Keep me posted.'

'Sure. Anything new on Tarawicz?'

'Nothing I've heard. No sign of Candice either, sorry.'

'Thanks again.'

''Bye.'

Curt was standing in the doorway. He'd stripped off gown and gloves, and his hands smelled of soap.

'Not much I can do till my assistants get in.' He looked at his watch. 'Fancy a spot of breakfast?'

'You have to appreciate how this looks, John. The media could be all over us. I can think of a few journalists who'd give their drinking-arm to nail you.'

Chief Superintendent Watson was in his element. Seated behind his desk, hands folded, he had the serenity of a large stone Buddha. The occasional crises with which John Rebus presented him had hardened the Farmer to life's lesser knocks and taught him calm acceptance.

'You're going to suspend me,' Rebus stated with conviction – he'd been here before. He finished the coffee his boss had given him, but kept his hands locked around the mug. 'Then you're going to open an investigation.'

'Not straight away,' Watson surprised him by saying. 'What I want first of all is your statement – and I mean a full and frank explanation – of your recent movements, your interest in Mr Matsumoto and Thomas Telford. Bring in anything you want about your daughter's accident, any suspicions you've had, and above all the *validity* of those suspicions. Telford already has a lawyer asking awkward questions about our Japanese friend's untimely end. The lawyer ...' Watson looked to Gill Templer, seated by the door, mouth a thin unimpressed line.

'Charles Groal,' she said flatly.

'Groal, yes. He's been asking at the casino. He got a description of a man who came in just after Matsumoto, and left immediately after him. He seems to think it's you.'

'Are you telling him otherwise?' Rebus asked.

'We're telling him nothing, not until our own inquiries have established ... et cetera. But I can't hold him off forever, John.'

'Have you asked anyone what Matsumoto was doing here?'

'He works for a firm of management consultants. He was here at a client's behest, finalising the takeover of a country club.'

'With Tommy Telford in tow.'

'John, let's not lose sight of ...'

'Matsumoto was a member of the Yakuza, sir. The closest I've come to one of those before has been on a TV screen. Now suddenly they're in Edinburgh.' Rebus paused. 'Don't you find that just a *wee* bit curious? I mean, doesn't it worry you at all? I don't know, maybe I'm getting my priorities all wrong, but it seems to me we're splashing about in puddles while a tidal wave's coming in!'

The pressure of his hands around the mug had been increasing by degrees. Now the thing broke, a piece falling to the floor as Rebus winced. He picked one ceramic shard out of his palm. Drops of blood hit the carpet. Gill Templer had come forward, was reaching for his hand.

'Here, let me.'

He spun away from her. 'No!' Way too loud. Fumbling in his pocket for a handkerchief.

'I've got some paper ones in my bag.'

'It's all right.' Blood dripping on to his shoes. Watson

244

was saying something about the mug having a crack; Templer was staring at him. He wrapped white cotton around the wound.

'I'll go wash it,' he said. 'With your permission, sir?'

'On you go, John. Sure you're all right?'

'I'll be fine.'

It wasn't a bad cut. Cold water helped. He dried off with paper towels, which he flushed down the toilet, waiting to see they'd gone. A first aid box next: half a dozen plasters, cover the nick good and proper. He bunched his fist, saw no sign of leakage. Had to be content with that.

Back at his desk, he started on his memoirs – as ordered by Watson. Gill Templer came past, decided he needed a few soft words.

'None of us thinks you did it, John. But something like this ... questions being asked by the Japanese consul ... it has to be done by the book.'

'It all comes down to politics in the end, eh?' He was thinking of Joseph Lintz.

At lunchtime he dropped in on Ned Farlowe, asked him if he needed anything. Farlowe wanted sandwiches, books, newspapers, company. He looked drawn, weary of imprisonment. Maybe soon he'd think to ask for a lawyer. A lawyer – any lawyer – would get him out.

Rebus handed his report to Watson's secretary and headed out of the station. He'd gone fifty yards when a car pulled up alongside. Range Rover. Pretty-Boy telling him to get in. Rebus looked into the back of the car.

Telford. Ointment on his blistered face. Looking like a scaled-down Jake Tarawicz ...

Rebus hesitated. The cop shop was a short sprint away.

'Get in,' Pretty-Boy repeated. Sucker for a free offer, Rebus got in.

Pretty-Boy turned the car. The giant yellow teddy had been strapped into the passenger seat.

'I don't suppose,' Rebus said, 'it's worth my while asking you to leave Ned Farlowe be?'

Telford's mind was on other things. 'He wants war, he's going to get war.'

'Who?'

'Your boss.'

'I don't work for Cafferty.'

'Don't give me that.'

'I'm the one who put him inside.'

'And you've been snuggling up ever since.'

'I didn't kill Matsumoto.'

Telford looked at him for the first time, and Rebus could see he was itching for violence.

'You know I didn't,' Rebus went on.

'What do you mean?'

'Because you did it, and you want me to –'

Telford's hands were around Rebus's neck. Rebus shrugged them off, tried pinning Telford down. Impossible with the car in motion, cramped in the back seat. Pretty-Boy stopped the car and got out, opened Rebus's door and dragged him on to the pavement. Telford followed, face beetroot-red, eyes bulging.

'You're not going to pin this on me!' he roared. Drivers slowed to watch. Pedestrians crossed the road to safety.

'Who else?' Rebus's voice was shaky.

'Cafferty!' Telford screeched. 'It's you and Cafferty, trying to shut me down!'

'I'm telling you, I didn't do it.'

'Boss,' Pretty-Boy was saying, 'let's screw the head, eh?' He was looking around, nervous of the attention they were attracting. Telford saw his point, let his shoulders relax a little.

'Get in the car,' he said to Rebus. Rebus just stared at

him. 'It's okay. Just get in. I want to show you a couple of things.'

Rebus, world's craziest cop, got back in.

There was silence for a couple of minutes, Telford rearranging the dressings on his fingers, which had come loose during the fight.

'I don't think Cafferty wants war,' Rebus said.

'What makes you so sure?'

Because I've done a deal with him – it's me who's going to shut you down. They were heading west. Rebus tried not to think about possible destinations.

'You were in the Army, weren't you?' Telford asked.

Rebus nodded.

'Paratroops, then the SAS.'

'I didn't get past training.' Rebus thinking: he's well-informed.

'So you decided to become a cop instead.' Telford was completely calm again. He'd brushed down his suit and checked the knot in his tie. 'Thing is, working for structures like those – Army, cops – you need to obey orders. I hear you're not very good at it. You wouldn't last long with me.' He looked out of the window. 'What's Cafferty planning?'

'No idea.'

'Why were you watching Matsumoto?'

'Because he tied into you.'

'Crime Squad pulled their surveillance.' Rebus said nothing. 'But you kept yours going.' Telford turned towards him. 'Why?'

'Because you tried to kill my daughter.'

Telford stared at him, unblinking. 'Is that what this is about?'

'It's why Ned Farlowe tried to blind you. He's her boyfriend.'

Telford choked out a disbelieving laugh, started to shake

his head. 'I'd nothing to do with your daughter. Where's the reason?'

'To get at me. Because she helped me with Candice.'

Telford was thoughtful. 'Okay,' he said, nodding, 'I can see your thinking, and I don't suppose my word's going to count for much, but for what it's worth, I know absolutely nothing about your daughter.' He paused. Rebus could hear sirens nearby. 'Is that what took you to Cafferty?'

Rebus said nothing, which seemed, to Telford's mind, to confirm his suspicions. He smiled again.

'Pull over,' Telford said. Pretty-Boy stopped the car. The road ahead was blocked anyway, police diverting traffic down side-streets. Rebus realised he'd been smelling smoke for some time. The tenements had hidden it from view, but now he could see the fire. It was in the lot where Cafferty kept his taxis. The shed used as an office had been reduced to ash. The garage behind, where the cabs were worked on and cleaned up, was about to lose its corrugated roof. A row of vehicles was burning nicely.

'We could have sold tickets,' Pretty-Boy said. Telford turned from the spectacle to Rebus.

'Fire Brigade's going to be stretched. Two of Cafferty's offices are spontaneously combusting ...' he checked his watch ... 'right about now, as is that beautiful house of his. Don't worry, we waited till his wife was out shopping. Final ultimatums have been delivered to his men – they can shuffle out of town or off this mortal coil.' He shrugged. 'Makes no odds to me. Go tell Cafferty: he's finished in Edinburgh.'

Rebus licked his lips. 'You've just said I'm wrong about you, that you had nothing to do with my daughter. What if *you're* wrong about Cafferty?'

'Wake up, will you? The stabbing at Megan's, then Danny Simpson ... Cafferty's not exactly subtle.'

'Did Danny say it was Cafferty's men?'

'He knows, same as I do.' Telford tapped Pretty-Boy's shoulder. 'Back to base.' To Rebus: 'Another little message for you to take to Barlinnie. Here's what I told Cafferty's men – any of them left in this city after midnight are fair game ... and I don't take prisoners.' He sniffed, seemed pleased with himself, settled back in the seat. 'You won't mind if I drop you at Flint Street? Only I've a business meeting in fifteen minutes.'

'With Matsumoto's bosses?'

'If they want Poyntinghame, they'll keep dealing with me.' He looked at Rebus. 'You should deal with me, too. Think about this: who'd want you pissed off with me? It comes back to Cafferty: hitting your daughter, setting up Matsumoto ... It *all* comes back to Cafferty. Think it over, then maybe we should talk again.'

After a couple of minutes, Rebus broke the silence.

'You know a man called Joseph Lintz?'

'Bobby Hogan mentioned him.'

'He phoned your office in Flint Street.'

Telford shrugged. 'I'll tell you what I told Hogan. Maybe it was a wrong number. Whatever it was, *I* didn't speak to any old Nazi.'

'You're not the only one uses that office though.' Rebus saw Pretty-Boy watching him in the rearview mirror. 'What about you?'

'Never heard of the cat.'

A car was parked in Flint Street – a huge white limousine with blackened windows. There was a TV aerial on the boot, and the hubcaps were painted pink.

'Christ,' Telford said in amusement, 'look at his latest toy.' He seemed to have forgotten all about Rebus. He was out of the car and loping towards the man who was emerging from the back of the limo. White suit, panama hat, big cigar, and a bright red paisley shirt. None of which stopped you staring at the scarred face and blue-tinted glasses. Telford was commenting on the attire, the car, the audacity, and Mr Pink Eyes was loving it. He put a hand around Telford's shoulder, steering him towards the amusement arcade. But then he stopped, clicked his fingers, turned back to the limo and reached out a hand.

And now a woman was emerging. Short black dress and black tights, fur jacket keeping out the chills. Tarawicz rubbed a hand over her backside; Telford kissed her on the neck. She smiled, eyes slightly glazed. Then Tarawicz and Telford turned towards the Range Rover. They were both staring at Rebus.

'Trip's over, Inspector,' Pretty-Boy said, telling Rebus it was time to get out. He did so, his eyes on Candice. But she wasn't looking at him. She was snuggling into Mr Pink Eyes, head on his chest. He was still rubbing her backside, the dress rising and falling. He was watching Rebus, eyes alight, face pulled into a latex grin. Rebus walked over to them, and now Candice saw him, and looked frightened.

'Inspector,' Tarawicz said, 'good to see you again. Come to whisk the damsel away to safety?'

Rebus ignored him. 'Come on, Candice.' His hand, not quite steady, held out towards her.

She looked at him and shook her head. 'Why would I want that?' she said, and was rewarded with another kiss from Tarawicz.

'You were abducted. You can press charges.'

Tarawicz was laughing, leading her into the café.

'Candice.' Rebus reached for her arm, but she pulled away and followed her master inside.

Two of Telford's men were blocking the door. Pretty-Boy was behind Rebus.

'No cheap heroics?' he asked, making to pass the policeman.

Back at St Leonard's, Rebus took Farlowe his food and

newspapers, then hitched a lift in a patrol car to Torphichen. The man he wanted was DI 'Shug' Davidson, and Davidson was in the CID office, looking frazzled.

'Somebody torched a taxi rank,' he told Rebus.

'Any idea who?'

Davidson's eyes narrowed. 'The rank was owned by Jock Scallow. Is there something you're trying to tell me?'

'Who really owned the outfit, Shug?'

'You know damned well.'

'And who's muscling in on Cafferty's patch?'

'I've heard rumours.'

Rebus rested against Davidson's desk. 'Tommy Telford's going into combat, unless we can stop him.'

' "We"?'

'I want you to take me somewhere,' Rebus said.

Shug Davidson was happily married to an understanding wife, and had kids who didn't see as much of him as they deserved. A year back, he'd won forty grand on the Lottery. Everyone in his station got a drink. The rest of the money had been salted away.

Rebus had worked with him before. He wasn't a bad cop, maybe lacking a little in imagination. They had to work their way around the scene of the fire. A further mile and a half on, Rebus told him to stop.

'What is it?' Davidson asked.

'That's what I want you to tell me.' Rebus was looking towards the brick building, the same one which so interested Tommy Telford.

'It's Maclean's,' Davidson said.

'And what's Maclean's when it's at home?'

Davidson smiled. 'You really don't know?' He opened his car door. 'Come on, I'll show you.'

They had to have their identities checked at the main entrance. Rebus noticed a lot of security, albeit subtle:

cameras trained down from the corners of the building, catching every angle of approach. A phone call was made, and a man in a white coat came down to sign them in. They pinned visitor's badges to their jackets, and the tour began.

'I've been here before,' Davidson confided. 'If you ask me, it's the best kept secret in the city.'

They climbed steps, walked down passageways. Everywhere there was security: guards checked their badges; doors had to be unlocked; cameras charted their progress. Which puzzled Rebus, for it was such an unassuming building, really. And nothing spectacular was happening.

'What is it, Fort Knox?' he asked. But then their guide handed them white coats to put on, before pushing open the door to a laboratory, and Rebus started to understand.

People were working with chemicals, examining testtubes, writing notes. There were all sorts of weird and wonderful machines, but in essence it was a school chemistry-lab on a slightly grander scale.

'Welcome,' Davidson said, 'to the world's biggest drugs factory.'

Which wasn't quite correct, for Maclean's was only the world's largest *legal* producer of heroin and cocaine, something the guide explained.

'We're licensed by the government. Back in 1961 there was an international agreement: every country in the world was allowed just one producer, and we're it for Britain.'

'So what do you make?' Rebus was staring at the rows of locked fridges.

'All sorts of things: methadone for heroin addicts, pethedine for women in labour. Diamorphine to ease terminal illnesses and cocaine for use in medical procedures. The company started out supplying laudanum to the Victorians.'

'And these days?'

'We produce about seventy tonnes of opiates a year,' the

guide said. 'And around two million pounds' worth of pure cocaine.'

Rebus rubbed his forehead. 'I begin to see the need for security.'

The guide smiled. 'The MoD has asked us for advice – that's how good our security is.'

'No break-ins?'

'A couple of attempts, nothing we couldn't deal with.'

No, Rebus thought, but then you've never had to deal with Tommy Telford and the Yakuza ... not yet.

Rebus walked around the lab, smiled and nodded at a woman who just seemed to be standing there, not doing anything.

'Who's she?' he asked the guide.

'Our nurse. She's on stand-by.'

'What for?'

The guide nodded towards where a man was operating one of the machines. 'Etorphine,' he said. 'Forty thousand pounds a kilo, and extremely potent. The nurse has the antidote, just in case.'

'So what's it used for, this etorphine?'

'Knocking out rhinos,' the guide said, like the answer should have been obvious.

The cocaine was produced from coca leaves flown in from Peru. The opium came from plantations in Tasmania and Australia. The pure heroin and cocaine were kept in a strongroom. Each lab had its share of locked safes. The storage warehouse boasted infrared detectors and move-ment sensors. Five minutes in the place told Rebus *exactly* why Tommy Telford was interested in Maclean's. And he'd brought the Yakuza in on the plan either because he needed their help – which was unlikely – or to brag about the exploit.

Back at the car, Davidson asked the obvious question. 'What's this all about, John?'

Rebus pinched the bridge of his nose. 'I think Telford's planning to hit this place.'

Davidson snorted. 'He'd never get in. Like you said yourself, it's Fort bloody Knox.'

'It's a prestige thing, Shug. If he can empty the place, it'll make his name. He'll have beaten Cafferty hands down.' It was the same with the fire-bombings: they weren't just a message to Cafferty, but a sort of 'red carpet' for Mr Pink Eyes – welcome to Edinburgh, and look what I can do.

'I'm telling you,' Davidson said, 'there's no way in. Christ, that's cheap!' Davidson's attention had been diverted by signs on the window of the corner shop. Rebus looked, too. Cut-price cigarettes. Cheap sandwiches and hot rolls. Plus five pence off any morning paper.

'Competition around here must be crippling,' Davidson said. 'Fancy a roll?'

Rebus was watching workers leaving the gates of Maclean's. Afternoon break maybe. Saw them cross the road, dodging traffic. Counting small change from their pockets as they pushed open the door to the shop.

'Yes,' Rebus said quietly, 'why not?'

The small shop was packed out. Davidson got in the queue, while Rebus looked at the rack of papers and magazines. The workers were sharing jokes and gossip. Two staff worked behind the counter – young males, mixing banter with less-than-efficient service.

'What do you fancy, John? Bacon?'

'Fine,' Rebus said. Remembered he hadn't had lunch. 'Make it two.'

Two bacon rolls came in at one pound exactly. They sat in the car to eat.

'You know, Shug, the usual ploy with a shop like that is to take a beating on one or two necessities to get the punters in.' Davidson nodded, attacked his roll. 'But that place looked like Bargain City.' Rebus had stopped eating. 'Do us both a favour: find out the shop's history, who owns it, who those two are behind the counter.'

Davidson's chewing slowed. 'You think ... ?'

'Just check it out, all right?'

22

Back at St Leonard's, his telephone was ringing. He sat down and prised the lid from a beaker of coffee. On the drive back he'd been thinking about Candice. Two swigs of coffee and he lifted the receiver.

'DI Rebus,' he said.

'What the fuck is that little shite up to?' The voice of Big Ger Cafferty.

'Where are you?'

'Where do you think I am?'

'Sounds like a mobile.'

'Amazing the things that find their way into Barlinnie. Now tell me, what is happening over there?'

'You've heard then.'

'He torched my house! My *house*! Am I supposed to let him get away with that?'

'Look, I think I may have found a way to get to him.'

Cafferty calmed a little. 'Tell me?'

'Not yet, I want to –'

'And all my taxis,' Cafferty exploded again. 'The little bastard!'

'Look, the point is: what's he expecting you to do? He's waiting for instant retaliation.'

'And he's going to get it.'

'He'll be ready. Wouldn't it be better to catch him off-guard?'

'That little bastard hasn't been off-guard since he was lifted from the cradle.'

'Shall I tell you why he did it?'

Cafferty's anger ebbed again. 'Why?'

'Because he says you killed Matsumoto.'

'Who?'

'A business acquaintance. Whoever did it made it look like I was behind the wheel.'

'It wasn't me.'

'Try telling Telford that. He thinks you ordered me to do it.'

'We know differently.'

'That's right. *We* know someone was setting me up, trying to get me out of the way.'

'What was his name again, the dead one?'

'Matsumoto.'

'Is that Japanese?'

Rebus wished he could see Cafferty's eyes. Even then, it was hard to tell when the man was playing games.

'He was Japanese,' Rebus stated.

'What the hell did he have to do with Telford?'

'Sounds to me like your intelligence has gone to pot.'

There was silence on the line. 'About your daughter ...'

Rebus froze. 'What about her?'

'A secondhand shop in Porty.' Meaning Portobello. 'The owner bought some stuff from a seller. Including opera tapes and Roy Orbison. Stuck in his mind. They don't naturally go together.'

Rebus's hand tightened on the receiver. 'Which shop? What did the seller look like?'

Cold laughter. 'We're working on it, Strawman, just leave everything to us. Now, about this Japanese fellow ...?'

'I said *I'd* put Telford out of the game. That was the agreement.'

'I've yet to see any action.'

'I'm working on it!'

'I want to hear about him anyway.'

Rebus paused.

'How is Samantha anyway?' Cafferty asked. 'That's her name, isn't it?'

'She's ...'

'Because it looks like I'll be fulfilling *my* side of our bargain any day. While you, on the other hand ...'

'Matsumoto was Yakuza: heard of them?'

A moment's silence. 'I've heard of them.'

'Telford's helping them buy a country club.'

'What in God's name do they want with that?'

'I'm not sure.'

Cafferty was silent again. Rebus almost thought his mobile had died. Then: 'He's got big ideas, hasn't he?' Like there was just a touch of respect there, battling the sense of territorial breach.

'We've both seen people overreach themselves.' An idea formed in Rebus's mind, a sudden notion of where everything was headed.

'Looks like Telford's got plenty of stretch left in him though,' Cafferty was saying. 'And me, I'm not even halfway through *my* stretch.'

'Know something, Cafferty? Every time you start to sound beaten, that's when I know you're just coming to the boil.'

'You know I'm going to have to retaliate, whether I want to or not. A little ritual we have to go through, like shaking hands.'

'How many men have you got?'

'More than enough.'

'Listen, one last thing ...' Rebus couldn't believe he was telling his arch-enemy this. 'Jake Tarawicz arrived here today. I think the fireworks were meant to impress him.'

'Telford torched my house just so he'd have something to show that ugly Russian bastard?'

Like a kid showing off to his elders, Rebus was thinking. Overreaching himself ...

'That's it, Strawman!' Cafferty was back to being furious. 'All bets are off. Those two want to get dirty with Morris Gerald Cafferty, I'll give them both anthrax. I'll infect the pair of them. They'll think they've caught full-blown fucking AIDS by the time I'm finished!'

Which was about as much as Rebus could take. He put down the phone, drank his cold coffee, checked his messages. Patience wondered if he could make it to supper. Rhona said they'd carried out another scan. Bobby Hogan wanted a word.

He called the hospital first. Rhona said something about a new scan to assess the amount of damage done to the brain.

'Then why the hell didn't they give her *that* scan straight away?'

'I don't know.'

'Did you ask?'

'Why don't *you* come down here? Why don't *you* ask? Seems like when I'm not here, you're happy enough spending time with Samantha, even sleeping in the chair. What is it – do I scare you off?'

'Look, Rhona, I'm sorry. It's been a rough day.'

'For you and everyone else.'

'I know. I'm a selfish bastard.'

The rest of their conversation was predictable. It was a relief to say goodbye. He tried Patience, got her answering machine, and told it he'd be happy to accept the invitation. Then he called Bobby Hogan.

'Hiya, Bobby, what've you got?'

'Not much. I had a word with Telford.'

'I know, he told me.'

'You've been speaking to him?'

'Says he never knew Lintz. Did you talk to The Family?'

'The ones who frequent the office. Same story.'

'Did you mention the five thou'?'

'Think I'm stupid? Listen, I thought you might be able to help me.'

'Fire away.'

'Lintz's address book, I found a couple of addresses for a Dr Colquhoun. Thought at first it must be his GP.'

'He's a Slavic Studies lecturer.'

'Only Lintz seems to have been keeping track of him. Three changes of address, going back twenty years. First two addresses have phone numbers with them, but not the most recent. I checked, and Colquhoun's only been at this latest address three years.'

'So?'

'So Lintz didn't have his home phone number. So if he wanted to speak to him …'

Rebus twigged. 'He'd phone the university.' The call on Lintz's bill: twenty-odd minutes. Rebus was remembering what Colquhoun had said about Lintz.

I met him at a few social functions … our departments weren't that close … As I say, we weren't close …

'They weren't in the same department,' Rebus said. 'Colquhoun told me they'd barely met …'

'So how come Lintz has been keeping up with Colquhoun's various moves around the city?'

'Beats me, Bobby. Have you asked him?'

'No, but I intend to.'

'He's lying low. I've been trying to talk to him for a week.' Last seen at the Morvena: did Colquhoun link Telford to Lintz?

'Well, he's back now.'

'What?'

'I've an appointment with him at his office.'

'Count me in,' Rebus said, getting to his feet.

*

As Rebus parked in Buccleuch Place – he was in an unmarked Astra, courtesy of St Leonard's – he saw the car in the neighbouring bay make to leave. He waved, but Kirstin Mede didn't see him, and by the time he'd found the horn, she'd pulled away. He wondered how well she knew Colquhoun. After all, she'd been the one to suggest him as a translator ...

Hogan, standing by the railings, had seen Rebus's attempts at communication.

'Someone you know?'

'Kirstin Mede.'

Hogan placed the name. 'The one who did those translations?'

Rebus looked up at the Slavic Studies building. 'Have you tracked down David Levy?'

'Daughter still hasn't heard from him.'

'How long has that been?'

'Long enough to seem suspicious in itself, only she doesn't seem too bothered.'

'How do you want to play this?' Rebus asked.

'Depends what he's like.'

'You ask your questions. Me, I just want to be there.'

Hogan looked at him, then shrugged and pushed open the door. They started to climb the worn stone steps. 'Hope they haven't put him in the penthouse.'

Colquhoun's name was on a piece of card stuck to a door on the second floor. They pushed it open, and were confronted with a short hallway and another five or six doors. Colquhoun's office was first on the right, and he was already standing in the doorway.

'Thought I heard you. Sound carries in this place. Come in, come in.' He wasn't expecting Hogan to have company. His words dried up when he saw Rebus. He walked back into his office, motioned for both officers to sit, then fussed about moving their chairs around so they'd be facing his desk.

'Terrible muddle,' he said, kicking over a pile of books.

'Know the feeling, sir,' Hogan said.

Colquhoun peered in Rebus's direction. 'My secretary says you used the library.'

'Filling in some of the gaps, sir.' Rebus kept his voice level.

'Yes, Candice ...' Colquhoun was thoughtful. 'Is she ... ? I mean, did she ... ?'

'But today, sir,' Hogan interrupted, 'we want to talk to you about Joseph Lintz.'

Colquhoun sat down heavily in his wooden chair, which creaked under the weight. Then he sprang to his feet again. 'Tea, coffee? You must excuse the mess. Not normally this disorganised ...'

'Not for us, sir,' Hogan said. 'If you'd just take a seat?'

'Of course, of course.' Again, Colquhoun collapsed on to his chair.

'Joseph Lintz, sir,' Hogan prompted.

'Terrible tragedy ... terrible. They think it's murder, you know.'

'Yes, sir, we do know.'

'Of course you do. Apologies.'

The desk in front of Colquhoun was venerable and spotted with woodworm. The shelves were bowed under the weight of textbooks. There were old framed prints on the walls, and a blackboard with the single word CHARACTER on it. University paperwork was piled on the window ledge, all but blacking out the bottom two panes. The smell in the room was that of intellect gone awry.

'It's just that Mr Lintz had your name in his address book, sir,' Hogan continued. 'And we're talking to all his friends.'

'Friends?' Colquhoun looked up. 'I wouldn't call us

"friends" exactly. We were colleagues, but I don't think I met him socially more than three or four times in twenty-odd years.'

'Funny, he seems to have taken an interest in you, sir.' Hogan flipped open his notebook. 'Starting with your address in Warrender Park Terrace.'

'I haven't lived there since the seventies.'

'He also has your telephone number there. After that, it's Currie.'

'I thought I was ready for the rural life ...'

'In Currie?' Hogan sounded sceptical.

Colquhoun tipped his head. 'I eventually realised my mistake.'

'And moved to Duddingston.'

'Not at first. I rented a few properties while I was looking for a place to buy.'

'Mr Lintz has your telephone number in Currie, but not for the Duddingston address.'

'Interesting. I went ex-directory when I moved.'

'Any reason for that, sir?'

Colquhoun swayed in his chair. 'Well, I'm sure it sounds awful ...'

'Try us.'

'I didn't want students bothering me.'

'Did they do that?'

'Oh, yes, phoning to ask questions, advice. Worried about exams or wanting deadlines extended.'

'Do you remember giving Mr Lintz your address, sir?'

'No, I don't.'

'You're sure of that?'

'Yes, but it wouldn't have been hard for him to find out. I mean, he could just have asked one of the secretaries.'

Colquhoun was beginning to look more agitated than ever. The little chair could barely contain him.

'Sir,' Hogan said, 'is there anything you want to tell us about Mr Lintz, anything at all?'

Colquhoun just shook his head, staring at the surface of his desk.

Rebus decided to use their joker. 'Mr Lintz made a phone call to this office. He was talking for over twenty minutes.'

'That's ... simply not true.' Colquhoun mopped his face with a handkerchief. 'Look, gentlemen, I'd like to help, but the fact is, I barely knew Joseph Lintz.'

'And he didn't phone you?'

'No.'

'And you've no idea why he'd keep note of your Edinburgh addresses for the past three decades?'

'No.'

Hogan sighed theatrically. 'Then we're wasting your time and ours.' He got to his feet. 'Thank you, Dr Colquhoun.'

The look of relief on the old academic's face told both detectives all they needed to know.

They said nothing as they walked back downstairs -- like Colquhoun had said, sound could travel. Hogan's car was nearest. They rested against it as they talked.

'He was worried,' Rebus said.

'Hiding something. Think we should go back up?'

Rebus shook his head. 'Let him sweat for a day or so, then hit him.'

'He didn't like the fact you were there.'

'I noticed.'

'That restaurant ... Lintz dining with an elderly gent.'

'We could tell him we've got a description from the restaurant staff.'

'Without going into specifics?'

Rebus nodded. 'See if it flushes him out.'

'What about the other person Lintz took to lunch, the young woman?'

'No idea.'

'Posh restaurant, old man, young woman ...'

'A call girl?'

Hogan smiled. 'Do they still call them that?'

Rebus was thoughtful. 'It might explain the phone call to Telford. Only I doubt Telford's daft enough to discuss business like that from his office. Besides, his escort agency runs from another address.'

'Fact is, he called Telford's office.'

'And nobody's owned up to talking to him.'

'Escort agency stuff, could be very innocent. He doesn't want to eat alone, hires some company. Afterwards, a peck on the cheek and separate taxis.' Hogan exhaled. 'This one's running in circles.'

'I know the feeling, Bobby.'

They looked up at the second-floor windows. Saw Colquhoun staring down, handkerchief to his face.

'Let's leave him to it,' Hogan said, unlocking his car.

'I've been meaning to ask: how did you get on with Abernethy?'

'He didn't give me too much trouble.' Hogan avoided Rebus's eyes.

'So he's gone?'

Hogan had disappeared into the driver's seat. 'He's gone. See you, John.'

Leaving Rebus on the pavement, a frown on his face. He waited till Hogan's car had turned the corner, then went back into the stairwell and climbed the steps again.

Colquhoun's office door was open, the old man fidgeting behind his desk. Rebus sat down opposite him, said nothing.

'I've been ill,' Colquhoun said.

'You've been hiding.' Colquhoun started shaking his

head. 'You told them where to find Candice.' Head still shaking. 'Then you got worried, so they hid you away, maybe in a room at the casino.' Rebus paused. 'How am I doing?'

'I've no comment to make,' Colquhoun snapped.

'What if I just keep talking then?'

'I want you to leave now. If you don't go, I'll have to call my lawyer.'

'Name of Charles Groal?' Rebus smiled. 'They might have spent the last few days tutoring you, but they can't change what you've done.' Rebus stood up. '*You* sent Candice back to them. *You* did that.' He leaned down over the desk. 'You knew all along who she was, didn't you? That's why you were so nervous. How come you knew who she was, Dr Colquhoun? How come you're so chummy with a turd like Tommy Telford?'

Colquhoun picked up the receiver, his hands shaking so badly he kept missing the digits.

'Don't bother,' Rebus said. 'I'm going. But we'll talk again. And you *will* talk. You'll talk because you're a coward, Dr Colquhoun. And cowards always talk eventually ...'

266

23

The Crime Squad office at Fettes: home of country and western; Claverhouse terminating a phone call. No sign of Ormiston and Clarke.

'They're out on a call,' Claverhouse said.

'Any progress on that stabbing?'

'What do you think?'

'I think there's something you should know.' Rebus seated himself behind Siobhan Clarke's desk, admiring its tidy surface. He opened a drawer: it was tidy, too. Compartments, he thought to himself. Clarke was very good at dividing her life into separate compartments. 'Jake Tarawicz is in town. He's got this outrageous white limo, hard to miss.' Rebus paused. 'And he's brought Candice with him.'

'What's he doing here?'

'I think he's here for the show.'

'What show?'

'Cafferty and Telford, fifteen rounds of bare-knuckle and no referee.' Rebus leaned forward, arms on the desk. 'And I've got an idea where it's headed.'

Rebus went home, called Patience and told her he might be late.

'How late?' she asked.

'How late can I be without us falling out?'

She thought about it. 'Half-nine.'

'I'll be there.'

He checked his answering machine: David Levy, saying he could be reached at home.

'Where the hell have you been?' Rebus asked, when Levy's daughter had put her father on.

'I had business elsewhere.'

'You know your daughter's been worried. You might have phoned her.'

'Does this counselling service come free?'

'My fee cancels out when you answer a few questions. You know Lintz is dead?'

'I've heard.'

'Where were you when you *heard*?'

'I've told you, I had business ... Inspector, am I a suspect?'

'Practically the only one we've got.'

Levy gave a harsh laugh. 'This is preposterous. I'm not a ...' He couldn't say the word. Rebus guessed his daughter was within hearing distance. 'Hold on a moment, please.' The receiver was muffled: Levy ordering his daughter out of the room. He came back on, voice lower than before.

'Inspector, for the record, I feel I must let you know how *angry* I felt when I heard the news. Justice may have been done or not done – I can't argue those points just now – but what is absolutely certain is that history has been cheated here!'

'Of the trial?'

'Of course! And the Rat Line, too. With each suspect who dies, we're that much less likely to prove its existence. Lintz isn't the first, you know. One man, the brakes failed on his car. Another fell from an upstairs window. There've been two apparent suicides, six more cases of what look like natural causes.'

'Am I going to get the full conspiracy theory?'

'This isn't a joke, Inspector.'

'Did you hear me laughing? What about you, Mr Levy? When did you leave Edinburgh?'

'Before Lintz died.'

'Did you see him?' Rebus knowing he had, but seeking a lie.

Levy paused. '*Confronted* would be a more apposite term.'

'Just the once?'

'Three times. He wasn't keen to talk about himself, but I stated my case nonetheless.'

'And the phone call?'

Levy paused. 'What phone call?'

'When he called you at the Roxburghe.'

'I wish I'd recorded it for posterity. Rage, Inspector. Foul-mouthed rage. I'm positive he was mad.'

'Mad?'

'You didn't hear him. He's very good at seeming perfectly normal – he must be, or he wouldn't have gone undetected for so long. But the man is ... was ... mad. Truly mad.'

Rebus was remembering the crooked little man in the cemetery, and how he'd suddenly let fly at a passing dog. Poise, to rage, to poise again.

'The story he told ...' Levy sighed.

'Was this in the restaurant?'

'What restaurant?'

'Sorry, I thought the two of you went out to lunch.'

'I can assure you we didn't.'

'So what story is this then?'

'These men, Inspector, they come to justify their actions by blanking them out, or by transference. Transference is the more common.'

'They tell themselves someone else did it?'

'Yes.'

'And that was Lintz's story?'

'Less believable than most. He said it was all a case of mistaken identity.'

'And who did he think you were mistaking him for?'
'A colleague at the university ... a Dr Colquhoun.'

Rebus called Hogan, gave him the story.
'I told Levy you'd want to speak to him.'
'I'll phone him right now.'
'What do you think?'
'Colquhoun a war criminal?' Hogan snorted.
'Me, too,' Rebus said. 'I asked Levy why he didn't think any of this worth telling us.'
'And?'
'He said as he gave it no credence, it was worthless.'
'All the same, we'd better talk to Colquhoun again. Tonight.'
'I've other plans for tonight, Bobby.'
'Fair enough, John. Look, I really appreciate all your help.'
'You're going to talk to him alone?'
'I'll have someone with me.'
Rebus hated being left out. If he cancelled that late supper ...
'Let me know how you get on.' Rebus put the telephone down. On the hi-fi: Eddie Harris, upbeat and melodic. He went and soaked in a bath, facecloth across his eyes. Everyone, it seemed to him, lived their lives out of little boxes, opening different ones for different occasions. Nobody ever gave their whole self away. Cops were like that, each box a safety mechanism. Most people you met in the course of your life, you never even learned their names. Everybody was boxed off from everybody else. It was called society.
He was wondering about Joseph Lintz, always question-ing, turning every conversation into a philosophy lesson. Stuck in his own little box, identity blocked off elsewhere, his past a necessary mystery ... Joseph Lintz, furious when

cornered, possibly clinically mad, driven there by … what? Memories? Or the lack of them? Driven there by other people?

The Eddie Harris CD was on its last track by the time he emerged from the bathroom. He put on the clothes he'd be wearing to Patience's. Only he had a couple of stops to make first: check on Sammy at the hospital, and then a meeting at Torphichen.

'The gang's all here,' he said, walking into the CID room.

Shug Davidson, Claverhouse, Ormiston, and Siobhan Clarke, all seated around the one big desk, drinking coffee from identical Rangers mugs. Rebus pulled a chair over.

'Have you filled them in, Shug?'

Davidson nodded.

'What about the shop?'

'I was just getting to that.' Davidson picked up a pen, played with it. 'The last owner went out of business, not enough passing trade. The shop was shut the best part of a year, then suddenly reopened – under new management and with prices that stopped the locals looking elsewhere.'

'And got the workers at Maclean's interested, too,' Rebus added. 'So how long's it been going?'

'Five weeks, selling cut-price everything.'

'No profit motive, you see.' Rebus looked around the table. This was mostly for the benefit of Ormiston and Clarke; he'd given Claverhouse the story already.

'And the owners?' Clarke asked.

'Well, the shop's *run* by a couple of lads called Declan Delaney and Ken Wilkinson. Guess where they come from?'

'Paisley,' Claverhouse said, keen to hurry things on.

'So they're part of Telford's gang?' Ormiston asked.

'Not in so many words, but they're connected to him, no doubt about that.' Davidson blew his nose loudly. 'Of course, Dec and Ken are running the shop, but they don't own it.'

'Telford does,' Rebus stated.

'Okay,' Claverhouse said. 'So we've got Telford owning a loss-making business, in the hope of gathering intelligence.'

'I think it goes further than that,' Rebus said. 'I mean, listening in on gossip is one thing, but I don't suppose any of the workers are standing around talking about the various security systems and how to beat them. Dec and Ken are garrulous, perfect for the job Telford's given them. But it's going to look suspicious if they start asking too many questions.'

'So what's Telford looking for?' Ormiston asked. Siobhan Clarke turned to him.

'A mole,' she said.

'Makes sense,' Davidson went on. 'That place *is* well-protected, but not impregnable. We all know any break-in's going to be a lot easier with someone on the inside.'

'So what do we do?' Clarke asked.

'We fight Telford's sting with our own,' Rebus explained. 'He wants a man on the inside, *we* give him one.'

'I'm seeing the head of Maclean's later on tonight,' Davidson said.

'I'll come with you,' Claverhouse said, keen not to be left out.

'So we put someone of our own inside the factory.' Clarke was working it out for herself. 'And they shoot their mouth off in the shop, making them an attractive proposition. And we sit and pray that Telford approaches *them* rather than anyone else?'

'The less luck we have to rely on the better,' Claverhouse said. 'Got to do this right.'

'Which is why we work it like this.' Rebus said. 'There's a bookie called Marty Jones. He owes me one big favour.

Say our man's just been into Telford's shop. As he's coming out, a car pulls up. Marty and a couple of his men. Marty wants some bets paid off. Big argy-bargy, and a punch in the guts as warning.'

Clarke could see it. 'He stumbles back into the shop, sits down to catch his breath. Dec and Ken ask him what's going on.'

'And he gives them the whole sorry story: gambling debts, broken marriage, whatever.'

'To make him more attractive still,' Davidson said, 'we make him a security guard.'

Ormiston looked at him. 'You think Maclean's will go for it?'

'We'll persuade them,' Claverhouse said quietly.

'More importantly,' Clarke asked, 'will *Telford* go for it?'

'Depends how desperate he is,' Rebus answered.

'A man on the inside ...' Ormiston's eyes were alight. 'Working for Telford – it's what we've always wanted.'

Claverhouse nodded. 'Just one thing.' He looked at Rebus and Davidson. 'Who's it going to be? Telford knows us.'

'We get someone from outside,' Rebus said. 'Someone I've worked with before. Telford won't have heard of him. He's a good man.'

'Is he willing?'

There was silence around the table.

'Depends who's asking,' a voice called from the doorway. A stocky man with thick, well-groomed hair and narrow eyes. Rebus got up, shook Jack Morton's hand, made the introductions.

'I'll need a history,' Morton said, all business. 'John's explained the deal, and I like it. But I'll need a flat, something scruffy and local.'

'First thing tomorrow,' Claverhouse said. 'Look, we need to talk to our bosses about this, make sure it's cleared.'

He looked at Morton. 'What did you tell your own boss, Jack?'

'I've got a few days off, didn't think it was worth mentioning.'

Claverhouse nodded. 'I'll talk to him as soon as we get the go–ahead.'

'We need that go–ahead *tonight*,' Rebus said. 'Telford's men may already have lined someone up. If we hang around, we might lose it.'

'Agreed,' Claverhouse said, checking his watch. 'I'll make a few phone calls, interrupt a few post-prandial whiskies.'

'I'll back you up if need be,' Davidson said.

Rebus looked at Jack Morton – his friend – and mouthed the word 'thanks'. Morton shrugged it off. Then Rebus got to his feet.

'I'm going to have to leave you to it,' he told the assembly. 'You've got my pager number and mobile if you need me.'

He was halfway down the hall when Siobhan Clarke caught him.

'I just wanted to say thanks.'

Rebus blinked. 'What for?'

'Ever since you got Claverhouse excited, the tape machine's stayed off.'

24

Supper was fine. He talked to Patience about Sammy, Rhona, his obsession with sixties music, his ignorance of fashion. She talked about work, an experimental cookery class she'd been taking, a trip to Orkney she was thinking of. They ate fresh pasta with a homemade mussel and prawn sauce, and shared a bottle of Highland Spring. Rebus tried his damnedest to forget about the sting operation, Tarawicz, Candice, Lintz ... She could see at least half his mind was elsewhere; tried not to feel betrayed. She asked him if he was going home.

'Is that an invitation?'

'I'm not sure ... I suppose so.'

'Let's pretend it wasn't, then I won't feel like complete scum when I turn it down.'

'That sounds reasonable. Things on your mind?'

'I'm surprised you can't see them leaking out of my ears.'

'Do you want to talk about any of it? I mean, you may not have noticed, but we've talked about practically everything tonight except *us*.'

'I don't think talking would help.'

'But bottling it up does?' She threw out an arm. 'Behold the Scottish male, at his happiest when in denial.'

'What am I denying?'

'For a start, you're denying *me* access to your life.'

'Sorry.'

'Christ, John, get the word put on a t-shirt.'

'Thanks, maybe I will.' He got up from the sofa.

'Oh, hell, I'm sorry.' She smiled. 'Look, you've got me at it now.'

'Yes, it's catching, all right.'

She stood up, touched his arm. 'You're worried about taking the test?'

'Right now, believe it or not, that's the least of my worries.'

'It should be. Everything's going to be fine.'

'Hunky dory.'

'Hunky dory,' she repeated, smiling again. She pecked him on the cheek. 'You know, I've never quite understood what that meant.'

'*Hunky Dory*?'

She nodded.

'It's a David Bowie album.' He kissed her brow.

He would never know what instinct made him decide on the detour, but he was glad he'd made it. For there, parked outside the Morvena casino, stood the white stretch limo. The driver leaned against it, smoking a cigarette, looking bored. From time to time he took out a mobile phone and had a short conversation. Rebus stared at the Morvena, thinking: Tommy Telford has a slice of the place; the hostesses come from Eastern Europe, provided by Mr Pink Eyes. Rebus wondered how closely entwined the two empires – Telford's and Tarawicz's – really were. And add a third strand: the Yakuza. Something refused to add up.

What was Tarawicz getting out of it?

Miriam Kenworthy had suggested muscle: Scottish hardmen trained in Telford's organisation then shipped south. But it wasn't *enough* of a trade. There had to be more. Was Mr Pink Eyes due a share of the Maclean's pay-out? Was Telford tempting him with some Yakuza action? What about the theory that Telford was Tarawicz's supplier?

At quarter to midnight, another phone call had the driver springing into action. He flicked his cigarette on to the road, started opening doors. Tarawicz and his entourage breezed out of the casino looking like they owned the world. Candice was wearing a black full-length coat over a shimmering pink dress which didn't quite reach her knees. She was carrying a bottle of champagne. Rebus counted three of Tarawicz's men, remembering them from the scrapyard. Two no-shows: the lawyer, and the Crab. Telford was there, too, with a couple of minders, one of them Pretty-Boy. Pretty-Boy was making sure his jacket hung right, trying to decide whether it would look better buttoned. But his eyes raked the darkened street. Rebus had parked away from the street-lights, confident he was invisible. They were piling into the limo. Rebus watched it move off, waited until it had signalled and turned a corner before switching on his own headlamps and starting the engine.

They drove to the same hotel Matsumoto had stayed at. Telford's Range Rover was parked outside. Pedestrians – late-night couples hurrying home from the pub – turned to stare at the limo. Saw the entourage spill out, probably mistook them for pop stars or film people. Rebus as casting director: Candice's starlet being mauled by sleazy producer Tarawicz. Telford a sleek young operator on his way up, looking to learn from the producer before toppling him. The others were bit players, except maybe Pretty-Boy, who was hanging on to his boss's coattails, maybe readying himself for his own big break ...

If Tarawicz had a suite, there might be room for them all. If not, they'd be in the bar. Rebus parked, followed them inside.

The lights hurt his eyes. The reception area was all mirrors and pine, brass and pot-plants. He tried to look like he'd been left behind by the party. They were settling down in the bar, through a double set of swing-doors with glass panels. Rebus hung back. Sitting target in the empty reception; bigger target in the bar. Retreat to the car? Someone was standing up, shrugging off a long black coat. Candice. Smiling now, saying something to Tarawicz, who was nodding. Took her hand and planted a kiss in the palm. Went further: a slow lick across the palm and up her wrist. Everyone laughing, whistling. Candice looking numb. Tarawicz got to the inside of her elbow and took a bite. She squealed, pulled back, rubbed her arm. Tarawicz had his tongue out, playing to the gallery. Give Tommy Telford credit: he wasn't grinning along with everyone else.

Candice stood there, a stooge to her owner's little act. Then he waved her off with a flick of his hand. Permission granted, she started for the doors. Rebus moved back into a recess where the public telephones sat. She turned right out of the doors, disappeared into the ladies'. At the table, they were busy ordering more champagne – and an orange juice for Pretty-Boy.

Rebus looked around, took a deep breath. Walked into the ladies' toilets like it was the most natural thing in the world.

She was splashing her face with water. A little brown bottle sat next to the sink. Three yellow tablets lying ready. Rebus swept them on to the floor.

'Hey!' She turned, saw him, put a hand to her mouth. She tried backing away, but there was nowhere to go.

'Is this what you want, Karina?' Using her real name as a weapon: friendly fire.

She frowned, shook her head: incomprehension on her face. He grabbed her shoulders, squeezed.

'Sammy,' he hissed. 'Sammy's in hospital. Very ill.' He pointed towards the hotel bar. '*They* tried to kill her.'

The gist got through. Candice shook her head. Tears were smudging her mascara.

'Did you tell Sammy anything?'

She frowned again.

'Anything about Telford or Tarawicz? Did you talk to Sammy about them?'

A slow, determined shake of the head. 'Sammy ... hospital?'

He nodded. Turned his hands into a steering-wheel, made engine noises, then slammed a fist into his open palm. Candice turned away, grabbed the sink. She was crying, shoulders jerking. She scrabbled for more tablets. Rebus tore them from her hand.

'You want to blank it all out? Forget it.' He threw them on to the floor, crushed them under his heel. She crouched down, licked a finger and dabbed at the powder. Rebus hauled her to her feet. Her knees wouldn't lock; he had to keep holding her upright. She wouldn't look him in the eyes.

'It's funny, we first met in a toilet, remember? You were scared. You hated your life so much you'd slashed your arms.' He touched her scarred wrists. 'That's how much you hated your life. And now you're straight back in it.'

Her face was against his jacket, tears dropping on to his shirt.

'Remember the Japanese?' he cooed. 'Remember Juniper Green, the golf club?'

She drew back, wiped her nose on her bare wrist. 'Juniper Green,' she said.

'That's right. And a big factory ... the car stopped, and everyone looked at the factory.'

She was nodding.

'Did anyone talk about it? Did they say *anything*?'

She was shaking her head. 'John ...' Her hands on his lapels. She sniffed, swiped at her nose again. She slid down his jacket, his shirt. She was on her knees, looking up at him, blinking tears, while her damp fingers scored white powder from the tiles. Rebus crouched down in front of her.

'Come with me,' he said. 'I'll help you.' He pointed towards the door, towards the world outside, but she was busy in her own world now, fingers going to her mouth. Someone pushed open the door. Rebus looked up.

A woman: young, drunk, hair falling into her eyes. She stopped and studied the two people on the floor, then smiled and headed for a cubicle.

'Save some for me,' she said, sliding the lock.

'Go, John.' There was powder at the corners of Candice's mouth. A tiny piece of tablet had lodged between her front two teeth. 'Please, go now.'

'I don't want you getting hurt.' He sought her hands, squeezed them.

'I do not hurt any more.'

She got to her feet and turned from him. Checked her face in the mirror, wiped away the powder and dabbed at her mascara. Blew her nose and took a deep breath.

Walked out of the toilets.

Rebus waited a moment, time enough for her to reach the table. Then he opened the door and made his exit. Walked back to his car on legs that seemed to belong to someone else.

Drove home, not quite crying.

But not quite not.

25

Four in the morning, the blessed telephone pulled him out of a nightmare.

Prison-camp prostitutes with teeth filed to points were kneeling in front of him. Jake Tarawicz, in full SS regalia, held him from behind, telling him resistance was useless. Through the barred window, Rebus could see black berets – the *maquis*, busy freeing the camp but leaving his billet till last. Alarm bells ringing, everything telling him that salvation was at hand ...

... alarm becoming his telephone ... he staggered from his chair, picked it up.

'Yes.'

'John?' The Chief Super's voice: Aberdonian, instantly recognisable.

'Yes, sir?'

'We've got a spot of bother. Get down here.'

'What kind of bother?'

'I'll tell you when you get here. Now *shift*.'

Night shift, to be precise. The city asleep. St Leonard's was lit up, the tenements around it dark. No sign of the Farmer's 'spot of bother'. The Chief Super's office: the Farmer in conference with Gill Templer.

'Sit down, John. Coffee?'

'No, thanks, sir.'

While Templer and the Chief Super were deciding who should speak, Rebus helped them out.

'Tommy Telford's businesses have been hit.'

Templer blinked. 'Telepathy?'

'Cafferty's offices and taxis got firebombed. So did his house.' Rebus shrugged. 'We knew there'd be payback.'

'Did we?'

What could he say? *I did, because Cafferty told me.* He didn't think they'd like that. 'I just put two and two together.'

The Farmer poured himself a mug of coffee. 'So now we've got open war.'

'What got hit?'

'The arcade on Flint Street,' Templer said. 'Not too much damage: the place has a sprinkler system.' She smiled: an amusement arcade with a sprinkler system ... not that Telford was careful or anything.

'Plus a couple of nightclubs,' the Farmer added. 'And a casino.'

'Which one?'

The Chief Super looked to Templer, who answered: 'The Morvena.'

'Any injuries?'

'The manager and a couple of friends: concussion and bruising.'

'Which they got ...?'

'Falling over each other as they ran down the stairs.'

Rebus nodded. 'Funny how some people have trouble with stairs.' He sat back. 'So what does all this have to do with me? Don't tell me: having disposed of Telford's Japanese partner, I decided to take up fire-raising?'

'John ...' The Farmer got up, rested his backside against the desk. 'The three of us, we know you had nothing to do with that. Tell me, we found an untouched half-bottle of malt under your driver's seat ...'

Rebus nodded. 'It's mine.' Another of his little suicide bombs.

'So why would you be drinking a supermarket blend?'

'Is that what the screw-top was? The cheap bastards.'

'No alcohol in your blood either. Meantime, as you say, Cafferty's in the frame for this. And Cafferty and you ...'

'You want me to talk to him?'

Gill Templer leaned forward in her chair. 'We don't want war.'

'Takes two to make a ceasefire.'

'I'll talk to Telford,' she said.

'He's a sharp little bugger, watch out for him.'

She nodded. 'Will you talk to Cafferty?'

Rebus didn't want a war. It would take Telford's mind off the Maclean's heist. He'd need all the troops he could get; the shop might even have to close. No, Rebus didn't want a war.

'I'll talk to him,' he said.

Breakfast-time at Barlinnie.

Rebus jangling after the drive, knowing a whisky would smooth out his nerve-endings. Cafferty waiting for him, same room as before.

'Top of the morning, Strawman.' Arms folded, looking pleased with himself.

'You've had a busy night.'

'On the contrary, I slept as well as I ever have done in this place. What about you?'

'I was up at four o'clock, checking damage reports. I could have done without driving all the way here. Maybe if you gave me the number of your mobile ...?'

Cafferty grinned. 'I hear the nightclubs were gutted.'

'I think your boys are making themselves look good.'

Cafferty's grin tightened. 'Telford's premises seem to have state of the art fire prevention. Smoke sensors, sprinklers, fire-doors. The damage was minimal.'

'This is just the start,' Cafferty said. 'I'll have that little arse-wipe.'

'I thought that was supposed to be *my* job?'

'I've seen precious little from you, Strawman.'

'I've got something in the pipeline. If it comes off, you'll like it.'

Cafferty's eyes narrowed. 'Give me details. Make me believe you.'

But Rebus was shaking his head. 'Sometimes, you just have to have faith.' He paused. 'Deal?'

'I must have missed something.'

Rebus spelled it out. 'Back off. Leave Telford to me.'

'We've been through this. He hits me and I do nothing, I look like something you'd step around on the pavement.'

'We're talking to him, warning him off.'

'And meantime I'm supposed to trust you to get the job done?'

'We shook hands on it.'

Cafferty snorted. 'I've shaken hands with a lot of bastards.'

'And now you've met an exception to the rule.'

'You're an exception to a lot of rules, Strawman.' Cafferty looked thoughtful. 'The casino, the clubs, the arcade ... they weren't badly hit?'

'My guess is the sprinklers will have done as much damage as anything.'

Cafferty's jaw hardened. 'Makes me look even more of a mug.'

Rebus sat in silence, waiting for him to finish whatever chess-game was being played inside his head.

'Okay,' the gangster said at last, 'I'll call off the troops. Maybe it's time to do some recruiting anyway.' He looked up at Rebus. 'Time for some fresh blood.'

Which reminded Rebus of another job he'd been putting off.

*

Danny Simpson lived at home with his mother in a terraced house in Wester Hailes.

This bleak housing-scheme, designed by sadists who'd never had to live anywhere near it, had a heart which had shrivelled but refused to stop pumping. Rebus had a lot of respect for the place. Tommy Smith had grown up here, practising with socks stuffed into the mouth of his sax, so as not to disturb the neighbours through the thin walls of the high-rise. Tommy Smith was one of the best sax players Rebus had ever heard.

In a sense, Wester Hailes existed outside the real world: it wasn't on a route from anywhere to anywhere. Rebus had never had cause to drive *through* it -- he only went there if he had business there. The city bypass flew past it, offering many drivers their only encounter with Wester Hailes. They saw: high-rise blocks, terraces, tracts of unused playing field. They didn't see: people. Not so much concrete jungle as concrete vacuum.

Rebus knocked on Danny Simpson's door. He didn't know what he was going to say to the young man. He just wanted to see him again. He wanted to see him without the blood and the pain. Wanted to see him whole and of a piece.

Wanted to see him.

But Danny Simpson wasn't in, and neither was his mother. A neighbour, lacking her top set of dentures, came out and explained the situation.

The situation took Rebus to the Infirmary, where, in a small, gloomy ward not easily found, Danny Simpson lay in bed, head bandaged, sweating like he'd just played a full ninety minutes. He wasn't conscious. His mother sat beside him, stroking his wrist. A nurse explained to Rebus that a hospice would be the best place for Danny, supposing they could find him a bed.

'What happened?'

'We think infection must have set in. When you lose your resistance ... the world's a lethal place.' She shrugged, looked like she'd been through it all once too often. Danny's mother had seen them talking. Maybe she thought Rebus was a doctor. She got up and came towards him, then just stood there, waiting for him to speak.

'I came to see Danny,' he said.

'Yes?'

'The night he ... the night of his accident, I was the one who brought him here. I just wondered how he was doing.'

'See for yourself.' Her voice was breaking.

Rebus thought: a five-minute walk from here, he'd be in Sammy's room. He'd thought her situation unique, because it was unique to *him*. Now he saw that within a short radius of Sammy's bed, other parents were crying, and squeezing their children's hands, and asking why.

'I'm really sorry,' he said. 'I wish ...'

'Me, too,' the woman said. 'You know, he's never been a bad laddie. Cheeky, but never bad. His problem was, he was always itching for something new, something to stop him getting bored. We all know where that can lead.'

Rebus nodded, suddenly not wanting to be here, not wanting to hear Danny Simpson's life story. He had enough ghosts to contend with as it was. He squeezed the woman's arm.

'Look,' he said, 'I'm sorry, but I have to go.'

She nodded distractedly, wandered off in the direction of her son's bed. Rebus wanted to curse Danny Simpson for the mere *possibility* that he'd passed on the virus. He realised now that if they'd met on the doorstep, that's the way their conversation would have gone, and maybe Rebus would have gone further.

He wanted to curse him ... but he couldn't. It would be every bit as efficacious as cursing the Big Man. A waste of time and breath. So instead he went to Sammy's room, to find that she was back on her own. No other patients, no nursing staff, no Rhona. He kissed her forehead. It tasted salty. Sweat: she needed wiping down. There was a smell he hadn't noticed before. Talcum powder. He sat down, took her warm hands in his.

'How are you doing, Sammy? I keep meaning to bring in some Oasis, see if that would bring you round. Your mum sits here listening to classical. I wonder if you can hear it. I don't even know if you like that sort of stuff. Lots of things we've never got round to talking about.'

He saw something. Stood up to be sure. Movement behind her eyelids.

'Sammy? Sammy?'

He hadn't seen her do that before. Pushed the button beside her bed. Waited for a nurse to come. Pushed it again.

'Come on, come on.'

Eyelids fluttering ... then stopping.

'Sammy!'

Door opening, nurse coming in.

'What is it?'

Rebus: 'I thought I saw ... she was moving.'

'Moving?'

'Just her eyes, like she was trying to open them.'

'I'll fetch a doctor.'

'Come on, Sammy, try again. Wakey-wakey, sweetheart.' Patting her wrists, then her cheeks.

The doctor arrived. He was the same one Rebus had shouted at that first day. Lifted her eyelids, shone a thin torch into them, pulling it away, checking her pupils.

'If you saw it, I'm sure it was there.'

'Yes, but does it mean anything?'

'Hard to say.'

'Try anyway.' Eyes boring into the doctor's.

'She's asleep. She has dreams. Sometimes when you dream you experience REM: Rapid Eye Movement.'

'So it could be ...' Rebus sought the word '... involuntary?'

'As I say, it's hard to tell. Latest scans show definite improvement.' He paused. '*Minor* improvement, but certainly there.'

Rebus nodding, trembling. The doctor saw it, asked if he needed anything. Rebus shaking his head. The doctor checking his watch, other places to be. The nurse shuffling her feet. Rebus thanked them both and headed out.

HOGAN: You agree to this interview being taped, Dr Colquhoun?

COLQUHOUN: I've no objections.

HOGAN: It's in your interests as well as ours.

COLQUHOUN: I've nothing to hide, Inspector Hogan. (*Coughs.*)

HOGAN: Fine, sir. Maybe we'll just start then?

COLQUHOUN: Might I ask a question? Just for the record, you want to ask me about Joseph Lintz – nothing else?

HOGAN: What else might there be, sir?

COLQUHOUN: I just wanted to check.

HOGAN: You wish to have a solicitor present?

COLQUHOUN: No.

HOGAN: Right you are, sir. Well, if I can begin ... it's really just a question of your relationship with Professor Joseph Lintz.

COLQUHOUN: Yes.

HOGAN: Only, when we spoke before, you said you didn't know Professor Lintz.

COLQUHOUN: I think I said I didn't know him very well.

HOGAN: Okay, sir. If that's what you said ...

COLQUHOUN: It is, to the best of my recollection.

HOGAN: Only, we've had some new information ...

COLQUHOUN: Yes?

HOGAN: That you knew Professor Lintz a little better than that.

COLQUHOUN: And this is according to …?

HOGAN: New information in our possession. The informant tells us that Joseph Lintz accused you of being a war criminal. Anything to say to that, sir?

COLQUHOUN: Only that it's a lie. An outrageous lie.

HOGAN: He didn't think you were a war criminal?

COLQUHOUN: Oh, he thought it all right! He told me to my face on more than one occasion.

HOGAN: When?

COLQUHOUN: Years back. He got it into his head … the man was mad, Inspector. I could see that. Driven by demons.

HOGAN: What did he say exactly?

COLQUHOUN: Hard to remember. This was a long time ago, the early 1970s, I suppose.

HOGAN: It would help us if you could …

COLQUHOUN: He came out with it in the middle of a party. I believe it was some function to welcome a visiting professor. Anyway, Joseph insisted on taking me to one side. He looked feverish. Then he came out with it: I was some sort of Nazi, and I'd come to this country by some circuitous route. He kept on about it.

HOGAN: What did you do?

COLQUHOUN: Told him he was drunk, babbling.

HOGAN: And?

COLQUHOUN: And he was. Had to be taken home in a taxi. I said no more about it. In academic circles, one becomes used to a certain amount of … eccentric behaviour. We're obsessive people, it can't be helped.

HOGAN: But Lintz persisted?

COLQUHOUN: Not really, no. But every few years … there'd … he'd say something, allege some atrocity …

HOGAN: Did he approach you outside the university?

COLQUHOUN: For a time, he telephoned my home.

HOGAN: You moved?

COLQUHOUN: Yes.

HOGAN: To an unlisted phone number?

COLQUHOUN: Eventually.

HOGAN: To stop him calling you?

COLQUHOUN: I suppose that was part of it.

HOGAN: Did you speak to anyone about Lintz?

COLQUHOUN: You mean the authorities? No, no one. He was a nuisance, nothing more.

HOGAN: And then what happened?

COLQUHOUN: Then these stories started appearing in the papers, saying Joseph might be a Nazi, a war criminal. And suddenly he was on my back again.

HOGAN: He phoned you at your office?

COLQUHOUN: Yes.

HOGAN: You lied to us about that?

COLQUHOUN: I'm sorry. I panicked.

HOGAN: What was there to panic about?

COLQUHOUN: Just ... I don't know.

HOGAN: So you met him? To straighten things out?

COLQUHOUN: We had lunch together. He seemed ... lucid. Only what he was saying, it was the stuff of madness. He had a whole history mapped out, only it wasn't mine. I kept saying to him, 'Joseph, when the war ended I wasn't out of my teens.' Besides, I was born and raised here. It's all on record.

HOGAN: What did he say to that?

COLQUHOUN: He said records could be faked.

HOGAN: Faked records ... one way Josef Linzstek could have gone undetected.

COLQUHOUN: I know.

HOGAN: You think Joseph Lintz was Josef Linzstek?

COLQUHOUN: I don't know. Maybe the stories got to him ... he started to believe ... I don't know.

HOGAN: Yes, but these accusations, they began before the media circus – decades before.

COLQUHOUN: That's true.

HOGAN: So he was hounding you. Did he say he would go to the media with his version of events?

COLQUHOUN: He may have ... I can't remember.

HOGAN: Mmm.

COLQUHOUN: You're looking for a motive, aren't you? You're looking for reasons why I'd want him dead.

HOGAN: Did you kill him, Dr Colquhoun?

COLQUHOUN: Emphatically not.

HOGAN: Any idea who did?

COLQUHOUN: No.

HOGAN: Why didn't you tell us? Why tell lies?

COLQUHOUN: Because I knew this would happen. These suspicions. Stupidly, I thought I could circumvent them.

HOGAN: Circumvent?

COLQUHOUN: Yes.

HOGAN: A young woman was seen dining with Lintz, same restaurant he took you to. Any idea who she might be?

COLQUHOUN: None.

HOGAN: You knew Professor Lintz a long time ... what did you think were his sexual proclivities?

COLQUHOUN: Never thought about it.

HOGAN: No?

COLQUHOUN: No.

HOGAN: What about yourself, sir?

COLQUHOUN: I don't see what that ... well, for the record, Inspector, I'm monogamous and heterosexual.

HOGAN: Thank you, sir. I appreciate your frankness.

Rebus switched off the tape.

'I'll bet you did.'

'What do you think?' Bobby Hogan asked.

'I think you mistimed the did–you–do–it. Otherwise, not bad.' Rebus tapped the tape machine. 'Is there much more?'

'Not a lot.'

Rebus switched it back on.

HOGAN: When you met in the restaurant, it was the same routine as before?

COLQUHOUN: Oh, yes. Names, dates ... countries I was taken through on my way into Britain from the continent.

HOGAN: He told you how this was achieved?

COLQUHOUN: He called it the Rat Line. Said it was operated by the Vatican, if you can believe that. And all the western governments were in cahoots to get the top Nazis – the scientists and intellectuals – away from the Russians. I mean, really ... it's Ian Fleming meets John Le Carré, isn't it?

HOGAN: But he was very detailed?

COLQUHOUN: Yes, but it can be that way with obsessives.

HOGAN: There have been books written alleging the same thing Professor Lintz was talking about.

COLQUHOUN: Have there?

HOGAN: Nazis smuggled overseas ... war criminals rescued from the gallows.

COLQUHOUN: Well, yes, but those are just stories. You don't seriously think ...?

HOGAN: I'm just collecting information, Dr Colquhoun. In my job, we don't throw anything away.

COLQUHOUN: Yes, I can see that. The problem is, sorting out the wheat from the chaff.

HOGAN: You mean the truths from the lies? Yes, that's one problem.

COLQUHOUN: I mean, the stories you hear about Bosnia

and Croatia ... slaughterhouses, mass torture, the guilty being spirited away ... It's hard to know what's *true*.

HOGAN: Just before we finish ... any idea what happened to the money?

COLQUHOUN: What money?

HOGAN: The withdrawal Lintz made from his bank. Five thousand pounds in cash.

COLQUHOUN: This is the first I've heard of it. Another motive?

HOGAN: Thank you for your time, Dr Colquhoun. It might be necessary for us to talk again. I'm sorry, but you shouldn't have lied to us, it makes our job that much more difficult.

COLQUHOUN: I'm sorry, Inspector Hogan. I quite understand, but I hope you can comprehend why I did it.

HOGAN: My mum always told me never to lie, sir. Thanks again for your time.

Rebus looked at Hogan. 'Your mum?'

Hogan shrugged. 'Maybe it was my granny.'

Rebus drained his coffee. 'So we know one of Lintz's mealtime companions.'

'And we know he was hounding Colquhoun.'

'Is he a suspect?'

'I'm not exactly snowed under with them.'

'Fair point, but all the same ...'

'You think he's on the level?'

'I don't know, Bobby. He sounded like he had it rehearsed. And he was relieved at the end.'

'You don't think I got it all? I could bring him in again.'

Rebus was thinking: *stories you hear ... the guilty being spirited away*. Not stories you *read*, but ones you *hear* ... Who might he have heard them from? Candice? Jake Tarawicz?

Hogan rubbed the bridge of his nose. 'I need a drink.'

Rebus dropped his beaker into a waste-bin. 'Message received and understood. By the way, any word from Abernethy?'

'He's a bloody nuisance,' Hogan said, turning away.

26

'He's in place,' Claverhouse said, when Rebus phoned him to ask about Jack Morton. 'Got him a little one-bedroom shit-hole in Polwarth. Measured him up for his uniform, and he's now officially a member of on-site security.'

'Is anyone else in on it?'

'Just the big boss. His name's Livingstone. We had a long session with him last night.'

'Won't the other security men find it a bit odd, a stranger arriving in their midst?'

'It's down to Jack to put them at ease. He was pretty confident.'

'What's his cover?'

'Secret drinker, open gambler, busted marriage.'

'He doesn't drink.'

'Yes, he told me. Doesn't matter, so long as everyone *thinks* he does.'

'Is he in character?'

'Getting there. He's going to be working double shifts. That way he makes more trips to the shop, some in the evening when the place is quieter. More chance to get to know Ken and Dec. We've no contact with him during the day. Debriefing takes place once he's reached home. Telephone only, can't risk too many meetings.'

'You think they'll watch him?'

'If they're being thorough. And *if* they fall for the plan.'

'Did you talk to Marty Jones?'

'That's set for tomorrow. He'll bring a couple of heavies, but they'll go easy on Jack.'

'Isn't tomorrow a bit soon?'

'Can we afford to wait? They might already have someone in mind.'

'We're asking a lot of him.'

'He was *your* idea.'

'I know.'

'You don't think he's up to it?'

'It's not that ... but he's stepping into a war.'

'Then get the ceasefire sorted out.'

'It is.'

'That's not what I hear ...'

Rebus heard it too, as soon as he got off the phone. He knocked on the Chief Super's door. The Farmer was in conference with Gill Templer.

'Did you talk to him?' the Farmer asked.

'He agreed to a ceasefire,' Rebus said. He was looking at Templer. 'What about you?'

She took a deep breath. 'I spoke to Mr Telford – his solicitor was present throughout. I kept telling him what we wanted, and the lawyer kept telling me I was blackening his client's name.'

'And Telford?'

'Just sat there, arms folded, smiling at the wall.' Colour was creeping up her face. 'I don't think he looked at me once.'

'But you gave him the message?'

'Yes.'

'You said Cafferty would comply?'

She nodded.

'Then what the hell's happening?'

'We can't let it get out of control,' the Farmer said.

'Looks to me like it already is.'

The latest score-line: two of Cafferty's men, their faces mashed to something resembling fruit-pulp.

'Lucky they're not dead,' the Farmer went on.

'You know what's happening?' Rebus said. 'It's Tarawicz, *he's* the problem. Tommy's playing up to him.'

'It's times like this you yearn for independence,' the Farmer agreed. 'Then we could just extradite the bugger.'

'Why don't we?' Rebus suggested. 'Tell him his presence here is no longer acceptable.'

'And if he stays?'

'We shadow him, make sure everyone knows we're doing it. We make *nuisances* of ourselves.'

'You think that would work?' Gill Templer sounded sceptical.

'Probably not,' Rebus agreed, slumping into a chair.

'We've no real leverage,' the Farmer said, glancing at his watch. 'Which isn't going to please the Chief Constable. He wants me in his office in half an hour.' He got on the phone, ordered a car, rose to his feet.

'Look, see if you can thrash something out between you.'

Rebus and Templer exchanged a look.

'I'll be back in an hour or two.' The Farmer looked around, as if he were suddenly lost. 'Lock the door when you leave.' With that and a wave of his hand, he left. There was silence in the room.

'Has to keep his office locked,' Rebus said, 'to stop people stealing the secret of his terrible coffee.'

'Actually, it's been getting better recently.'

'Maybe your taste buds are being corroded. So, Chief Inspector ...' Rebus turned his chair to face hers. 'What about thrashing it out then, eh?'

She smiled. 'He thinks he's losing it.'

'Is he in for a bollocking?'

'Probably.'

'So it's down to us to come to the rescue?'

'I don't really see us as the Dynamic Duo, do you?'

'No.'

'Then there's always that part of you that says, let them tear each other apart. So long as no civilians get caught in the crossfire.'

Rebus thought of Sammy, of Candice. 'Thing is,' he said, 'they always do.'

She looked at him. 'How are you doing?'

'Same as ever.'

'As bad as that?'

'It's my calling.'

'You're done with Lintz though?'

Rebus shook his head. 'There's half a chance he ties in to Telford.'

'You still think Telford was behind the hit-and-run?'

'Telford or Cafferty.'

'Cafferty?'

'Setting up Telford, the way someone tried to set *me* up for Matsumoto.'

'You know you're not out of the woods?'

He looked at her. 'An internal inquiry? The men with rubber soles?' She nodded. 'Bring them on.' He sat forward in his chair, rubbed his temples. 'No reason they should be left out of the party.'

'What party?'

'The one inside my head. The party that never stops.' Rebus leaned across the desk to answer the phone. 'No, he's not here. Can I take a message? This is DI Rebus.' A pause; he was looking at Gill Templer. 'Yes, I'm working that case.' He found pen and paper, started writing. 'Mmm, I see. Yes, sounds like. I'll let him know when he gets back.' Eyes *boring into* hers. Then the punchline: 'How many did you say were dead?'

Just the one. Another fled the scene, holding his arm, all

but severed from the shoulder. He turned up at a local hospital later, needing surgery and a huge transfusion of blood.

In broad daylight. Not in Edinburgh, but Paisley. Telford's hometown, the town he still ruled. Four men, dressed in council work jackets, like a road team. But in place of picks and shovels, they'd toted machetes and a large-calibre revolver. They'd chased two men into a housing scheme. Kids playing on tricycles; kicking a ball up the street. Women hanging out of their windows. And grown men itching to hurt one another. A machete swung overhead, coming down hard. The wounded man kept running. His friend tried hurdling a fence, wasn't agile enough. Three inches higher and he'd have made it. As it was, his toe caught, and he fell. He was pushing himself back up when the barrel of the gun touched the back of his head. Two shots, a fine drizzle of blood and brain. The children not playing any more, the women screaming for them to run. But something had been satisfied by those two shots. The chase was over. The four men turned and jogged back down the street, towards a waiting van.

A public execution, in Tommy Telford's heartland.

The two victims: known money-lenders. The one in hospital was called 'Wee' Stevie Murray, age twenty-two. The one in the mortuary was Donny Draper – known since childhood as 'Curtains'. They'd be making jokes about that. Curtains was two weeks shy of his twenty-fifth birthday. Rebus hoped he'd made the most of his short time on the planet.

Paisley police knew about Telford's move to Edinburgh, knew there were some problems there. A courtesy call had been placed to Chief Superintendent Watson.

The caller said: the men were two of Telford's brightest and best.

The caller said: descriptions of the attackers were vague.

The caller said: the children weren't talking. They were being shielded by their parents, fearful of reprisals. Well, they might not be talking to the *police*, but Rebus doubted they'd be so reticent when Tommy Telford came calling, armed with his own questions and determined to have answers.

This was bad. This was *escalation*. Fire-bombings and beatings: these could be remedied. But murder ... murder put the grudge-match on to a much higher plane.

'Is it worth talking to them again?' Gill Templer asked. They were in the canteen, sandwiches untouched in front of them.

'What do you think?'

He knew what she thought. She was talking because she thought talking was better than doing nothing. He could have told her to save her breath.

'They used a machete,' he said.

'Same thing they took to Danny Simpson's scalp.' Rebus nodded. 'I've got to ask ...' she said.

'What?'

'About Lintz ... what you said?'

He drained the last inch of his cold coffee. 'Fancy another?'

'John ...'

He looked at her. 'Lintz had some phone calls he was trying to hide. One of them was to Tommy Telford's office in Flint Street. We don't know how it ties in, but we think it *does* tie in.'

'What could Lintz and Telford have had in common?'

'Maybe Lintz went to him for help. Maybe he rented prossies off him. Like I say, we don't *know*. Which is why we're keeping it under the table.'

'You want Telford very badly, don't you?'

Rebus stared at her, thought about it. 'Not as much as I did. He's not enough any more.'

'You want Cafferty, too?'

'And Tarawicz ... and the Yakuza ... and anybody else who's along for the ride.'

She nodded. 'This is the party you were talking about?'

He tapped his head. 'They're all in here, Gill. I've tried kicking them out, but they won't leave.'

'Maybe if you stopped playing their kind of music?'

He smiled tiredly. 'Now there's an idea. What do you reckon: ELP? The Enid? How about a Yes triple album?'

'Your department, not mine, thank God.'

'You don't know what you're missing.'

'Yes, I do: I was there first time round.'

Old Scottish proverb: he who has had knuckles rapped will want to rap someone else's. Which is why Rebus found himself back in Watson's office. The Farmer's cheeks were still red from his meeting with the Chief Constable. When Rebus made to sit, Watson told him to get back on his feet.

'You'll sit when you're told and not before.'

'Thank you, sir.'

'What the bloody hell's going on, John?'

'Pardon, sir?'

The Farmer looked at the note Rebus had left on his desk. 'What's this?'

'One dead, one seriously wounded in Paisley, sir. Telford's men. Cafferty's hitting him where it hurts. Probably reckons that Telford's territory's spun a bit thin. Leaves him open to breaches.'

'Paisley.' The Farmer stuffed the note in his drawer. 'Not our problem.'

'It will be, sir. When Telford hits back, it'll be right here.'

'Never mind that, Inspector. Let's talk about Maclean's Pharmaceuticals.'

Rebus blinked, relaxed his shoulders. 'I was going to tell you, sir.'

'But instead I had to hear it from the Chief Constable?'

'Not really my baby, sir. Crime Squad are pushing the pram.'

'But who put the baby *in* the pram?'

'I was going to tell you, sir.'

'Know how it makes me look? I walk into Fettes and I don't know something one of my junior officers knows? I look like a mug.'

'With respect, sir, I'm sure that's not the case.'

'I look like a *mug*!' The Farmer slammed the desk with both palms. 'And it's not as though this was the first time. I've always tried to do my best for you, you know that.'

'Yes, sir.'

'Always been fair.'

'Absolutely, sir.'

'And you pay me back like this?'

'It won't happen again, sir.'

The Farmer stared at him; Rebus held it, returned it.

'I bloody well hope not.' The Farmer leaned back in his chair. He'd calmed down a little. Bollocking as therapy. 'Nothing else you want to tell me, is there, while I've got you here?'

'No, sir. Except ... well ...'

'Go on.' The Farmer sat forward again.

'It's the man in the flat above me, sir,' Rebus said. 'I think he might be Lord Lucan.'

27

Leonard Cohen: 'There is a War'.

They were waiting for Telford's retaliatory strike. The Chief Constable's idea: 'visible presence as deterrent'. It came as no surprise to Rebus: probably even less so to Telford, who had Charles Groal ready, claiming harassment the minute the patrol cars turned up in Flint Street. How was his client supposed to carry on with his legitimate and substantial business interests, as well as his many community developments, under the pressure of unwarranted and intrusive police surveillance? 'Community developments' meaning the pensioners and their rent-free flats: Telford wouldn't hesitate to use them as pawns. The media would love it.

The patrol cars would be pulled, it was just a matter of time. And afterwards: firework night all over again. That's what everyone was expecting.

Rebus went to the hospital, sat with Rhona. The room, so familiar to him now, was an oasis where calm and order reigned, where each hour of the day brought its comforting rituals.

'They've washed her hair,' he said.

'She's had another scan,' Rhona explained. 'They had to get the gunk off afterwards.' Rebus nodded. 'They said you'd noticed eye movement?'

'I thought I did.'

Rhona touched his arm. 'Jackie says he might manage to come up again at the weekend. Call this fair warning.'

'Received and understood.'

'You look tired.'

He smiled. 'One of these days someone's going to tell me how terrific I'm looking.'

'But not today,' Rhona said.

'Must be all the booze, clubbing and women.'

Thinking: Coke, the Morvena Casino, and Candice.

Thinking: why do I feel like piggy in the middle? Are Cafferty and Telford *both* playing games with me?

Thinking: I hope Jack Morton's okay.

The phone was ringing when he got back to Arden Street. He picked up just as the answering machine was cutting in.

'Hold on till I stop this thing.' Found the right button and hit it.

'Technology, eh, Strawman?'

Cafferty.

'What do you want?'

'I've heard about Paisley.'

'You mean you've been talking to yourself?'

'I had nothing to do with it.'

Rebus laughed out loud.

'I'm telling you.'

Rebus fell into his chair. 'And I'm supposed to believe you?' Games, he was thinking.

'Whether you believe me or not, I wanted you to know.'

'Thanks, I'm sure I'll sleep better for that.'

'I'm being set up, Strawman.'

'Telford doesn't *need* to set you up.' Rebus sighed, stretched his neck to left and right. 'Look, have you considered another possibility?'

'What?'

'Your men have lost it. They're going behind your back.'

'I'd know.'

'You'd know what your own lieutenants tell you. What if

304

they're lying? I'm not saying it's the whole gang, could be just two or three gone rogue.'

'I'd know.' The emotion had drained from Cafferty's voice. He was thinking it over.

'Fine, okay, you'd know: who'd be the first to tell you? Cafferty, you're on the other side of the country. You're in *prison*. How hard would it be to keep stuff from you?'

'These are men I'd trust with my life.' Cafferty paused. 'They'd tell me.'

'*If* they knew. *If* they hadn't been warned not to tell you. See what I'm saying?'

'Two or three gone rogue ...' Cafferty echoed.

'You must have candidates?'

'Jeffries would know.'

'Jeffries? Is that the Weasel's name?'

'Don't let him hear you call him that.'

'Give me his number. I'll talk to him.'

'No, but I'll get him to call you.'

'And if he's part of the breakaway?'

'We don't know there is one.'

'But you admit it makes sense?'

'I admit Tommy Telford's trying to put me in a box.' Rebus stared from his window. 'You mean literally?'

'I've heard word of a contract.'

'But you've got protection?'

Cafferty chuckled. 'Strawman, you almost sound concerned.'

'You're imagining things.'

'Look, there are only two ways out of this. One, *you* deal with Telford. Two, *I* deal with him. Are we agreed on that? I mean, I'm not the one who went poaching players and territory and putting out frighteners.'

'Maybe he's just more ambitious than you. Maybe he reminds you of the way you used to be.'

'Are you saying I've gone soft?'

'I'm saying it's adapt or die.'

'Have *you* adapted, Strawman?'

'Maybe a little.'

'Aye, a fucking speck, if that.'

'We're not talking about me though.'

'You're as involved as anyone. Remember that, Strawman. And sweet dreams.'

Rebus put down the phone. He felt exhausted, and depressed. The kids across the way were in bed, shutters closed. He looked around the room. Jack Morton had helped him paint it, back when Rebus was thinking of selling. Jack had helped him off the sauce, too ...

He knew he wouldn't be able to sleep. Got back into the car and headed for Young Street. The Oxford Bar was quiet. A couple of philosophers in the corner, and through in the back-room three musicians who'd packed up their fiddles. He drank a couple of cups of black coffee, then drove to Oxford Terrace. Parked the car outside Patience's flat, turned off the ignition and sat there for a while, jazz on the radio. He hit a good streak: Astrid Gilberto, Stan Getz, Art Pepper, Duke Ellington. Told himself he'd wait till a bad record came on, then go knock on Patience's door.

But by then it was too late. He didn't want to turn up unannounced. It would be ... it wouldn't look right. He didn't mind that it smacked of desperation, but he didn't want her to think he was pushing. He started the engine again and moved off, drove around the New Town and down to Granton. Sat by the edge of the Forth, window down, listening to water and the nighttime traffic of HGVs.

Even with eyes closed, he couldn't shut out the world. In fact, in those moments before sleep came, his images were at their most vivid. He wondered what Sammy dreamed about, or even if she dreamed at all. Rhona said that Sammy had come north to be with him. He couldn't think what he'd done to deserve her.

Back into town for an espresso at Gordon's Trattoria, then the hospital: easy to find a parking space this time of night. A taxi was idling outside the entrance. He made his way to Sammy's room, was surprised to see someone there. His first thought: Rhona. The only illumination in the room was that given through the closed curtains. A woman, kneeling by the bed, head resting on the covers. He walked forwards. She heard him, turned, face glistening with tears.

Candice.

Her eyes widened. She stumbled to her feet.

'I wanting see her,' she said quietly.

Rebus nodded. In shadows, she looked even more like Sammy: same build, similar hair and shape to her face. She wore a long red coat, fished in the pocket for a paper hankie.

'I like her,' she said. He nodded again.

'Does Tarawicz know where you are?' he asked.

She shook her head.

'The taxi outside?' he guessed.

She nodded. 'They went casino. I said sore head.' She spoke falteringly, checking each word was right before using it.

'Will he find out you've gone?'

She thought about it, shook her head.

'You sleep in the same room?' Rebus asked.

She shook her head again, smiled. 'Jake not liking women.'

This was news to Rebus. Miriam Kenworthy had said something about him marrying an Englishwoman ... but put that down to immigration. He remembered the way Tarawicz had pawed Candice, realised now it had been for *Telford's* benefit. He'd been showing Telford that he could control his women. While Telford ... well, Telford had let her get arrested, then be taken in by the Crime Squad. A small sign of rivalry between the two partners. Something to be exploited?

'Is she ... will she ...?'

Rebus shrugged. 'We hope so, Candice.'

She looked down at the floor. 'My name is Karina.'

'Karina,' he echoed.

'Sarajevo was ...' She looked up at him. 'You know, like *really*. I was escaping ... lucky. They all said to me: "You lucky, you lucky".' She stabbed at her chest with a finger. 'Lucky. Survivor.' She broke down again, and this time he held her.

The Stones: 'Soul Survivor'. Only sometimes it was the body alone that survived, the soul eaten into, chewed up by experience.

'Karina,' he said, repeating her name, reinforcing her true identity, trying to get through to the one part of her she'd kept hidden since Sarajevo. 'Karina, sshhh. It's going to be all right. Sshhh.' And stroking her hair, her face, his other hand on her back, feeling her tremble. Blinking back his own tears, and watching Sammy's body. The atmosphere in the room crackled like electricity: he wondered if any part of it was reaching Sammy's brain.

'Karina, Karina, Karina ...'

She pulled away, turned her back on him. He wouldn't let her go. Walked up to her and rested his hands on her shoulders.

'Karina,' he said, 'how did Tarawicz find you?' She seemed not to understand. 'In Anstruther, his men found you.'

'Brian,' she said quietly.

Rebus frowned. 'Brian Summers?' Pretty-Boy ...

'He tell Jake.'

'He told Tarawicz where you were?' But why not just take her back to Edinburgh? Rebus thought he knew: she was too dangerous; she'd been too close to the police. Best get her out of the way. Not a killing: that would have implicated all of them. But Tarawicz could control her. Mr Pink Eyes bailing out his friend one more time ...

'He brought you here so he could gloat over Telford.' Rebus was thoughtful. He looked at Candice. What could he do with her? Where would be safe? She seemed to sense his thoughts, squeezed his hand.

'You know I have a ...' She made a cradling motion with her hands.

'A boy,' Rebus said. She nodded. 'And Tarawicz knows where he is?'

She shook her head. 'The lorries ... they took him.'

'Tarawicz's refugee lorries?' She nodded again. 'And you don't know where he is?'

'Jake knows. He says his man ...' she made scuttling motions with her hands '... will kill my boy if ...'

Scuttling motions: the Crab. Something struck Rebus. 'Why isn't the Crab up here with Tarawicz?' She was looking at him. 'Tarawicz here,' he said, 'Crab in Newcastle. Why?'

She shrugged, looked thoughtful. 'He don't come.' She was remembering some snippet of conversation. 'Danger.'

'Dangerous?' Rebus frowned. 'Who for?'

She shrugged again. Rebus took her hands.

'You can't trust him, Karina. You have to leave him.'

She smiled up at him, eyes glinting. 'I tried.'

They looked at one another, held one another for a while. Afterwards, he walked her back out to her taxi.

28

In the morning he called the hospital, found out how Sammy was doing, then asked to be transferred.

'How's Danny Simpson getting on?'

'I'm sorry, are you family?'

Which told him everything. He identified himself, asked when it had happened.

'In the night,' the nurse said.

Body at its lowest ebb: the dying hours. Rebus called the mother, identified himself again.

'Sorry to hear the news,' he said. 'Is the funeral ...?'

'Just family, if you don't mind. No flowers. We're asking for donations to be sent to an ... to a charity. Danny was well thought of, you know.'

'I'm sure.'

Rebus took down details of the charity – an AIDS hospice; the mother couldn't bring herself to say the word. Terminated the call. Got an envelope out and put in ten pounds, plus a note: 'In memory of Danny Simpson'. He wondered about going for that test ... His phone rang and he picked it up.

'Hello?'

Lots of static and engine noise: car-phone, on the move at speed.

'This takes persecution to new levels.' *Telford*.

'What do you mean?' Rebus trying to compose himself.

'Danny Simpson's been dead six hours, and already you're on the phone to his mum.'

'How do you know?'

'I was *there*. Paying my respects.'

'Same reason I phoned then. Know what, Telford? I think *you're* taking persecution complexes to new levels.'

'Yes, and Cafferty's not out to shut me down.'

'He says he didn't have anything to do with Paisley.'

'I bet you believed in the Tooth Fairy when you were a kid.'

'I still do.'

'You'll need more than a good fairy if you side with Cafferty.'

'Is that a threat? Don't tell me: Tarawicz is in the car with you?' Silence. Bingo, Rebus thought. 'You think Tarawicz will respect you because you bad-mouth cops? He's got no respect for you whatsoever – look how he's waving Candice in your face.'

Mixing levity with fury: 'Hey, Rebus, you and Candice in that hotel – what was she like? Jake tells me she's vindaloo.' Background laughter: Mr Pink Eyes, who, according to Candice, had never touched her. For 'laughter' read 'bravado'. Telford and Tarawicz, playing games between themselves, playing games with the world.

Rebus found the tone of voice he wanted. 'I tried to help her. If she's too stupid to know that, she deserves the likes of you and Tarawicz.' Telling them he had no further interest in her. 'Anyway, Tarawicz didn't have any trouble taking her off *your* hands.' Rebus jabbing away, looking for gaps in the armour of the Telford/Tarawicz relationship.

'What if Cafferty wasn't behind Paisley?' he asked into the silence.

'It was his men.'

'Gone rogue.'

'He can't control them, that's his look-out. He's a *joke*, Rebus. He's finished.'

Rebus didn't say anything; listened instead to a muted

conversation. Then Telford again: 'Mr Tarawicz wants a word.' The phone was handed over.

'Rebus? I thought we were civilised men?'

'In what way?'

'When we met in Newcastle ... I thought we came to an understanding?'

The unspoken agreement: leave Telford alone, have nothing more to do with Cafferty, and Candice and her son would be safe. What was Tarawicz getting at?

'I've kept my side.'

A forced chuckle. 'You know what Paisley represents?

'What?'

'The beginning of the end of Morris Gerald Cafferty.'

'And I bet you'd send flowers to the grave.'

Dead flowers at that.

Rebus went into St Leonard's, got settled in front of his computer screen, and took a look at the Crab.

The Crab: William Andrew Colton. Plenty of form. Rebus decided he'd like to read the files. Phoned in and requested them, backed up the request in writing. Buzzed from downstairs: a man to see him, no name supplied. Description: the Weasel.

Rebus went downstairs.

The Weasel was outside, smoking a cigarette. He was wearing a green waxed jacket, torn at both pockets. A lumberjack hat with its flaps down protected his ears from the wind.

'Let's walk,' Rebus said. The Weasel got into step with him. They wandered through an estate of new flats: satellite dishes and windows picked from Lego boxes. Behind the flats sat Salisbury Crags.

'Don't worry,' Rebus said, 'I'm not in the mood for rock-climbing.'

'I'm in the mood for indoors.' The Weasel tucked his chin into the upturned collar of his coat.

'What's the news on my daughter?'

'We're close, I told you.'

'How close?'

The Weasel measured his response. 'We've got the tapes from the car, the guy who sold them. He says he got them from another party.'

'And he is …?'

A sly smile: the Weasel knew he had control over Rebus. He'd play it out as long as possible.

'You're going to be meeting him fairly shortly.'

'Even so … say the tapes got taken from the car after it was abandoned?'

The Weasel was shaking his head. 'That's not how it was.'

'Then how was it?' He wanted to pull his tormentor down on to the ground and start hammering his skull on the pavement.

'Give us a day or two, we'll have everything you need.' The wind gusted some grit towards them. They turned their faces. Rebus saw a heavy-set man loitering sixty yards behind.

'Don't worry,' the Weasel said, 'he's with me.'

'Getting jittery?'

'After Paisley, Telford's out for blood.'

'What do you know about Paisley?'

The Weasel's eyes became slits. 'Nothing.'

'No? Cafferty's beginning to suspect some of his own men might have gone rogue.' Rebus watched the Weasel shake his head.

'I don't know the first thing about it.'

'Who's your boss's main man?'

'Ask Mr Cafferty.' The Weasel was looking around, as if bored by the conversation. He made a signal to the back-marker, who passed it along. Seconds later, a newish Jaguar – arterial-red paint-job – cruised to a stop beside them. Rebus saw: a driver itching for a less sedentary occupation; cream leather interior; the back-marker jogging forwards, opening the door for the Weasel.

'It's you,' Rebus said. The Weasel: Cafferty's eyes and ears on the street; the man with the look and dress-code of a down-and-out. The Weasel was running the show. All the lieutenants in the various outposts ... all the tailor-made suits ... the collective which, according to police intelligence, ran Cafferty's kingdom in their master's absence ... they were a smokescreen. The hunched man pulling off his lumberjack hat, the man with bad teeth and a blunt razor, *he* was in charge.

Rebus actually laughed. The bodyguard got into the car's passenger seat, having made sure his boss was comfortable in the back. Rebus tapped on the window. The Weasel lowered it.

'Tell me,' Rebus asked, 'have you got the bottle to wrest it away from him?'

'Mr Cafferty trusts me. He knows I'll do right by him.'

'What about Telford?'

The Weasel stared at him. 'Telford's not my concern.'

'Then who is?'

But the window was rising again, and the Weasel – Cafferty had called him Jeffries – had turned his face away, dismissing Rebus from his mind.

He stood there, watching the car drive off. Was Cafferty making a big mistake, putting the Weasel in charge? Was it just that his best men had scarpered or gone over to the other side?

Or was the Weasel every bit as sly, clever and vicious as his namesake?

Back at the station, Rebus sought out Bill Pryde. Pryde was

shrugging his shoulders even before Rebus had reached his desk.

'Sorry, John, no news.'

'Nothing at all? What about the stolen tapes?' Pryde shook his head. 'That's funny, I've just been talking to someone who claims to know who sold them on, and who *he* got them from.'

Pryde sat back in his chair. 'I wondered why you hadn't been chasing me up. What've you done, hired a private eye?' Blood was rising to his face. 'I've been working my arse off on this, John, you know I have. Now you don't trust me to do the job?'

'It's not like that, Bill.' Rebus suddenly found himself on the defensive.

'Who've you got working for you, John?'

'Just people on the street.'

'Well-connected people by the sound of it.' He paused. 'Are we talking villains?'

'My daughter's in a coma, Bill.'

'I'm well aware of that. Now answer my question!'

People around them were staring. Rebus lowered his voice. 'Just a few of my grasses.'

'Then give me their names.'

'Come on, Bill ...'

Pryde's hands gripped the table. 'These past days, I've been thinking you'd lost interest. Thinking maybe you didn't *want* an answer.' He was thoughtful. 'You wouldn't go to Telford ... Cafferty?' His eyes widened. 'Is that it, John?'

Rebus turned his head away.

'Christ, John ... what's the deal here? He hands over the driver, what do *you* hand *him*?'

'It's not like that.'

'I can't believe you'd trust Cafferty. You put him away, for Christ's sake!'

'It's not a question of trust.'

But Pryde was shaking his head. 'There's a line we don't cross.'

'Get a grip, Bill. There's no line.' Rebus spread his arms. 'If there is, show me it.'

Pryde tapped his forehead. 'It's up here.'

'Then it's a fiction.'

'You really believe that?'

Rebus sought an answer, slumped against the desk, ran his hands over his head. He remembered something Lintz had once said: *when we stop believing in God, we don't suddenly believe in 'nothing' ... we believe anything.*

'John?' someone called. 'Phone call.'

Rebus stared at Pryde. 'Later,' he said. He walked across to another desk, took the call.

'Rebus here.'

'It's Bobby.' Bobby Hogan.

'What can I do for you, Bobby?'

'For a start, you can help get that Special Branch arsehole off my back.'

'Abernethy?'

'He won't leave me alone.'

'Keeps phoning you?'

'Christ, John, aren't you listening? He's *here*.'

'When did he get in?'

'He never went away.'

'Whoah, hold on.'

'And he's driving me round the twist. He says he knows you from way back, so how about having a word?'

'Are you at Leith?'

'Where else?'

'I'll be there in twenty minutes.'

'I got so pissed off, I went to my boss – and that's something I seldom have to resort to.' Bobby Hogan was drinking coffee like it was something best taken intravenously. The top button of his shirt was undone, tie hanging loose.

'Only,' he went on, '*his* boss had a word with my *boss's* boss, and I ended up with a warning: co-operate or else.'

'Meaning?'

'I wasn't to tell anyone he was still around.'

'Thanks, pal. So what's he actually doing?'

'What *isn't* he doing? He wants to be in on any interviews. He wants copies of tapes and transcripts. He wants to see all the paperwork, wants to know what I'm planning to do next, what I had for breakfast ...'

'I don't suppose he's managing to be helpful in any shape or form?'

Hogan's look gave Rebus his answer.

'I don't mind him taking an interest, but this verges on the obstructive. He's slowing the case to a dead stop.'

'Maybe that's his plan.'

Hogan looked up from his cup. 'I don't get it.'

'Neither do I. Look, if he's being obstructive, let's put on a show, see how he reacts.'

'What sort of show?'

'What time will he be in?'

Hogan checked his watch. 'Half an hour or so. That's when my work stops for the day, while I fill him in.'

'Half an hour's enough. Mind if I use your phone?'

29

When Abernethy arrived, he didn't manage not to look surprised. The space put aside for the investigation – Hogan's space – now contained three bodies, and they were working at the devil's own pace.

Hogan was on the telephone to a librarian. He was asking for a run-down of books and articles about the 'Rat Line'. Rebus was sorting through paperwork, putting it in order, cross-referencing, laying aside anything he didn't think useful. And Siobhan Clarke was there, too. She appeared to be on the phone to some Jewish organisation, and was asking them about lists of war criminals. Rebus nodded towards Abernethy, but kept on working.

'What's going on?' Abernethy asked, taking off his raincoat.

'Helping out. Bobby's got so many leads to work on ...' He nodded towards Siobhan. 'And Crime Squad are interested, too.'

'Since when?'

Rebus waved a piece of paper. 'This might be bigger than we think.'

Abernethy looked around. He wanted to speak to Hogan, but Hogan was still on the phone. Rebus was the only one with time to talk.

Which was just the way Rebus had planned it.

He'd only had five minutes in which to brief Siobhan, but she was a born actress, even holding a conversation with the dialling tone. Hogan's fantasy librarian, meantime, was asking him all the right questions. And Abernethy was looking glazed.

'What do you mean?'

'In fact,' Rebus said, putting down a file, 'you might be able to help.'

'How?'

'You're Special Branch, and Special Branch has access to the secret services.' Rebus paused. 'Right?'

Abernethy licked his lips and shrugged.

'See,' Rebus went on, 'we're beginning to wonder something. There could be a dozen reasons why someone would want to kill Joseph Lintz, but the one we've been practically ignoring' (ignoring at Abernethy's suggestion, according to Hogan) 'is the one that just might provide the answer. I'm talking about the Rat Line. What if Lintz's murder had something to do with that?'

'How could it?'

It was Rebus's turn to shrug. 'That's why we need your help. We need any and all information we can get on the Rat Line.'

'But it never existed.'

'Funny, a lot of books seem to say it did.'

'They're wrong.'

'Then there are all these survivors ... except they haven't survived. Suicides, car crashes, a fall from a window. Lintz is just one of a long line of dead men.'

Siobhan Clarke and Bobby Hogan had finished their calls and were listening.

'You're climbing the wrong tree,' Abernethy said.

'Well, you know, if you're in a forest, climbing any tree will give you a better view.'

'There is no Rat Line.'

'You're an expert?'

'I've been collating ...'

'Yes, yes, all the investigations. And how far have you got? Is any one of them going to make it to trial?'

'It's too early to tell.'

'And soon it may be too late. These men aren't getting any younger. I've seen the same thing all around Europe: delay the trial until the defendants are so old they snuff it or go doolally. Result's the same: no trial.'

'Look, this has nothing to do with ...'

'Why are you here, Abernethy? Why did you come up that time to speak to Lintz?'

'Look, Rebus, it's not ...'

'If you can't tell us, talk to your boss. Get *him* to do it. Otherwise, the way we're digging, we're bound to throw up an old bone sooner or later.'

Abernethy stood back a pace. 'I think I get it,' he said. And he began to smile. 'You're trying to stiff me.' He was looking at Hogan. 'That's what this is.'

'Not at all,' Rebus answered. 'What I'm saying is: we'll redouble our efforts. We'll sniff into every little corner. The Rat Line, the Vatican, turning Nazis into cold war spies for the allies ... it could all count as evidence. The other men on your list, the other suspects ... we'll need to talk to all of them, see if they knew Joseph Lintz. Maybe they met him on the trip over.'

Abernethy was shaking his head. 'I'm not going to let you do that.'

'You're going to obstruct the investigation?'

'That's not what I said.'

'No, but it's what you'll *do*.' Rebus paused. 'If you think we're climbing the wrong tree — and, incidentally, that should be *barking up* — go ahead and prove it. Give us everything you've got on Lintz's past.'

Abernethy's eyes were fierce.

'Or we go on digging and sniffing.' Rebus opened another file, lifted out the first sheet. Hogan picked up his telephone, made another call. Siobhan Clarke looked at a list of numbers and chose one.

'Hello, is that the City Synagogue?' Hogan was saying. 'Yes, it's Detective Inspector Hogan here, Leith CID. Do you by any chance have information on a Joseph Lintz?'

Abernethy grabbed his coat, turned on his heels and left. They waited thirty seconds, then Hogan put the receiver down.

'He looked nettled.'

'That's one Christmas wish I can chalk off,' Siobhan Clarke said.

'Thanks for your time, Siobhan,' Rebus said.

'Happy to oblige. But why did it have to be me?'

'Because he knows you're Crime Squad. I wanted him to think interest was escalating. And because the two of you didn't exactly hit it off last time you met. Antagonism always helps.'

'And what did we accomplish?' Bobby Hogan asked, beginning to gather together the files, half of which belonged to other cases.

'We rattled his cage,' Rebus said. 'He's not up here for the good of his health – or yours, come to that. He's here because Special Branch in London want to know all about the investigation. And to me, that means they're scared of something.'

'The Rat Line?'

'That would be my guess. Abernethy's been keeping an eye on all the new cases nationwide. Someone in London is getting a bit sweaty.'

'They're worried this Rat Line will connect to whoever killed Lintz?'

'I'm not sure it goes that far,' Rebus said.

'Meaning?'

He looked at Clarke. 'Meaning I'm not sure it goes that far.'

321

'Well,' Hogan said, 'looks like he's off my back for a little while at least, for which I'm grateful.' He got to his feet. 'Get anyone a coffee?'

Clarke checked her watch. 'Go on then.'

Rebus waited till Hogan was gone, then thanked Siobhan again. 'I wasn't sure you'd be able to spare the time.'

'We're giving Jack Morton a wide berth,' she explained. 'Nothing to do but bite our fingernails and wait. What about you, what are you up to?'

'Keeping my nose clean.'

She smiled. 'I'll bet.'

Hogan came back with three coffees. 'Powdered milk, sorry.'

Clarke wrinkled her nose. 'Actually, I've got to be getting back.' She stood up and put on her coat.

'That's one I owe you,' Hogan said, shaking her hand.

'I won't let you forget.' She turned to Rebus. 'See you later.'

'Cheers, Siobhan.'

Hogan put her cup beside his own. 'So we got Abernethy off my back, but did we get anything else?'

'Wait and see, Bobby. I didn't exactly have much time to devise a strategy.'

The phone rang, just as Hogan took a mouthful of scalding coffee. Rebus picked up.

'Hello?'

'Is that you, John?' Country and western twanging in the background: Claverhouse.

'You've just missed her,' Rebus told him.

'It's not Clarke I wanted, it's you.'

'Oh?'

'Something I thought you might be interested in. It's just filtered down from NCIS.' Rebus heard Claverhouse pick up a sheet of paper. 'Sakiji Shoda ... I think I've pronounced that right. Flew into Heathrow from Kansai

Airport yesterday. South-East Regional Crime Squad were apprised.'

'Terrific.'

'He didn't hang around, caught a connection to Inverness. Stayed the night in a local hotel, and now I hear he's in Edinburgh.'

Rebus looked out of the window. 'Not exactly golfing weather.'

'I don't think he's up here for the golf. According to the original report, Mr Shoda is a high-ranking member of the ... can't make it out on the fax. Socky-something.'

'Sokaiya?' Rebus sat up.

'That looks about right.'

'Where is he now?'

'I tried a couple of hotels. He's staying at the Caly. What's the Sokaiya?'

'It's the upper echelons of the Yakuza.'

'How does it read to you?'

'I was going to suggest he's Matsumoto's replacement, but it sounds to me like he's a few grades higher.'

'Matsumoto's boss?'

'Which means he's probably here to find out what happened to his boy.' Rebus tapped a pen against his teeth. Hogan was listening, but not getting any of it. 'Why Inverness? Why not direct to Edinburgh?'

'I've been wondering that.' Claverhouse sneezed. 'How pissed off will he be?'

'Somewhere between "mildly" and "very". More importantly, how are Telford and Mr Pink Eyes going to react?'

'You think Telford will drop Maclean's?'

'On the contrary, I think he'll want to show Mr Shoda that he can do *some* things right.' Rebus thought back to something Claverhouse had said. 'South-East Crime Squad?'

'Yes.'

'Rather than Scotland Yard?'

'Maybe the two are the same?'

'Maybe. Do you have a contact number?'

Claverhouse gave it to him.

'You'll speak to Jack Morton tonight?' Rebus asked.

'Yes.'

'Better tell him about this.'

'Talk to you again.'

Rebus put down the receiver, picked it up again, got an outside line and made the call. Explained his reason for calling and asked if there was anyone who could help him.

He was told to hold.

'Is this to do with Telford?' Hogan asked. Rebus nodded.

'Hey, Bobby, did you ever talk to Telford again?'

'I tried a couple of times. He just kept saying: "It must've been a wrong number".'

'And this was echoed by his staff?'

Hogan nodded, smiled. 'Tell you a funny thing. I walked into Telford's office, and someone was at his desk, back to me. I apologised, said I'd come back when he'd finished with the lady. Well, the "lady" turns, face like fury ...'

'Pretty-Boy?'

Hogan nodded. 'And pretty fucking angry the last I saw him.' Hogan laughed.

'Putting you through,' the switchboard told Rebus.

'How can I help you?' The voice sounded Welsh.

'My name's DI Rebus, Scottish Crime Squad.' Rebus winked at Hogan: the lie would give him more clout.

'Yes, Inspector?'

'And you are ...?'

'DI Morgan.'

'We had this message this morning ...'

'Yes?'

'Concerning Sakiji Shoda.'

324

'That would be my boss has sent you that.'

'What I'm wondering is, what's your interest?'

'Well, Inspector, I'm more of an expert on *vory v zakone*.'

'That clears things up then.'

Morgan chuckled. ' "Thieves within the code". Meaning *mafiya*.'

'Russian mafia?'

'That's it.'

'You'll have to help me here. What's that got to do with ...?'

'Why do you want to know?'

Rebus took a sip of coffee. 'We've had a spot of bother with the Yakuza up here. One victim so far. My guess is that Shoda is the victim's boss.'

'And he's up there for a sort of unofficial committal?'

'We don't have the committal stage in Scotland, DI Morgan.'

'Well, pardon me for breathing.'

'Thing is, we've also got a Russian gangster up here. I say he's Russian, word is he's Chechen.'

'Is it Jake Tarawicz?'

'You've heard of him?'

'That's my job, sonny boy.'

'Well, anyway, with the Yakuza and the Chechens in town ...'

'You've got a nightmare scenario. Understood. Well, look ... What about if you give me your number there, and I'll call back in five minutes? Need to put some facts together first.'

Rebus gave him the number, then waited ten minutes for the call back.

'You were checking me out,' he told the Welshman.

'Got to be careful. Bit naughty of you to say you were Crime Squad.'

'Let's just say I'm the next best thing. So is there anything you can tell me?'

Morgan took a deep breath. 'We've been chasing a lot of dirty money around the world.'

Rebus couldn't find a clean sheet of paper to write on. Hogan gave him a pad.

'See,' Morgan was saying, 'the old Soviet Asia is now the biggest supplier of raw opium in the world. And wherever there's drugs, there's money needs laundering.'

'And this money makes its way to Britain?'

'On its way elsewhere. Companies in London, private banks in Guernsey ... the money gets filtered down, getting cleaner all the time. Everyone wants to do business with the Russians.'

'Why?'

'Because they make everyone money. Russia's one giant bazaar. You want weapons, counterfeit goods, money, fake passports, even plastic surgery? You want any of that, it's in Russia. The place has open borders, airports nobody knows exist ... it's ideal.'

'If you happen to be an international mobster.'

'Exactly. And the *mafiya* have made links with their Sicilian cousins, with the Camorra, the Calabrians ... I could go on forever. British villains go shopping there. They all love the Russians.'

'And now they're here?'

'Oh, they're here all right. Running protection and prossies, dealing drugs ...'

Prostitutes, drugs: Mr Pink Eyes's territory; Telford's territory.

'Any evidence of a hook-up with the Yakuza?'

'Not that I know of.'

'But if they moved into Britain ...?'

'They'd be trying to control drugs and prostitution. They'd be laundering money.'

Ways to launder money: through legitimate businesses such as country clubs and the like; by swopping dirty money for casino chips at an establishment like the Morvena.

Rebus already knew that the Yakuza liked to smuggle artworks back into Japan. Rebus already knew Mr Pink had made his early money smuggling icons out of Russia. Put the two together.

Then add Tommy Telford to the equation.

Did they need the haul from Maclean's? It didn't sound to Rebus like they did. So why was Tommy Telford doing it? Two possible reasons: one, to show off; two, *because they'd told him to*. Some rite of passage ... If he wanted to play with the big boys, he had to prove himself. He had to wipe out Cafferty, and pull off what would be the biggest heist in Scottish history.

Something hit Rebus between the eyes.

Telford wasn't meant to succeed. Telford was meant to fail.

Telford was being set up by Tarawicz and the Yakuza.

Because he had something they wanted: a steady supply of drugs; a kingdom waiting to be plucked from his grasp. Miriam Kenworthy had said as much: rumour was, the drugs were going south from Scotland. Which meant Telford had a supply ... something *nobody* knew about.

With Cafferty out of the way, there'd be no competition. The Yakuza would have their British base – solid, respectable, reliable. The electronics factory would act as perfect cover, maybe even as a laundering operation itself. Every way Rebus looked at it, Telford was unnecessary to the equation, like a zero that could be safely cancelled out.

Which was where Rebus wanted Telford ... only not at the price being asked.

'Thanks for your help,' he said. He noticed that Hogan

had stopped listening and was staring into space. Rebus put the phone down.

'Sorry to have bored you.'

Hogan blinked. 'No, nothing like that. It's just that I thought of something.'

'What?'

'Pretty-Boy. I mistook him for a woman.'

'You're probably not the first.'

'Exactly.'

'I'm not sure I follow you?'

'In the restaurant ... Lintz and a young woman.' Hogan shrugged. 'It's a long shot.'

Rebus saw it. 'Talking business?'

Hogan nodded. 'Pretty-Boy runs Telford's stable.'

'And takes a personal interest in the higher-price models. It's worth a try, Bobby.'

'What do you think – bring him in?'

'Definitely. Beef up the restaurant angle. Say there's a positive ID. See what he says to that.'

'Same gag we pulled with Colquhoun? Pretty-Boy's bound to deny it.'

'Doesn't mean it ain't so.' Rebus patted Hogan on the shoulder.

'What about your call?'

'My call?' Rebus looked at his scrawled notes. Gangsters preparing to carve up Scotland. 'It wasn't the worst news I've ever had.'

'And is that saying much?'

'Afraid not, Bobby,' Rebus said, putting on his jacket. 'Afraid not.'

30

By the end of play, Rebus still hadn't received the files on the Crab, but he had fielded a frank and foul-mouthed call from Abernethy, accusing him of everything from obstruction — which was pretty rich, considering — to racism, which Rebus thought nicely ironic.

They'd given him back his car. Someone had run their finger through the dirt crusted on the boot, creating two messages: TERMINAL CASE, and WASHED BY STEVIE WONDER. The Saab, affronted, started first time and seemed to have shrugged off some of its repertoire of clanks and thunks. On the drive home, Rebus kept the windows open so he wouldn't smell the whisky that had soaked into the upholstery.

The evening had turned out fine, the sky clear, temperature dropping sharply. The low red sun, curse of the city's drivers, had disappeared behind the rooftops. Rebus left his coat unbuttoned as he walked down to the chip shop. He bought a fish supper, two buttered rolls, and a couple of cans of Irn-Bru, then returned to the flat. Nothing on the TV, so he put on a record. Van Morrison: *Astral Weeks*. The record had more scratches than a dog with eczema.

The opening track contained the refrain 'To be born again'. Rebus thought of Father Leary, shored up by a fridge full of medicine. Then he thought of Sammy, crowned with electrodes, machines rising either side of her, like she was being offered to them in sacrifice. Leary often talked of faith, but it was hard to have faith in a human race that never learned, that seemed ready to accept torture, murder, destruction. He opened his newspaper: Kosovo, Zaire, Rwanda. Punishment beatings in Northern Ireland. A young girl found murdered in England, another girl's disappearance termed 'a cause for concern'. The predators were out there, no doubt about it. Strip the veneer, and the world had moved only a couple of steps from the cave.

To be born again ... But sometimes only after a baptism of fire.

Belfast, 1970. A sniper's bullet blew open the skull of a British squaddie. The victim was nineteen, came from Glasgow. Back in the barracks, there'd been little mourning, just an overspill of anger. The assassin would never be caught. He'd slipped back into the shadows of a tower-block, and from there deep into the Catholic housing estate.

Leaving one more newspaper story, one early statistic in the 'Troubles'.

And anger.

The ring-leader went by the nickname of 'Mean Machine'. He was a lance-corporal, came from somewhere in Ayrshire. Cropped blond hair, looked like he'd played rugby, liked to work out, even if it was just press-ups and sit-ups in the barracks. He started the campaign for retribution. It was to be covert – meaning behind the backs of the 'brass'. It was to be a release-valve for the frustration, the pressure that was building in the cramped confines of the barracks. The world outside was enemy terrain, everyone a potential foe. Knowing there was no way to punish the sniper, Mean Machine had decided to hold the entire community to blame: collective responsibility, for which there would be collective justice.

The plan: a raid on a known IRA bar, a place where sympathisers drank and colluded. The pretext: a man with a handgun, chased into the bar, necessitating a search.

Maximum harassment, ending with the beating of the local IRA fundraiser.

And Rebus went along with it ... because it *was* collective. You were either part of the team, or you were dead meat. And Rebus wasn't in the market for pariah status.

But all the same, he knew the line between 'good guys' and 'bad guys' had become blurred. And during the incursion, it disappeared altogether.

Mean Machine went in hardest, teeth bared, eyes ablaze. He swung with his rifle, cracking skulls. Tables flew, pint glasses shattered. Initially the other soldiers seemed shocked by the sudden violence. They looked to each other for guidance. Then one of them lashed out, and the others fell in beside him. A mirror dissolved into glittering stars, stout and lager washed over the wooden floor. Men were shouting, begging, crawling on hands and knees across the glass minefield. Mean Machine had the IRA man pinned to a wall, kneeing him in the groin. He twisted his body, threw him to the floor, then started pummelling him with the rifle-butt. More soldiers were pouring into the drinking-club: armoured cars arriving outside. A chair crashed into the row of optics. The smell of whisky was almost overpowering.

Rebus tried to shut it out, his own teeth bared not in anger but anguish. Then he aimed his rifle at the ceiling and let loose a single shot, and everything froze ... A final kick to the bloodied figure on the floor and Mean Machine turned and walked out of the club. The others hesitated again, then followed. He'd proved something to the other men: for all his lowly rank, he'd become their leader.

They enjoyed themselves that night in the barracks, chiding Rebus for letting his trigger-finger slip. They cracked open cans of beer and told stories, stories which were already being exaggerated, turning the event into a myth, giving it a grandeur it had lacked.

Turning it into a lie.

A few weeks later, the same IRA man was found shot dead in a stolen car south of the city, on a farm road with a view of hills and grazing land. Protestant paramilitaries took the blame, but Mean Machine, though he admitted nothing, would wink and grin when the incident was mentioned. Bravado or confession – Rebus was never sure. All he knew was that he wanted out, away from Mean Machine's newly minted code of ethics. So he did the one thing he could – applied to join the SAS. Nobody would think him a coward or a turncoat for applying to join the elite.

To be born again.

Side one had finished; Rebus turned the record over, switched off the lights and went to sit in his chair. He felt a chill run through him. Because he *knew* how events like Villefranche could come to be. Because he *knew* how the world's continuing horrors could come to be perpetrated at the cusp of the twentieth century. He knew that mankind's instinct was raw, that every act of bravery and kindness was countered by so many acts of savagery.

And he suspected that if his daughter had been that sniper's victim, he'd have run into the bar with his trigger-finger already working.

Telford's gang ran in a pack, too, trusted their leader. But now *he* wanted to run with an even bigger gang ...

The phone rang and he picked up.

'John Rebus,' he said.

'John, it's Jack.' Jack Morton. Rebus put down his can.

'Hello, Jack. Where are you?'

'In the poky one-bedroomed flat our friends at Fettes so graciously provided.'

'It has to fit the image.'

'Aye, I suppose so. Got a phone though. Coin job, but you can't have everything.' He paused. 'You okay, John? You sound ... not all there.'

'That just about sums me up, Jack. What's it like being a security guard?'

'A dawdle, pal. Should have taken it up years ago.'

'Wait till your pension's safe.'

'Aye, right.'

'And it went okay with Marty Jones?'

'Oscars all round. They were just heavy enough. I stumbled back into the shop, said I had to sit down. The Gruesome Twosome were very solicitous, then started asking me all these questions ... Not very subtle.'

'You don't think they twigged?'

'Like you, I was a bit dubious about setting it up so fast, but I think they fell for it. Whether their boss goes along is a different story.'

'Well, he's under a lot of pressure.'

'With the war going on?'

'I don't think that's the whole story, Jack. I think he's under pressure from his partners.'

'The Russian and the Japs?'

'I think they're setting him up for a fall, and Maclean's is the precipice.'

'Evidence?'

'Gut feeling.'

Jack was thoughtful. 'So where do I stand?'

'Just ca' canny, Jack.'

'I never thought of that.'

Rebus laughed. 'When do you think they'll make contact?'

'They followed me home – that's how desperate they are. They're sitting outside right now.'

'They must think you're a good thing.'

Rebus could see the way it was going. Dec and Ken

getting panicky, needing a quick result – feeling vulnerable so far away from Flint Street, not knowing if they'd be Cafferty's next victims. Telford, pressure applied by Tarawicz, and now with the Yakuza boss in town ... needing a result, something to show he was top dog.

'What about you, John? It's been a while.'

'Yes.'

'How are you holding up?'

'I'm on soft drinks only, if that's what you mean.' And a car doused in whisky ... he could taste it in his lungs.

'Hang on,' Jack said. 'Someone's at the door. I'll call you back.'

'Be careful.'

The phone went dead.

Rebus gave it an hour. When Jack hadn't called, he got on the blower to Claverhouse.

'It's okay,' Claverhouse told him from his mobile. 'Tweedledee and Tweedledum came calling, took him off somewhere.'

'You're watching the flat?'

'Decorator's van parked down the street.'

'So you've no idea where they've taken him?'

'I'd guess he's at Flint Street.'

'With no back-up?'

'That's how we all wanted it.'

'Christ, I don't know ...'

'Thanks for the vote of confidence.'

'It's not you in the firing line. And I'm the one who volunteered him.'

'He knows the score, John.'

'So now you wait for him either to come home or end up on a slab?'

'Christ, John, Calvin was Charlie Chester compared to you.' Claverhouse had lost all patience. Rebus tried to think of a comeback, slammed the phone down instead.

Suddenly he couldn't be doing with Van the Man; put on Bowie instead, *Aladdin Sane*: nicely discordant, Mike Garson's piano in key with his thoughts.

Empty juice cans and a dead pack of cigarettes stared up at him. He didn't know Jack's address. The only person who'd give it to him was Claverhouse, and he didn't want to pick up their conversation. He took Bowie off halfway through side one, substituted *Quadrophenia*. Liner notes: 'Schizophrenic? I'm bleeding Quadrophenic'. Which was just about right.

Quarter past midnight, the phone rang. It was Jack Morton.

'Back home safe and sound?' Rebus asked.

'Right as nails.'

'Have you spoken to Claverhouse?'

'He can wait his turn. I said I'd phone you back.'

'So what did you get?'

'The third degree, basically. Some guy with dyed black hair, frizzy ... tight jeans.'

'Pretty-Boy.'

'Wears mascara.'

'Looks like. So what was the gist?'

'Second hurdle passed. Nobody's mentioned what the job is yet. Tonight was a sort of preface. Wanted to know all about me, told me my money worries could be over. If I could help them with a "little problem" – Pretty-Boy's words.'

'You asked what the problem was?'

'He wasn't saying. If you ask me, he goes to Telford, talks it through. Then there's another meeting, and that's where they tell me the plan.'

'And you'll be miked up?'

'Yes.'

'And if they strip you?'

335

'Claverhouse has access to some miniaturised stuff, cuff-links and the like.'

'And your character would obviously wear cuff-links.'

'True enough. Maybe fit a transmitter into a bookie's pencil.'

'Now you're thinking.'

'I'm thinking I'm wiped out.'

'What was the mood like?'

'Fraught.'

'Any sign of Tarawicz or Shoda?'

'Nope, just Pretty-Boy and the Gruesome Twosome.'

'Claverhouse calls them Tweedledum and Tweedledee.'

'He's obviously classically educated.' Morton paused. 'You've spoken to him?'

'When you didn't call back.'

'I'm touched. Do you think he's up to it?'

'Claverhouse?' Rebus thought about it. 'I'd feel better if *I* was in charge. But that probably puts me in a minority.'

'I didn't say that.'

'You're a pal, Jack.'

'They're running a check on me. But that's all in place. With luck, I'll pass.'

'What did they say to your sudden arrival at Maclean's?'

'I've been transferred from another plant. If they go looking, I'm in the personnel files.' Morton paused again. 'One thing I want to know ...'

'What?'

'Pretty-Boy handed me a hundred quid on account: what do I do with it?'

'That's between you and your conscience, Jack. See you soon.'

'Night, John.'

For the first time in a while, Rebus actually made it as far as his bed. His sleep was deep and dreamless.

31

Doctors in white coats were doing things to Sammy when
Rebus arrived at the hospital next morning: taking her
pulse, shining lights in her eyes. They were setting up
another scanner, a nurse trying to untangle the thin
coloured leads. Rhona looked like she'd lost some sleep.
She jumped up and ran towards him.

'She woke up!'

It took him a second to take it in. Rhona was holding his
arms, shaking him.

'She woke *up*, John!'

He pushed his way to the bedside.

'When?'

'Last night.'

'Why didn't you phone me?'

'I tried three, four times. You were engaged. I tried
Patience, but there was no answer there.'

'What happened?' To him, Sammy looked the same as
ever.

'She just opened her eyes ... No, first off, it was like she
was moving her eyeballs. You know, with her eyelids
closed. Then she opened her eyes.'

Rebus could see that the medical personnel were finding
their work hampered. Half of him wanted to lash out –
We're her fucking parents! The other half wanted them to do
all they could to bring her round again. He took Rhona by
the shoulder and guided her out into the hallway.

'Did she ... Did she look at you? Did she say anything?'

'She was just staring at the ceiling, where the strip–light is. Then I thought she was going to blink, but she closed her eyes again and they stayed shut.' Rhona burst into tears. 'It was like ... I lost her all over again.'

Rebus took her in his arms. She hugged him back.

'She did it once,' he whispered into her ear, 'she'll do it again.'

'That's what one of the doctors said. He said they're "very hopeful". Oh, John, I wanted to tell you! I wanted to tell *everyone*!'

And he'd been busy with work: Claverhouse, Jack Morton. And he'd got Sammy into all this in the first place. Sammy and Candice – pebbles dropped into a pool. And now the ripples had grown so that he'd all but forgotten about the centre, the starting point. Just like when he was married, work consuming him, becoming an end in itself. And Rhona's words: *You've exploited every relationship you ever had.*

To be born again ...

'I'm sorry, Rhona,' he said.

'Can you let Ned know?' She started crying again.

'Come on,' he said, 'let's get some breakfast. Have you been here all night?'

'I couldn't leave.'

'I know.' He kissed her cheek.

'The person in the car ...'

'What?'

She looked at him. 'I don't care any more. I don't care who they were or whether they get caught. All I want is for her to wake up.'

Rebus nodded, told her he understood. Told her breakfast was on him. He kept the talk going, his mind not really on it. Instead, her words bounced around in his head: *I don't care who they were or whether they get caught ...*

Whichever stress he put on it, he couldn't make it sound like surrender.

At St Leonard's, he broke the news to Ned Farlowe. Farlowe wanted to go to the hospital, but Rebus shook his head. Farlowe was crying as Rebus left his cell. Back at his desk, the files on the Crab were waiting.

The Crab: real name, William Andrew Colton. He had form going back to his teens, celebrated his fortieth birthday on Guy Fawkes Day. Rebus hadn't had many dealings with him during his time in Edinburgh. Looked like the Crab had lived in the city for a couple of years in the early-80s, and again in the early-90s. 1982: Rebus gave evidence against him in a conspiracy trial. Charges dropped. 1983: he was in trouble again – a fight in a pub left one man in a coma and his girlfriend needing sixty stitches to her face. Sixty stitches: you could knit a pair of mittens with less.

The Crab had held various jobs: bouncer, bodyguard, general labourer. The Inland Revenue had a go at him in 1986. By '88, he was on the West Coast, which was presumably where Tommy Telford had found him. Knowing good muscle when he saw it, he'd put the Crab on the doors of his club in Paisley. More blood-spilling; more accusations. Nothing came of them. The Crab had lived a charmed life, the sort of life that niggled at cops the world over: witnesses too scared to testify; withdrawing or refusing to give evidence. The Crab didn't often make it to trial. He'd served three adult sentences – a total of twenty-seven months – in a career that was now entering its fourth decade. Rebus went through the paperwork again, picked up the phone and called CID in Paisley. The man he wanted to speak to had been transferred to Motherwell. Rebus made the call, eventually got through to Detective Sergeant Ronnie Hannigan, and explained his interest.

'It's just that reading between the lines, you suspected the Crab of a lot more than ever got put down on paper.'

'You're right.' Hannigan cleared his throat. 'Never got close to proving anything though. You say he's south of the border now?'

'Telford placed him with a gangster in Newcastle.'

'Have criminal tendencies, will travel. Well, let's hope they keep him. He was a one-man reign of terror, and that's no exaggeration. Probably why Telford palmed him off on someone else: the Crab was getting out of control. My theory is, Telford tried him out as a hit-man. Crab wasn't suitable, so Telford needed to jettison him.'

'What was the hit?'

'Down in Ayr. Must've been ... four years ago? Lot of drugs swilling around, most of them inside a dance-club ... can't remember its name. I don't know what happened: maybe a deal went sour, maybe someone was skimming. Whatever, there was a hit outside the club. Guy got his face half torn off with a carving knife.'

'You put the Crab in the frame?'

'He had an alibi, of course, and the eye-witnesses all seemed to have suffered temporary blindness. Could be a plot for the *X-Files* in that.'

A knife attack outside a nightclub ... Rebus tapped his desk with a pen. 'Any idea how the attacker got away?'

'On a motorbike. The Crab likes bikes. Crash helmet makes a good disguise.'

'We had an almost identical attack recently. Guy on a motorbike went for a drug dealer outside one of Tommy Telford's nightclubs. Killed a bouncer instead.'

And Cafferty denied any involvement ...

'Well, like you say, the Crab's in Newcastle.'

Yes, and staying put ... *scared* to come north. Warned off by Tarawicz. Because Edinburgh was too dangerous ... people might *remember* him.

'Do you know how far away Newcastle is?'

'A couple of hours?'

'No distance at all by bike. Anything else I should know?'

'Well, Telford tried the Crab in the van, but he wasn't much good.'

'What van?'

'The ice-cream van.'

Rebus nearly dropped the phone. 'Explain,' he said.

'Easy: Telford's boys were selling dope from an ice-cream van. The "five-pound special", they called it. You handed over a fiver and got back a cone or wafer with a wee plastic bag tucked inside ...'

Rebus thanked Hannigan and terminated the call. Five-pound specials: Mr Taystee with his clients who ate ice-cream in all weathers. His daytime pitches: near schools. His nighttime pitches: outside Telford's clubs. Five-pound specials on the menu, Telford taking his cut ... The new Merc: Mr Taystee's big mistake. Telford's moneymen wouldn't have taken long to work out their boy was skimming. Telford would have decided to turn Mr Taystee into a lesson ...

It was coming together. He spun his pen, caught it, and made another call, this time to Newcastle.

'Nice to hear from you,' Miriam Kenworthy said. 'Any sign of your lady friend?'

'She's turned up here.'

'Great.'

'In tow with Mr Pink Eyes.'

'Not so great. I wondered where he'd gone.'

'And he's not here to see the sights.'

'I'll bet he isn't.'

'Which is really why I'm calling.'

'Mmm?'

'I'm just wondering if he's ever been linked to machete attacks.'

'Machetes? Let me think ...' She was so quiet for so long, he thought the connection had failed. 'You know, that *does* ring a bell. Let me put it up on the screen.' Clackety-clack of her keyboard. Rebus was biting his bottom lip, almost drawing blood.

'God, yes,' she said. 'A year or so back, a battle on an estate. Rival gangs, that was the story, but everyone knew what was behind it: namely, drugs and pitch incursions.'

'And where there's drugs, there's Tarawicz?'

'There was a rumour his men were involved.'

'And they used machetes?'

'One of them did. His name's Patrick Kenneth Moynihan, known to all and sundry as "PK".'

'Can you give me a description?'

'I can fax you his picture. But meantime: tall, heavy build, curly black hair and a black beard.'

He wasn't part of the Tarawicz retinue. Two of Mr Pink's best muscle-men had been left behind in Newcastle. For safety's sake. Rebus put PK down as one of the Paisley attackers – Cafferty again in the clear.

'Thanks, Miriam. Listen, about that rumour ...'

'Remind me.'

'Telford supplying Tarawicz rather than the other way round: anything to back it up?'

'We tracked Pink Eyes and his men. A couple of jaunts to the continent, only they came back clean.'

'Leading you up the garden path?'

'Which made us start reassessing.'

'Where would Telford be getting the stuff?'

'We didn't reassess that far.'

'Well, thanks again ...'

'Hey, don't leave me hanging: what's the story?'

'Morning Glory. Cheers, Miriam.'

Rebus went and got a coffee, put sugar in it without realising, had finished half the cup before he noticed. Tarawicz was attacking Telford. Telford was blaming Cafferty. The resulting war would destroy Cafferty and weaken Telford. Then Telford would pull off the Maclean's break-in but be grassed up ...

And Tarawicz would fill the vacuum. That had been the plan all along. Bluesbreakers: 'Double-Crossing Time'. Christ, it was beautiful: set the two rivals against one another and wait for the carnage to end ...

The prize: something Rebus didn't yet know. There had to be something big. Tarawicz, the theory went, was sourcing his drugs not from London but from Scotland. From Tommy Telford.

What did Telford know? What was it that made *his* supply so valuable? Did it have something to do with Maclean's? Rebus got another coffee, washed down three Paracetamol with it. His head felt ready to explode. Back at his desk, he tried Claverhouse, couldn't get him. Paged him instead, and got an immediate call back.

'I'm in the van,' Claverhouse said.

'I've something to tell you.'

'What?'

Rebus wanted to know what was happening. Wanted in on the action. 'It's got to be face to face. Where are you parked?'

Claverhouse sounded suspicious. 'Down from the shop.'

'White decorator's van?'

'This definitely isn't a good idea ...'

'You want to hear what I've got?'

'Sell me the idea.'

'It clears everything up,' Rebus lied.

Claverhouse waited for more, but Rebus wasn't obliging. Theatrical sigh: life was hard on Claverhouse.

'I'll be there in half an hour,' Rebus said. He put down

the phone, looked around the office. 'Anyone got a set of overalls?'

'Nice disguise,' Claverhouse said, as Rebus squeezed into the front seat.

Ormiston was in the driver's seat, plastic piece-box open in front of him. A flask of tea had been opened, steaming up the windscreen. The back of the van was full of paint-tins, brushes and other paraphernalia. A ladder was strapped to the roof, and another was leaning against the wall of the tenement beside which the van had been parked. Claverhouse and Ormiston were in white overalls, daubed with swatches of old paint. The best Rebus could come up with was a blue boilersuit, tight at the waist and chest. He pulled the first few studs open as he settled in.

'Anything happening?'

'Jack's been in twice this morning.' Claverhouse looked towards the shop. 'Once for ciggies and a paper, once for a can of juice and a filled roll.'

'He doesn't smoke.'

'He does for this operation: perfect excuse to nip to the shop.'

'He hasn't given you any signal?'

'You expecting him to put the flags out?' Ormiston exhaled fish-paste.

'Just asking.' Rebus checked his watch. 'Either of you want a break?'

'We're fine,' Claverhouse said.

'What's Siobhan up to?'

'Paperwork,' Ormiston said with a smile. 'Ever come across a woman house painter?'

'Done much house painting yourself, Ormie?'

This brought a smile from Claverhouse. 'So, John,' he said, 'what is it you've got for us?'

Rebus filled them in quickly, noting Claverhouse's mounting interest.

'So Tarawicz is planning to double-cross Telford?' Ormiston said at the end.

Rebus shrugged. 'That's my guess.'

'Then why the hell are we bothering to set up a sting? Just let them get on with it.'

'That wouldn't give us Tarawicz,' Claverhouse said, his eyes slitted in concentration. 'If he sets up Telford for a fall, *he's* home and dry. Telford gets put away, and all we've done is replace one villain with another.'

'And an altogether nastier species at that,' Rebus said.

'What? And Telford's Robin Hood?'

'No, but at least with him, we know what we're dealing with.'

'And the old dears in his flats love him,' Claverhouse said.

Rebus thought of Mrs Hetherington, readying herself for her trip to Holland. The only drawback: she had to fly from Inverness ... Sakiji Shoda had flown from London to Inverness ...

Rebus started laughing.

'What's so funny?'

He shook his head, still laughing, wiping his eyes. It wasn't funny, not really.

'We could let Telford know what we know,' Claverhouse said, studying Rebus. 'Set him against Tarawicz, let them eat each other alive.'

Rebus nodded, took a deep breath. 'That's certainly one option.'

'Give me another.'

'Later,' Rebus said. He opened the door.

'Where are you off to?' Claverhouse asked.

'Got to fly.'

32

But in fact he was driving. A long drive, too. North through Perth and from there into the Highlands, taking a route which could be cut off during the worst of the winter. It wasn't a bad road, but traffic was heavy. He'd get past one slow-moving lorry only to catch up with another. He knew he should be thankful for small mercies: in the summer, caravans could end up fronting mile-long tail-backs.

He did pass a couple of caravans outside Pitlochry. They were from the Netherlands. Mrs Hetherington had said it was out of season for a trip to Holland. Most people her age would go in the spring, ready to fill their senses with the bulb-fields. But not Mrs Hetherington. Telford's offer: go when I say. Telford probably provided spending money, too. Told her to have a good time, not worry about a thing ...

As he neared Inverness, Rebus hit dual carriageway again. He'd been on the road well over two hours. Sammy might be coming round again; Rhona had his mobile number. Inverness Airport was signposted from the road into town. Rebus parked and got out, stretched his legs and arched his back, feeling the vertebrae pop. He went into the terminal and asked for security. He got a small balding man with glasses and a limp. Rebus introduced himself. The man offered coffee, but Rebus was jumpy enough after the drive. Hungry though: no lunch. He gave the man his story, and eventually they tracked down a representative of

Her Majesty's Customs. During his tour of the facilities, Rebus got the impression of a low-key operation. The Customs official was in her early thirties, rosy-cheeked and with black curly hair. There was a purple birthmark, the size of a small coin, in the middle of her forehead, looking for all the world like a third eye.

She took Rebus into the Customs area and found a room they could use for their conversation.

'They've just started direct international flights,' she said, in answer to his question. 'It's shocking really.'

'Why?'

'Because at the same time, they've cut back on man-power.'

'You mean in Customs?'

She nodded.

'You're worried about drugs?'

'Of course.' She paused. 'And everything else.'

'Are there flights to Amsterdam?'

'There will be.'

'But as of now … ?'

She shrugged. 'You can fly to London, make the connection there.'

Rebus was thoughtful. 'There was a guy a few days ago, flew from Japan to Heathrow, then got a flight to Inverness.'

'Did he stop off in London?'

Rebus shook his head. 'Caught the first connection.'

'That counts as an international connection.'

'Meaning?'

'His luggage would be put on the plane in Japan, and he wouldn't see it again until Inverness.'

'So you'd be the first Customs point?'

She nodded.

'And if his flight came in at some horrible hour …?'

She shrugged again. 'We do what we can, Inspector.'

Yes, Rebus could imagine: a lone, bleary-eyed Customs official, wits not at their sharpest ...

'So the bags change planes at Heathrow, but no one checks them there?'

'That's about it.'

'And if you were flying from Holland to Inverness via London?'

'Same deal.'

Rebus knew now, knew the brilliance of Tommy Telford's thinking. *He* was supplying drugs for Tarawicz, and Christ knew how many others. His little old ladies and men were bringing them in past early-morning or late-night Customs posts. How difficult would it be to slip something into a piece of luggage? Then Telford's men would be on hand to take everyone back to Edinburgh, carry their luggage upstairs ... and surreptitiously remove each package.

Old age pensioners as unwitting drugs couriers. It was stunning.

And Shoda hadn't flown into Inverness so he could check out the local tourist amenities. He'd flown in so he could see how easy it was, what a brilliant route Telford had found, quick and efficient with a minimum of risk. Rebus had to laugh again. The Highlands had its own drugs problem these days: bored teenagers and cash-rich oil-workers. Rebus had smashed one north-east ring back in early summer, only to have Tommy Telford come along ...

Cafferty would never have thought of it. Cafferty would never have been so daring. But Cafferty would have kept it quiet. He wouldn't have sought to expand, wouldn't have brought partners into the scheme.

Telford was still a kid in some respects. The passenger-seat teddy bear was proof of that.

Rebus thanked the Customs official and went in search of food. Parked in the middle of town and grabbed a burger, sat at a window table and thought it all through. There were still aspects that didn't make sense, but he could cope with that.

He made two calls: one to the hospital; one to Bobby Hogan. Sammy hadn't woken up again. Hogan was interviewing Pretty-Boy at seven o'clock. Rebus said he'd be there.

The weather was kind on the trip south, the traffic manageable. The Saab seemed to enjoy long drives, or maybe it was just that at seventy miles an hour the engine noise disguised all the rattles and bumps.

He drove straight to Leith cop-shop, looked at his watch and found he was quarter of an hour late. Which didn't matter, since they were just starting the interview. Pretty-Boy was there with Charles Groal, all-purpose solicitor. Hogan was sitting with another CID officer, DC James Preston. A tape-recorder had been set up. Hogan looked nervous, realising how speculative this whole venture was, especially with a lawyer present. Rebus gave him a reassuring wink and apologised for having been detained. The burger had given him indigestion, and the coffee he'd had with it had done nothing for his frayed nerves. He had to shake his head clear of Inverness and all its implications and concentrate on Pretty-Boy and Joseph Lintz.

Pretty-Boy looked calm. He was wearing a charcoal suit with a yellow t-shirt, black suede winkle-picker boots. He smelt of expensive aftershave. In front of him on the desk: a pair of tortoiseshell Ray-Bans and his car keys. Rebus knew he'd own a Range Rover – it was mandatory for Telford employees – but the key-ring boasted the Porsche marque, and on the street outside Rebus had parked behind a cobalt blue 944. Pretty-Boy showing a touch of individuality …

Groal had his briefcase open on the floor beside him. On the desk in front of him: an A4 pad of ruled paper, and a fat black Mont Blanc pen.

Lawyer and client oozed money easily made and just as easily spent. Pretty-Boy used his money to buy class, but Rebus knew his background: working-class Paisley, a granite-hard introduction to life.

Hogan identified those present for the benefit of the tape-recorder, then looked at his own notes.

'Mr Summers ...' Pretty-Boy's real name: Brian Summers. 'Do you know why you're here?'

Pretty-Boy made an O of his glossy lips and stared ceilingwards.

'Mr Summers,' Charles Groal began, 'has informed me that he is willing to co-operate, Inspector Hogan, but that he'd like some indication of the accusations against him and their validity.'

Hogan stared at Groal, didn't blink. 'Who said he's accused of anything?'

'Inspector, Mr Summers works for Thomas Telford, and your police force's harassment of that individual is on record ...'

'Nothing to do with me, Mr Groal, or this station.' Hogan paused. 'Nothing at all to do with my present inquiries.'

Groal blinked half a dozen times in quick succession. He looked at Pretty-Boy, who was now studying the tips of his boots.

'You want me to say something?' Pretty-Boy asked the lawyer.

'I'm just ... I'm not sure if ...'

Pretty-Boy cut him off with a wave of his hand, then looked at Hogan.

'Ask away.'

Hogan made show of studying his notes again. 'Do you know why you're here, Mr Summers?'

'General vilification as part of your witch-hunt against my employer.' He smiled at the three CID men. 'Bet you didn't think I'd know a word like "vilification".' His gaze rested on Rebus, then he turned to Groal.

'DI Rebus isn't based at this station.'

Groal took the hint. 'That's true, Inspector. Might I ask by what authority you've been allowed to sit in on this interview?'

'That will become clear,' Hogan said, '*if* you'll allow us to begin?'

Groal cleared his throat, but said nothing. Hogan let the silence lie for a few moments, then began.

'Mr Summers, do you know a man called Joseph Lintz?'

'No.'

The silence stretched out. Summers recrossed his feet. He looked up at Hogan, and blinked, the blink deteriorating into a momentary twitch of one eye. He sniffed, rubbed at his nose – trying to make out that the twitch meant nothing.

'You've never met him?'

'No.'

'The name means nothing to you?'

'You've asked me about him before. I'll tell you same as I told you then: I never knew the cat.' Summers sat up a bit straighter in his chair.

'You've never spoken to him by telephone?'

Summers looked at Groal.

'Hasn't my client made himself clear, Inspector?'

'I'd like an answer.'

'I don't know him,' Summers said, forcing himself to relax again, 'I've never spoken to him.' He gave Hogan his stare again, and this time held it. There was nothing behind the eyes but naked self-interest. Rebus wondered how anyone could ever think him 'pretty', when his whole outlook on life was so fundamentally ugly.

'He didn't phone you at your ... business premises?'

'I don't have any business premises.'

'The office you share with your employer.'

Pretty-Boy smiled. He liked those phrases: 'business premises'; 'your employer'. They all knew the truth, yet played this little game ... and he liked playing games.

'I've already said, I never spoke to him.'

'Funny, the phone company says differently.'

'Maybe they made a mistake.'

'I doubt that, Mr Summers.'

'Look, we've been through this before.' Summers sat forward in his chair. 'Maybe it was a wrong number. Maybe he spoke to one of my associates, and they *told* him he had a wrong number.' He opened his arms. 'This is going nowhere.'

'I agree with my client, Inspector,' Charles Groal said, scribbling something down. 'I mean, is this leading anywhere?'

'It's leading, Mr Groal, to an identification of Mr Summers.'

'Where and by whom?'

'In a restaurant with Mr Lintz. The same Mr Lintz he claims never to have met, never to have spoken to.'

Rebus saw hesitation cross Pretty-Boy's face. *Hesitation*, rather than surprise. He made no immediate denial.

'An identification made by a member of staff at the restaurant,' Hogan continued. 'Corroborated by another diner.'

Groal looked to his client, who wasn't saying anything, but the way he was staring at the table, Rebus wondered a smoking hole didn't start appearing in it.

'Well,' Groal went on, 'this is fairly irregular, Inspector.'

Hogan wasn't interested in the lawyer. It was Pretty-Boy and him now.

'What about it, Mr Summers? Care to revise your version of events? What were you talking about with Mr

Lintz? Was he looking for female company? I believe that's your particular area of expertise.'

'Inspector, I must insist ...'

'Insist away, Mr Groal. It won't change the facts. I'm just wondering what Mr Summers will say in court when he's asked about the phone call, the meeting ... when the witnesses identify him. I'm sure he's got a fund of stories, but he'll have to find a bloody good one.'

Summers slapped the desk with both palms, half-rose to his feet. There wasn't an ounce of fat on him. Veins stood out on the backs of his hands.

'I told you, I've never met him, never talked to him. Period, end of story, finito. And if you've got witnesses, they're lying. Maybe *you've* told them to lie. And that's all I've got to say.' He sat back down, put his hands in his pockets.

'I've heard,' Rebus said, as though attempting to liven up a flagging conversation between friends, 'that you run the more upmarket girls, the three-figure jobs rather than the gam-and-bam merchants.'

Summers snorted and shook his head.

'Inspector,' Groal said, 'I can't allow these accusations to continue.'

'Was that what Lintz wanted? Did he have expensive tastes?'

Summers continued shaking his head. He seemed about to say something, but caught himself, laughed instead.

'I would like to remind you,' Groal went on, unheeded by anyone, 'that my client has co-operated fully throughout this outrageous ...'

Rebus caught Pretty-Boy's eyes, held their stare. There was so much he wasn't telling ... so much he very nearly *wanted* to tell. Rebus thought of the length of rope in Lintz's house.

'He liked to tie them up, didn't he?' Rebus asked quietly.

Groal stood up, yanking Summers to his feet.

'Brian?' Rebus asked.

'Thank you, gentlemen,' Groal said. He was stuffing his notepad into his case, closing its brass locks. 'If you should find yourselves with any questions worth my client's time, we'll be pleased to assist. But otherwise, I'd advise you to …'

'Brian?'

DC Preston had turned off the tape recorder and gone to open the door. Summers picked up his car keys, slipped his sunglasses on.

'Gentlemen,' he said, 'it's been educational.'

'S&M,' Rebus persisted, getting in Pretty-Boy's face. 'Did he tie them up?'

Pretty-Boy snorted, shook his head again. He paused as his lawyer led him past Rebus.

'It was for *him*,' he said in an undertone.

It was for him.

Rebus drove to the hospital. Sat with Sammy for twenty minutes. Twenty minutes of meditation and head-clearing. Twenty reviving minutes, at the end of which he squeezed his daughter's hand.

'Thanks for that,' he said.

Back at the flat, he thought of ignoring the answering-machine until after he'd had a bath. His shoulders and back were aching from the drive to Inverness. But something made him press the button. Jack Morton's voice: 'I'm on for a meeting with TT. Let's meet after. Half-ten at the Ox. I'll aim for that, but can't promise. Wish me luck.'

He walked in at eleven.

There was folk music in the back room. The front would have been quiet if it weren't for two loud-mouths who looked like they'd been at it since their office closed for the

354

night. They still wore work-suits, newspapers rolled in their pockets. They were drinking G&T.

Rebus asked Jack Morton what he wanted.

'A pint of orange and lemonade.'

'So how did it go?' Rebus ordered the drink. In forty minutes, he'd managed to put away two Cokes, and was now on coffee.

'They seem keen.'

'So who was at the meeting?'

'My sponsors from the shop, plus Telford and a couple of his men.'

'The transmitter worked okay?'

'Sound as a pound.'

'Did they search you?'

Morton shook his head. 'They were sloppy, seemed really sweaty about something. Want to hear the plan?' Rebus nodded. 'Middle of the night, truck arrives at the factory, and I let it through the gates. My story is, I had a phone call from the boss okaying the delivery. So I wasn't suspicious.'

'Only your boss never made the call?'

'That's right. So I was duped by a voice. And that's all I need to tell the police.'

'We'd sweat the truth out of you.'

'Like I say, John, the whole plan's half-baked. I'll give them this though – they did check my background. Seemed satisfied.'

'Who's going to be in the truck?'

'Ten men, armed to the teeth. I'm to get a rough plan of the place to Telford tomorrow, let him know how many people will be around, what the alarm system's like ...'

'What's in it for you?'

'Five grand. He's judged that right: five gets my debts repaid and puts a wedge in my pocket.'

Five grand: the amount Joseph Lintz had taken out of his bank ...

'Your story's holding?'

'They've staked out my flat.'

'And they didn't follow you here?'

Morton shook his head, and Rebus filled him in on what he'd learned and what he suspected. While Morton was taking it in, Rebus threw a question at him.

'How does Claverhouse want to play it?'

'The tape evidence is good: Telford talking, me making sure I called him "Mr Telford" and "Tommy" a few times. It's obviously him on the recording. But ... Claverhouse wants Telford's crew caught red-handed.'

' "Got to do it right".'

'That seems to be his catch-phrase.'

'Is there a date?'

'Saturday, all being well.'

'What's the betting we get a tip-off on Friday?'

'If your theory's right.'

'If I'm right,' he agreed.

33

The tip-off didn't come until Saturday lunchtime, but when it did, Rebus knew his hunch had been right.

Claverhouse was the first to congratulate him, which surprised Rebus, because Claverhouse had a lot on his plate and had acted very casually when the call had come. Pinned to the walls of the Crime Squad office were detailed maps of the drugs plant, along with staff rosters. Coloured stickers showed where personnel would be stationed. During the night, it was security only, unless some big order was demanding overtime. Tonight, the usual security staff would be augmented by Lothian & Borders Police. Twenty people inside the plant, with marksmen stationed on roofs and at certain key windows. A dozen cars and vans as back-up. It was the biggest operation of Claverhouse's career; a lot was expected of him. He kept saying 'it has to be done right'. He said he would leave 'nothing to chance'. Those two phrases had become his mantra.

Rebus had listened to a recording of the snitch call: 'Be at Maclean's factory in Slateford tonight. Two in the morning, it's going to be turned over. Ten men, tooled up, driving a lorry. If you're canny, you can catch all of them.'

Scots accent, but sounding long distance. Rebus smiled, looked at the turning spools, and said 'Hello again, Crab' out loud.

No mention of Telford, which was interesting. Telford's men were loyal: they'd go down without saying a word. And Tarawicz wasn't grassing up Telford. He couldn't know the police already had taped evidence of Telford's involvement. Which meant he was planning on letting Telford go ... No, think it through. With the plan dead in the water and ten of his best men in custody, Tarawicz didn't *need* Telford under lock and key. He wanted him out in the open and worried, Yakuza breathing down his neck, all his frailties exposed. He could be picked off at any time, or made to hand over *everything*. No blood-letting required; it would be a simple business proposition.

'It has to be ...'

'Done right,' Rebus said. 'Claverhouse, we *know*, okay?'

Claverhouse lost it. 'You're only here because I tolerate you! So let's get that straight for a start. I snap my fingers and you're out of the game, understood?'

Rebus just stared at him. A line of sweat was running down Claverhouse's left temple. Ormiston was looking up from his desk. Siobhan Clarke, briefing another officer beside a wall-chart, stopped talking.

'I promise I'll be a good boy,' Rebus said quietly, 'if you'll promise to stop with the broken record routine.'

Claverhouse's jaw was working, but eventually he produced a near-smile of apology.

'Let's get on with it then.'

Not that there was much for them to do. Jack Morton was working a double shift, wouldn't start till three o'clock. They'd be watching the place from then on, just in case Telford changed the game-plan. This meant personnel were going to miss the big match: Hibs against Hearts at Easter Road. Rebus had his money on a 3–2 home win.

Ormiston's summing-up: 'Easiest quid you'll ever lose.'

Rebus retired to one of the computers and got back to work. Siobhan Clarke had already come round snooping.

'Writing it up for one of the tabloids?'

'No such luck.'

He tried to keep it simple, and when he was happy with

the finished product he printed off two copies. Then he went out to buy a couple of nice, bright folders ...

He dropped off one of the folders, then returned home, too restless to be much use at Fettes. Three men were waiting in his tenement stairwell. Two more came in behind him, blocking the only escape route. Rebus recognised Jake Tarawicz and one of his muscle-men from the scrapyard. The others were new to him.

'Up the stairs,' Tarawicz ordered. Rebus was a prisoner under escort as they climbed the steps.

'Unlock the door.'

'If I'd known you were coming, I'd have got in some beers,' Rebus said, searching his pockets for keys. He was wondering which was safer: let them in, or keep them out? Tarawicz made the decision for him, nodded some signal. Rebus's arms were grabbed, hands went into his jacket and trousers, found his keys. He kept his face blank, eyes on Tarawicz.

'Big mistake,' he said.

'In,' Tarawicz ordered. They pushed Rebus into the hallway, walked him to the living room.

'Sit.'

Hands pushed Rebus on to the sofa.

'At least let me make a pot of tea,' he said. Inside he was trembling, knowing everything he couldn't afford to give away.

'Nice place,' Mr Pink Eyes was saying. 'Lacks the feminine touch though.' He turned to Rebus. 'Where is she?' Two of the men had peeled off to search the place.

'Who?'

'I mean, who else would she turn to? Not your daughter ... not now she's in a coma.'

Rebus stared at him. 'What do you know about that?' The two men returned, shook their heads.

'I hear things.' Tarawicz pulled out a dining-chair and sat down. There were two men behind the sofa, two in front.

'Make yourselves at home, lads. Where's the Crab, Jake?' Reasoning: a question he might be expected to ask.

'Down south. What's it to you?'

Rebus shrugged.

'Shame about your daughter. Going to make a recovery, is she?' Rebus didn't answer. Tarawicz smiled. 'National Health Service ... I wouldn't trust it myself.' He paused. 'Where is she, Rebus?'

'Using my finely honed detective's skills, I'll assume you mean Candice.' Meaning she'd done a runner. Trusting to herself for once. Rebus was proud of her.

Tarawicz snapped his fingers. Arms grabbed Rebus from behind, pinning back his shoulders. One man stepped forward and punched him solidly on the jaw. Stepped back again. Second man forward: gut punches. A hand tugged his hair, forcing his eyes up to the ceiling. He didn't see the flat-handed chop aiming for his throat. When it came, he thought he was going to cough out his voice-box. They let him go, and he pitched forward, hands going to his throat, retching for breath. A couple of teeth felt loose, and the skin inside his cheek had burst. He got out a handkerchief, spat blood.

'Unfortunately,' Tarawicz was saying, 'I have no sense of humour. So I hope you'll understand I'm not joking when I say that I'll kill you if I have to.'

Rebus shook his head free of all the secrets he knew, all the power he held over Tarawicz. He told himself: *you don't know anything.*

He told himself: *you're not going to die.*

'Even ... if ... I did know ...' Fighting for breath. 'I wouldn't tell you. If the two of us were standing in a minefield, I wouldn't let you know. Want me ... to tell you why?'

'Sticks and stones, Rebus.'

'It's not because of *who* you are, it's *what* you are. You trade in human beings.' Rebus dabbed at his mouth. 'You're no better than the Nazis.'

Tarawicz put a hand to his chest. 'I'm struck to the quick.'

'Chance would be a fine thing.' Rebus coughed again. 'Tell me, why do you want her back?' Rebus knowing the answer: because he was about to head south, leaving Telford in Shit Street. Because to return to Newcastle without her was a small but palpable defeat. Tarawicz wanted it *all*. He wanted every last crumb on the plate.

'My business,' Tarawicz said. Another signal, and the hands grabbed him again, Rebus resisting this time. Packing-tape was being wound around his mouth.

'Everybody tells me how *genteel* Edinburgh is,' Tarawicz was saying. 'Can't have the neighbours complaining about the screams. Put him on a chair.'

Rebus was lifted up. He struggled. A kidney punch buckled his knees. They forced him down on to a dining-chair. Tarawicz was removing his jacket, undoing gold cufflinks so he could roll up the sleeves of his pink and blue striped shirt. His arms were hairless, thick, and the same mottled colour as his face.

'A skin complaint,' he explained, removing his blue-tinted glasses. 'Some distant cousin of leprosy, they tell me.' He loosened his top button. 'I'm not as pretty as Tommy Telford, but I think you'll find me his master in every other respect.' A smile to his troops, a smile Rebus wasn't supposed to understand. 'We can start anywhere you want, Rebus. And *you* get to choose when we stop. Just nod your head, tell me where she is, and I walk out of your life forever.'

He got in close to Rebus, the sheen on his face like a protective seal. His pale blue eyes had tiny black pupils. Rebus thought: consumer as well as pusher. Tarawicz waited for a nod which didn't come, then retreated. Found an anglepoise lamp next to Rebus's chair. Planted both feet on its base and yanked on the mains cable, ripping it free.

'Bring him over here,' he ordered. Two men pulled both Rebus and chair over towards where Tarawicz was checking that the cable was plugged into the wall and that the socket was switched on. Another man closed the curtains: no free show for the kids across the way. Tarawicz was dangling the cable, letting Rebus see the loose wires – the very *live* wires. Two-hundred-and-forty volts just waiting to make his acquaintance.

'Believe me,' Tarawicz said, 'this is nothing. The Serbs had torture down to a fine art. Much of the time, they weren't even looking for a confession. I've helped a few of the more intelligent ones, the ones who knew when it was time to run. There was money to be made in the early days, power for the taking. Now the politicians are moving in, bringing trial-judges with them.' He looked at Rebus. 'The intelligent ones always know when it's time to quit. One last chance, Rebus. Remember, a nod of the head ...' The wires were inches from his cheek. Tarawicz changed his mind, moved them towards his nostrils, then his eyeballs.

'A nod of the head ...'

Rebus was twisting, arms holding him down – his legs, arms, shoulders. Hands holding his head, chest. Wait! The shock would pass straight through Tarawicz's men! Rebus saw it for a bluff. His eyes met Tarawicz's, and they both knew. Tarawicz pulled back.

'Tape him to the chair.' Two-inch-wide runs of tape, fixing him in place.

'This time for real, Rebus.' To his men: 'Hold him till I get close. Pull away when I say.'

Rebus thinking: there'd be a split-second after they let go ... A moment in which to break free. The tape wasn't the strongest he'd seen, but there was plenty of it. Maybe too much. He flexed his chest against it, felt no sign that it would break.

'Here we go,' Tarawicz said. 'First the face ... then the genitals. You *will* tell me, we both know it. How much bravado you want to show is up to you, but don't think it means anything.'

Rebus said something behind the gag.

'No point talking,' Tarawicz said. 'The only thing I want from you is a nod, understood?'

Rebus nodded.

'Was that a nod?'

Forcing a smile, Rebus shook his head.

Tarawicz didn't look impressed. His mind was on business. That was all Rebus was to him. He aimed the wire at Rebus's cheek.

'Let go!'

The pressure on Rebus fell away. He pushed against his bonds, couldn't budge them. Electricity flashed through his nervous system, and he went rigid. His heart felt like it had doubled in size, his eyeballs bulged, tongue pushing against the gag. Tarawicz lifted the cable away.

'Hold him.'

Arms fell on Rebus again, finding less resistance than before.

'Doesn't even leave a mark,' Tarawicz said. 'And the real beauty is, you end up paying for it from your own electric bill.'

His men laughed. They were beginning to enjoy themselves.

Tarawicz crouched down, face to face. His eyes sought Rebus's.

'For your information, that was a five-second jolt.

Things only start to get interesting at the half-minute mark. How's your heart? For your sake, I hope it's in good condition.'

Rebus felt like he'd just mainlined adrenaline. Five seconds: it had seemed much longer. He was changing strategies, trying to think up some new lies Mr Pink might believe, anything to get him out of the flat ...

'Undo his trousers,' Tarawicz was saying. 'Let's see what a jolt down there will do.'

Behind the gag, Rebus started screaming. His tormentor was looking around the room again.

'Definitely lacks the feminine touch.'

Hands were loosening his trouser-belt. They stopped when a buzzer sounded. There was someone at the main door.

'Just wait,' Tarawicz said quietly. 'They'll go away.'

The buzzer sounded again. Rebus wrestled with his bonds. Silence. Then the buzzer again, more insistent now. One of the men went for the window.

'Don't!' Tarawicz snapped.

Buzzer again. Rebus hoped it would go on forever. Couldn't think who it might be: Rhona? Patience? A sudden thought ... what if they persisted, and Tarawicz decided to allow them inside? Rhona or Patience ...

Time stretched. No more buzzing. They'd gone away. Tarawicz was beginning to relax, focusing his mind on his work once more.

Then there was a knock at the flat door. The person had got into the tenement. Now they were on the landing outside. Knocking again. Lifting the flap of the letterbox.

'Rebus!'

A male voice. Tarawicz looked to his men, nodded another signal. Curtains were opened; Rebus's bonds cut; the tape ripped from his face. Tarawicz rolled down his sleeves, put his jacket back on. Left the flex lying on the floor. One last word to Rebus: 'We'll speak again.' Then he marched his men to the door, opened it.

'Excuse us.'

Rebus was left sitting on the chair. He couldn't move, felt too shaky to stand up.

'Hang on a minute, chief!'

Rebus placed the voice: Abernethy. It didn't sound as if Tarawicz was heeding the Special Branch man.

'What's the score?' Now Abernethy was in the living-room, looking around.

'Business meeting,' Rebus croaked.

Abernethy came forward. 'Funny old business where you have to unzip your flies.'

Rebus looked down, started to make repairs.

'Who was that?' Abernethy persisted.

'A Chechen from Newcastle.'

'Likes to travel mob-handed, does he?' Abernethy walked around the room, found the bare flex and tut-tutted, unplugged it at the socket. 'Fun and games,' he said.

'Don't worry,' Rebus told him, 'it's under control.'

Abernethy laughed.

'What do you want anyway?'

'Brought someone to see you.' He nodded towards the doorway. A distinguished-looking man was standing there, dressed in three-quarter-length black woollen coat and white silk scarf. He was completely bald, with a huge dome of a head and cheeks reddened from cold. He had a sniffle, and was wiping his nose with a handkerchief.

'Thought we might pop out somewhere,' the man said, locution impeccable, his eyes everywhere but on Rebus. 'Get a spot to eat, if you're hungry.'

'I'm not,' Rebus said.

'Something to drink then.'

'There's whisky in the kitchen.'

The man looked reluctant.

365

'Look, pal,' Rebus told him, 'I'm staying right here. You can join me or you can bugger off.'

'I see,' the man said. He put the handkerchief away and stepped forward, stretched out a hand. 'Name's Harris, by the way.'

Rebus took the hand, expecting sparks to leap from his fingertips.

'Mr Harris, let's sit at the dining-table.' Rebus got to his feet. He was shaky, but his knees held till he'd crossed the floor. Abernethy appeared from the kitchen with the bottle and three glasses. Left again, and returned with a milk-jug of water.

Ever the host, Rebus poured, sizing up the trembling in his right arm. He felt disoriented. Adrenaline and electricity coursing through him.

'*Slainte*,' he said, lifting the glass. But he paused with it at his nostrils. Pact with the Big Man: no drinking, and Sammy back. His throat hurt when he swallowed, but he put the glass down untouched. Harris was pouring too much water into his own glass. Even Abernethy looked disapproving.

'So, Mr Harris,' Rebus said, rubbing his throat, 'just who the hell are you?'

Harris affected a smile. He was playing with his glass.

'I'm a member of the intelligence community, Inspector. I know what that probably conjures up in your mind, but I'm afraid the reality is far more prosaic. Intelligence-gathering means just that: lots of paperwork and filing.'

'And you're here because of Joseph Lintz?'

'I'm here because DI Abernethy says you're determined to link the murder of Joseph Lintz with the various accusations which have been made against him.'

'And?'

'And that, of course, is your prerogative. But there are

matters not necessarily germane which might prove ... embarrassing, if brought into the open.'

'Such as that Lintz really was Linzstek, and was brought to this country by the Rat Line, probably with help from the Vatican?'

'As to whether Lintz and Linzstek were the same man ... I can't tell you. A lot of the documentation was destroyed just after the war.'

'But "Joseph Lintz" was brought to this country by the Allies?'

'Yes.'

'And why did we do that?'

'Lintz was useful to this country, Inspector.'

Rebus poured a fresh whisky for Abernethy. Harris hadn't touched his. 'How useful?'

'He was a reputable academic. As such he was invited to attend conferences and give guest lectures all round the world. During this time, he did some work for us. Translation, intelligence-gathering, recruitment ...'

'He recruited people in other countries?' Rebus stared at Harris. 'He was a *spy*?'

'He did some dangerous and ... influential work for this country.'

'And got his reward: the house in Heriot Row?'

'He earned every penny in the early days.'

Harris's tone told Rebus something. 'What happened?'

'He became ... unreliable.' Harris lifted the glass to his nose, sniffed it, but put it down again untouched.

'Drink it before it evaporates,' Abernethy chided. Harris looked at him, and the Londoner mumbled an apology.

'Define "unreliable",' Rebus said, pushing aside his own glass.

'He began to ... fantasise.'

'He thought a colleague at the university had been in the Rat Line?'

Harris was nodding. 'He became obsessed with the Rat Line, began to imagine that everyone around him had been involved in it, that we were *all* culpable. Paranoia, Inspector. It affected his work and eventually we had to let him go. This was years back. He hasn't worked for us since.'

'So why the interest? What does it matter if any of this comes out?'

Harris sighed. 'You're right, of course. The problem is not the Rat Line *per se*, or the notion of Vatican involvement or any of the other conspiracy theories.'

'Then what is ...?' Rebus broke off, realised the truth. 'The problem is the personnel,' he stated. 'The other people brought in by the Rat Line.' He nodded to himself. 'Who are we talking about? Who might be implicated?'

'Senior figures,' Harris admitted. He'd stopped playing with the glass. His hands were flat on the table. He was telling Rebus: this is *serious*.

'Past or present?'

'Past ... plus people whose children have gone on to achieve positions of power.'

'MPs? Government ministers? Judges?'

Harris was shaking his head. 'I can't tell you, Inspector. I haven't been trusted with that knowledge myself.'

'But you could hazard a guess.'

'I don't deal in guesswork.' He looked at Rebus. There was steel behind the eyes. 'I deal in known quantities. It's a good maxim – one you should try.'

'But whoever killed Lintz did so *because* of his past.'

'Are you sure?'

'It doesn't make sense otherwise.'

'DI Abernethy tells me there's a link with some criminal elements in Edinburgh, perhaps a question of prostitution. It all sounds sordid enough to be believable.'

'And if it's believable, that's good enough for you?'

368

Harris stood up. 'Thank you for listening.' He blew his nose again, looked to Abernethy. 'Time to go, I believe. DI Hogan is waiting for us.'

'Harris,' Rebus said, 'you said yourself, Lintz had gone loopy, become a liability. Who's to say *you* didn't have him killed?'

Harris shrugged. 'If we'd arranged it, his demise would not have been quite so obvious.'

'Car crash, suicide, falling from a window ...?'

'Goodbye, Inspector.'

As Harris walked to the door, Abernethy stood up and locked eyes with Rebus. He didn't say anything, but the message was there.

This is deeper water than either of us wants to be in. So do yourself a favour, swim for shore.

Rebus nodded, reached out a hand. The two men shook.

34

Two in the morning.

Frost on the car windscreens. They couldn't clear them: had to blend in with the other cars on the street. Back-up – four units – parked in a builder's yard just round the corner. Bulbs had been removed from street-lights, leaving the area in almost total darkness. Maclean's was like a Christmas tree: security lights, every window blazing, same as every other night.

No heating in the unmarked cars: heat would melt the frost; exhaust fumes a dead giveaway.

'This all seems very familiar,' Siobhan Clarke said. The surveillance on Flint Street seemed a lifetime ago to Rebus. Clarke was in the driving seat, Rebus in the back. Two to each car. That way, they had space to duck should anyone come snooping. Not that they expected anyone to do that: the whole heist was half-baked. Telford desperate *and* with his mind on other things. Sakiji Shoda was still in town – a quiet word with the hotel manager had revealed a Monday morning check-out. Rebus was betting Tarawicz and his men had already gone.

'You look pretty snug,' Rebus said, referring to her padded ski-jacket. She brought a hand out of her pocket, showed him what it was holding. It looked like a slim lighter. Rebus lifted it from her palm. It was warm.

'What the hell is it?'

Clarke smiled. 'I got it from one of those catalogues. It's a handwarmer.'

'How does it work?'

'Fuel rods. Each one lasts up to twelve hours.'

'So you've got one warm hand?'

She brought her other hand out, showed him an identical rod. 'I bought two,' she said.

'You might have said.' Rebus closed his fingers around the handwarmer, stuck it deep into his pocket.

'That's not fair.'

'Call it a privilege of rank.'

'Lights,' she warned. They dived for cover, surfaced again when the car had sped past: false alarm.

Rebus checked his watch. Jack Morton had been told to expect the truck some time between one-thirty and two-fifteen. Rebus and Clarke had been in the car since just after midnight. The snipers on the roof, poor bastards, had been in position since one o'clock. Rebus hoped they had a good supply of fuel rods. He still felt jittery from the afternoon's events. He didn't like that he owed Abernethy such a huge favour; indeed, maybe owed him his life. He knew he could cancel it out by agreeing – along with Hogan – to soft-pedal on the Lintz inquiry. He didn't like the idea, but all the same ... And the day's silver lining: Candice had made the break from Tarawicz.

Clarke's police radio was silent. They had maintained silence since before midnight. Claverhouse's words: 'The first person to speak will be me, understood? Anyone uses a radio before me, they're in farmyard shit. And I won't utter a sound until the truck's entered the compound. Is that clear?' Nods all around. 'They could be listening in, so this is *important*. We've got to do this *right*.' Averting his eyes from Rebus as he said it. 'I'd wish us all luck, but the less luck's involved the better I'll like it. A few hours from now, if we stick to the plan, we should have broken up Tommy Telford's gang.' He paused. 'Just let that sink in. We'll be heroes.' He swallowed, realising the immensity of the prize.

Rebus couldn't get so excited. The whole enterprise had shown him a simple truth: no vacuum. Where you had society, you had criminals. No belly without an underbelly.

Rebus knew his own criteria came cheaply: his flat, books, music and clapped-out car. And he realised that he had reduced his life to a mere shell in recognition that he had completely failed at the important things: love, relationships, family life. He'd been accused of being in thrall to his career, but that had never been the case. His work sustained him only because it was an easy option. He dealt every day with strangers, with people who didn't mean anything to him in the wider scheme. He could enter their lives, and leave again just as easily. He got to live other people's lives, or at least portions of them, experiencing things at one remove, which wasn't nearly as challenging as the real thing.

Sammy had brought home to him these essential truths: that he was not only a failed father but a failed human being; that police work kept him sane, yet was a substitute for the life he could have had, the kind of life everyone else seemed to lead. And if he became obsessed with his case-work, well, that was no different from being obsessed with train numbers or cigarette cards or rock albums. Obsession came easy – especially to men – because it was a cheap way of achieving *control*, albeit control over something practically worthless. What did it matter if you could reel off the track listing to every '60s Stones album? It didn't matter a damn. What did it matter if Tommy Telford got put away? Tarawicz would take his place, and if he didn't, there was always Big Ger Cafferty. And if not Cafferty, then someone else. The disease was endemic, no cure in sight.

'What are you thinking about?' Clarke asked, switching her rod from left hand to right.

'My next cigarette.' Patience's words: *happiest when in denial* ...

They heard the truck before they saw it: changing gears noisily. Slid down into their seats, then up again as it made to pull into Maclean's. A wheeze of air-brakes as it jolted to a stop at the gates. A guard came out to talk to the driver. He carried a clip-board.

'Jack really suits a uniform,' Rebus said.

'Clothes maketh the man.'

'You reckon your boss has got it right?' He meant Claverhouse's plan: when the truck was in the compound, they'd use a megaphone and show the marksmen to whoever was in the driver's cab, tell them to come out. The rest of the men could stay locked in the back of the vehicle. They'd have them toss out any arms and then come out one at a time.

It was either that or wait until they were *all* out of the truck. Merit of this second plan: they'd know what they were dealing with. Merit of the first: most of the gang would be nicely stowed in the truck, and could be dealt with as and when.

Claverhouse had plumped for plan one.

Marked and unmarked cars were to move in as soon as the truck had come to a stop – engine off – in the compound. They would block the exit, then watch from safety while Claverhouse, at a first-floor window with his megaphone, and the marksmen (roof; ground-floor windows) did their stuff. 'Negotiation with force' was how Claverhouse had described it.

'Jack's opening the gates,' Rebus said, peering through the side window.

Engine roar, and the truck jerked forward.

'Driver seems a bit nervous,' Clarke commented.

'Or isn't used to HGVs.'

'Okay, they're in.'

Rebus stared at the radio, willing it to burst into life. Clarke had turned the ignition one click away from starting.

Jack Morton was watching the truck move into the compound. He turned his head towards the line of cars parked across the way.

'Any second ...'

The truck's brake-lights came on, then went off again. Air-brakes sounded.

The radio fizzed a single word: '*Now!*'

Clarke turned the engine, revved hard. Five other cars did the same. Exhaust smoke billowed suddenly into the night air. The noise was like the start of a stock-car race. Rebus wound his window down, the better to hear Claverhouse's megaphone diplomacy. Clarke's car leaped forward, first to the gates. Both she and Rebus jumped out, keeping their heads down, the car a shield between themselves and the truck.

'Engine's still running,' Rebus hissed.

'What?'

'The truck. Its engine's still running!'

Claverhouse's voice, warbling – partly nerves, partly megaphone quality: 'Armed police. Open the cab doors slowly and come out one at a time, hands held high. I repeat: armed police. Discard weapons before coming out. I repeat: discard weapons.'

'Do it!' Rebus hissed. Then: 'Tell them to switch off the bloody engine!'

Claverhouse: 'The gate is blocked, there's no escape, and we don't want anyone getting hurt.'

'Tell them to throw out the keys.' Cursing, Rebus dived back into the car, grabbed the handset. 'Claverhouse, tell them to ditch the bloody keys!'

Windscreen frosted over; he couldn't see a thing. Heard Clarke's yell: '*Get out!*'

Saw: dim white lights. The truck was reversing. At speed. A roar from its engine, veering crazily but heading for the gates.

374

Heading straight for him.

An explosion: bricks flying from the factory's front wall. Rebus dropped the handset, got his arm stuck in the seatbelt. Clarke was screaming as he leaped clear.

A second later, truck and car connected in a rending of metal and smashing of glass. Domino effect: Clarke's car hit the one behind, throwing officers off balance. The road was like a skating rink, the truck pushing one car, two cars, then three cars back on to the highway.

Claverhouse was on the megaphone, choking on dust: 'No shooting! Officers too close! Officers too close!'

Yes, all they needed now was to be pinned down by sniper fire. Men and women were slipping, losing their footing, clambering from their cars. Some of them armed, but dazed. The truck's back doors, buckled by the initial collision, flew open, seven or eight men hit the ground running. Two of them had handguns, and loosed off three or four shots apiece.

Shouts, screams, the megaphone. The glass wall of the gatehouse exploded as a bullet hit it. Rebus couldn't see Jack Morton ... couldn't see Siobhan. He was lying on his front on a section of grass verge, hands over his head: classic defence/defeat posture and bloody useless with it. The whole area was picked out by floodlights, and one of the gunmen – Declan from the shop – was now aiming at those. Other members of the gang had headed out into the street and were running for it. They carried shotguns, pickaxe handles. Rebus recognised a few more faces: Ally Cornwell, Deek McGrain. The streetlights were dead, of course, giving them all the cover they could want. Rebus hoped the backup cars from the builder's yard were coming.

Yes: turning the corner now, all lights blazing, sirens howling. Tenement curtains were twitching, palms rubbing at windows. And right in front of Rebus, about an inch from his nose, a thickly rimed blade of grass. He could make out each sliver of frost, and the complex patterns which had formed. But he realised it was melting fast as his breath hit it. And his front was growing cold. And the marksmen were running from the building, lit up like a firing-range.

And Siobhan Clarke was safe: he could see her lying beneath a car. Good girl.

And one policewoman, also lying low, had been wounded in the knee. She kept touching it with her hand, then pulling the hand away to stare at the blood.

And there was still no sign of Jack Morton.

The gunmen were returning fire, scattering shots, smashing windscreens. Uniforms were ordered out of the front back-up car. Four of the gang got in.

Second car: uniforms out, three of the gang got in. No windscreens, but they were rolling. Yelling and whooping, waving their weapons. The two remaining gunmen were cool. They were taking a good look round, assessing the situation. Did they want to be here when the marksmen arrived? Maybe they did. Maybe they fancied their chances in that arena, too. Their luck had held *this* far, after all. Claverhouse: *the less luck's involved, the better I'll like it*.

Rebus got on to his knees, then his feet, staying at a crouch. He felt moderately safe. After all, *his* luck had held today, too.

'You okay, Siobhan?' Voice low, eyes on the gunmen. The two getaway cars added up to seven men. Two still left. Where was number ten?

'Fine,' Clarke said. 'What about you?'

'I'm okay.' Rebus left her, worked his way round to the front of the truck. The driver was unconscious behind his wheel, head bleeding where it had connected after the collision. There was some kind of grenade launcher on the seat beside him. It had left a bloody great hole in the wall of

Maclean's. Rebus checked the driver for firearms, found none. Then checked the pulse: steady. Recognised the face: one of the arcade regulars; looked about nineteen, twenty. Rebus took out his handcuffs, hooked the driver to the steering-wheel, threw the grenade launcher on to the road.

Then headed for the gatehouse. Jack Morton, in uniform but missing his cap, prone on the floor, covered by a glass shroud. The bullet had pierced his right breast-pocket. Pulse was weak.

'Christ, Jack ...'

There was a telephone in the booth. Rebus punched 999 and asked for ambulances.

'Police officers down at the Maclean's factory on Slateford Road!' Staring down at his friend.

'Whereabouts on Slateford Road?'

'Believe me, they won't be able to miss it.'

Five marksmen, dressed in black, aimed rifles at Rebus from outside. Saw him on the phone, saw him shake his head, moved on. Saw their targets out on the road, getting into a patrol car. Yelled the order to stop, warning that they would fire.

Response: muzzle-flash. Rebus ducked again. Fire was returned, the noise deafening but momentary.

Shouts from the road: 'Got them!'

A plaintive wail: one of the gunmen wounded. Rebus looked. The other was lying quite still on the road. Marksmen yelling to the wounded man: 'Drop the weapon, turn on to your front, hands behind your back.'

Response: 'I'm shot!'

Rebus to himself: 'Bastard's only wounded. Finish him off.'

Jack Morton unconscious. Rebus knew better than to move him. He could staunch the bleeding, that was all. Removed his jacket, folded it and pressed it to his friend's chest. Must've hurt, but Jack was out of it. Rebus dug the fuel rod out of his own pocket, the tiny canister still warm. Pressed it into Jack's right hand, curled the fingers around it.

'Stick around, pal. Just keep sticking around.'

Siobhan Clarke at the doorway, tears welling in her eyes.

Rebus pushed past her, slid his way across the road to where the Armed Response Team were cuffing the wounded man. Nobody much bothering with his dead partner. A little group of onlookers, keeping their distance. Rebus walked right up to the corpse, prised the handgun from its fingers, walked back around the front of the car. Heard someone call out: 'He's got a gun!'

Rebus bending down until the barrel of the gun touched the back of the wounded man's neck. Declan from the shop: breath coming in short gasps, hair matted with sweat, burrowing his face into the tarmac.

'John ...'

Claverhouse. No megaphone needed. Standing right behind him. 'You really want to be like them?'

Like them ... Like Mean Machine. Like Telford and Cafferty and Tarawicz. He'd crossed the line before, made several trips forth and back. His foot was on Declan's neck, the gun barrel so hot it was singeing nape-skin.

'Please, no ... oh, Christ, please ... don't ... don't ...'

'Shut up,' Rebus hissed. He felt Claverhouse's hand close over his, flick on the safety.

'My responsibility, John. My fuck-up, don't make it yours, too.'

'Jack ...'

'I know.'

Rebus's vision blurred. 'They're getting away.'

Claverhouse shook his head. 'Road blocks. Back-up are already on it.'

'And Telford?'

Claverhouse checked his watch. 'Ormie will be picking him up right about now.'

Rebus grabbed Claverhouse's lapels. 'Nail him!'

Sirens nearing. Rebus shouted for the drivers to move their cars, make room for the ambulance. Then he ran back to the gatehouse. Siobhan Clarke was kneeling beside Jack, stroking his forehead. Her face was streaked with tears. She looked up at Rebus and shook her head.

'He's gone,' she said.

'No.' But he knew the truth. Which didn't stop him saying the word over and over again.

35

They divided the gang between two different locations – Torphichen and Fettes – and took Telford and a few of his 'lieutenants' to St Leonard's. Result: a logistical nightmare. Claverhouse was washing Pro-Plus down with double-strength coffee, part of him wanting to do things right, the other part knowing he was answerable for the blood-bath at Maclean's. One officer dead, six wounded or otherwise injured – one of them seriously. One gunman dead, one wounded – not seriously enough to some people's minds.

The getaway cars had been apprehended and arrests made – shots exchanged but no bloodshed. None of the gang was saying anything, not a single damned word.

Rebus was sitting in an empty Interview Room at St Leonard's, arms on the table, head resting on arms. He'd been sitting there for a while, just thinking about loss, about how suddenly it could strike. A life, a friendship, just snatched away.

Irretrievable.

He hadn't cried, and didn't think he would. Instead, he felt numb, as if his soul had been spiked with novocaine. The world seemed to have slowed, like the mechanism was running down. He wondered if the sun would have the energy to rise again.

And I got him into it.

He had wallowed before in feelings of guilt and inadequacy, but nothing to measure up to this. This was overwhelming. Jack Morton, a copper with a quiet patch in

Falkirk ... murdered in Edinburgh because a friend had asked a favour. Jack Morton, who'd brought himself back to life by swearing off cigarettes and booze, getting into shape, eating right, taking *care* of himself ... Lying in the mortuary, deep-body temperature dropping.

And I put him there.

He jumped up suddenly, threw the chair at the wall. Gill Templer walked into the room.

'All right, John?'

He wiped his mouth with the back of his hand.

'Fine.'

'My office is empty if you want to get your head down.'

'No, I'll be fine. Just ...' He looked around. 'Is this place needed?'

She nodded.

'Right. Okay.' He picked up the chair. 'Who is it?'

'Brian Summers,' she said.

Pretty-Boy. Rebus straightened his back.

'I can make him talk.'

Templer looked sceptical.

'Honest, Gill.' Hands trembling. 'He doesn't know what I've got on him.'

She folded her arms. 'And what's that?'

'I just need ...' He checked his watch. 'An hour or so; two hours tops. Bobby Hogan needs to be here. And I want Colquhoun brought in pronto.'

'Who's he?'

Rebus found the business card and handed it over. 'Pronto,' he repeated. He worked at his tie, making himself presentable. Smoothed back his hair. Said nothing.

'John, I'm not sure you're in any state to ...'

He pointed at her, turned it into a wagging finger. 'Don't presume, Gill. If I say I can break him, I mean it.'

'No one else has said a single word.'

'Summers will be different.' He stared at her. 'Believe me.'

Looking back at him, she believed. 'I'll hold him back till Hogan gets here.'

'Thanks, Gill.'

'And, John?'

'Yes?'

'I'm really sorry about Jack Morton. I didn't know him, but I've heard what everyone's saying.'

Rebus nodded.

'They're saying he'd be the last one to blame you.'

Rebus smiled. 'Right at the back of the queue.'

'There's only one person in the queue, John,' she said quietly. 'And you're it.'

Rebus phoned the night-desk at the Caledonian Hotel, learned that Sakiji Shoda had checked out unexpectedly, less than two hours after Rebus had dropped off the green folder which had cost him fifty-five pence at a stationer's on Raeburn Place. Actually, the folders had come in three-packs at one sixty-five. He had the other two in his car, only one of them empty.

Bobby Hogan was on his way. He lived in Portobello. He said to give him half an hour. Bill Pryde came over to Rebus's desk and said how sorry he was about Jack Morton, how he knew the two of them had been old friends.

'Just don't get too close to me, Bill,' Rebus told him. 'The people closest to me tend to lose their health.'

He got a message from reception: someone there to see him. He headed downstairs, found Patience Aitken.

'Patience?'

She had all her clothes on, but not necessarily in the right order, like she'd dressed in a power-cut.

'I heard on the radio,' she said. 'I couldn't sleep, so I had the radio on, and they said about this police raid and how people were dead … And you weren't in your flat, so I …'

He hugged her. 'I'm okay,' he whispered. 'I should have called you.'

'It's my fault, I …' She looked at him. 'You were there, I can see it on your face.' He nodded. 'What happened?'

'I lost a friend.'

'Oh, Christ, John.' She hugged him again. She was still warm from the bedclothes. He could smell shampoo on her hair, perfume on her neck. *The people closest to me* … He pulled away gently, planted a kiss on her cheek.

'Go get some sleep,' he told her.

'Come for breakfast.'

'I just want to go home and crash.'

'You could sleep at my place. It's Sunday. We could stay in bed.'

'I don't know what time I'll finish here.'

She found his eyes. 'Don't feed on it, John. Don't keep it all inside.'

'Okay, Doc.' He pecked her cheek again. 'Now vamoose.'

He managed a smile and a wink: both felt treacherous. He stood at the door and watched her leave. A lot of times while he'd been married, he'd thought of just walking. There were times when all the responsibilities and the shite at work and the pressure and the *need* would make him dream of escape.

He was tempted again now. Push open the door and head off to somewhere that wasn't here, to do something that wasn't this. But that, too, would be treachery. He had scores to settle, and a reason to settle them. He knew Telford was somewhere in the building, probably consulting with Charles Groal, saying nothing to anyone else. He wondered how the team were playing it. When would they let Telford know about the tape? When would they tell him the security guard had been a plant? When would they tell him that same man was now dead?

He hoped they were being clever. He hoped they were rattling Telford's cage.

He couldn't help wondering – and not for the first time – if it was all worth it. Some cops treated it like a game, others like a crusade, and for most of the rest it was neither, just a way of earning their daily bread. He asked himself why he'd invited Jack Morton in. Answers: because he'd wanted a *friend* involved, someone who'd keep *him* in the game; because he'd thought Jack was bored, and would enjoy the challenge; because tactics had demanded an outsider. There were plenty of reasons. Claverhouse had asked if Morton had any family, anyone who should be informed. Rebus had told him: divorced, four kids.

Did Rebus blame Claverhouse? Easy to be wise after the event, but then Claverhouse's reputation had been built on being wise *before* the event. And he'd failed ... monumentally.

Icy roads: they'd needed the gates closed. The blockade had been too easy to move with the horsepower available to a truck.

Marksmen in the building: fine in the enclosed space of the yard, but they'd failed to keep the truck there, and the marksmen had been ineffectual once the truck had reversed out.

More armed officers *behind* the truck: producing little but a crossfire hazard.

Claverhouse should have got them to turn off the ignition, or – better still – waited for it to be turned off before making his presence known.

Jack Morton should have kept his head down.

And Rebus should have warned him.

Only, a shout would have turned the gunmen's attention towards him. Cowardice: was that what was at the bottom of his feelings? Simple human cowardice. Like in the bar in Belfast, when he hadn't said anything, fearing Mean Machine's wrath, fearing a rifle-butt turned on *him*. Maybe that was why – no, *of course* that was why – Lintz had got beneath Rebus's skin. Because when it came down to it, if Rebus had been in Villefranche ... drunk on failure, the dream of conquest over ... if he'd been under orders, just a lackey with a gun ... if he'd been primed by racism and the loss of comrades ... who was to say what he'd have done?

'Christ, John, how long have you been out here?'

It was Bobby Hogan, touching his face, prising the folder from frozen fingers.

'You're like ice, man, let's get you inside.'

'I'm fine,' Rebus breathed. And it had to be true: how else to explain the sweat on his back and his brow? How else to explain that he only started shivering *after* Bobby led him indoors?

Hogan got two mugs of sweet tea into him. The station was still buzzing: shock, rumour, theories. Rebus filled Hogan in.

'They'll have to let Telford walk, if nobody talks.'

'What about the tape?'

'They'll want to spring that later ... if they're being canny.'

'Who's in with him?'

Rebus shrugged. 'Farmer Watson himself, last time I heard. He was doing a double-act with Bill Pryde, but I saw Bill later, so they've either taken a break or else done a swop.'

Hogan shook his head. 'What a fucking business.'

Rebus stared at his tea. 'I hate sugar.'

'You drank the first mug all right.'

'Did I?' He took a mouthful, squirmed.

'What the hell did you think you were doing out there?'

'Catching a breath.'

'Catching your death more like.' Hogan patted down an unruly clump of hair. 'I had a visit from a man called Harris.'

'What are you going to do?'

Hogan shrugged. 'Let it go, I suppose.'

Rebus stared at him. 'You might not have to.'

36

Colquhoun didn't look happy to be there.

'Thanks for coming in,' Rebus told him.

'I didn't have much choice.' He had a solicitor sitting beside him, a middle-aged man: one of Telford's? Rebus couldn't have cared less.

'You might have to get used to not having choices, Dr Colquhoun. Know who else is in here tonight? Tommy Telford; Brian Summers.'

'Who?'

Rebus shook his head. 'You're getting your script wrong. It's okay for you to know who they are: we talked about them in front of Candice.'

Colquhoun's face flushed.

'You remember Candice, don't you? Her real name's Karina: did I ever tell you that? She's got a son somewhere, only they took him away. Maybe she'll find him one day, maybe not.'

'I don't see what this —'

'Telford and Summers are going to be spending a while behind bars.' Rebus sat back. 'If I want to, I could have a damned good go at putting you in there with them. How would you like that, Dr Colquhoun? Conspiracy to pervert, et cetera.'

Rebus could feel himself relaxing into his work; doing it for Jack.

The solicitor was about to say something, but Colquhoun got in first. 'It was a mistake.'

'A mistake?' Rebus hooted. 'One way of putting it, I suppose.' He sat forward, resting his elbows on the table. 'Time to talk, Dr Colquhoun. You know what they say about confession ...'

Brian 'Pretty-Boy' Summers looked immaculate.

He had a lawyer with him, too, a senior partner who looked like an undertaker and wasn't taking kindly to being kept waiting. As they settled at the table in the Interview Room, and Hogan slotted tapes into cassette machine and video recorder, the lawyer started the protest he'd spent the past hour or two preparing in his head.

'On behalf of my client, Inspector, I feel duty bound to say that this is some of the most appalling behaviour I've –'

'You think you've seen appalling behaviour?' Rebus answered. 'In the words of the song, you ain't seen nothing yet.'

'Look, it's clear to me that you –'

Rebus ignored him, slapped the folder down on to the table, slid it towards Pretty-Boy.

'Take a look.'

Pretty-Boy was wearing a charcoal suit and purple shirt, open at the neck. No sunglasses or car-keys. He'd been brought in from his flat in the New Town. Comment from one of the men who'd gone to fetch him: 'Biggest hi-fi I've seen in my life. Bugger was wide awake, listening to Patsy Cline.'

Rebus started whistling 'Crazy': that got Pretty-Boy's attention and a wry smile, but he kept his arms folded.

'I would if I were you,' Rebus said.

'Ready,' Hogan said, meaning he had the tapes running. They went through the formalities: date and time, location, individuals present. Rebus looked towards the lawyer and smiled. He looked pretty expensive. Telford would have ordered the best, same as always.

'Know any Elton John, Brian?' Rebus asked. 'He's got this song: "Someone Saved My Life Tonight". You'll be singing it to me once you've looked inside.' He tapped the folder. 'Go on, you know it makes sense. I'm not playing some trick, and you don't have to say anything. But you really should do yourself a favour ...'

'I've got nothing to say.'

Rebus shrugged. 'Just open the folder, take a look.'

Pretty-Boy looked to his lawyer, who seemed uncertain.

'Your client won't be incriminating himself,' Rebus explained. 'If you want to read what's in there first, that's fine. It might not mean much to you, but go ahead.'

The lawyer opened the folder, found a dozen sheets of paper.

'Sorry in advance for any mistakes,' Rebus said. 'I typed it in a bit of a rush.'

Pretty-Boy didn't so much as glance towards the material. He kept his eyes on Rebus, while the lawyer sifted through the papers.

'These allegations,' the lawyer finally said, 'you must realise they're worthless?'

'If that's your opinion, fair enough. I'm not asking Mr Summers to admit or deny anything. Like I said, he can do a deaf and dumb routine for all I care, so long as he uses his *eyes*.'

A smile from Pretty-Boy, then a glance towards his lawyer, who shrugged his shoulders, saying there was nothing here to fear. A glance back at Rebus, and Pretty-Boy unfolded his arms, picked up the first sheet, and started reading.

'Just so we have a record for the tape,' Rebus said, 'Mr Summers is now reading a draft report prepared by myself earlier today.' Rebus paused. 'Actually, I mean yesterday, Saturday. He's reading my interpretation of recent events in and around Edinburgh, events concerning his employer,

Thomas Telford, a Japanese business consortium – which is really, in my opinion, a Yakuza front – and a gentleman from Newcastle by the name of Jake Tarawicz.'

He paused. The lawyer said: 'Agreed, thus far.' Rebus nodded and continued.

'My version of events is as follows. Jake Tarawicz became an associate of Thomas Telford only because he wanted something Telford had: namely, a slick operation to bring drugs into Britain without raising suspicion. Either that or it was only later on, once their relationship had become established, that Tarawicz decided he could move in on Telford's turf. To facilitate this, he manufactured a war between Telford and Morris Gerald Cafferty. This was easily accomplished. Telford had moved in aggressively on Cafferty's territory, probably with Tarawicz egging him on. All Tarawicz had to do was make sure things escalated. To this end, he had one of his men attack a drug dealer outside one of Telford's night-clubs, Telford immediately placing the blame on Cafferty. He also had some of his men attack a Telford stronghold in Paisley. Meanwhile, there were attacks on Cafferty's territory and associates, retaliation by Telford for perceived wrongs.'

Rebus cleared his throat, took a sip of tea – a fresh cup, no sugar.

'Does this sound familiar, Mr Summers?' Pretty-Boy said nothing. He was busy reading. 'My guess is that the Japanese were never meant to become involved. In other words, they had no knowledge of what was happening. Telford was showing them around, easing the way for them as they tried to buy a country club. Rest and recreation for their members, plus a good way of laundering money – less suspect than a casino or similar operation, especially when an electronics factory is about to open, so that the Yakuza slip into the country as just a few more Japanese businessmen.

'I think when Tarawicz saw this, he began to worry. He didn't want to get rid of Tommy Telford just to leave the way open for other competitors to muscle in. So he decided they'd have to become part of his plan. He had Matsumoto followed. He had him killed, and in a nice twist made *me* the chief suspect. Why? Two reasons. First, Tommy Telford had me pegged as Cafferty's man, so by fingering me, Tarawicz was fingering Cafferty. Second, he wanted me out of the game, because I'd gone to Newcastle, and had met one of his men, a guy called William 'The Crab' Colton. I knew the Crab of old, and it so happened Tarawicz had used him for the hit on the drug dealer. He didn't want me putting two and two together.'

Rebus paused again. 'How's it sounding, Brian?'

Pretty-Boy had finished reading. His arms were folded again, eyes on Rebus.

'We've yet to see any evidence, Inspector,' the lawyer said.

Rebus shrugged. 'I don't need evidence. See, the same file you've got there, I delivered a copy to a Mr Sakiji Shoda at the Caledonian Hotel.' Rebus watched Pretty-Boy's eyelids flutter. 'Now, the way I see it, Mr Shoda is going to be a bit pissed off. I mean, he's already pissed off, that's why he was here. He'd seen Telford screw up, and wanted to see if he could do anything *right*. I don't suppose the raid on Maclean's will have given him any renewed sense of confidence. But he was also here to find out why one of his men had been killed, and who was responsible. This report tells him Tarawicz was behind it, and if he chooses to believe that, he'll go after Tarawicz. In fact, he checked out of his hotel yesterday evening – seems he was in a bit of a rush. I'm wondering if he was on his way home via Newcastle. Doesn't matter. What matters is that he'll *still* be pissed off at Telford for letting it happen. And meantime Jake Tarawicz is going to be wondering who shopped him to Shoda. The Yakuza are not nice people, Brian. You lot are nursery school by comparison.' Rebus sat back in his chair.

'One last point,' he said. 'Tarawicz's base is Newcastle. I'm betting he had eyes and ears here in Edinburgh. In fact, I know he did. I've just been having a chat with Dr Colquhoun. You remember him, Brian? You'd heard about him from Lintz. Then when Tarawicz offered East Europeans as working girls, you reckoned maybe Tommy should have a few foreign phrases to hand. Colquhoun did the teaching. You told him stories about Tarawicz, about Bosnia. Catch was, he's the only person round these parts who knew the subject, so when we picked up Candice, we ended up using him, too. Colquhoun sussed straight off what was happening. He wasn't sure if he had anything to fear: he'd never met her, and her answers were reassuringly vague – or he kept them that way. All the same, he came to you. Your solution: ship Candice to Fife, then snatch her, and take Colquhoun out of the game till the heat died.'

Rebus smiled. 'He told *you* about Fife. Yet it was *Tarawicz* who got Candice. I think Tommy will find that a bit odd, don't you? So, here we sit. And I can tell you that the minute you walk out of here, you're going to be a marked man. Could be the Yakuza, could be Cafferty, could be your own boss or Tarawicz himself. You haven't got any friends, and nowhere's safe any more.' Rebus paused. 'Unless *we* help you. I've talked to Chief Superintendent Watson, and he's agreeing to witness protection, new identity, whatever you want. There may be a short sentence to serve – just so it looks right – but it'll be a soft option, room of your own, no other prisoners allowed near. And afterwards, you'll be home and dry. That's a big commitment on our part, and we'll need a big commitment from *you*. We'll want everything.' Rebus counted off on his fingers. 'The drug shipments, the war with Cafferty, the

Newcastle connection, the Yakuza, the prostitutes.' He paused again, drained his tea. 'Tall order, I know. Your boss had a meteoric rise, Brian, and he nearly made it. But that's all over. Best thing you can do now is talk. It's either that or spend the rest of your days waiting for the bullet or the machete to strike ...'

The lawyer started to protest. Rebus held up a hand.

'We'll need all of it, Brian. Including Lintz.'

'Lintz,' Pretty-Boy said dismissively. 'Lintz is nothing.'

'So where's the harm?'

The look in Pretty-Boy's eyes was a mix of anger, fear and disorientation. Rebus stood up.

'I need something else to drink. What about you gentlemen?'

'Coffee,' the lawyer said, 'black, no sugar.'

Pretty-Boy hesitated, then said, 'Get me a Coke.' And at that point – for the very first time – Rebus knew a deal might be done. He stopped the interview, Hogan switched off the tapes, and both men left the room. Hogan patted him on the back.

Farmer Watson was coming along the corridor towards them. Rebus moved to meet him, leading them away from the door.

'I think we might be in with a shout, sir,' Rebus said. 'He'll try to twist the deal, give us less than we want, but I think there's a chance.'

Watson beamed a smile, as Rebus leaned against the wall, eyes closed. 'I feel about a hundred years old.'

'Experience tells,' Hogan said.

Rebus growled at him, then they went to fetch the drinks.

'Mr Summers,' the lawyer said, as Rebus handed him his cup, 'would like to tell you the story of his relationship with Joseph Lintz. But first we'll need some assurances.'

'What about everything else I mentioned?'

'These can be negotiated.'

Rebus stared at Pretty-Boy. 'You don't trust me?'

Pretty-Boy picked up his can, said 'No', and drank.

'Fine.' Rebus walked over to the far wall. 'In that case, you're free to go.' He checked his watch. 'Soon as you've finished your drinks, I want you out of here. Interview Rooms are at a premium tonight. DI Hogan, mark up the tapes, will you?'

Hogan ejected both cassettes. Rebus sat down beside him and they started discussing work, as though Pretty-Boy had been dismissed from their minds. Hogan examined a sheet of paper, checking who was due to be interviewed next.

From the corner of his eye, Rebus saw Pretty-Boy leaning in towards his lawyer, whispering something. He turned on them.

'Can you do that outside, please? We need to vacate this room.'

Pretty-Boy *knew* Rebus was bluffing ... knew the policeman needed him. But he realised, too, that Rebus was *not* bluffing about giving the file to Shoda, and he was far too intelligent not to be scared. He didn't move from the chair, and held his lawyer's arm so he had to stay and listen. Eventually the lawyer cleared his throat.

'Inspector, Mr Summers is willing to answer your questions.'

'*All* my questions?'

The lawyer nodded. 'But I must insist on hearing more of the "deal" you're proposing.'

Rebus looked at Hogan. 'Go get the Chief Super.'

Rebus left the room, stood in the hallway while Hogan was away. Cadged a cigarette off a passing uniform. He'd just got it lit when Farmer Watson came barrelling towards him, Hogan behind as though attached to Watson by an invisible leash.

'No smoking, John, you know that.'

'Yes, sir,' Rebus said, crimping the tip. 'I was just holding it for Inspector Hogan.'

Watson nodded towards the door. 'What do they want?'

'We've been talking possible immunity from prosecution. At the very least, he'll want a soft sentence, and a safe one, plus new ID afterwards.'

Watson was thoughtful. 'We haven't had a cheep out of any of them. Not that it matters greatly. There's the gang we caught red-handed, plus Telford on the audio tape ...'

'Summers is a real insider, knows Telford's organisation.'

'So how come he's willing to spill?'

'Because he's scared, and his fear is overwhelming his loyalty. I'm not saying we'll get every last detail out of him, but we'll probably get enough to start pressing the other members. Once they know someone's yapping, they'll all want a trade.'

'What's his lawyer like?'

'Expensive.'

'No point shilly-shallying then.'

'I couldn't have put it better myself, sir.'

The Chief Super pinned back his shoulders. 'All right, let's do a deal.'

'When did you first meet Joseph Lintz?'

Pretty-Boy's arms were no longer folded. He was resting them on the desk, head in his hands. His hair flopped forward, making him look younger than ever.

'About six months ago. We'd spoken on the phone before that.'

'He was a punter?'

'Yes.'

'Meaning what exactly?'

Pretty-Boy looked at the turning spools. 'You want me to explain for all our listeners?'

'That's right.'

'Joseph Lintz was a client of the escort service for which I worked.'

'Come on, Brian, you were a bit more than a flunkey. You ran it, didn't you?'

'If you say so.'

'Anytime you want to walk, Brian ...'

Eyes burning. 'Okay, I *ran* it for my employer.'

'And Mr Lintz phoned wanting an escort?'

'He wanted one of our girls to go to his home.'

'And?'

'And that was it. He'd sit there opposite her and just stare for half an hour.'

'Both of them fully clothed?'

'Yes.'

'Nothing else?'

'Not at first.'

'Ah.' Rebus paused. 'You must have been curious.'

Pretty-Boy shrugged. 'Takes all sorts, doesn't it?'

'I suppose it does. So how did your business relationship progress?'

'Well, on a gig like that, there's always a chaperone.'

'Yourself?'

'Yes.'

'You didn't have better things to do?'

Another shrug. 'I was curious.'

'About what?'

'The address: Heriot Row.'

'Mr Lintz had ... class?'

'Coming out his ears. I mean, I've met plenty fat cats, corporate types looking for a shag in their hotel, but Lintz was a long way from that.'

'He just wanted to look at the girls.'

'That's right. And this huge house he had …'

'You went in? You didn't just wait in the car?'

'Told him it was company policy.' A smile. 'Really, all I wanted was to snoop.'

'Did you talk to him?'

'Later, yes.'

'You became friends?'

'Not really … maybe. He knew things, had a real brain on him.'

'You were impressed.'

Pretty-Boy nodded. Yes, Rebus could imagine. His previous role model had always been Tommy Telford, but Pretty-Boy had aspirations. He *wanted* class. He wanted people to acknowledge him for his mind. Rebus knew how seductive Lintz's storytelling could be. How much more seductive would Pretty-Boy have found it?

'Then what happened?'

Pretty-Boy shifted. 'His tastes changed.'

'Or his real tastes started to emerge?'

'That's what I wondered.'

'So what did he want?'

'He wanted the girls … he had this length of rope … he'd made it into a noose.' Pretty-Boy swallowed. His lawyer had stopped writing, was listening intently. 'He wanted the girls to slip it over their heads, then lie down like they were dead.'

'Dressed or naked?'

'Naked.'

'And?'

'And he'd … he'd sit on his chair and get off. Some of the girls wouldn't go along. He wanted the works: bulging eyes, tongue sticking out, neck twisted …' Pretty-Boy rubbed his hands through his hair.

'Did you ever talk about it?'

'With him? No, never.'

'So what did you talk about?'

'All sorts of things.' Pretty-Boy looked up at the ceiling, laughed. 'He told me once, he believed in God. Said the problem was, he wasn't sure God believed in him. That seemed clever at the time ... he always managed to get me thinking. And this was the same guy who tossed himself off over bodies with ropes round their necks.'

'All this personal attention you were giving him,' Rebus said, 'you were sizing him up, weren't you?'

Pretty-Boy looked into his lap, nodded.

'For the tape, please.'

'Tommy always wanted to know if a punter was worth squeezing.'

'And ... ?'

Pretty-Boy shrugged. 'We found out about the Nazi stuff, realised we couldn't hurt him any more than he was already being hurt. Turned into a bit of a joke. There we were, thinking of threatening him with exposure as a perv, and at the same time the papers were saying he was a mass murderer.' He laughed again.

'So you dropped that idea?'

'Yes.'

'But he paid you five grand?' Rebus fishing.

Pretty-Boy licked his lips. 'He'd tried topping himself. He told me that. Tying the rope to the top of his banister and jumping off. Only it didn't work. Banister snapped and he fell half a flight.'

Rebus remembering: the broken stair-rail.

Rebus remembering: Lintz with a scarf around his neck, his voice hoarse. Telling Rebus he had a throat bug.

'He told you this?'

'He phoned the office, said we had to meet. That was unusual. In the past, he'd always used phone boxes and got me on my mobile. Safe old bugger, I'd always thought. Then he calls from home, right to the office.'

'Where did you meet?'

'In a restaurant. He bought me lunch.' The young woman ... 'Told me he'd tried killing himself and couldn't do it. He kept saying he'd proved himself a "moral coward", whatever that means.'

'So what did he want?'

Pretty-Boy stared up at Rebus. 'He needed someone to help him.'

'You?'

Pretty-Boy shrugged.

'And the price was right?'

'No haggling necessary. He wanted it done in Warriston Cemetery.'

'Did you ask him why?'

'I knew he liked the place. We met at his house, really early. I drove him down there. He seemed the same as ever, except he kept thanking me for my "resolve". I wasn't sure what he meant by that. To me, Resolve is something you take after a hard night.'

Rebus smiled, as was expected. 'Go on,' he said.

'Not much more to tell, is there? *He* put the noose over his head. *He* told me to pull on the rope. I had a last go at talking him out of it, but the bugger was determined. It's not murder, is it? Assisted suicide: a lot of places, it's legal.'

'How did the dunt get on his head?'

'He was heavier than I thought. First time I hauled him up, the rope slipped and he fell, thumped himself on the ground.'

Bobby Hogan cleared his throat. 'Brian, did he say anything ... right at the end?'

'Famous last words and all that?' Pretty-Boy shook his head. 'All he said was "thank you". Poor old sod. One thing: he wrote it all down.'

'What?'

'About me helping him. A sort of insurance, in case

anyone ever linked us. Letter says he paid me, begged me to help.'

'Where is this?'

'In a safe. I can get it for you.'

Rebus nodded, stretched his back. 'Did you ever talk about Villefranche?'

'A little bit, mostly about the way the papers and TV were hounding him, how difficult it made it when he wanted ... company.'

'But not the massacre itself?'

Pretty-Boy shook his head. 'Know something else? Even if he *had* told me, I wouldn't tell you.'

Rebus tapped his pen against the desk. He knew the Lintz story was as closed as it was ever going to be. Bobby Hogan knew it, too. They had the secret at last, the story of how Lintz had died. They knew he'd been helped by the Rat Line, but they'd never know whether he'd been Josef Linzstek or not. The circumstantial evidence was over-whelming, but so was the evidence that Lintz had been hounded to death. He'd started putting the escorts into nooses only *after* the accusations had been made.

Hogan caught Rebus's eye and shrugged, as if to say: what does it matter? Rebus nodded back. Part of him wanted to take a break, but now that Pretty-Boy was rolling it was important to keep up the steam.

'Thanks for that, Mr Summers. We may come back to Mr Lintz if we think of any more questions. But meantime, let's move on to the relationship between Thomas Telford and Jake Tarawicz.'

Pretty-Boy shifted, as if trying to get comfortable. 'This could take a while,' he said.

'Take as long as you like,' Rebus told him.

37

They got it all, in time.

Pretty-Boy had to rest, and so did they. Other teams came in, worked on different areas. The tapes were filling up, being listened to elsewhere, notes and transcripts made. Back-up questions were forwarded to the Interview Room. Telford wasn't talking. Rebus went and took a look at him, sat across from him. Telford didn't blink once. He sat ramrod-straight, hands on knees. And all the while, Pretty-Boy's confession was being used to squeeze other gang members – without letting slip who was singing.

The ranks broke, slowly at first and then in a cataract of accusation, self-defence and denial. And they got it all.

Telford and Tarawicz: European prostitutes heading north; muscle and dope heading south.

Mr Taystee: taking more than his fair share; dealt with accordingly.

The Japanese: using Telford as their introduction to Scotland, finding it a good base of operations.

Only now Rebus had scuppered that. In his folder to Shoda he'd warned the gangster to leave Poyntinghame alone, or he'd be 'implicated in ongoing criminal investigations'. The Yakuza weren't stupid. He doubted they'd be back ... for a while at least.

His last trip of the night: Rebus went down to the cells, unlocked one of the doors and told Ned Farlowe he was free. Told him he had nothing to fear ...

Unlike Mr Pink Eyes. The Yakuza had a score to settle.

And it didn't stay unsettled long. He was found in his car-crusher, seatbelt welded shut. His men had started running. Some of them were running still.

Rebus sat in his living-room, staring at the door Jack Morton had stripped and varnished. He was thinking about the funeral, about how the Juice Church would be there in force. He wondered if they'd blame him. Jack's kids would be there, too. Rebus had never met them; didn't think he wanted to see them.

Wednesday morning, he was back in Inverness, meeting Mrs Hetherington off her flight. She'd been delayed in Holland, answering Customs questions. They'd laid a little trap, caught a man called De Gier – a known trafficker – planting the kilo package of heroin in Mrs Hetherington's luggage: a secret compartment in her suitcase, the suitcase itself a gift from her landlord. Several of Telford's other elderly tenants were enjoying short breaks in Belgium. They'd be questioned by local police.

Home again, Rebus telephoned David Levy.

'Lintz committed suicide,' he told him.

'That's your conclusion?'

'It's the truth. No conspiracy, no cover-up.'

A sigh. 'It's of little consequence, Inspector. What matters is that we've lost another one.'

'Villefranche doesn't mean a thing to you, does it? The Rat Line, that's all you care about.'

'There's nothing we can do about Villefranche.'

Rebus took a deep breath. 'A man called Harris came to see me. He works for British Intelligence. They're protecting some big names, high-level people. Rat Line survivors, maybe their children. Tell Mayerlink to keep digging.'

There was silence for a moment. 'Thank you, Inspector.'

Rebus was in a car. It was the Weasel's Jag. The Weasel

was in the back with him. Their driver was missing a big chunk of his left ear. The shape made him resemble a pixie – but only from the side, and you wouldn't want to tell him to his face.

'You did well,' the Weasel was saying. 'Mr Cafferty's pleased.'

'How long have you been holding him?'

The Weasel smiled. 'Nothing gets past you, Rebus.'

'Rangers have offered me a trial in goal. How long have you had him?'

'A few days. Had to be sure we had the right one, didn't we?'

'And now you're sure?'

'Absolutely positive.'

Rebus looked out of the window at the passing parade of shops, pedestrians, buses. The car was heading down towards Newhaven and Granton. 'You wouldn't be setting up some loser to take the blame?'

'He's genuine.'

'You could have spent the past few days making sure he was going to say the right things.'

The Weasel seemed amused. 'Such as?'

'Such as that he was in Telford's pay.'

'Rather than Mr Cafferty's, you mean?' Rebus glared at the Weasel, who laughed. 'I think you'll find him a pretty convincing candidate.'

The way he said it made Rebus shiver. 'He's still alive, isn't he?'

'Oh, yes. How long he remains so is entirely up to you.'

'You think I want him dead?'

'I know you do. You didn't go to Mr Cafferty because you wanted justice. You went out of *revenge*.'

Rebus stared at the Weasel. 'You don't sound like yourself.'

'You mean I don't sound like my persona – different thing entirely.'

'And do many people get behind the persona?' The Who: 'Can You See the Real Me?'

The Weasel smiled again. 'I thought you deserved it, after all the trouble you've gone to.'

'I didn't break Telford just to please your boss.'

'Nevertheless ...' The Weasel slid across his seat towards Rebus. 'How's Sammy, by the way?'

'She's fine.'

'Recuperating?'

'Yes.'

'That's good news. Mr Cafferty will be pleased. He's disappointed you haven't been to see him.'

Rebus took a newspaper from his pocket. It was folded at a story: FATAL STABBING AT JAIL.

'Your boss?' he said, handing the paper over.

The Weasel made show of reading it. ' "Aged twenty-six, from Govan ... stabbed through the heart in his cell ... no witnesses, no weapon recovered despite a thorough search." ' He tutted. 'Bit careless.'

'He'd taken up the contract on Cafferty?'

'Had he?' The Weasel looked amazed.

'Fuck off,' Rebus said, turning back to his window.

'By the way, Rebus, if you decide not to go to trial with the driver ...' The Weasel was holding something out. A homemade screwdriver, filed to a point, grip covered in packing-tape. Rebus looked at it in disgust.

'I washed the blood off,' the Weasel assured him. Then he laughed again. Rebus felt like he was being ferried straight to hell. In front of him he could see the grey expanse of the Firth of Forth, and Fife beyond it. They were coming into an area of docks, gas-plant and ware-houses. It had been earmarked for a development spill-over from Leith. The whole city was changing. Traffic routes and priorities were altered overnight, cranes were kept busy on building-sites, and the council, who always complained about being broke, had all manner of schemes underway to further alter the shape and scope of his chosen home.

'Nearly there,' the Weasel said.

Rebus wondered if there'd be any turning back.

They stopped at the gates to a warehouse complex. The driver undid the padlock, pulled the chain free. The gates swung open. In they went. The Weasel ordered the driver to park around the back. There was a plain white van there, more rust than metal. Its back windows had been painted over, turning it into a suitable hearse should occasion demand.

They got out into a salt wind. The Weasel shuffled over towards a door and banged once. The door was pushed open from within. They stepped inside.

A huge open space, filled with only a few packing cases, a couple of pieces of machinery covered with oil-cloth. And two men: the one who'd let them in, and another at the far end. This man was standing in front of a wooden chair. There was a figure tied to the chair, half-hidden by the man. The Weasel led the procession. Rebus tried to control his breathing, which was growing painfully shallow. His heart was racing, nerves jangling. He pushed back the anger, wasn't sure he could hold it.

When they were eight feet from the chair, the Weasel nodded and the man stood away, revealing to Rebus the terrified figure of a kid.

A boy.

Nine or ten, no older.

One black eye, nose caked with blood, both cheeks bruised and a graze on his chin. Burst lip beginning to heal, trousers torn at the knees, one shoe missing.

And a smell, as if he'd wet himself, maybe even worse.

'What the hell is this?' Rebus asked.

'This,' the Weasel said, 'is the little bastard who stole the car. This is the little bastard who lost his nerve at a red light and gunned through it, losing control of the pedals because he could barely reach them. This ...' The Weasel stepped forward, planted a hand on the kid's shoulder. 'This is the culprit.'

Rebus looked at the faces around him. 'Is this your idea of a joke?'

'No joke, Rebus.'

He looked at the boy. Dried tear-tracks. Eyes bloodshot from crying. Shoulders trembling. They'd tied his arms behind him. Tied his ankles to the chair-legs.

'Puh-please, mister ...' Dry, cracked voice. 'I ... help me, puh-please ...'

'Nicked the car,' the Weasel recited, 'then did the hit and run, got scared, and dumped the car near where he lives. Took the cassette and the tapes. He wanted the car for a race. That's what they do, race cars around the schemes. This little runt can start an engine in ten seconds flat.' He rubbed his hands together. 'So ... here we all are.'

'Help me ...'

Rebus recalling the city's graffiti: Won't Anyone Help? The Weasel nodding towards one of his men, the man producing a pickaxe-handle.

'Or the screwdriver,' the Weasel said. 'Or whatever you like, really. We are at your command.' And he gave a little bow.

Rebus could hardly speak. 'Cut the ropes.'

Silence in the warehouse.

'*Cut those fucking ropes!*'

A sniff from the Weasel. 'You heard the man, Tony.'

Ca-chink of a flick-knife opening. Ropes severed like cutting through butter. Rebus walked to within inches of the boy.

'What's your name?'

'J-Jordan.'

'Is that your first name or your second?'

The boy looked at him. 'First.'

'Okay, Jordan.' Rebus leaned down. The boy flinched, but did not resist as Rebus picked him up. He weighed almost nothing. Rebus started walking with him.

'What now, Rebus?' the Weasel asked. But Rebus didn't answer. He carried the boy to the threshold, kicked open the door, stepped out into sunshine.

'I'm ... I'm really sorry.' The boy had a hand across his eyes, unused to the light. He was starting to cry.

'You know what you did?'

Jordan nodded. 'I've been ... ever since that night. I knew it was bad ...' Now the tears came.

'Did they say who I was?'

'Please don't kill me.'

'I'm not going to kill you, Jordan.'

The boy blinked, trying to clear tears from his eyes, the better to know whether he was being lied to.

'I think you've been through enough, pal,' Rebus said. Then added: 'I think we both have.'

So after everything, it had come to this. Bob Dylan: 'Simple Twist of Fate'. Segue to Leonard Cohen: 'Is This What You Wanted?'

Rebus didn't know the answer to that.

38

Clean and sober, he went to the hospital. An open ward this time, set hours for visitors. No more darkened vigils. No return visit by Candice, though nurses spoke of regular phone calls by someone foreign-sounding. No way of knowing where she was. Maybe out there searching for her son. It didn't matter, so long as she was safe. So long as she was in control.

When he reached the ward's far end, two women rose from their chairs so he could kiss them: Rhona and Patience. He had a carrier-bag with him, magazines and grapes. Sammy was sitting up, supported by three pillows, Pa Broon propped beside her. Her hair had been washed and brushed, and she was smiling at him.

'Women's magazines,' he said, shaking his head. 'They should be on the top-shelf.'

'I need a few fantasies to sustain me in here,' Sammy said. Rebus beamed at her, said hello, then bent down and kissed his daughter.

The sun was shining as they walked through The Meadows – a rare day off for both. They held hands and watched people sunbathing and playing football. He knew Rhona was excited, and thought he knew why. But he wasn't going to spoil things with speculation.

'If you had a daughter, what would you call her?' she asked.

He shrugged. 'Haven't really thought about it.'

'What about a son?'

'I quite like Sam.'

'Sam?'

'When I was a kid, I had a bear called Sam. My mum knitted it for me.'

'Sam …' She tried the name out. 'It would work both ways, wouldn't it?'

He stopped, circled his arms around her waist. 'How do you mean?'

'Well, it could be Samuel or Samantha. You don't get many of those – names that work both ways.'

'I suppose not. Rhona, is there …?'

She put a finger to his lips, then kissed him. They walked on. There didn't seem to be a cloud in the whole damned sky.

Afterword

My fictional French village of Villefranche d'Albarede owes its existence to .the real village of Oradour-sur-Glâne, which was the subject of an attack by the 3rd Company of the SS 'Der Führer' regiment.

On the afternoon of Saturday 10 June 1944, 3rd Company – known as 'Das Reich' – entered the village and rounded up everyone. The women and children were herded into the church, while the men were split into groups and marched to various barns and other buildings around the village. Then the slaughter began.

Some 642 victims have been accounted for, but the estimate is that up to a thousand people may have perished that day. Only fifty-three corpses were ever identified. One boy from Lorraine, having first-hand knowledge of SS atrocities, managed to flee when the troops entered the village. Five men escaped the massacre in Laudy's barn. Wounded, they were able to crawl from the burning building and hide until the next day. One woman escaped from the church, climbing out of a window after playing dead beside the corpse of her child.

Soldiers went from house to house, finding villagers too sick or elderly to leave their beds. These people were shot and their houses set alight. Some of the bodies were hidden in mass graves, or dumped down wells and in bread ovens.

General Lammerding was the commanding officer. On 9 June he'd ordered the deaths of ninety-nine hostages in Tulle. He also gave the order for the Oradour massacre.

Later on in the war, Lammerding was captured by the British, who refused his extradition to France. Instead, he was returned to Düsseldorf, where he ran a successful company until his death in 1971.

In the general euphoria of the Normandy landings, the tragedy at Oradour went almost unnoticed. Eventually, in January 1953, the trial opened in Bordeaux of sixty-five men identified as having been involved in the massacre. Of these sixty-five, only twenty-one were present: seven Germans, and fourteen natives of French Alsace. None of the men was of officer rank.

Every individual found guilty at the Bordeaux trial left court a free man. A special Act of Amnesty had been passed, in the interests of national unity. (People in Alsace were disgruntled that their countrymen had been picked out for condemnation.) Meantime, the Germans were said to have already served their terms.

As a result, Oradour broke off all relations with the French state, a rupture which lasted seventeen years.

In May 1983, a man stood trial in East Berlin, charged with having been a lieutenant in 'Das Reich' during the Oradour massacre. He admitted everything, and was sentenced to life imprisonment.

In June 1996, it was reported that around 12,000 foreign volunteers to the Waffen SS are still receiving pensions from the Federal German government. One of these pensioners, a former Obersturmbannführer, was a participant at Oradour ...

Oradour still stands as a shrine. The village has been left just the way it was on that day in June 1944.

1

'Then why are you here?'

'Depends what you mean,' Rebus said.

'Mean?' The woman frowned behind her glasses.

'Mean by "here",' he explained. 'Here in this room? Here in this career? Here on the planet?'

She smiled. Her name was Andrea Thomson. She wasn't a doctor – she'd made that clear at their first meeting. Nor was she a 'shrink' or a 'therapist'. 'Career Analysis' was what it had said on Rebus's daily sheet.

2.30–3.15: Career Analysis, Rm 3.16.

With *Ms* Thomson. Which had become Andrea at the moment of introduction. Which was yesterday, Tuesday. A 'get to know' session, she'd called it.

She was in her late thirties, short and large-hipped. Her hair was a thick mop of blond with some darker streaks showing through. Her teeth were slightly oversized. She was self-employed, didn't work for the police full-time.

'Do any of us?' Rebus had asked yesterday. She'd looked a bit puzzled. 'I mean, do any of us work full-time . . . that's why we're here, isn't it?' He'd waved a hand in the direction of the closed door. 'We're not pulling our weight. We need a smack on the wrists.'

'Is that what you think you need, Detective Inspector?'

He'd wagged a finger. 'Keep calling me that and I'll keep calling you "Doc".'

'I'm not a doctor,' she'd said. 'Nor am I a shrink, a therapist, or any other word you've probably been thinking in connection with me.'

'Then what are you?'

1

'I deal with Career Analysis.'

Rebus had snorted. 'Then you should be wearing a seat-belt.'

She'd stared at him. 'Am I in for a bumpy ride?'

'You could say that, seeing how my *career*, as you call it, has just careered out of control.'

So much for yesterday.

Now she wanted to know about his feelings. How did he feel about being a detective?

'I like it.'

'Which parts?'

'All of me.' Fixing her with a smile.

She smiled back. 'I meant—'

'I know what you meant.' He looked around the room. It was small, utilitarian. Two chrome-framed chairs either side of a teak-veneered desk. The chairs were covered in some lime-coloured material. Nothing on the desk itself but her A4-sized lined pad and her pen. There was a heavy-looking satchel in the corner; Rebus wondered if his file was in there. A clock on the wall, calendar below it. The calendar had come from the local fire brigade. A length of net curtaining across the window.

It wasn't her room. It was a room she could use on those occasions when her services were required. Not quite the same thing.

'I like my job,' he said at last, folding his arms. Then, wondering if she'd read anything into the action – defensiveness, say – he unfolded them again. Couldn't seem to find anything to do with them except bunch his fists into his jacket pockets. 'I like every aspect of it, right down to the added paperwork each time the office runs out of staples for the staple-gun.'

'Then why did you blow up at Detective Chief Superintendent Templer?'

'I don't know.'

'She thinks maybe it has something to do with professional jealousy.'

2

The laugh burst from him. 'She said that?'

'You don't agree?'

'Of course not.'

'You've known her some years, haven't you?'

'More than I care to count.'

'And she's always been senior to you?'

'It's never bothered me, if that's what you're thinking.'

'It's only recently that she's become your commanding officer.'

'So?'

'You've been at DI level for quite some time. No thoughts of improvement?' She caught his look. 'Maybe "improvement" is the wrong word. You've not wanted promotion?'

'No.'

'Why not?'

'Might be I'm afraid of responsibility.'

She stared at him. 'That smacks of a prepared answer.'

'Be prepared, that's my motto.'

'Oh, you were a Boy Scout?'

'No,' he said. She stayed quiet, picking up her pen and studying it. It was one of those cheap yellow Bics. 'Look,' he said into the silence, 'I've got no quarrel with Gill Templer. Good luck to her as a DCS. It's not a job I could do. I like being where I am.' He glanced up. 'Which doesn't mean here in this room, it means out on the street, solving crimes. The reason I lost it is . . . well, the way the whole inquiry's being handled.'

'You must have had similar feelings before in the middle of a case?' She had taken her glasses off so she could rub the reddened skin either side of her nose.

'Many a time,' he admitted.

She slid the glasses back on. 'But this is the first time you've thrown a mug?'

'I wasn't aiming for her.'

'She had to duck. A full mug, too.'

'Ever tasted cop-shop tea?'

3

She smiled again. 'So you've no problem then?'

'None.' He folded his arms in what he hoped was a sign of confidence.

'Then why are you here?'

Time up, Rebus walked back along the corridor and straight into the men's toilets, where he splashed water on his face, dried off with a paper towel. Watched himself in the mirror above the sink as he pulled a cigarette from his packet and lit it, blowing the smoke ceilingwards.

One of the lavatories flushed; a door clicked its lock off. Jazz McCullough came out.

'Thought that might be you,' he said, turning on the tap.

'How could you tell?'

'One long sigh followed by the lighting of a cigarette. Had to be a shrink session finishing.'

'She's not a shrink.'

'Size of her, she looks like she's shrunk.' McCullough reached for a towel. Tossed it in the bin when he'd finished. Straightened his tie. His real name was James, but those who knew him seemed never to call him that. He was Jamesy, or more often Jazz. Tall, mid-forties, cropped black hair with just a few touches of grey at the temples. He was thin. Patted his stomach now, just above the belt, as if to emphasise his lack of a gut. Rebus could barely see his own belt, even in the mirror.

Jazz didn't smoke. Had a family back home in Broughty Ferry: wife and two sons about his only topic of conversation. Examining himself in the mirror, he tucked a stray hair back behind one ear.

'What the hell are we doing here, John?'

'Andrea was just asking me the same thing.'

'That's because she knows it's a waste of time. Thing is, we're paying her wages.'

'We're doing some good then.'

4

Jazz glanced at him. 'You dog! You think you're in there!'

Rebus winced. 'Give me a break. All I meant was . . .' But what was the point? Jazz was already laughing. He slapped Rebus on the shoulder.

'Back into the fray,' he said, pulling open the door. 'Three thirty, "Dealing with the Public".'

It was their third day at Tulliallan: the Scottish Police College. The place was mostly full of recent recruits, learning their lessons before being allowed out on to public streets. But there were other officers there, older and wiser. They were on refresher courses, or learning new skills.

And then there were the Resurrection Men.

The college was based at Tulliallan Castle, not in itself a castle but a mock-baronial home to which had been added a series of modern buildings, connected by corridors. The whole edifice sat in huge leafy grounds on the outskirts of the village of Kincardine, to the northern side of the Firth of Forth, almost equidistant between Glasgow and Edinburgh. It could have been mistaken for a university campus, and to some extent that was its function. You came here to learn.

Or, in Rebus's case, as punishment.

There were four other officers in the seminar room when Rebus and McCullough arrived. 'The Wild Bunch', DI Francis Gray had called them, first time they'd been gathered together. A couple of faces Rebus knew – DS Stu Sutherland from Livingston; DI Tam Barclay from Falkirk. Gray himself was from Glasgow, and Jazz worked out of Dundee, while the final member of the party, DC Allan Ward, was based in Dumfries. 'A gathering of nations,' as Gray had put it. But to Rebus they acted more like spokesmen for their tribes, sharing the same language but with different outlooks. They were wary of each other. It was especially awkward with officers from the same region. Rebus and Sutherland were both Lothian and Borders, but the town of Livingston was F Division, known to anyone in Edinburgh as 'F Troop'. Sutherland was just waiting for Rebus to say something to the others, something disparaging. He had the look of a haunted man.

The six men shared only one characteristic: they were at Tulliallan because they'd failed in some way. Mostly it was an issue with authority. Much of their free time the previous two days had been spent sharing war stories. Rebus's tale was milder than most. If a young officer, fresh out of uniform, had made the mistakes they had made, he or she would probably not have been given the Tulliallan life-line. But these were lifers, men who'd been in the force an average of twenty years. Most were nearing the point where they could leave on full pension. Tulliallan was their last-chance saloon. They were here to atone, to be resurrected.

As Rebus and McCullough took their seats, a uniformed officer walked in and marched briskly to the head of the oval table where his chair was waiting. He was in his mid-fifties and was here to remind them of their obligation to the public at large. He was here to train them to mind their p's and q's.

Five minutes into the lecture, Rebus let his eyes and mind drift out of focus. He was back on the Marber case . . .

Edward Marber had been an Edinburgh art and antique dealer. Past tense, because Marber was now dead, bludgeoned outside his home by assailant or assailants unknown. The weapon had not yet been found. A brick or rock was the best guess offered by the city pathologist, Professor Gates, who had been called to the scene for a PLE: Pronouncement of Life Extinct. Brain haemorrhage brought on by the blow. Marber had died on the steps of his Duddingston Village home, front-door keys in his hand. He had been dropped off by taxi after the private viewing night of his latest exhibition: New Scottish Colourists. Marber owned two small, exclusive galleries in the New Town, plus antique shops in Dundas Street, Glasgow and Perth. Rebus had asked someone why Perth, rather than oil-rich Aberdeen.

'Because Perthshire's where the wealth goes to play.'

The taxi-driver had been interviewed. Marber didn't drive, but his house was at the end of an eighty-metre driveway, the gates to which had been open. The taxi had pulled up at the door, activating a halogen light to one side of the steps. Marber had paid and tipped, asking for a receipt, and the taxi-driver had U-turned away, not bothering to look in his mirror.

'I didn't see a thing,' he'd told the police.

The taxi receipt had been found in Marber's pocket, along with a list of the sales he'd made that evening, totalling just over £16,000. His cut, Rebus learned, would have been twenty per cent, £3,200. Not a bad night's work.

It was morning before the body was found by the postman. Professor Gates had given an estimated time of death of between nine and eleven the previous evening. The taxi had picked Marber up from his gallery at eight thirty, so must have dropped him home around eight forty-five, a time the driver accepted with a shrug.

The immediate police instinct had screamed robbery, but problems and niggles soon became apparent. Would someone have clobbered the victim with the taxi still in sight, the scene lit by halogen? It seemed unlikely, and yet by the time the taxi turned out of the driveway, Marber should have been safely on the other side of his door. And though Marber's pockets had been turned out, cash and credit cards evidently taken, the attacker had failed to use the keys to unlock the front door and trawl the house itself. Scared off perhaps, but it still didn't make sense.

Muggings tended to be spontaneous. You were attacked on the street, maybe just after using a cash machine. The mugger didn't hang around your door waiting for you to come home. Marber's house was relatively isolated: Duddingston Village was a wealthy enclave on the edge of Edinburgh, semi-rural, with the mass of Arthur's Seat as its neighbour. The houses hid behind walls, quiet and secure. Anyone approaching Marber's home on foot would have triggered the same halogen security light. They would then have had to hide – in the undergrowth, say, or behind one of the trees. After a couple of minutes, the lamp's timer would finish its cycle and go off. But any movement would trigger the sensor once again.

The Scene of Crime officers had looked for possible hiding places, finding several. But no traces of anyone, no footprints or fibres.

Another scenario, proposed by DCS Gill Templer:

'Say the assailant was already inside the house. Heard the door being unlocked and ran towards it. Smashed the victim on the head and ran.'

But the house was high-tech: alarms and sensors everywhere. There was no sign of a break-in, no indication that anything was missing. Marber's best friend, another art dealer called Cynthia Bessant, had toured the house and pronounced that she could see nothing missing or out of place, except that much of the deceased's art collection had been removed from the walls and, each painting neatly packaged in bubble-wrap, was stacked against the wall in the dining room. Bessant had been unable to offer an explanation.

'Perhaps he was about to re-frame them, or move them to different rooms. One *does* get tired of the same paintings in the same spots . . .'

She'd toured every room, paying particular attention to Marber's bedroom, not having seen inside it before. She called it his 'inner sanctum'.

The victim himself had never been married, and was quickly assumed by the investigating officers to have been gay.

8

'Eddie's sexuality,' Cynthia Bessant had said, 'can have no bearing on this case.'

But that would be something for the inquiry to decide. Rebus had felt himself side-lined in the investigation, working the telephones mostly. Cold calls to friends and associates. The same questions eliciting almost identical responses. The bubble-wrapped paintings had been checked for fingerprints, from which it became apparent that Marber himself had packaged them up. Still no one – neither his secretary nor his friends – could give an explanation.

Then, towards the end of one briefing, Rebus had picked up a mug of tea – someone else's tea, milky grey – and hurled it in the general direction of Gill Templer.

The briefing had started much as any other. Rebus washing down three aspirin caplets with his morning latte. The coffee came in a cardboard beaker. It was from a concession on the corner of The Meadows. Usually his first and last decent cup of the day.

'Bit too much to drink last night?' DS Siobhan Clarke had asked. She'd run her eyes over him: same suit, shirt and tie as the day before. Probably wondering if he'd bothered to take any of it off between times. The morning shave erratic, a lazy run-over with an electric. Hair that needed washing and cutting.

She'd seen just what Rebus had wanted her to see.

'And a good morning to you too, Siobhan,' he'd muttered to himself, crushing the empty beaker.

Usually he stood towards the back of the room at briefings, but today he was nearer the front. Sat there at a desk, rubbing his forehead, loosening his shoulders, as Gill Templer spelt out the day's mission.

More door-to-door; more interviews; more phone calls.

His fingers were around the mug by now. He didn't know whose it was, the glaze cold to the touch – could even have been left from the day before. The room was stifling and already smelt of sweat.

'More bloody phone calls,' he found himself saying, loud enough to be heard at the front. Templer looked up.

'Something to say, John?'

'No, no . . . nothing.'

Her back straightening. 'Only if you've anything to add – maybe one of your famous deductions – I'm all ears.'

'With respect, ma'am, you're not all ears – you're all talk.' Noises around him: gasps and looks. Rebus rising slowly to his feet.

'We're getting nowhere fast.' His voice was loud. 'There's nobody left to talk to, and nothing worth them saying!'

The blood had risen to Templer's cheeks. The sheet of paper she was holding – the day's duties – had become a cylinder which her fingers threatened to crush.

'Well, I'm sure we can all learn something from *you*, DI Rebus.' Not 'John' any more. Her voice rising to match his. Her eyes scanned the room: thirteen officers, not quite the full complement. Templer was working under pressure: much of it fiscal. Each investigation had a ticket attached to it, a costing she daren't overstep. Then there were the illnesses and holidays, the latecomers . . . 'Maybe you'd like to come up here,' she was saying, 'and give us the benefit of your thoughts on the subject of just exactly *how* we should be proceeding with this inquiry.' She stretched an arm out, as if to introduce him to an audience. 'Ladies and gentlemen . . .'

Which was the moment he chose to throw the mug. It travelled in a lazy arc, spinning as it went, dispensing cold tea. Templer ducked instinctively, though the mug would have sailed over her head in any case. It hit the back wall just above floor level, bouncing off and failing to break. There was silence in the room as people rose to their feet, checking their clothes for spillage.

Rebus sat down then, one finger punching the desk as if trying to find the rewind on life's remote control.

*

'DI Rebus?' The uniform was talking to him.

'Yes, sir?'

'Glad you've decided to join us.' Smiles all around the table. How much had he missed? He didn't dare look at his watch.

'Sorry about that, sir.'

'I was asking if you'd be our member of the public.' Nodding to the opposite side of the table to Rebus. 'DI Gray will be the officer. And you, DI Rebus, will be coming into the station with what could turn out to be some vital information pertaining to a case.' The teacher paused. 'Or you could be a crank.' Laughter from a couple of the men. Francis Gray was beaming at Rebus, nodding encouragement.

'Whenever you're ready, DI Gray.'

Gray leaned forward on the table. 'So, Mrs Ditchwater, you say you saw something that night?'

The laughter was louder. The teacher waved them quiet. 'Let's try to keep this serious, shall we?'

Gray nodded, turned his eyes to Rebus again. 'You definitely saw something?'

'Yes,' Rebus announced, coarsening his voice. 'I saw the whole thing, Officer.'

'Though you've been registered blind these past eleven years?'

Gales of laughter in the room, the teacher thumping the table-top, trying to restore order. Gray sitting back, joining the laughter, winking across at Rebus, whose shoulders were rocking.

Francis Gray was fighting hard against resurrection.

'I thought I was going to wet myself,' Tam Barclay said, lowering the tray of glasses on to the table. They were in the larger of Kincardine's two pubs, lessons finished for the day. Six of them forming a tight circle: Rebus, Francis Gray, Jazz McCullough, plus Tam Barclay, Stu Sutherland and Allan Ward. At thirty-four, Ward was the youngest of the group and the lowest-ranking officer on the course. He had a tough, spoilt look to him. Maybe it came from working in the south-west.

Five pints, one cola: McCullough was driving home afterwards, wanted to see his wife and kids.

'I do my damnedest to *avoid* mine,' Gray had said.

'No joking,' Barclay said, squeezing into his seat, 'near wet myself.' Grinning at Gray. '"Blind these past eleven years".'

Gray picked up his pint, raised it. 'Here's tae us, wha's like us?'

'Nobody,' Rebus commented. 'Or they'd be stuck on this damned course.'

'Just got to grin and bear it,' Barclay said. He was late thirties, thickening around the waist. Salt-and-pepper hair brushed back from the forehead. Rebus knew him from a couple of cases: Falkirk and Edinburgh were only thirty minutes apart.

'I wonder if Wee Andrea grins when she bares it,' Stu Sutherland said.

'No sexism, please.' Francis Gray was wagging a finger.

'Besides,' McCullough added, 'we don't want to stoke John's fantasies.'

Gray raised an eyebrow. 'That right, John? Got the hots for your counsellor? Better watch, you might make Allan jealous.'

Allan Ward looked up from the cigarette he was lighting, just glowered.

'That your sheep-frightening look, Allan?' Gray said. 'Not much to do down in Dumfries, is there, except round up the usual ewes?'

More laughter. It wasn't that Francis Gray had made himself the centre of attention; it seemed to happen naturally. He'd been first into his seat, and the others had congregated around him, Rebus sitting directly opposite. Gray was a big man, and the years told on his face. And because he said everything with a smile, a wink or a glint

12

in his eye, he got away with it. Rebus hadn't heard anyone making a joke about Gray himself yet, though they'd all been his target. It was as if he were challenging them, testing them. The way they took his comments would tell him everything he needed to know about them. Rebus wondered how the big man would react to a jibe or joke directed against him.

Maybe he'd have to find out.

McCullough's mobile sounded, and he got up, moving away.

'His wife, odds-on,' Gray stated. He was halfway down his pint of lager. Didn't smoke, told Rebus he'd given up a decade back. The two of them had been outside during a break, Rebus offering the packet. Ward and Barclay smoked too. Three out of six: it meant Rebus could feel comfortable lighting up.

'She's keeping tabs on him?' Stu Sutherland was saying.

'Proof of a deep and loving relationship,' Gray commented, tipping the glass to his mouth again. He was one of those drinkers, you never saw them swallow: it was as if they could hold their throat open and just pour the stuff down.

'You two know each other?' Sutherland asked. Gray glanced over his shoulder to where McCullough was standing, his head bowed towards the mobile phone.

'I know the type,' was all Gray said by way of answer.

Rebus knew better. He rose to his feet. 'Same again?'

Two lagers, three IPAs. On his way to the bar, Rebus pointed towards McCullough, who shook his head. He still had most of his cola, didn't want another. Rebus heard the words 'I'll be on the road in ten minutes . . .' Yes, he was on the phone to his wife. Rebus had a call he wanted to make too. Jean was probably finishing work right around now. Rush hour, the journey from the museum to her home in Portobello might take half an hour.

The barman knew the order: this was their third round of the evening. The previous two nights, they'd stuck to the college premises. First night, Gray had produced a good bottle of malt, and they'd sat in the common room, getting to know each other. Tuesday, they'd met in the college's own bar for an after-dinner session, McCullough sticking to soft drinks and then heading out for his car.

But at lunchtime today, Tam Barclay had mentioned a bar in the village, good rep.

'No trouble with the locals,' was the way he'd put it. So here they were. The barman looked comfortable, which told Rebus he'd dealt with intakes from the college before. He was efficient, not over-friendly. Midweek, only half a dozen regulars in the place. Three at one table, two at one end of the bar, another standing alone next to Rebus. The man turned to him.

'Up at the cop school, are you?'

Rebus nodded.

'Bit old for recruits.'

Rebus glanced at the man. He was tall, completely bald, his head shining. Grey moustache, eyes which seemed to be retracting into the skull. He was drinking a bottle of beer with what looked like a dark rum in the glass next to it.

'Force is desperate these days,' Rebus explained. 'Next thing, they'll be press-ganging.'

The man smiled. 'I think you're having me on.'

Rebus shrugged. 'We're here on a refresher course,' he admitted.

'Teaching old dogs new tricks, eh?' The man lifted his beer.

'Get you one?' Rebus offered. The man shook his head. So Rebus paid the barman and, deciding against a tray, hoisted three of the pints, making a triangle of them between his hands. Went to the table, came back for the last two, including his own. Thinking: best not leave it too late to phone Jean. He didn't want her to hear him drunk. Not that he was planning on getting drunk, but you could never tell . . .

'This you celebrating the end of the course?' the man asked.

'Just the beginning,' Rebus told him.

St Leonard's police station was mid-evening quiet. There were prisoners in the holding cells waiting for next morning's court appearance, and two teenagers being booked for shoplifting. Upstairs, the CID offices were almost empty. The Marber inquiry had wound down for the day, and only Siobhan Clarke was left, in front of a computer, staring at a screen-saver in the form of a banner message: WHAT WILL SIOBHAN DO WITHOUT HER SUGAR DADDY? She didn't know who had written it: one of the team, having a bit of a laugh. She surmised it referred to John Rebus, but couldn't quite work out the meaning. Did the author know what a sugar daddy was? Or did it just mean that Rebus looked after her, watched out for her? She was annoyed to find herself so irritated by the message.

She went into the screen-saver options and clicked on 'banner', erased the present message and replaced it with one of her own: I KNOW WHO YOU ARE, SUCKER. Then she checked a couple of other terminals, but their screen-savers were asteroids and wavy lines. When the phone on her desk started ringing, she considered not answering. Probably another crank wanting to confess, or ready with spurious information. A respectable middle-aged gent had called yesterday and accused his upstairs neighbours of the crime. Turned out they were students, played their music too loud and too often. The man had been warned that wasting police time was a serious matter.

'Mind you,' one of the uniforms had commented afterwards, 'if I'd to listen to Slipknot all day, I'd probably do worse.'

Siobhan sat down in front of her computer, lifted the receiver.

'CID, DS Clarke speaking.'

'One thing they teach at Tulliallan,' the voice said, 'is the importance of the quick pick-up.'

She smiled. 'I prefer to be wooed.'

'A quick pick-up,' Rebus explained, 'means picking up the phone within half a dozen rings.'

'How did you know I was here?'

'I didn't. Tried your flat first, got the answering machine.'

'And somehow sensed I wasn't out on the town?' She settled back in her chair. 'Sounds like you're in a bar.'

'In beautiful downtown Kincardine.'

'And yet you've dragged yourself from your pint to call me?'

'I called Jean first. Had a spare twenty-pence piece . . .'

'I'm flattered. A whole twenty pee?' She listened to him snort.

'So . . . how's it going?' he asked.

'Never mind that, how's Tulliallan?'

'As some of the teachers would say, we have a new tricks–old dog interface scenario.'

She laughed. 'They don't talk like that, do they?'

'Some of them do. We're being taught crime *management* and victim *empathy response*.'

'And yet you still have time for a drink?'

Silence on the line; she wondered if she'd touched a nerve.

'How do you know I'm not on fresh orange?' he said at last.

'I just do.'

'Go on then, impress me with your detective skills.'

'It's just that your voice gets slightly nasal.'

'After how many?'

'I'll guess four.'

'The girl's a marvel.' The pips started sounding. 'Hang on,' he said, putting in more money.

'Another spare twenty pee?'

'A fifty, actually. Which gives you plenty of time to update me on Marber.'

'Well, it's all been very quiet since the coffee incident.'

'I think it was tea.'

'Whatever it was, the stain's not budging. For what it's worth, I think they over-reacted, sending you into purdah.'

'I'm wasting money here.'

She sighed, sat forward. The screen-saver had just kicked in: I KNOW WHO YOU ARE, SUCKER scrolling right to left across the screen. 'We're still looking at friends and associates. Couple of interesting stories: an artist Marber had fallings-out with. Not unusual in the business, apparently, but this came to blows. Turns out the artist is one of these New Scottish Colourists, and leaving him out of the exhibition was a definite snub.'

'Maybe he whacked Marber with his easel.'

'Maybe.'

'And the second story?'

'That one I've been saving up to tell you. Did you ever see the guest list for the preview?'

'Yes.'

'Turns out not everyone who turned up was on the list. What we had were people who'd signed Marber's guest book. But now we've printed off a list of the people who actually got invites. Some of them were at the exhibition, hadn't bothered to RSVP or sign the book.'

'This artist was one of them?' Rebus guessed.

'God, no. But a certain M. G. Cafferty was.'

She heard Rebus whistle. Morris Gerald Cafferty – Big Ger, to those in the know – was the east coast's biggest gangster, or the biggest one they knew about. Cafferty and Rebus went back a long way.

'Big Ger a patron of the arts?' Rebus mused.

'He collects paintings, apparently.'

'What he doesn't do is smack people over the head on their doorsteps.'

17

'I bow to your superior knowledge.'

There was a pause on the line. 'How's Gill doing?'

'Much better since you left. Is she going to take it any further?'

'Not if I finish this course – that was the deal. How about the L-plate?'

Siobhan smiled. By L-plate Rebus meant the latest addition to CID, a detective constable called Davie Hynds. 'He's quiet, studious, industrious,' she recited. 'Not your type at all.'

'But is he any good?'

'Don't worry, I'll slap him into shape.'

'That's one of the prerogatives, now you've been promoted.'

The pips were sounding again. 'Do I get to go now?'

'A concise and helpful report, DS Clarke. Seven out of ten.'

'Only seven?'

'I'm deducting three for sarcasm. You need to address this attitudinal problem of yours, or—'

The sudden hum on the line told her his time was up. It was taking some getting used to, being addressed as 'DS'. She sometimes still introduced herself as Detective Constable Clarke, forgetting that the recent round of promotions had been kind to her. Could jealousy be behind the message on her screen? Silvers and Hood had stayed the same rank – as had most of the rest of CID.

'Narrowing the field nicely, girl,' she told herself, reaching for her coat.

Back at the table, Barclay lifted a mobile phone and told Rebus he could have borrowed it.

'Thanks, Tam. I've actually got one.'

'Are the batteries flat?'

Rebus lifted his glass, shook his head slowly.

'I think,' Francis Gray said, 'John just prefers things done the old-fashioned way. Isn't that right, John?'

18

Rebus shrugged, tipped the glass to his lips. Above the rim, he could see the bald man standing sideways on to the bar, watching the group intently . . .

available from
THE ORION PUBLISHING GROUP

☐ **Beggars Banquet** £6.99
IAN RANKIN
0 75284 959 X

☐ **Black & Blue** £6.99
IAN RANKIN
0 75280 948 2

☐ **The Black Book** £6.99
IAN RANKIN
1 85797 413 1

☐ **Bleeding Hearts** £6.99
IAN RANKIN (writing as
Jack Harvey)
0 75284 332 X

☐ **Blood Hunt** £6.99
IAN RANKIN (writing as
Jack Harvey)
0 75284 406 7

☐ **Dead Souls** £6.99
IAN RANKIN
0 75282 684 0

☐ **The Falls** £6.99
IAN RANKIN
0 75284 405 9

☐ **A Good Hanging & Other
Stories** £6.99
IAN RANKIN
0 75280 943 1

☐ **The Hanging Garden** £6.99
IAN RANKIN
0 75281 711 6

☐ **Hide & Seek** £6.99
IAN RANKIN
0 75280 941 5

☐ **Knots & Crosses** £6.99
IAN RANKIN
0 75280 942 3

☐ **Let It Bleed** £6.99
IAN RANKIN
0 75280 401 4

☐ **Mortal Causes** £6.99
IAN RANKIN
1 85797 863 3

☐ **A Question of Blood** £6.99
IAN RANKIN
0 75285 896 3

☐ **Resurrection Men** £6.99
IAN RANKIN
0 75284 822 4

☐ **Set in Darkness** £6.99
IAN RANKIN
0 75283 708 7

☐ **Strip Jack** £6.99
IAN RANKIN
0 75280 956 3

☐ **Tooth & Nail** £6.99
(previously published as *Wolfman*)
IAN RANKIN
0 75280 940 7

☐ **Witch Hunt** £6.99
IAN RANKIN (writing as
Jack Harvey)
0 75284 289 7

All Orion/Phoenix titles are available at your local bookshop or from the following address:

Mail Order Department
Littlehampton Book Services
FREEPOST BR535
Worthing, West Sussex, BN13 3BR
telephone 01903 828503, *facsimile* 01903 828802
e-mail MailOrders@lbsltd.co.uk
(Please ensure that you include full postal address details)

Payment can be made either by credit/debit card (Visa, Mastercard, Access and Switch accepted) or by sending a £ Sterling cheque or postal order made payable to *Littlehampton Book Services*.
DO NOT SEND CASH OR CURRENCY.

Please add the following to cover postage and packing

UK and BFPO:
£1.50 for the first book, and 50p for each additional book to a maximum of £3.50

Overseas and Eire:
£2.50 for the first book plus £1.00 for the second book and 50p for each additional book ordered

---

BLOCK CAPITALS PLEASE

name of cardholder _____

delivery address
(if different from cardholder)

address of cardholder _____

_____

_____

postcode _____

postcode _____

☐ I enclose my remittance for £_____

☐ please debit my Mastercard/Visa/Access/Switch (delete as appropriate)

card number ☐☐☐☐☐☐☐☐☐☐☐☐☐☐☐☐☐☐

expiry date ☐☐☐☐   Switch issue no. ☐☐

signature _____

prices and availability are subject to change without notice